CRAZED

MAFIA WARS NEW YORK - BOOK THREE

MAGGIE COLE

PULSE PRESS

PROLOGUE

MC

Katiya Nikitin

EACH SECOND THAT PASSES IS A GIFT. I'M ON BORROWED TIME and fully aware there are multiple bullets ready to end my life. Normally, I don't worry about the decisions I've made. At this moment, I'm regretting everything, but it's not due to the extra danger surrounding me.

If only I'd chosen a different path.

I tried.

Really, I did.

Not until it was too late though.

I didn't know he would tear my heart to pieces.

Once I realized I was in too deep, I attempted to get out. Yet nothing I said could persuade the powerful men in charge to give me another assignment.

Staying in my role was like diving off a boat and never coming up for air. For the first time in my life, I had something—someone—beautiful, loving, and real. It gave me hope for the future. But I was naive. And once I realized how stuck I was, it was as if the cold depths of the ocean swallowed me whole.

Now, I don't know how I'm ever going to do what they're demanding of me.

Four sets of beady eyes glare at me, assessing every word and movement I make. They all attempt to determine if I'm lying or telling the truth. The voice in my head screams they aren't buying a word I say, but I force myself to play it cool and not ramble.

Every breath I take becomes more difficult. The pain in my chest I can't seem to get rid of intensifies. Blood boils hotter in my veins, on the verge of making me break out into a full-out sweat. I struggle not to shift on my feet while maintaining my composure.

Leo Abruzzo steps closer. He's the youngest brother of Jacopo, who runs the Abruzzo dynasty. It's the first time in months I've seen Leo. I can't say I missed him.

After my father died, Ludis Petrov, heir to the Russian mafia, claimed me as his own. Ludis said my father worked for him. I had no knowledge of it. All I saw was how hard my father worked in his woodworking business. Yet, Ludis declared there was an unpaid debt. I had no money, so he informed me that he now owned me. I was fifteen at the time and had no way to fight when his men arrived to take me. And the first night in Ludis's house, he showed no mercy, taking my virginity.

I didn't want to be with him. When he ordered me to sleep in his bed, my stomach flipped. The maid told me not to fight him, claiming it would be easier to get through it if I didn't resist. Then she showed me the knife scars on her stomach and legs. It was from when she tried to fight him off.

Her disfigured body etched itself in my mind. So I took her advice when Ludis came back into the room, not making a sound while silent tears fell down my cheeks.

For years, I was his. Then he lost a bet. Before I knew it, I was sold to the Abruzzos to pay off his gambling debt. And they weren't any better than the Petrovs. I quickly learned they dealt with things in a similar fashion.

I no longer live with the Abruzzos, but they still own me. As I stare at the guns pointed at me and the muscular men who would snap me in two without warning, Leo's stale breath from last night's alcohol flares in my nostrils. He pins his bloodshot gaze on me, seething in Italian, "You bring us nothing. Should I remind you what we do to those who betray us?" Even though my native tongue is Russian, I speak Italian fluently, and therefore have no problem under-standing him.

My stomach churns. The memory of Leo's heavy body on mine makes me nauseous. Half of what I say is a lie. The other part is the truth. In a confident voice, I assert, "I haven't betrayed you. I never would. And he doesn't know. But I can only push so much before he knows who I am. He already suspects—"

"If he suspects, then you convince him otherwise!" Leo barks, slamming his hand on the table.

I refrain from jumping or showing any emotion. Most people see me as a cold, Russian woman. It's something I learned as a child from my father. He always said, *"Katiya, your emotions will kill you someday. You must learn to control them."*

It's something I've only gotten better at since Ludis first touched me. There's no room in life for weakness, which is another thing my father taught me.

I raise my chin and state to Leo, "I need more time."

"More time?" Leo spits, and some hits my cheek.

I don't react, freezing in my spot, resisting the urge to wipe his saliva off my face. I once did that and quickly learned my lesson when Leo kept me chained to a bench in a sauna for a week. He'd come in from time to time, taunting me with water, giving me only enough to stay alive.

Silence fills the brownstone. I struggle to push the lingering memories out of my mind. A beam of sunlight gets hotter, shining through the window, tormenting me further. My body feels overheated, as if I'm back in the sauna.

Leo nods to his thug. The sound of a magazine slamming into a Glock fills my ears right as one of the goons tugs on my hair and then holds the gun to my head.

My heart races. I tear my eyes off the ceiling, locking my gaze on Leo, staying as nonreactive as possible. In a firm tone, I say, "If he kills me, you're starting all over. Is that what you want?"

More tension fills the quiet room. The overpowering scent of men's sweat, alcohol, and smoke mix with musk. It closes in around me until I feel so suffocated, I think I might faint.

Leo steps closer, grabs my chin, and squeezes. His fingers dig so deep, I wonder if he cut the skin and is touching my jawbone.

"Ow!" I cry out, unable to not react.

A bead of sweat drips down his forehead. His hot breath gets more pungent. His eyes dart around my face then down to my breasts. He drills his orbs into me, pausing for what seems like forever. He finally threatens, "This is your last chance. If you don't find out who the Marino suppliers are by next week—"

"His brother's getting married in a few months. Give me until a month after the event. I'll gain the family's trust. The women. The men. The kids. Everyone. Then I'll have the information you need," I blurt out.

"A few months. That's convenient," one of the thugs mutters.

"Shut up," Leo growls, then his head snaps back toward me. A few more minutes pass as he silently studies me.

My pulse pounds in my neck while his fingers remain grasped tightly on my chin. I break the silence, claiming, "It'll be worth the wait. I'll find out a lot more. I promise."

"More? Such as...?" Leo questions.

Panic hits me. This is why I shouldn't blurt things out without thinking. My father would have lectured me for weeks about this mistake.

When I don't respond, Leo says, "You don't know—"

"Everything. Not just names, but how to contact them, their location, everything," I interject, once again not thinking about how impossible it's going to be but needing to get Leo out of the brownstone.

Leo studies me further before holding his face over mine.

My insides quiver harder. I push the memories of all the sadistic things he did to me to the back of my mind. I try to stay present in the moment so I don't lose all control of my emotions.

"Two weeks after the wedding. If you don't provide every detail we've discussed, I won't just kill you. I'll keep you locked up, ready for anyone who wants to defile you. You'll be begging for me to end your life. Do you understand?" he warns.

My stomach flips, and bile rises in my throat. I swallow it and nod. "Yes."

He squeezes harder then releases my chin, stepping back. Another moment passes as he attempts to intimidate me further. He sniffs and motions toward the door, saying nothing to his goons. They each scowl at me before leaving.

When the four men step outside, I run to the door and lock it. Not that it would matter, but it gives me a sliver of relief. I lean against the wood, trying to regulate my breathing, and finally let a tear escape.

As soon as it hits my chin, I brush it away. There's no time for emotions. Weakness will only get me killed.

Only a few months.

I'm never getting that information.

Why the heck did I ever say I would get everything?

I gently bang my head against the door, wishing my entire life wasn't a nightmare. All I want to do is escape the Abruzzo-Petrov nightmare I'm in.

But I can't.

Massimo is never going to tell me any of that information.

How could I even betray him at this point?

I close my eyes, and more tears fall. There's only one man, other than my father, who's ever loved me. When I met him, the world seemed to stop. I was at work at the library where the Abruzzos assigned me. We flirted, but I didn't think twice about it. When he asked me out, I declined. My life didn't have room for anyone else in it. I was damaged and owned by Leo. Plus, Massimo was a Marino, the Abruzzo's main enemy.

If only Massimo hadn't kept coming back.

The Abruzzos eventually caught wind about his interest in me. When they told me my assignment, I cringed. Yet there was nothing I could do unless I defied them. My fate would be nothing short of vile.

I'm unsure when I fell in love with Massimo. It might have been the first moment I laid eyes on him. But I guess it doesn't really matter. After I fulfill Leo's wishes, he's going to hate me.

Scratch that. I'm going to be dead. Either Leo is going to kill me, or Massimo will. Once I do what's required, there's no way Massimo will show me mercy. And I'm going to deserve every moment of pain.

I go into the bathroom and toss cold water on my face. As I stare in the mirror, everything is clear.

There will never be a happily ever after for me. The last few months, I've been fooling myself. No matter how much I want a life with Massimo, it isn't possible. I'm a former Petrov and now an Abruzzo, and there's no escaping them.

Even Massimo can't save me.

1

M C

Massimo Marino

Several Days Later

"WHERE HAVE YOU BEEN?" DANTE SNAPS, INTERROGATING ME the moment I step into the gym.

Irritation instantly replaces my good mood. Lately, no matter what I do, my brothers are all over my back. I place my water bottle on the table then slide on my weight-lifting gloves. To piss off my brother, I don't look at him. While walking toward the free weights, I answer, "Out."

"Where?" Tristano asks, setting the bar on the rack and rising off the bench.

"None of your business," I bark. I sit on the ground and reach for my toes, leaning into the stretch while attempting to avoid my brothers' steely gazes pinned on me.

The constant questions about where I'm at and who I'm with are getting old. All they want to do is lecture me about seeing Katiya. It's creating a real rift between us, and I'm unsure how to repair it. If they don't cease their accusations, they're going to leave me no choice but to turn violent on them. It's all getting old, and I'm over it. The number of times I held myself back from punching them is too many to count.

Their constant notions about Katiya and insinuations that I don't even know the person I'm seeing are beyond insulting. It's the first time in my life my brothers don't have faith in me. It's as if they think I've lost all my wits. And I'm sick of their demands to end it with her.

Nothing will stop me from being with Katiya—nothing. For the first time in my life, a woman actually gets me. I'm in love, and that's something I never thought would happen to me. It might be a bit messy due to my family's circumstances, but when I'm with Katiya, everything feels good. She fills a void inside me I didn't realize I had. Plus, since the moment I laid eyes on her, I've thought about no one except her.

My heart beats faster as I envision her long blonde hair, eyelashes that stretch for miles over deep-blue eyes, and pouty red lips that I'll gladly allow anywhere on my body.

Every time she speaks, my dick aches. Her Russian accent just does something to me. She has a no-one-messes-with-me aura, but I see the real her. Inside, she's fragile. And the shit the Abruzzos have put her through only deepens my hatred toward them.

I'll take them all down.

That's the one thing my brothers and I still agree upon, no matter my status with Katiya.

Every Abruzzo on Earth needs to die.

Immediately.

I release my toes then bend my arm above my head, pushing on my elbow to stretch my shoulder. Gianni crouches in front of me.

Our eyes lock, and all the rage I'm holding inside me ignites. He's wearing an arrogant scowl. Before I can speak, he states, "I called you all night."

I crack my neck then sniff hard. "And?"

"Since when don't you pick up?" Dante interjects.

I jump off the mat, grab two fifty-pound weights, and do warm-up squats, responding, "If it were important, you would have texted our code."

"So, from now on, if we need to talk to you and you're with *her*, we'll just use the code," Tristano sarcastically states.

"Watch your mouth. If you can't show my woman basic respect, I'll teach you a lesson," I warn, unhappy with his tone regarding Katiya.

My little brother crosses his arms. His mocking expression turns into a scowl. "Your woman?"

"Jesus, you're an idiot," Gianni mutters.

I drop the weights and shove him against the wall. "What was that?"

He recovers from the shock and pushes back. "How fucking stupid can you be?"

All the rage I've bottled up comes bursting out. I pull my arm back, make a fist, and swing. My knuckles connect with his cheek, but he turns his face, so it barely connects and doesn't do the damage I intended.

"Enough!" Dante shouts, pulling Gianni back while Tristano tugs at my arms.

"Get off me!" I order, yanking my limbs, but he has a strong grasp on me.

"Calm down!" he commands.

I escape his hold and spin, landing a punch on Tristano's bicep.

"What the fuck, Massimo!" he declares. His eyes turn cold. He rushes at me, and I lose my balance, taking him to the floor.

The next few minutes are chaos. My brothers and I are all screaming at each other while trying to throw punches.

"Enough!" Papà's voice rips through the air, but we don't stop. He continues screaming at us, yet none of us back down.

Men pull us apart, and it's only after I'm pinned to the ground that I realize it's the O'Connor brothers.

"You boys still have a lot of fight in you." Tully's Irish accent hits my ears.

I scowl at Brody, who has his arm across my throat. I choke out, "Get off me."

His brother Tynan tugs my arms over my head.

"I'm going to kill you," I threaten.

"Easy," he mutters.

"Get up. Now!" Papà orders.

Slowly, we all rise. Blood continues to pulse hotly through my veins. My brothers glare at me, and I return their angry stares.

"What is this about?" Papà demands.

No one speaks. The tension builds in the air. I cross my arms and refrain from leaving the room. I don't need another lecture from Papà about anything, either. Lately, it seems like all my family wants to do is tell me how they don't like my decisions. I'd happily run to my wing of the house, but that would be a cowardly move, and I'm not a chicken.

"Sorry, but can you deal with your family drama later? I've got things to do today," Devin states.

Tully flings his hand across Devin's head.

"Ow! What was that for?"

Tully points in his face. "Figure it out."

"Why are you all here? Bridget has already left to take the kids to school. Are you here to see her?" Dante asks, glancing at each O'Connor.

"No. You're all the reason I'm here. It seems we have a little issue to discuss," Tully states, his eyes turning into green slits.

Gianni scrubs his face. "What would that be? I don't have time for your games today, Tully."

13

Papà warns, "Do not disrespect Tully. And leave your cockiness out of this discussion."

"Well, don't let us waste any more of your time. Spit it out," Gianni challenges, his expression hardening.

"Don't push me right now," Papà cautions.

I shift on my feet as the room turns silent, waiting for Tully or Papà to tell us the reason for their visit. My brothers and I have so many different issues we're dealing with right now, I have no clue what he wants to discuss.

Tully questions, "Whose idea was it to utilize my property?"

"What are you talking about?" Dante asks.

Papà's nostrils flare. His dark eyes drill into Gianni. He snarls, "Who gave you permission to take out two detectives and an FBI agent?"

My stomach sinks. A little over a month ago, the authorities interrogated Cara and tried to turn her against our family. Gianni didn't hesitate to have us pick them up, claiming they crossed the line by harassing his wife. But we couldn't bring them to the dungeon below our house. We needed another place to torture them.

Papà didn't tell us not to do it, but we never actually asked permission. Something of this nature would have required his approval. We've all been at odds with him on too many topics lately. So, my brothers and I kept it from him. We called the O'Connors to utilize Tully's newest torture chamber to help us execute the three men.

It figures Tully and Papà would find out what we did. It's not the first time my brothers and I acted without Papà's permission or the first time we got caught. Yet each incident seems to send my father into a bigger tizzy.

Gianni doesn't flinch. He mimics Papà's leer and asserts, "They crossed the line by harassing my wife. I don't need permission."

Papà's face turns maroon. He angrily hurls, "Is that so?"

Tully sarcastically laughs. "When you utilize my property and kill the authorities on it, you need mine."

"All the evidence is gone. Aidan and Brody took care of it. Those three bastards are dead. They won't harass my wife, or anyone else's, again," Gianni proclaims.

Tully steps closer. He pulls a cigar out of his pocket then cuts the end with his knife.

"Not in the gym," I bellow. The last thing I want is to smell leftover cigar smoke while I work out.

Tully turns toward me. He lights it up, puffing on it, so a thick cloud of smoke fills the air. Defiance is all over his expression, and I hold myself back from smacking it off.

"Goddamnit, Tully," Dante mutters.

"Really? You had to in our gym?" Tristano mutters.

Tully blows more smoke, and he motions between my brothers and his sons. "You all owe me."

"Excuse me?" I blurt out. I'll be damned if I have to bend over for Tully.

He nods then inhales another puff, studying all of us. "Next time you decide to bring any authority figure, much less a

Fed, on my property, you better make sure I'm fully aware. Then you better have my permission. In the meantime, you all owe me a favor."

"We did *you* a favor," I claim. When Gianni told Tristano and me to pick up the detectives, we didn't argue. If anyone held Katiya in custody, questioning her and not giving her a phone call or access to her attorney, I'd want them dead, too.

"You did *me* a favor?" Tully questions.

"How did I raise such stupid men?" Papà seethes.

"Mine apparently aren't that bright, either," Tully replies, then scowls at Aidan.

He clenches his jaw, staring at Tully.

"Why am I here? I didn't do anything," Devin claims.

"Me, either," Tynan agrees.

"Shut up, you two," Brody orders.

"You're here so you can learn. And here's the lesson," Tully states, walking to the bathroom, stubbing out his cigar, then returning to us. He motions between Papà and him. "You all seem to have forgotten that we call the shots. None of you do. Yet you disregard us when there are decisions to make that have consequences beyond the scope of your engagement."

"This ends. Now," Papà sneers.

I glance at my brothers and the O'Connors. All of us have the same hardened expressions. If the O'Connors feel half as frustrated with Tully as we have with Papà lately, then I can only assume what they've done behind Tully's back.

"*We* run our families. That means *we* make the decisions. You run things past us first. No exceptions ever," Tully asserts.

Papà's glare throws more daggers at my brothers and me.

Tully adds, "Now that you've taken out the authorities, we're going to have to clean up your mess."

Brody blurts out, "What mess? I made sure there was nothing left of any of them. We distributed the ashes at the docks. Any DNA from those bastards is spread out all over the Atlantic."

Papà's face turns redder. He seethes, "You're all ignorant. You can't kill authorities right after they question you. Who do you think they are looking at now?"

I shrug. "Who cares. There's no proof. This isn't an issue."

"Idiot! Of course it's an issue. And now it's going to cost your father and me more with the guys on our payroll," Tully admits.

"Why? There aren't any bodies. No DNA. No proof. Why would you pay those bastards any more than they already get?" I question.

Papà roars, "Who do you think the top suspects are?"

"So what? No proof," I restate, then grind my molars.

"So what? Are you that naive?" Papà accuses.

I glance at my brothers. The look in their eyes tells me they feel the same way I do. This isn't a big deal. We have other issues to attend to, but this isn't one. This entire conversation is wasting our time.

Dante interjects, "Massimo is right. No proof. This is like any other thug we've taken care of in the past."

Papà spins toward Tully. "I've failed. My successor can't even see the damage he and his brothers have caused."

Gianni comes to Dante's rescue, confessing, "He wasn't there."

It only upsets Papà further. He points at Dante. "You may not have been there, but you knew. You said nothing to me. Did you give Gianni the go-ahead, too?"

Gianni snorts. "I don't need anyone's approval to take out someone who harasses and threatens my wife."

"The man's got a point," Brody offers.

Tully snaps his head toward him. "Apparently, my successor isn't ready to lead, either, Angelo."

Brody sniffs hard. He locks eyes with Dante. "Have you lost track of the number of times your father has said that to you?"

"Yep," Dante replies.

Papà steps closer. He shakes his head at Dante and Brody, then declares, "Grow up. Both of you. We have real issues. The Feds are looking at us closer. Every move we make is getting scrutinized. You all did this. When I'm dead someday, you're going to inherit these issues. Mark my word, you're going to regret making these amateur moves."

"I don't consider elimination an amateur move," Gianni cockily claims.

Rage flares on Papà's expression. He roars, "Did you like being arrested? Was it enjoyable for you to be locked in a cell, with no idea when or if you were getting released?"

Gianni grinds his molars, staying quiet.

"Yeah. I thought so. You put both our families at risk," Papà insists.

"And you two," Tully seethes, motioning to Brody and Aidan.

Tense silence hangs in the air. Every moment that passes gets more uncomfortable. Tully and Papà leer at all of us.

Dante runs his hand through his hair. "We need to move forward. What's done is done."

Tully's lips curve into a tight smile. My gut flips. Every time I've seen that expression, it means he has something up his sleeve we aren't going to like. He replies, "Oh, we're going to move forward all right. Everyone in this room owes us."

"What? Devin and I weren't even part of this," Tynan asserts.

"Way to have our back, bro," Aidan mutters.

Tristano and I exchange an uneasy glance. The last time we owed Tully, he made us rummage through sewage for some thug's lost finger. It was the most disgusting thing I've ever done. Tully watched us while he smoked his cigar and drank a tumbler of Irish whiskey. If I think hard enough, I can still smell the rotten feces.

Gianni snaps, "Enough of the dramatics, Tully. What do you want us to do?"

Tully and Papà lock eyes. More minutes of silence pass.

Tristano says, "I have a meeting this morning. Can we get on with this?"

"With who?" Papà asks, assessing my brother.

A brief hesitation flickers in Tristano's expression. Papà doesn't catch it, but I don't miss it, probably since I'm the closest to him. There isn't much he can do and get past me. I'm pretty sure he's lying when he responds, "Meeting at the docks."

Papà arches his eyebrows. "With who?"

Tristano shrugs. "My guys."

"About what?" Papà interrogates.

"Since when do we go over every meeting detail with you?" Tristano hurls back.

My big brother instincts take over. I don't know what he's up to, but I'll find out later. If he doesn't want our father to know, he must have his reasons. I interject, "He's meeting about the accident we had at the docks last week. His guys all need an assessment."

"We already did that," Papà replies, sizing up Tristano and me further.

"Not good enough. We still don't know why the container caught fire. Someone planted it. No one has been on our turf. I scanned all the videos. The only explanation is one of the guys is involved," Tristano quickly adds, avoiding my gaze.

"He's right. You need to figure that out, Angelo," Tully points out.

Papà sighs, then glances at the ceiling.

"So, can we move on with this conversation now?" Tristano asks again.

Tully's grin reappears. "Next Thursday night at nine. Angelo knows the address. Don't be late."

I groan, fed up with this entire scene. "And here we go again with Tully's games."

"Do not disrespect Tully," Papà barks, scowling at me.

"Tully, tell us what we'll be doing," Dante demands.

"Yeah, Dad. Don't keep us in suspense for several days," Brody dryly adds.

Tully smirks. "What fun would that be for me?" He turns to Papà. "Bring your best bottle."

Papà nods. "Will do."

Tristano gives me a worried glance. The scent of sewage flares in my nostrils. I try to breathe through it. I've had all sorts of bodily fluids on me, torn men's guts out, and done heinous acts. Those smells never stay with me. I wish I could somehow forget Tully's last payback. From the looks of it, my brother has the same horrible memories as I do.

"Fine. Anything else, or can I resume my workout?" Dante asks.

Tully's arrogant, happy smile makes me cringe inside. He glances at Papà. "I'm good. How about you, Angelo?"

Papà assesses all of us. He shakes his head. "I have nothing else to say right now." He turns, and Tully follows him out the door.

"What does your father have up his sleeve?" I ask the O'Connors.

Aidan shakes his head. "No idea."

"Well, I need to go," Tristano proclaims, walking toward the exit.

"Me, too," I mutter, following him.

"You just got here," Dante calls out.

I ignore him and grab Tristano's bicep once we turn the corner. "Want to tell me where you're really going?"

He glances behind us then clenches his jaw.

"What is it?" I ask.

He still doesn't answer.

"I just covered for you," I remind him.

He keeps his poker face. "Thanks. I'll tell you about it later."

The hairs on the back of my neck rise. I cross my arms tight to my chest. "Why don't you tell me now."

"It's not a big deal. I have to go. We'll talk later," he repeats, then takes off.

I watch him until I can't see him anymore, wondering what he's hiding. My phone rings, pulling me out of my trance. Katiya's name pops up on the screen, and the butterflies in my stomach flutter. It's another thing I've never felt before her.

I answer, "Hey, dolce."

Her Russian accent shows me no mercy. My cock hardens the moment she responds. She keeps her voice low, asking, "Are you tied up all day?"

I run through my schedule in my head then reply, "No."

She softly laughs. "Good. Then why don't you come over and tie me up?"

I slowly inhale, trying to calm my racing pulse. Images of my rope draped around her naked body flash in my mind. I can't stop my grin from forming. Making my way through the house to my wing, I lower my voice, ordering, "Turn on your video chat. I need to shower. You can play with yourself and let me watch until I get there."

Her breath hitches. Her voice is barely audible. "When can you get here?"

I step inside my room and go straight to the bathroom, turning on the shower. "I'll leave in five minutes. Now, be a good girl. Turn on your video and play with your pretty pussy the way I showed you to."

2

MC

Katiya

"STOP TOUCHING YOURSELF," MASSIMO COMMANDS VIA VIDEO chat.

My shallow breaths match the thumping beat of my heart. I squeeze my eyes shut and bite my lip while removing my hand from my lower body. I whine, "Why aren't you here yet?"

He half chuckles, half grunts. "I'm driving over 100 miles per hour. Now, look at me."

I obey, taking in every feature that pulled me in the moment I first saw him. His full lips, chiseled cheekbones, and wavy dark hair were enough to grab my attention. But what mesmerized me to the point of no return were his gray-blue eyes.

I've never seen anything like his authoritative, piercing gaze. Sure, I've had enough dangerous men over the years intimidate me, but none of their orbs ever hypnotized me the way Massimo's do.

Every emotion possible passes over his facial features. When he's angry, a storm rages so violently, goose bumps pop out on my skin. When we get intimate, he'll size me up with an intense, powerful stare filled with so much heat my cheeks burn. And it isn't only lust in his scrutiny. There's a vulnerability in his eyes so potent, my heart feels like it might explode. All I want to do is drop my guard, confess everything to him, and run away where no one will find us.

Then reality hits, and I come to my senses.

They'll always find us.

They own me.

My death will be at their hands, unless Massimo gets to me first.

The irony is I shouldn't feel anything for him. He's a Marino. My assumption is his family isn't any more law-abiding than the Petrovs or Abruzzos. And I may not know a lot about his affairs, but it's no secret he hates the Abruzzos. If he ever found out the truth, there's no way he'd still love me or protect me. I'd be his enemy, and he'd no doubt crush me the first moment he could.

If only I hadn't fallen for him. My life would be much simpler.

And I'd be lonely again.

It would be better than hurting him, which will happen eventually.

If only I could pull myself out of this situation and get away.

About eighteen months ago, Leo got bored and decided I was no longer suitable for his bed. He brought a new girl to his mansion. She was at least a decade younger than me. The moment I locked eyes with her horror-filled ones, my heart dropped.

I knew that look.

I was once that girl.

I wanted to help save her, but it was impossible. Guards filled Leo's estate, watching my every move. It's something I never got used to, either. Not that I believe Leo wanted me to. He liked the fact I lived in fear, even if I did my best to hide it. So there was no way to save the poor girl.

Within forty-eight hours of her arrival, Leo's thug escorted me out of his house. He took me to the brownstone I live in now. A new set of clothes was already in the closet. They were nothing like the designer ones Leo made me wear. A box on the dresser held a few pieces of non-flashy costume jewelry. Personal products you can buy at the grocery store were stocked in the bathroom. They were unlike the name brand, expensive ones I had at Leo's.

Within minutes of arriving, more of his goons came inside my new home. They sat me down and explained that I would be working as a librarian.

Everything they said was confusing. None of it made any sense to me. I had no training to do that job. There were no instructions other than to wait for their orders. They also said I would need to live off my salary. Besides my rent and utilities, they wouldn't pay for my food or anything else. Before they left, one of them slammed me against the wall and reminded me who owned me. If I ran or tried anything, there would be consequences. For weeks, I couldn't sit in a chair without feeling the sting of the bruise on my back.

After a few months, I fell into my librarian role, learning everything I needed to excel. I heard nothing from the Abruzzos and prayed they had forgotten about me. Most of all, I loved my job at the library. It was quiet and felt safe, which wasn't the case at the Petrov or Abruzzo estates. I also had a lot of free time when my manager put me on desk duty, so reading became a way to escape my reality.

Of course, I was only fooling myself. The Abruzzos didn't forget me. One day, a man named Donato came in. He made it clear he was with them and only came to see me. He wanted access to the basement rooms, which weren't public. I didn't even know how to give it to him at the time. I had never been down there.

Within a few weeks, I stole keys from my manager, made copies, then replaced her set before she knew they were gone. I gave them to Donato. From time to time, he'd arrive and sneak into the creepy space. But he always left me alone, so I didn't bother to learn what he was doing.

I later found out he used that room to keep Massimo's sister Arianna hostage. She got rescued, and Donato never returned to the library. I'm assuming Massimo's family killed him, but nothing was ever confirmed.

And that's how I got into the current predicament I'm in now.

Before Arianna's abduction, Massimo came to the library. I was putting returned books on the shelf, and a bolt of energy seared through my spine. When I turned, I had to hold my breath.

27

No one had ever affected me like that before. He oozed confident sexiness, but I knew he wasn't ordinary after being around so many dangerous men.

His twinkling, flirtatious eyes also screamed, *don't mess with me.* I had no doubt he'd kill anyone who got in his way. When he interrogated me about Donato, I played dumb, only giving him basic details. Whenever he returned to the library, my heart skipped a beat, even though I knew he was a Marino and I should stay away.

But that was impossible.

For a few weeks, it got harder to ignore his advances. It was like playing a game. He'd ask me out. I'd turn him down. He'd return the next day and we'd do it all over.

Yet his mesmerizing charm presented a problem I didn't anticipate. I couldn't help my face heating whenever he looked at me. It was as if he was undressing me with his eyes and debating what he wanted to do with me first. Plus, I'm sure my nervous laughter, the huge grin that hurt my cheeks, and my inability to tear myself away from his indecent ogle gave my feelings away.

Even when he'd lean forward and ask me to dinner, he'd also assert in his hushed voice what we'd be doing later that night in his bed. I'd only been with men who forced me to be with them. All I wanted was for them to leave me alone. But the electric zings lighting up my soul whenever Massimo was around confused me. I couldn't stop or ignore the chemistry between us. It's probably why I failed at turning him down in a way that made him stop trying. If anything, it made him try harder.

It was a problem for several reasons. One, I vowed never to let any man ever touch me again. Ludis and Leo were enough. Nothing about sex with them was fun or even slightly enjoyable. I had learned to block it all out during the event. So why did I imagine what it would be like to be with Massimo?

The second issue created a more serious complication. And I should have predicted it. I knew the Abruzzos were never far. They were watching me even though I never saw them. It wasn't long before they decided to use Massimo's persistence to date me to their advantage.

One day, Leo showed up at my brownstone. He laid out my new assignment. I was to find out everything I could about Massimo and who the Marinos' business contacts were. Leo wanted access to their jewelry suppliers, and he wouldn't rest until he had them.

Now, I'm officially dead meat. Not only did I convince Leo I'd get them, but I added more to my plate by promising him I'd find out how to contact them and where they reside.

It's the stupidest thing I've ever done. Massimo's never discussed his business with me, minus a few details anyone outside his circle could know. Plus, it doesn't help that we've had several angry conversations about the Abruzzos. His family doesn't trust me. And he didn't know I spoke Italian, so I overheard and understood several of his phone calls.

When he found out I was bilingual, he got irritated all over again, but I had already heard enough. It's clear the Marinos think I was involved in Arianna's abduction. It doesn't surprise me since Massimo is a smart man, and he knew I gave the key to Donato. Yet, somehow, I convinced Massimo I wasn't involved.

Even though it was the truth, something about that conversation triggered me. That evening, I woke up in a sweat, sobbing from a nightmare of being back in the sauna. I was so hysterical, I revealed some of the things Ludis and Leo did to me.

Massimo held me, trying to calm me from my panicked state, but I saw the deadly anger in his expression. It should have freaked me out more, but there's as much comfort in his rage-filled eyes as there is in his vulnerability. He vowed to kill them all. I begged him to forget I said anything. The last thing I want is his life in danger, especially because of me. I know the extent of Ludis and Leo's wrath. But Massimo isn't going to forget it.

The ironic part about that night is I saw the killer in Massimo. I know in my heart he'd not think twice about killing them. That look was about getting revenge, not just because they're his enemies but because he loves me. Yet one day, I'll pay for my sins. I shudder whenever I think about him turning those unforgiving eyes on me.

Lately, he's questioning me again regarding my involvement with the Abruzzos. I've barely skated past his interrogations. It's getting harder. Every time he drills me, I want to admit everything and beg him for his forgiveness.

The only thing I've ever wanted is for him to continue loving me. However, I know it's not possible. Eventually, it'll all come crashing down.

As our relationship has developed, I've witnessed the extremes of his need for vengeance and his vulnerability.

And Massimo isn't dumb. No matter how much I fake stupidity, there have been too many close calls. He's called me out on it, questioning me over and over again. One minute, a fierce hurricane will swirl in his expression, making me worry he knows the truth. The next minute, we'll be in bed, wrapped around each other, and his soul-crushing, vulnerable scrutiny almost kills me.

Everything about his wrathful stance means I should be scared of him. I don't doubt Massimo would invoke the same pain on me as the Abruzzos if he ever found out who I really am. Yet there's a strange comfort knowing he's capable of harming me. Maybe I subconsciously convinced myself it would be better for him than for them to end my life.

When Massimo and I are lying in bed, and his body is pretzeled around mine, I tell myself it's time to end it between us before it's too late. I'll listen to him breathing, feeling his heartbeat against my back, ordering myself to sneak out and finally do what I've been planning.

For years, I've stashed cash to try and escape the Abruzzos. I have enough for a fresh start in the little beach town of St. Pete, Florida. I've never been there, but the photos and videos I've seen online make me believe I could be happy there. At least, I thought that until Massimo had to enter my life.

Too many nights, I lay in bed, plotting out my escape and reassuring myself it's better to try than continue to be at their mercy. When I met him, I was close to the amount I always told myself I needed. And if he weren't in my life, I wouldn't have thought twice about leaving. I'd be gone. However, I always chicken out when I try to work up the nerve to leave.

I can't even blame staying on the fear of the Abruzzos finding me. For years I saved my cash, diligently hiding it and mapping out how I would break free. Every task in my plan has a check mark. I'm unsure if I'd truly escape them forever, but I'm willing to die trying. So there's no reason to stay, especially since it's impossible for Massimo and me to have a legitimate future.

But I never even move an inch. Every night, I kick myself for my inability to leave. It's like paralysis replaced my motivation to go. Each time I think about not seeing Massimo, I feel like I can't breathe. I might as well take a knife and slice it through my heart. And that's why every day, I look at myself in the mirror, trying to find the strength to tell him we're through. But I'm in too deep. I don't know how to go back to the time when I only worried about myself.

Then there are these moments, like right now. I'm fixated on Massimo and his intense expression, even though it's only through the phone. All my self-talk to have him come over and discover the information I need for Leo falls to the wayside. Massimo's already commanding me, and he's not even next to me. Every word that flies out of his mouth might as well be a commandment. And I curse myself for the millionth time for being so weak.

"Let me in," he demands.

I blink, noticing the sunshine behind him for the first time. That's how pulled in I am. I didn't even realize he got out of his car.

I jump off the couch and press the button to release the lock to the building. My heart pounds with anticipation while I try to convince myself to manipulate him into telling me the information I promised Leo I'd obtain.

Get it, give it to Leo, then skip town, I repeat, over and over. If I give it to Leo, the best-case scenario is that he won't look for me. Yet I also can't shut up the voice in my head telling me it's a fat chance he won't.

I have to try.

Maybe I can disappear, and by the time Leo wants me to do another job, he won't be able to find me.

Fat chance.

By the time Massimo gets to my door, I feel stronger.

I can do this. Once I'm gone, I can attempt to have a life.

Without him? How?

Don't worry about that problem right now. This is survival.

My father's voice says in my head, "There's no room for weakness."

Massimo knocks. I take a deep breath, vowing to choose the chance for freedom over him.

Like all my previous attempts, my promise to myself falls to the wayside the moment he steps inside. Before I can even exhale, he tosses his jacket on the floor and has me against the wall, with his lips and tongue all over mine. His hands hold my cheeks. The woodsy scent of his cologne makes my butterflies go crazy. But the look in his eyes, the one that has both danger and vulnerability in it, that's the final bullet to my plan.

He's my quicksand. I'd happily drown in him forever. There's no pulling myself out. Instead of staying focused on my task, all I can do is fall further.

His steely gaze locks on mine. He studies me, the danger in his orbs flaring.

I panic that he knows something. My pulse beats in my neck while a lump grows bigger in my throat. I swallow it then ask, "What's wrong?"

Another moment passes under his scrutiny. His thumbs trace my lips. More anxiety builds, mixed with the uncontrollable desire I always have for him. The thought passes in my mind that maybe he could run away with me, but I scold myself. That's only an unattainable fairy tale.

His deep voice sends heat through my veins. And it makes zero sense why his statement turns me on so much. I shouldn't like what he does to me. Yet lately, it's like the more I experience being at his mercy, the more I crave it. He states, "You disobeyed me."

I sharply inhale. That phrase is one I used to wish I'd never hear again. Ludis and Leo used to say that, and a horrible punishment always followed. The first time Massimo said it, it was like I woke up from a deep sleep. Tingles raced down my spine, creating a feeling I'd never experienced before.

Right now, my pulse races so fast I feel dizzy. Maybe I'd fall if his muscular frame didn't have me trapped against the wall. I barely breathe out, "How?"

The corners of his mouth twitch, but then he gains control of it, sternly assessing me again. More silence fills the air, adding to the tension. He sniffs hard, cocking one eyebrow, dragging his knuckles over my cheek.

I close my eyes, melting into him.

His hot breath hits my ear. "Does it matter?" He flicks his tongue on my lobe then places his face in front of mine.

Zings burst in all my cells. I open my lids, admitting, "No."

Satisfaction fills his expression, but it dies quickly. He wraps a lock of my hair around his finger. "Did you get the rope I ordered?"

My butterflies spread their wings faster. He presses closer, and I whimper while nodding. "It's under my bed."

He gives me an authoritative glance then grabs my wrists and pins them above my head. I gasp as he asks, "How badly do you want me to tie you up?"

I take a few breaths, attempting to calm my racing heartbeat, then admit, "It's all I thought about since it arrived."

His lips curve into an arrogant smirk. Without releasing my wrists, he fists my hair and tugs it with the perfect amount of force. He sniffs hard, digging his erection against my belly.

Moments pass, increasing the electricity between us. His chest presses closer, and I feel his heartbeat. He commands, "There won't be any begging today."

"No?" I question. Massimo usually makes me plead for my orgasms until I'm crying. Then he gives me a release so strong, I'd die happy if it were my last breath.

His face hovers over mine. The blue in his eyes twinkles. "No. I'm putting a gag in your mouth."

3

Massimo

KATIYA INHALES SHARPLY. HER BLUE EYES WIDEN, AND THE longer I stare at her, the darker a sexy blush colors her cheeks.

I've never gagged her before. I've tied her up, restraining her for hours, doing all sorts of wicked things to her. After she told me what Ludis and Leo used to do to her, including the days they kept her captive in a sauna, I stopped doing it. I didn't want to trigger her. We still had sex, but it was different. She knew I was being cautious and told me to stop.

We had a long conversation about things. She said it was different with me, but I was still hesitant. We ended up fighting so much about it that she convinced me to do it again. I eventually gave in, and I have to say, it was a relief. Not taking control of her was like a punishment from God himself. It's like it's in my blood to dominate her, to have her helplessly at my mercy.

Even though we went back to normal, I held off gagging her. It's only been a thought in my head, but the urge has grown to the point I can no longer ignore it. I've never even discussed it with her. Now that I've stated what I want to do, I'm studying her to see what she thinks without giving her any clue she's the decision-maker for this activity.

Because she thinks I'm always in control.

Always.

No matter what.

But every time I have her in a vulnerable state, she's the one who makes the decisions. I'll study how her breathing turns shorter. Or the expressions on her face. Then her voice will change, and the desperation for whatever she needs is so potent, it makes me want to cum in my pants.

Right now, there's nervous anticipation in her eyes. I don't miss the way her red-stained lips slightly tremble. It's perfection, and I drag my thumb over her bottom one. I assert, "Did you wear this to match the rope?"

A few days ago, I found a blood-red cotton, silk-blend rope. I was in the sex toy store. I didn't even know why I went in. Maybe subconsciously, I knew time was up. I could no longer prohibit myself from holding back. My urges were only receiving more fuel every time I had her naked with rope or metal around her. The moment I spotted the luxury rope, I knew I needed it. Then I went looking for a black ball gag, imagining her lips in the exact shade she's now wearing.

Her hot breath hits my thumb. She responds, "I did."

"Then you called me?"

She nods, her eyes sparkling brighter, admitting, "Yes."

My dick strains against my zipper, pulsing against the designer denim. I fight to keep my control, not wanting her to know she's the one who holds the cards. I tighten my fist around her blonde locks and peck her on the lips, pulling away the moment she attempts to stick her tongue in my mouth. I grunt, taunting, "So you disobeyed me, and you decided to be a tease?"

She furrows her eyebrows then bites on her lip, further torturing me. Her voice cracks as she says, "I'm...umm... I still don't know what I did to disobey you."

I pause, tilting my head. She squirms, but it results in her pushing her body against my aching cock. I slide my hand under her chin and grip it so she can't move, then declare, "I said you couldn't come."

"I-I didn't."

"No?" I question, then release her hair. I slide my hand to her pussy, cupping it over her skimpy, matching blood-red lingerie. Heat sears into my palm. I hold in a groan, exhaling slowly.

"I swear I waited," she claims.

I glide my thumb under the lace, running it over her swollen clit.

She shudders, closing her eyes and whispering, "Massimo."

I keep the same pace and pressure, ordering, "Open your eyes."

Her lids fly open. She swallows hard.

I lean closer so I'm touching her mouth. To see her reaction, I ask her as if she has no choice, "You're a dirty little girl, aren't you? You can't wait for me to gag you, tie you up, and torture you all night. Can you?"

She shakes her head. "No. Please do it."

Her answer couldn't be any more perfect. Satisfaction swells in my gut while adrenaline pools in my veins. I sniff hard, not tearing my gaze off hers, sliding my index and middle finger up her soaked pussy and keeping my thumb on her clit.

She moans, pinning her eyebrows together.

I yank my hand out then shove my fingers in her mouth. She sucks as I claim, "Get it all. Then get on your knees. Before that ball goes into your mouth, you're sucking me off. You're going to swallow all of me. And then you're going to taste both of us while you suck on the gag, understand?"

Her chest rises and falls faster. She slides her hands down my chest, and I allow her to spin me into the wall. She gracefully dips to her knees, unfastening my belt and pants and shoving them to the floor.

A loud clang hits the tile. Her tongue and hand stroke my shaft.

I fist her hair again, positioning her head so she glances at me. It doesn't faze her. She never stops working my cock. Her teeth graze my vein, and I groan.

A smirk appears on her lush lips. She may be full of me, but I don't miss it.

I make a mental note to give her an extra punishment later. I gaze at the curve of her creamy, round ass with a tiny strip of lace between the cheeks, then proclaim, "You better be prepared, my dolce. I'm marking you as mine once that gag goes in your filthy little mouth."

She blushes again, making me pulse inside her.

Visions of the ball in her mouth while she's tied up in rope make me feel semi-crazy. I palm her head and take control of her movements.

Like always, she submits, opening the back of her throat and taking in all of me. Not once does she fight me, even when she makes a small gagging noise.

I keep her positioned on me, not showing her any mercy. Her eyes glisten, and one tear drips down her cheek. She fights through it, finding her breath and swallowing every time my head hits the back of her throat.

"Christ," I blurt out. She's the only woman who's ever done that to me. Hell, she's the only woman who's ever taken all of me in her mouth and pussy, yet never complained about the speed or force with which I take her. It's like our bodies were designed for each other. I never have to worry about whether she's ready or not. Her body always opens for me, no matter how long she or I play with her.

Plus, Katiya is one of the strongest women I know. Others may think she's cold, but I respect her guarded attitude. These moments where she submits to me only serve to stroke my ego. It's rare to find a woman like her who knows how to drop her hard act and allow herself to be at my mercy.

I debate about extending this little show, but my hand clenches the ball gag in my pocket. More images erupt in my mind, and the issue gets sorted. I move her faster, and adrenaline surges through me so rapidly, I have to press my hand against the wall to steady myself.

"Fuuuck," I bellow, my cock pumping like a machine gun in her mouth.

She takes every drop of my cum, swallowing it until there's nothing left. When the white light disappears, and I can focus again, I lock my gaze on her watery blues. Her plump lips twitch. I release her hair, and she resubmits, looking down at the floor.

I pull up my pants and fasten them. Then I remove my T-shirt, kneel, and trace the lace over her hard nipple. The sound of her inhale hits my ear. "This looks nice on you, but remove it."

I stand then leave the room, saying nothing else. I find the rope in her bedroom, untying the loose knot. My cock jumps back to attention, as if we didn't just do what we did.

I assess the room, wishing we were at my place.

That will never happen.

I close my eyes for a moment, pushing the thought to the back of my head. I'm unsure how to solve the issues my family has with Katiya. They've never even met her, but they insist she's working for the Abruzzos. I know the truth though. She was kidnapped by Ludis Petrov then sold to Leo Abruzzo, and they both raped her.

When Katiya first told me about it, I had questioned her association with the Abruzzos. She swore she wasn't part of them. No matter what my gut said, I couldn't seem to end it with her and leave.

Instead, I tied her up, sexually torturing her so she would tell me the truth.

She never changed her story. We finally fell asleep, and I still didn't know what to believe. Then she woke up screaming in terror. There was no way she was faking her horror. I made her tell me everything. As soon as she did, I felt guilty for our previous sexual encounters where I restrained her. I could barely stop myself from going over to Leo's and shooting up whoever got in my way to kill him. If it hadn't meant leaving her, I would have. But pulling myself away when she was so fragile wasn't possible.

I finally got her to sleep. The next day, I asked her how she was here if Leo had owned her. And, if she wasn't working for them, how had he not killed her?

According to Katiya, Leo got drunk one night and pissed his wife, Ramona, off. Katiya said she was always angry about why Katiya was there. Leo made a loud declaration in front of his men that he would make her a wager in a game of cards. If he won, Ramona had to shut up forever about Katiya and the other girls he brought into the house. If Ramona won, Katiya would go free, and she was to never step foot in the house again.

Ramona won, and they left Katiya out in the street that night. She claimed she had never met Donato until he showed up at the library, but no other Abruzzos have talked to her since.

I asked her many more questions, but she had answers for them all. They all made sense and connected. I believed her.

I *still* believe her, even if my family can't get past it.

My gut churns for a moment. I've never been at odds with my brothers. Sure, we've had the occasional disagreement about how to do things, but this is new territory. I'm not sure how to show them who Katiya is, especially since they've made it clear she's not welcome.

Snap out of it. This isn't the time to analyze.

Tristano's words pop into my mind. *"Once an Abruzzo, always an Abruzzo."*

Jesus. It's Katiya. She loves me.

I love her.

Fuck all of them.

I wrap the blood-red rope around my fist, determined not to let my family ruin my time with her. Katiya doesn't deserve anything but the best part of me.

I turn on the air conditioner. I've always kept things cool during these types of sessions, but I'm extra conscious of it since hearing about the sauna. I walk into the main living space and freeze. Not because I'm surprised about her current position but because she's so stunning. No matter how often I look at her, she never fades. The deeper I fall for her, the more beautiful she gets.

43

A strong, powerful woman like her can submit to me.

Jesus.

I finally found my girl.

Forever.

I study all of her. She's still kneeling, her head tilted toward the ground, her back straight. Her blonde hair cascades to the middle of her waist in waves. The barely there lace lingerie she wore is folded neatly on the floor next to her.

I walk over, kneel in front of her, and command, "Look at me."

She lifts her face, locking her gaze with mine.

My heart beats faster. I take the ball gag out of my pocket, ordering, "Lie on your back and spread your pussy lips open."

She obeys, opening her long legs, then slowly grazing her fingertips up her body. The sparkle in her eyes brightens, and her nipples stick straight in the air. She arches her back, tilting her hips slightly up, then placing her hands between her thighs. She licks her lips, bats her lashes, and waits.

Jesus. She's the sexiest woman on Earth.

I squeeze the ball, running my palm a few times over the back of her thighs. Her breath hitches, and the scent of her arousal flares in my nostrils. "Do you know why I'm having you open your sweet pussy up, dolce?"

Her index finger twitches.

I put my finger over hers and circle it over her clit.

She whimpers.

"You want to start playing now, greedy girl? Hmm?" I ask, then put my finger next to hers, continuing to circle.

"Oh," she breathes.

"So wet for me. Good girl," I praise, then take the ball and start to slip it inside her.

She gasps, her eyes widening.

I keep my finger over hers and press harder on her clit while sliding the ball gag in and out of her.

"Massimo!" she cries out.

I stop all motion, grabbing her finger with mine.

A desperate expression appears. She begs, "Please."

"You want this?" I taunt and resume gliding the ball gag in and out of her.

"Yes. Oh God," she whispers.

"Hands on your breasts," I order.

She moves them to her nipples and waits for my command.

"Play with them."

"Thank you, sir," she replies, her Russian accent coming out thicker than normal.

I work her clit and the ball gag. She cups her breasts, rubbing her thumbs over the edge of her nipples. A soft pink colors her cheeks, making the blue in her eyes appear lighter. Her skin glistens. Soft moans rotate with her pleas. "Massimo. Please."

I slow everything down, provoking, "What's going to happen when I shove this in your mouth and secure it? You won't be able to beg me. How will I know what you want?"

"Massimo. Please!" She makes a few tiny circles with her hips, but I grab them.

I tug the ball gag out, grab her wrists, and pin them over her head.

"Oh!"

I kiss her, sliding my tongue so deep I can't go any farther, then release her hands.

She consumes me, holding my head as close as possible and making me forget for a moment about everything.

Life.

Who my family is.

The ball gag.

When her nails dig into my shoulders, I sit back with my knees next to her hips. I hold the ball gag near her lips. "Do you smell yourself?"

"Yes."

"But you still taste me on you?" I question.

She nods. "Yes."

"Lick," I order.

She takes a long swipe, and heat ignites my blood. Her tongue swirls the ball then traces over my fingers.

I start to slide it in her mouth, saying, "Open."

She obeys, widening her lips. The ball goes all the way in and then a panicked expression takes over. Her eyes glisten.

I hold one hand over the ball so she can't spit it out. With the other, I caress her cheek with the back of my knuckles and instruct, "Breathe through your nose while sucking on the ball. Let's do it together, dolce."

She blinks a few times, mimicking the deep inhales and exhales I make through my nostrils. Her body relaxes, and her expression calms.

"Good girl. You don't need to be scared of this, okay?"

She nods, and an uninterpretable sound fills the air.

I kiss her forehead then roll next to her, demanding, "Hold the gag and sit up."

She places her hand over it and sits with her back to me.

I secure the black leather strap then kiss the back of her head. I jump up and pull her on her feet.

She's a magnificent piece of art. Her blue eyes and pink cheeks, and those red lips around the black gag, are priceless. Tingles flicker in my cells, and I wonder for a moment how I'm going to hold back releasing inside of her.

Stay focused, I reprimand myself.

She waits patiently, not moving or taking her gaze off mine.

Something in me switches. It's like a light flicking on. Or maybe in my case, it's off.

All the things I want to do to her that others think belong in the dark.

But they don't.

And they're wrong.

My warped, sexually-deviant self takes over. I steer her toward the window and position her in front of it. The blinds are half-open, letting in bright lights from the midmorning sun.

I open the slats all the way then glance down at the sidewalk. It's a busy weekday. The city is bustling like normal. I let my eyes roam over the buildings across the street.

I turn toward Katiya and point at the window. "If anyone went to the glass, they could see us standing here right now."

She tilts her head. I don't miss the fear mixed with excitement glowing in her orbs. It would be the first time there was any possibility of anyone seeing us while doing anything sexual.

I cup her chin. I tease, "I'd have you face the window, but then I'd miss all the fun, wouldn't I?"

A mumbled noise that sounds like agreement fills the air.

"Then again, we have the hook I installed, don't we? I can turn you if I use that," I state.

A muffled, "Mm-hmm," comes from her.

I kiss her forehead, guide her a few steps back, then sling the rope in the air. It catches on the large hook I attached to the ceiling over a month ago.

I position the middle of the rope on the metal then motion with my finger for her to come to me.

Her hips sway as she steps forward. She pauses in front of me.

"Hands above your head, fingers laced together," I order.

She obeys.

I slide my hands over her arms and secure the rope around her wrists. With the excess rope, I twist it down her arms. Then I put the rest over her chest and around her breasts. I make a final loop one time around her rib cage before securing it.

I stand back and stare with pride at my beautiful blonde bombshell.

A cloud moves in the sky, and more sunlight streams through the window. She's a Michelangelo, fascinating enough to go into any museum. She looks helpless. And innocent. Neither are things anyone on the street would ever say about her. The blood-red rope against her pale Russian skin competes with the black ball gag peeking out of her blood-red lips. It's pure perfection.

I turn her halfway so I'm on one side and the window is on her other. The wall in front of her has a floor-length mirror. If anyone is watching, they'll get a good show. And I can see every angle of her from behind her. I lick her earlobe and assert, "It's time to lean over, dolce. Daddy's ready to spank you."

4

MC

Katiya

MASSIMO'S WARM FLESH PRESSES INTO MY SKIN. HIS HAND circles my waist then traces the rope around my breast.

I stare at the mirror, getting turned on about everything I see.

Sunlight beams hotter through the window, and it only fuels the tension in the air. The more I stare at the red rope around my body or the black gag in my mouth, the more turned on I get.

I'm unsure why I love it when Massimo restrains me, or why I'm suddenly excited to do explicit things in front of my neighbors, or how I can wear this gag and not freak out.

I used to when they put one on me.

I shudder, remembering all the times I had panic attacks. The balls were bigger than the one Massimo slipped in my mouth. I don't know if it's the size that makes it okay or just because it's Massimo. Everything I do with him turns me on, and nothing feels off-limits.

He kisses the back of my neck. I reprimand myself for thinking of my past, and I try to push the thought as far away from me as possible.

I'm with Massimo now.

For how long though?

It doesn't matter. He's mine at this moment.

He's going to kill me one day.

"What's wrong?" Massimo frets, moving in front of me.

I snap out of my internal debate and try to talk, forgetting about the gag. I turn quiet when I realize I can't speak and begin to panic.

"Breathe," Massimo commands, demonstrating what I should do.

I follow his lead and return to sucking on the ball and breathing through my nose as he instructed. When I'm calm, he asks, "Do you want me to stop?"

I furrow my eyebrows and shake my head.

"You sure? You seemed far away."

I shake my head again.

He cups my cheek, studying me how he always does whenever he worries. He finally asks, "Then you're okay? You want to resume?"

There's no doubt in my mind. Now that I'm restrained and at his mercy, there's no way I would tell him to stop. My entire body is humming with anticipation, so I eagerly nod.

He assesses me for another moment, and I think he might stop. I nod again, and his expression morphs into the one I crave to see. It's as if he's going to devour me in pieces until he has all of me. Relief fills me when he kisses my forehead. Stepping back, he states, "You've disobeyed me. Naughty girls need to learn their lessons."

My pulse quickens, beating so hard in my neck, I wonder if he can see it. I focus on my breathing, maintaining control of the extra surge of energy shooting through my veins.

He clenches his jaw and drags his fingertips over my collarbone, down my arm, and across my stomach.

Tingles erupt under his touch. I squirm, pushing my hips closer to him, wishing he had his pants off so I could wrap my legs around his waist and have him inside me.

However, it's not how this works. And I'm feeling extra needy today. Maybe it's because I'm desperate not to lose him, but I know I eventually will.

It's impossible to survive what I have to do to even have a chance to live.

I'm a fool. Massimo will hunt me down just like the Abruzzos. But he won't stop until he finds me. Perhaps they won't care about me anymore once I'm not of value to them anymore, but Massimo won't be forgiving.

Massimo softly chuckles, pulling me out of my thoughts again. He tucks my locks behind my ear. The scent of his skin and his woodsy citrus cologne flare in my nostrils. I inhale deeper, wanting to take as much of it in as possible. His lips hit my ear as he asserts, "I didn't tell you that you could touch me, did I?" He grasps my neck and squeezes, tilting my head back. I can still breathe, but any more strength and I won't be able to. "Now you have to take the consequences."

My butterflies go wild. Massimo's punishments are another thing I don't understand. The pain he bestows on me gives me pleasure. It baffles me. He's not as rough as Ludis or Leo, but he somehow knows how to take me to the edge, break me, then put me back together.

He circles his hand around my waist and caresses my ass cheek. Warmth contrasts with the cool air. It's something else he always does. He keeps the temperature chilly even though it's barely spring. It creates a deeper sting when he doles out my punishments.

He continues rubbing my ass and fists my hair with his other hand. He tugs my head back until my neck can't physically go any farther and I'm facing the ceiling. He states, "Should we review the rules?"

A tiny sound comes out of me. I'm unsure if he wants me to try and answer, but he demonstrates the consequences every time he reviews the rules. And that turns both of us on.

"Rule number one. I determine when you touch me. You broke it, and now, I need to remind you what happens."

Before the last word is out of his mouth, he takes his hand and smacks my ass.

A loud slap echoes in the air.

A sting erupts along my backside. My pussy pulses, and I whimper as he spanks me three more times before rubbing my tender skin.

He repositions my head so I'm facing him. Darkness fills his expression. It should scare me, but all it does is make my body throb more. His deep voice declares, "The rest of the rules, we'll review with you watching in the mirror."

Zings ping-pong in my cells.

"There's one more thing, dolce."

I arch my eyebrows, trying to inhale more oxygen and keep myself calm, but the anticipation I always feel swirls with endorphins.

He drags his fingers over my nipple then pinches them.

I moan, closing my lids, refraining from moving my body closer to his.

"Open your eyes, Katiya," he demands.

I obey, and his commanding expression sends delicious chills down my spine. He studies me a moment then says, "I think it's time we upgrade, don't you?"

A temporary shot of fear passes through me.

Massimo acknowledges it, challenging, "You're breaking rules. We need to make sure you're a good girl in the future.

Your actions leave me no choice. Or do you want to stop now?"

Panic he'll untie me replaces my fear. I shake my head.

His lips curl up. "Good girl. Now, look out the window for a moment. See if anyone is watching. Think about all your neighbors who might see that you're a dirty, naughty girl. When I return, you'll only look at the mirror. Every part of your punishment, you'll watch. If you take your focus off the mirror, there will be consequences. Do you understand?"

"Mm-hmm," I agree.

His grin widens. He kisses me on the forehead and turns my head toward the window. "Look closely, my little dolce."

I keep my eyes focused on the glass, missing the heat of his body when he steps away. I don't know what he's doing, but I don't dare disobey him. I scan the buildings, wondering if some of the people I can see are looking back at me. My adrenaline pumps harder, and by the time he comes back, a drop of my juice rolls down my thigh.

"Fucking dirty girl," he murmurs in my ear, his body pressed against my back. He wipes his finger over my thigh, turns my head to the mirror, and slides his finger in his mouth. Then he arrogantly proclaims, "I'm going to whip you until you remember the rules."

He's gripping a flogger with a black handle, dark-red leather straps, and tiny black metal balls on the ends. The fear mixes with anticipation again, and every sensation in my body seems to heighten.

"Everyone is watching you get punished, including you. If I see your eyes move from the mirror, you'll pay." He takes the flogger and drags it over my quads, pinning his steel-blue eyes on mine in the mirror.

I swallow hard, tearing my eyes off his and watching him move the flogger around my body.

He nibbles the curve of my neck, continuing to observe me, and glides his one palm up my arm until his hand is over the rope on my wrists. He murmurs, "You're the sexiest woman I've ever seen. All those people watching, they want you and can't have you. You're mine. No one will ever have you again besides me. Understand?"

It's all I want—to be his, and only his, forever. A pain grows within my heart, blending with the love I can't escape and wish I didn't feel toward him.

He slides his hand down my arm and turns my chin so I'm looking at him. The contrasting vulnerability and dominant expression take my breath away while the affection I feel expands. He strokes my cheek with his thumb, tracing the leather from the gag. His voice softens, and he demands, "Tell me you agree. No one else ever again will touch you besides me."

Tears well in my eyes. I blink hard, nodding, trying to breathe correctly and not choke, so he doesn't have to remove the ball.

He softly smiles then kisses my cheek. His eyes darken again, and he orders, "Grab the rope and focus on the mirror. Let everyone see what they'll never have."

I wrap my fingers around the soft fibers and stare at my gagged, bound body in the mirror. The sound of the air conditioner echoes in the room. A blast of cold shoots out of the ceiling.

Goose bumps pop out on my skin. My nipples grow larger, hardening from the cold. Massimo steps back, and the loss of his body heat makes a shiver roll down my spine.

He trails the flogger down my back. It fills me with more anticipation. I watch in the mirror, and he pulls his arm back, then smacks my ass with the flogger.

A new type of sting sprawls over my ass cheek. I blurt out, "Ugh!"

He rubs my ass in a circle four times then hits me four times with the flogger.

I suck the ball harder, grip the rope tighter, and try to keep my emotions in check.

"Two people across from you are watching. A man and a woman," he claims, giving me a challenging stare in the mirror.

Zings fly to my core. I fight the urge to look but stay focused on the glass in front of me.

The devil lights up in his eyes. Ludis, Leo, and Massimo all have him in them. I've seen him ignite in all their orbs too many times. When he appeared in Ludis and Leo's, I would be scared. I knew bad things were about to happen. When he pops up in Massimo's, relief fills me. It's as if I need to see he's just as dangerous as they are, yet he never pushes me past the point he should.

"You don't want to look?" Massimo taunts.

I don't move, never tearing my glare off his. Somehow, in these moments where he eggs me on to break my submission, I feel my strength. In some ways, it's the only time I don't feel weak, even when others see me as a cold Russian woman.

Massimo's blues twinkle. "Ah. I see. You're going to behave today." He slides his hand around my body. Two fingers glide inside me, and he rolls his thumb on my clit. "You want a reward, dolce?"

I attempt to say please, but it comes out muffled.

He buries his face in my neck, inhaling deeply and manipulating my body until my legs are trembling and I'm about to fly over the edge.

Then he stops, goading in my ear, "You didn't think I'd forget about the rest of your punishment, did you?"

Desperation fills me. "Please," I say again, but it's incoherent around the gag.

His hand moves the rope over my breast, teasing my nipple. Everything feels so much more sensitive than in the past. Maybe it's the softness of the rope. Perhaps it's the cold air mixing with his body heat. It's possible that the thought of others watching us while I see everything he's doing to me makes it more erotic. Whatever the reason, my entire body craves a release, and I can't stop moaning.

He keeps tormenting my breasts, repositions himself to the side of me, then takes the flogger and smacks my ass harder than before.

I yelp, my pussy spasms, and tears roll down my cheek.

"How many times did you come when I wasn't here?" he questions.

I shake my head.

He flogs my ass again. I jump, but he moves in front of me, using his body as a wall. "Did you forget about the shower when I left this morning?"

A guilty flush fills my cheeks.

Arrogance flares on his face. "You think I didn't know you played with that sweet pussy? It wasn't enough, though, was it?"

My blush deepens. I can't deny it. I was still in bed when Massimo went home. He woke me up with a kiss, gave me a quick orgasm with his tongue, then left. It only made me need more. I got myself off in the shower, but that didn't work, either. All I wanted was him back in my arms, so I put on my red outfit and called. I didn't think he'd be free but was happy when he came right over.

"You practically pulled my hair out when you came in my mouth this morning. But you're a needy girl, aren't you?" he states.

I nod, wanting nothing else but for him to do it all over again.

He steps back, sniffs hard, then glances at the window.

I struggle not to look but keep focused on the mirror. A long silence passes, then he turns back to me. "We have more viewers. Should I show them how long I can eat you, keeping you on edge until your entire body is full of sweat and shaking?"

I don't answer, wanting him to do it but aware he'll drive me crazy. When Massimo decides to punish me, he can go hours making me wait for my orgasm. My clit's already swollen. My walls are dying for his body. And my legs started shaking as soon as he started doling out my punishment for disobeying him.

He traces the outline of my hair, repeating on my other breast the same thing he did with the rope earlier.

I whimper, once again wondering why everything feels so much more sensitive.

He drops the flogger and cups my pussy. "If I lick and suck your pretty little cunt, everyone is going to see how greedy you are. Is that what you want?"

I don't respond, knowing he might do the exact opposite of what he's suggesting if I do. Right now, my senses are so overloaded, I need him more than ever before.

"You aren't sure? I'll decide, then," he states, then positions the ropes so they rest against the top of my nipples. He drops to his knees and tugs my thighs on top of his shoulders.

I push my hips closer to his face, and he freezes, arching an eyebrow and glancing up. "Did I say you can look at me or move?"

I reprimand myself then shake my head. I refocus on the mirror.

"If you take your eyes off the mirror or move your body before I give you permission, I'm stopping."

I vow not to disobey him. All the training I had from Massimo about how to obey and have control over my body, I muster. I focus on the scene in front of me, unable to stop my muffled cries as his tongue and lips slowly work me over.

It's erotic torture, a scene better than any porno film could ever be because it's not two strangers. It's Massimo and me. I reposition my hands and squeeze the blood-red rope so I don't move. The muscles in Massimo's back flex. His warm skin makes me hotter, and I'm soon glistening with sweat, shaking, and begging him. Not that anyone could understand my pleas with the gag stuffed in my mouth.

He taunts and teases me without mercy. I want to grind into his face and look at him, or even the window, but I refrain. When Massimo warns he'll stop, he will. I learned that lesson early on. And I want to come, but he hasn't told me I'm allowed.

It feels like hours pass before he slaps my ass and commands, "Ride my face."

It's another form of his punishment. The more I circle my hips, the worse my urge to release gets. I can no longer hold my emotions in, and my tears drip off my chin. The mirror becomes blurry. I barely hear him order, "Come now," when adrenaline explodes in my cells. White light mixes with the heat of the sun's hot rays, and my entire body shakes.

He doesn't let up, extending my orgasm from a mix of biting, sucking, and flicking his tongue. Everything intensifies—the dizziness, the tremors, and the never-ending supply of endorphins racing through my veins.

The only sound in the room is my suppressed cries. I don't even know if I'm still looking at the mirror. Nothing is in focus. It's all heat, surges of adrenaline, and so much sweat and tears.

I barely hear his metal belt clang on the floor. He rises, keeping his palms on the back of my thighs, and enters me.

"Oh!" I scream, his length and girth stretching me. It's another thing I love about him. No matter how much he prepares me, taking him all at once is a delicious shock.

He presses his forehead to mine, thrusting at a slow pace, breathing in shallow breaths. The scent of my orgasm flares in my nostrils. His fingers grip deeper into my thighs. The control in his eyes strengthens. In a firm voice, he declares, "If you come with my cock in you before I say to, I'm leaving you here for the rest of the day, tied up for all of Queens to see."

Fear and newfound determination fill me. I don't dare test him. He'd do it to teach me a lesson. When we're like this, we aren't equals. He's the boss. My role is to submit fully. Anything less, and he has no choice but to follow through on his word.

He kisses my nose, slowing his thrusts more, creating havoc on my walls. His voice softens. "Good, dolce. Stay with me. From now on, you only look in my eyes."

So that's what I do. I focus on all the different blues swirling in them as he studies me with his scrutinizing stare. I control the things I can, and when fresh tears are rolling down my cheeks, only then does he bark, "Come now!"

He thrusts harder, and my body collapses around him, spasming with euphoria.

"Fuuuuck," he moans, gritting his teeth. His cock pumps and swells even bigger, pushing me higher.

My body gives out. I squirt all over him, unable to control anything, receiving a surge of adrenaline unlike anything I've ever experienced.

Silence fills the air, except for my heavy breaths through my nose. His heart thumps against my chest, matching my rapid beats. And all I can think is how much I don't want this to end—how I would give anything to never lose us.

But it's impossible.

5

Massimo

IF I COULD HAVE CREATED A PERFECT WOMAN, KATIYA WOULD be it. She's beyond gorgeous, but it's not just her outer appearance.

She took it.

All of it.

And she loved it and me.

I release her legs from around my waist and unlatch the leather strap. The ball stays in her mouth, so I gently command, "Open up, dolce."

She obeys.

I remove the ball and kiss her, sliding my tongue in her mouth the moment we make contact. She returns my affection as if I'm her everything, which is ironic since she's the one who's mine.

"Let me untie you," I mumble, then reach up for her wrists, unknot the rope, then untwist it from her body. I pick her up and carry her through her bedroom and into the bathroom.

She curls into me, kissing my neck, sending a new wave of emotions through my chest.

Before Katiya, I never knew what it was like to love someone so fiercely that I couldn't imagine my life without them. I'd had women tell me they loved me, but I never said it back. They'd get pissed, but I wasn't going to confess something that wasn't true. Maybe it also was because I never felt the love they claimed to have for me.

Everything is different with Katiya. She's an onion, and with every layer I peel back, I find something new about her I love. Plus, she never judges me. No matter what kind of deviant act I want to do with her or how harsh I come across at times, she accepts all my faults. And these moments after I've dominated and controlled her until she's in tears before giving her the release she's desperate for does something to me. She clings to me as if she needs my love more than I need hers. It's like she knows exactly how to reach into my soul and wrap hers tighter around mine.

I kiss the top of her head and turn on the shower. The water heats quickly, so I kiss her again and ask, "Can you stand, dolce?"

"Yes," she replies. She lifts her head and drills me with her blues. They appear tired and content, but something else swirls in them.

Alarm bells ring in my head. I set her on her feet in the shower and keep hold of her to ensure she has her footing. "Is something wrong?"

She hesitates then shakes her head. "No. Everything is perfect right now."

"You sure?" I ask, studying her face.

She smiles and nods, sliding her arms around my shoulders and lacing her fingers in my hair. "Yes. I wish you wouldn't have left this morning."

My chest tightens. My brothers had been sending me messages all day yesterday. I was with Katiya and ignored them. Their accusations about her are getting old. I suppose I could tell them everything she told me about Ludis and Leo, but it's not their business. Besides, they should believe my word, but somewhere along the way, they stopped. I spin her so the warm water is on her back, and respond, "I'm sorry. I had business to deal with."

She reaches up and cups my cheek while wrapping the other arm around my waist. She asks, "Is everything okay?"

I step as close as possible to her. After we have sex is my time to take care of her. I don't need her worrying about my family issues. Plus, I can't tell her what's going on. It would hurt her. The last thing I'm ever going to do is cause her any harm. I kiss her then state, "Everything is perfect. I'm with you."

She tilts her head. "But your business...did something happen?"

I shift on my feet and grab the shampoo bottle, squirting a handful in my palm, wanting to change the subject back to us. "Yep. Same old shit, different day. All good, except it required me to leave you. But now that I'm here, you have me the rest of the day. Spin."

She opens her mouth then shuts it.

"Go on," I encourage.

She turns, and I massage the shampoo on her scalp, keeping my body close to hers.

"That always feels so nice," she admits.

I do it for a little longer than normal then take the shower-head and hold it over her to rinse the soap out. Then I condition her hair before quickly shampooing mine.

"You're missing out on the scalp perks," she teases, reaching for my head. It's something she always does when we're in the shower. I never let her massage my scalp very long because taking care of her after sex is something I love.

I divert my attention back to her and wash her body with soap. When we're clean, I wrap a towel around her hair, then dry the rest of her off before myself. Then I scoop her in my arms.

She yelps, laughing. "What are you doing?"

I peck her on the lips. "Taking you to bed."

Her smile widens. "It's not even noon. Shouldn't we get dressed and go do something?"

I ogle her body and cock an eyebrow. It's Sunday, and she doesn't have to work. If my brothers hadn't been on my ass, texting me all night, I never would have left her this morning. Either way, I planned on keeping her naked all day, so in my eyes, nothing has changed. I question, "Is there something important you wish to do today?"

She bites her lip.

I groan inside. If she has something to do, I'll take her wherever or help with whatever. But I'd rather stay here with no one else around. I ask, "Do you?"

She slowly shakes her head.

Relief fills me. I almost feel giddy at the thought of getting my way. "Thank God!" I step into the bedroom and tear the covers back. Then I set her down and slip under the sheets beside her. She giggles, and I tug her toward me so her head rests on my bicep. I drag the back of my knuckles down her cheek and ask, "What should we order?"

She raises her eyebrows. "Order?"

"Yep. I'm hungry. I missed breakfast." I glance at the clock on her nightstand. It reads 10:15 A.M. I continue, "So it's time for brunch."

"You mean lunch?"

"No. I mean brunch."

"It's really just an early lunch," she claims.

I gasp. "You can't be serious."

"Why not?"

I wag my finger at her. "Tsk, tsk, tsk. Brunch is a combination of breakfast and lunch foods. You still get to eat three meals, just later in the day."

"Is that so?" She traces my lips with a finger, so I slide it in my mouth and suck on it for a moment.

I release her finger and palm her ass. "Yes. And you're going to need all the energy you can get today."

A blush creeps into her cheeks. "Is that right?"

"No doubt about it," I cockily reply.

Her face falls. She puts the butt of her hand on her forehead. "Crap!"

"What's wrong?"

She squeezes her eyes shut and scrunches her face. "I forgot about something I need to do today."

I groan. "What is it? Hopefully, something here?"

She makes a face then answers, "Unfortunately not."

"Okay, what is it?"

"I need to get some jewelry fixed."

I sit straighter. Jewelry is something I know all about. "What's wrong with it?"

She hesitates.

"Well?" I prod.

"Can I show you?"

"Sure," I reply, wondering what she owns. I've never seen her wear anything. It's one of the things I love about her. She doesn't need to be flashy. She shines brighter than any gem. But I still have our family jeweler Ettore making a necklace, earring, and bracelet set for her. Her birthday is around the corner, and I plan on making sure it's the best one yet.

Plus, I asked him to design an engagement ring based on an idea I had in my head. There's no doubt she's my future.

She slides out of bed, takes the towel off her head, and hangs it on her door hook. She shakes out her hair then walks to her dresser.

There's a wooden jewelry box I don't remember ever seeing. I'm guessing it's cedar. But it's not like me to miss details, so I inquire, "Where've you been keeping that box?"

She reaches for it then brings it back to the bed. "In the bottom drawer."

"Why there?" I question, then circle my arm around her as she slides under the covers.

Katiya shrugs. "So it isn't obvious if someone ever breaks in."

I kiss her. "Smart girl. So what's up with the box?"

She takes a deep breath, and something passes in her eyes. It leaves as quickly as it came, so I wonder if I imagined it. She puts her hand on the top and traces the engraved flower. "It's the only thing I have left from my father. He gave it to me on my twelfth birthday."

My heart squeezes. I tighten my arm around her. She told me how her mother died when she was three and her father when she was fifteen. It's still painful for her, and I imagine it always will be. My mama died of a heart attack over a decade ago. It was sudden and came from nowhere. I still have times when I get emotional over her death. I miss her. As much as my papà and I are at odds these days, I can't imagine not having him here. I soften my voice when I ask, "Can I see it?"

She hands me the box, watching me for my reaction.

I do the same thing she did and trace the ornate flower. "This is beautiful."

"My father made it," she admits.

I freeze, staring at the box then at her. "He designed this?"

A sad smile fills her face. She blinks hard and clears her throat. "He owned a woodworking business. When he wasn't making furniture, he would make these. He'd gift them to his customers on their birthdays."

I trace the flower's petal and take in all the little details, completely in awe. Impressed, I proclaim, "He was talented."

Her voice is so low I can barely hear. "Yes."

I kiss her forehead. "Can I see your jewelry?"

"Oh, it's not mine."

"No? Whose is it?"

"Well..." She furrows her eyebrows then bites on her bottom lip.

"Katiya?" I inquire.

She scratches the back of her neck, shifting on the mattress while avoiding my gaze.

My red flags fly full mast. There are so many ways she's innocent even though she's been through so much. Plus, she's fifteen years younger than I am. I'll be forty in a few months, and she's only turning twenty-five.

As smart as Katiya is, my gut says she's gotten herself into some sort of trouble. I can't imagine what, but all the warning bells are ringing in my head. The hairs on the back of my neck rise. In a firm voice, I demand, "Katiya, tell me what's going on."

She locks eyes with mine. "Promise you won't get mad at me?"

Every urge I have to protect her consumes me. I warn myself to stay calm, but the feeling I get when I'm ready to kill someone ignites. If she's done something wrong and now has a problem, I'll do whatever it takes to solve it for her. Yet, I don't want to scare her before she tells me what's going on. I keep my voice level and emotionless. "Of course I won't."

She hesitates, glancing around the room.

I take her hand and kiss it. "Katiya, please tell me."

She lets out a long sigh, turns on the mattress, and pretzels her legs. Her lip slightly trembles. She pins her scared orbs on me, confessing, "I shouldn't have done it."

My heart races. I tighten my fingers around hers, asking, "Done what?"

She closes her eyes briefly then states, "Let me show you." She carefully unclasps the gold latch on the box and starts to lift the lid then stops.

"Katiya—"

"I don't want you to think I'm a thief. I'm not. I promise you that I'm not," she blurts out.

I try to hide my shock. "Why would I think that?"

She stays quiet.

I point to the wood. "You stole what's in that box?"

She rubs her hand over her face. When she removes it, she squeezes her eyes shut, confessing, "Yes, but...but it wasn't how it sounds."

I've done a lot of bad things in my days. While I don't consider myself a thief, there have been times I've stolen something. In my eyes, the end always justifies the means. So while I don't normally agree with stealing, there are certain circumstances when I can condone it.

I tug her so she's on my lap. I place the box on her thighs and caress her jaw. I assure her, "Dolce, whatever you did, tell me. I won't judge you. Scouts' honor."

She smirks. "You were in the Boy Scouts?"

I arrogantly grin. "No. I got kicked out of the Cub Scouts."

A tiny laugh flies out of her mouth. She covers it. "How did that happen?"

"You really want to know?"

She nods. "Absolutely."

I give her several kisses. "Fine. But after I tell you, it's your turn to spill it."

Anxiety fills her expression, but she agrees. "Okay. Now tell me."

"Well, Ms. Bossy Pants," I tease.

She pushes my chest. "Hey, now!"

I chuckle then continue, "If you must know, Little Danny didn't like me playing with his sister instead of him when I went to his house."

Amusement floods her face. "And?"

"He said something to me about it. I might have challenged him to a duel during one of the meetings," I admit.

She laughs, blurting out, "A duel?"

"Yep. I brought the squirt guns. But instead of filling mine with water, I filled it with wine."

"Wine!" she shrieks.

I can't help my grin from widening. "Yep."

"Why did you do that?"

I feign shock. "Wine is the color of blood. I was out to win."

"Okay. So, what happened? Did you win?" she asks.

"Of course I won. Little Danny's still a horrible shot. But our Cub Scout leader didn't appreciate us using his new office or the wine stains all over his new white carpet," I answer.

She gapes. "You didn't?"

"Oh, I did."

"Wow!"

I shrug. "I was young. Okay, now your turn. What's in the box?"

The atmosphere turns serious. She slowly opens the wooden lid and pulls out a man's ring. The gold is set with a very pure, deep-green emerald. A foreign letter, I think Russian, is on it. Plus, this is an emerald you would only get from that region.

I take it from her and hold it to the light. Based on my initial assessment, someone with lots of money had this ring made.

I hand it back to her. "Where did you get this?"

Her face flushes with embarrassment. She licks her lips. "I..." She scratches her neck, and the red marks from her nails match her cheeks. "After Ludis gave me to Leo, I strategized how I could run away. One night, Ludis came to visit. He and Leo..." She swallows hard and puts her hand on her stomach.

Rage fills me. I growl, "He and Leo did what?"

She holds her hands in the air. "Nothing happened, but they were talking about sharing me."

My stomach pitches. I fight through the urge to leave and find them both now. I will kill them someday. I have men looking for Ludis right now. Leo is easy to find, but once I know where Ludis is, I'm going to abduct him. Then I'll get Leo. They're going to listen to each other scream while I stretch out their last breaths. I keep my cool and prod, "Go on."

She puts the box on the mattress and gets on her knees, straddling me. I wrap my arms around her and stroke her shoulder with my thumb. Her body relaxes, and she confesses, "All I could think was that I had to get away. There's no way I could have taken them both at the same time. One was..." She takes a deep breath, focusing on the ceiling, then meets my eyes again. "Enough."

Bile creeps up my throat, and I struggle to swallow it. Too afraid of what I'll say or do, I tighten my hold around her.

"Anyway, I found some of Leo's sleeping pills in the medicine cabinet. When they weren't looking, I mixed them into their drinks. I wasn't even thinking about taking the ring, but Ludis had put it on the desk. Leo told him he had to pay for the privilege to..."

I grit my teeth, seething. "To take you with Leo?"

She scrunches her face and nods. "Something in me snapped. I-I thought I could escape and sell it. But...but I couldn't. They were always watching."

It takes me a few moments before I can speak.

She misinterprets my silence and blurts out, "I promise I'm not a thief!"

I slide my hands over her cheeks. "Of course you aren't. I understand what you did. Now, tell me why you're taking it to a jeweler."

More nerves cross her features. Her voice breaks as she answers, "I need him to take the pieces apart so I can sell them. I-I shouldn't keep this here. It's not safe."

I can't disagree with her. Having anything of Ludis's is dangerous. I ask, "Didn't Leo ask where the ring was?"

I shake my head. "It never came up. They were both super drunk when Ludis put the ring down."

I exhale deeply. "That's good, but, dolce, you can't just walk into a jewelry store and have them take it apart."

Her eyes widen. "Why not?"

I slide my hands up and down her arms, calmly stating, "You don't have proof it's yours. If he thinks it's stolen, he may call the police. Even if he doesn't, you don't want word getting out you have this."

"Then how do I get rid of it?" she frets.

"Easy. I'll take you to my family jeweler. He's been with us forever and knows his stuff. Plus, he'd never talk, and he'll know who to offload it to."

She arches her eyebrows. "You'll take me to him? Today?"

Cockily, I puff up my chest. "How much do you love me?"

She tilts her head, smiling. "More than you'll ever understand."

I kiss her hand. "It's a good thing the feeling is mutual, then. I guess we're going to have to put on some clothes today."

6

MC

Katiya

GUILT EATS AT ME. WHILE MY FATHER DID GIVE ME THE BOX, and I did steal Ludis's ring, I still need to offload it. So I'm using it to my advantage. Massimo's jeweler is the first step in finding out more information about his other contacts. I assume if he trusts me with Ettore, he'll start to trust me with other information.

Everything about my underlying motives feels horrible. Massimo didn't hesitate to take care of my problem. All he does is care for me. Since my father died, he's the only person who's put me first. Yet, I don't know how to avoid the wrath of Leo.

Massimo's vengeance will be worse. It'll be personal.

I shudder at the thought.

"You cold?" he asks, pushing the button to increase the heat in his Ferrari.

"A bit," I lie again.

He veers to the right, entering the expressway, then guns it, weaving in and out of traffic. The sun is bright. I take my sunglasses out of my purse and put them on.

"You look sexy in your glasses," Massimo states, wiggling his eyebrows under his own pair.

"Thanks."

"Of course, the cat-eyed ones you wear in the library are pretty hot, too. In fact, I think I'm going to require you to wear them next time I tie you up," he adds.

My lips curl up. "Is that so?"

"Yep."

"Whatever you want, sir," I flirt, pulling my sunglasses down and batting my eyelashes.

Satisfaction fills his expression. It's no secret that Massimo loves it when I call him sir. But I love it, too. Something about submitting to him makes me feel alive.

And I'm going to throw it all away and destroy his life so Leo can get what he wants.

I don't have a choice.

Maybe I should tell Massimo.

No. He's never going to forgive me for lying to him about how I "earned" my freedom from Leo.

"You know what I want to do?" Massimo asks, turning on the radio.

A Bob Marley reggae song comes on. I don't know the name but know it's his. He's singing about if you could be loved.

How ironic. I finally get it and can't keep it.

"Dolce?" Massimo questions.

"What do you want to do?"

Massimo turns up the music and sings, "Oh no!"

I smirk. "I didn't know you were into reggae."

Massimo acts insulted. "It's island music."

"O-kay. And you know we live in New York?" I tease.

His grin widens. "Yep. Which is why I want to do what I want to do."

"What's that?"

"Take you to a hot, secluded beach, rub suntan lotion all over you, and serve you fruity drinks." He checks the lane to his left and guns the engine, flying past several cars and semis.

My butterflies go crazy. I've never gone on vacation with anyone except my father, which was years ago and only a few hours to a lake in upstate New York. Time in the sun with no one around except Massimo sounds like heaven.

Leo will never allow you to leave New York.

Maybe I can convince him.

No way. He'd follow us.

I wonder if he's following us now.

Goose bumps break out on my skin. One thing I've learned is Leo's men are never far. Anytime I have a temporary lapse of memory and don't think about them, they show up.

"Well, do you want to go?" he questions.

"Sorry! That sounds amazing, I ummm..."

"What?" he inquires, furrowing his eyebrows.

I blurt out, "I have to work."

He snorts. "Take some days off. They must give you vacation days."

I honestly don't know what the vacation policy is with the library. Leo's men dropped me off the first day and introduced me to the manager. I didn't even sign any paperwork. I add, "I can't pay my bills if I don't work."

It's not a lie. The library pays very little. If Leo didn't supply my housing, I wouldn't be able to survive. I'm pinching pennies to buy food most days.

Massimo shrugs. "Not a problem. I'll give you money."

I turn my head toward him. "What? I can't have you paying my bills."

He moves from the third lane into the first then zooms past several vehicles and ends up in the fourth. He looks at me, his lips twitching. "Dolce, you know I've got money, right?"

I roll my eyes. "Duh. I'm not stupid, Mr. Ferrari."

He chuckles. "Okay. So, no offense, but I doubt whatever you make in a month would even make a dent in my bank account."

"Ouch," I reprimand, but I know he's right. Still, I may have been put in my position by the Abruzzos, but I take pride in my work. Even though I don't have to worry about my brownstone, I still want to be independent. I want to know that I can support myself and I don't have to rely on anyone.

Except for Leo for rent.

"Don't get insulted, Katiya. Consider it the perks of being with me," Massimo claims.

I push the voice out of my head, replying, "Is that how you see it? Perks?"

He removes his hand off the stick shift and slides it between my thighs until he's cupping my pussy. In a cocky voice, he proclaims, "I come with all sorts of perks. Money isn't the best one." He squeezes his palm on me.

I slap his arm, and he laughs, removing his hand. I turn in my seat. "I don't want to rely on you for money."

He picks up my hand and kisses it. "One of the many reasons I love you. All the women I've been with see a big fat bank account. You aren't a vulture. So you shouldn't feel bad if I want to spoil you. Besides, think of it as me being selfish to get what I want."

My heart soars and sinks at the same time. I love how he sees I don't want anything from him, but more guilt devours me that it's not entirely true. I'm trying to figure out how to trick him into telling me who his contacts are and where they reside.

God, I'm a horrible person.

He maneuvers through more traffic, shifting to decelerate off the ramp. The Ferrari comes to a stop at the light, and he reaches for my chin. He turns my face toward his and demands, "Tell me you'll come with me."

I open my mouth, but nothing comes out.

He cocks his eyebrows. "You don't want to go?"

I shake my head. "No. It's not that."

"If money weren't an issue, would you say yes?"

I hesitate.

His eyes turn to slits. I can see them through the lenses of his sunglasses. "What's the real issue?"

A horn blares, breaking our gaze. He accelerates, turning left, then in an annoyed voice, says, "So you don't want to go with me?"

Panic mixed with annoyance fills me. I let my irritation rule and reply, "I care about my job. I don't know how taking time off would work. Just because you have money doesn't mean I can neglect my responsibilities."

"I didn't say that," he snaps.

"Really? Then what did you say?"

He cuts off a car and turns on a side road. "Are we seriously fighting about me wanting to take you on vacation?"

Shame fills me. Massimo isn't doing anything wrong. He's a man used to getting what he wants. He has the money to do it, and he's always generous to me. Yet I don't know how to get around the Leo issue. I drop my voice, admitting, "I'm not trying to fight. I've never taken a day off, even when I've been sick. It makes me nervous."

He exhales deeply, softening his voice, too, asserting, "That's why it'll be okay. They probably owe you a ton of vacation days."

"I-I don't know."

He pulls up to a building and parks in a fire lane. "Tell you what. Why don't we stop arguing about this? You talk to your manager tomorrow and then we can figure this out."

Relief floods me that he's dropping it. Maybe I can convince Leo it's necessary for me to find out what he wants. I nod. "Okay."

Massimo's expression lights up. He pecks me on the lips. "Good girl." He jumps out of the car, races around the vehicle, and opens my door. He reaches in, helps me out, then tugs me into him.

I tilt my head and state, "You can't park here."

He grunts. "Sure I can."

"You'll get towed."

He steers me toward the zit-filled, red-headed, barely an adult valet who's bolting toward us. "Make sure nothing happens to my Ferrari." He holds the keys out.

"Sir, that's a fire lane," the valet frets, his voice cracking.

Massimo stands taller and puts his hand on the young man's shoulder. "So what? That's why I have you. Two hundred big ones are coming your way if you keep it safe. However, if anything happens, I'll find out where you live."

Red burns the valet's cheeks. Fear flies into his face. He stammers, "I-I-I can get fired for letting you park here."

"Letting me? No one lets me do anything. I make my own choices," Massimo declares, shoves the keys in his hands, and guides me past him.

"Sir," the man shouts.

Massimo doesn't turn. He leads me inside the building.

I turn to him, asking, "Was that necessary?"

"What?" he asks, as if he has no clue why I'm asking him about it.

"To scare that poor kid."

More arrogance washes over him. In a firm tone, he asserts, "You ever try to find parking in Manhattan? Besides, he's going to get two hundred bucks." He nods to the security guard and moves us in front of the elevator, removing his sunglasses and putting them in his pocket.

"So that makes it okay? What if there's a fire?" I ask.

The elevator opens, and Massimo motions for me to go first. I step in, he follows, and the doors shut. He hits a code for the penthouse. He steps in front of me until I'm against the wall and puts both hands on my cheeks. "There are two types of people in this world, dolce. Those who take what they need and those who wait for scraps. Guess which one I am."

I say nothing.

A moment of silence passes, and he chuckles. "Don't tell me you'd have looked at me twice if I were someone who waited for scraps."

I bite my lip, not able to deny that the power Massimo displays is a huge turn on for me.

The elevator dings, and Massimo's cockiness grows. "Thought so." He kisses my forehead and grabs my hand, leading me into the corridor before I can respond. He knocks on a door and slides his arm around my shoulder, tugging me close to his muscular frame.

I lean into him, unable to stop my body from molding to his.

He says into my ear, "I'm punishing you when we get home."

Zings bounce through my body. "Oh? Why is that?"

He murmurs, "I need to show you what I'll do to you when I have you at my full disposal for a week."

I take a deep inhale.

"Sun. Sand. Drinks. You submitting to me with no interruptions."

"I didn't agree to go," I say, but it comes out weak.

He sniffs my hair. "There's one other thing you should know, dolce."

"What's that?"

"I always get my way."

The door opens, and a gray-haired, older man stands in front of us. Wrinkles cover the corners of his eyes, and smile lines indent his cheeks. His deep voice reminds me of a cigar smoker. He reaches his arms around Massimo, patting him on the back. "Massimo. Good to see you. And who's this beautiful woman?"

Massimo's face lights up. He puffs his chest out, circling his arm around my waist. "This is Katiya. Katiya, meet Ettore, the best jeweler in New York."

"Ah," Ettore states, waving his hand in front of his face, then kissing me on the cheek. "It's nice to meet you."

"You, too," I reply.

Ettore steps back. "Come in." We follow him to a sitting room, and he motions for us to sit on the couch. He asks, "Can I get you a drink?"

"I'm okay. Katiya?" Massimo asks.

"No, thank you."

Massimo and I sit on the couch.

Ettore takes a seat in a chair across from us. "So, to what do I owe this visit?"

My stomach somersaults. I worry about what to say, suddenly wondering why I'm doing this. Maybe I should just tell Leo I can't get it and let him do whatever it is he is going to eventually do anyway.

Massimo takes my hand. In a serious tone, he declares, "Katiya has a ring she needs taken apart then offloaded."

Ettore's seriousness matches Massimo's. "I see. And is it safe to assume this needs to be discreet?"

"That would be correct," Massimo replies. He turns toward me. "Katiya, show Ettore the ring."

My gut continues to twist. I put my hand in my pocket and squeeze the ring. For so long, I've wanted to get rid of this.

Now the opportunity is here, but I'm questioning everything.

Maybe I should tell Massimo I forgot it at home.

What am I thinking? Of course I can't do that!

I pull the ring out and hold it in front of me. My hand shakes, but I don't know how to stop it.

Ettore acts like he doesn't see my tremors. He picks up the gem, holds it in the air, and studies it. After a moment, he whistles. He drills his icy-blue eyes into mine. "This is quite the piece."

My mouth turns dry. I swallow, and it feels like my throat is cracking.

Massimo squeezes my hand. "Yes. We're aware. Can you take care of it for us?"

Ettore sets the ring on the side table. He takes a few breaths, studying us.

"What is it?" Massimo asks while my nerves escalate.

"Who's the owner of this ring? I need to know so I don't offload it to the wrong person."

Dizziness hits me. I grip the edge of the couch with my free hand. Why did I decide to do this? How stupid could I be? Of course he would want to know the details.

Massimo caresses the back of my hand with his thumb. He answers, "Ludis Petrov."

Deafening silence fills the air. Ettore's eyes sear like fire into Massimo's. The tension increases the longer no one speaks.

Massimo repeats, "Can you offload it?"

"Of course I can."

"So you'll do it for me?"

Ettore sits back in his chair, pinning his suddenly cold orbs on me again. A chill runs down my spine. I attempt not to move or appear intimidated, but everything about this feels off-balance. He slowly addresses Massimo, asking, "Does your papà know you're here?"

Massimo doesn't hesitate. "No. I'd like this to be between the three of us."

Annoyance fills Ettore's expression. He scowls at Massimo. "You bring me Ludis Petrov's ring—and not just any ring. This ring is an heirloom. It dates back to the 1800s."

My pulse pounds between my ears. I jump up and grab the ring, blurting out, "I'm sorry we brought it here. Thanks for your time." I spin to leave the room.

Massimo leaps in front of me. "Katiya, chill out. Everything is okay."

I blink hard, not wanting to cry but suddenly feeling nothing like my usual strong self. I curse myself, unable to stop the chaotic emotions annihilating me.

"Sit down, Katiya. Please," Ettore orders, but it's in a softer tone.

I freeze, unsure what to do, staring at Massimo.

"Dolce, sit down," Massimo reaffirms.

Not knowing how to get out of this, I take my seat.

Massimo slides next to me and puts his arm around my shoulders, hugging me close to him. He orders, "Ettore, this needs to stay between the three of us. I expect your discretion, as usual. Now, are you going to offload this for me or not?"

Ettore sighs. "You need to tell your papà about this."

"No," Massimo declares.

"Why not?"

"This isn't his business."

Ettore scrubs his face. He closes his eyes for a moment then refocuses on us. "How did you get this ring? I assume you stole it?"

"I'm not a thief!" I cry out, but shameful heat burns my cheeks.

He scrutinizes me, making me feel like an ant in a labyrinth with no way out.

Massimo starts, "Ettore—"

"A ring like this, an owner wouldn't forget about, especially Ludis Petrov," Ettore claims.

I can't deny it. Even I don't understand how I haven't been caught by now.

"It's been several years. No one knows she has it. Are you going to do this for me, or should I find someone else?" Massimo barks.

Ettore points at him. "You better think before you go waving this around."

Massimo grunts. "Please. I'm not stupid. I brought it to you for a reason. But if you aren't going to help me—"

"I didn't say that," Ettore interjects.

The room turns silent again. A stare-down between the two men reignites.

In a no-nonsense voice, Ettore proclaims, "Does anyone besides Ludis know this is missing? Has she told anyone?"

"No! Of course I didn't!" I declare.

"But you stole it?" he asks again.

I've never felt so small. I lift my chin and square my shoulders.

"She had justifiable reasons," Massimo claims.

Ettore arches his eyebrows, continuing to make me feel like a schoolgirl in trouble.

With as much confidence as I can muster, I state, "I've never stolen anything in my life besides this ring. If you were in my shoes, you would have done the same thing. And to answer your question, no one else knows about it."

A few seconds pass, and Ettore's expression softens. He nods and says, "Okay. Let's keep it that way."

"You'll do it?" Massimo questions.

"Yes. But there is one person you need to tell," Ettore insists.

Massimo groans. "Drop it. I'm not telling Papà."

Ettore shakes his head. "Then I'm not doing it. I don't keep things from your papà, and neither should you."

"This doesn't concern him," Massimo fumes.

Ettore snaps, "Everything concerns him. And this is Ludis Petrov's property we're discussing."

Massimo grinds his molars, giving Ettore a look so evil, chills run down my spine.

When he kills me, that's what I'll see.

My lungs turn stale. Everything about this conversation, I should have anticipated. And the last thing I want is Massimo's family to be more upset with him.

"Fine. I'll tell Papà. But I want this offloaded quickly," Massimo demands as he rises and pulls me off the couch.

Ettore stands. "It'll take me a little more time. This isn't something I can put through my normal channels."

"Whatever you have to do, just do it," Massimo orders and steers me out of his house before I can even thank him.

When the doors to the elevator shut, I turn toward him. "I'm sorry."

"For what?"

"Creating issues with Ettore and your papà."

Massimo snorts, pulling me into him. "Those aren't problems. Don't worry about this, dolce. But I think you owe me something."

"What's that?"

"A vacation. Tomorrow, talk to your manager and find out when you can get a week off. And make sure it isn't months away."

MC

Massimo

"Don't forget to talk to your supervisor," I remind Katiya and press my lips to hers.

The chaste kiss I meant to give her turns into a deeper one. It shouldn't surprise me. I always have a hard time touching her and letting her leave my arms.

"I have to go," she murmurs, then slides her tongue back in my mouth.

I chuckle and squeeze her ass. "Mm-hmm."

She pushes her palms against my chest, breaking our kiss. "Are you sure you have time to pick me up? I can take the bus. It's not a big deal."

"Yep. I'll be here. If anything changes, I'll send a car," I reply.

She scrunches her forehead. "That's not necessary."

I fist her hair, tug her head back, then lean over her face. She inhales sharply, and the floral scent of her perfume flares in my nostrils. The expression in her blue eyes, the growing flush in her cheeks, and those plump blood-red lips remind me of everything we did yesterday morning when she was gagged and restrained. My dick strains against my zipper. I state, "Let's get something straight, dolce."

"What's that?" she breathes.

I run my thumb over her stained lips, unable to resist. "We're past the point of beginnings."

Confusion fills her expression. "I don't understand."

I deeply inhale more of her scent, deciding it's the roses that make me like it so much. My stomach has flutters going crazy when I declare, "I don't need to be with you any longer to know you're the one. What's mine is yours. You won't be taking any more bus rides. From now on, I'll pick you up, or one of my drivers will. And I want to move in together."

She gapes at me. The color drains from her cheeks and her breath hitches.

The sound of my pulse between my ears gets louder. I've never asked anyone to live with me before. I didn't plan to ask her right now, either. Yet that's always been my problem. I don't have any patience. If I want something, I make it happen. Now, I'm questioning my inability to make it a little more special for her. Her silence and shock are increasing the nerves in my belly, and I'm not used to that feeling.

I don't like it one bit. I prefer knowing the outcome of something. Maybe she's not as sure about us as I am. I blurt out, "You don't want to live with me?"

"No! That's...that's not it!" she claims.

My pulse doesn't slow. "Then what is it?"

"I... I..." She blinks hard then looks away.

"Katiya," I say, trying to stay calm and not feel rejected. I move her chin so she can't avoid me. Her eyes glisten, and it feels like someone is squeezing my heart. "Tell me what's upsetting you."

A moment passes, and she finally reveals, "How can we live together? Your family hates me."

"They don't hate you," I claim, even though they might.

"Massimo, you've interrogated me, and we've fought a lot about these issues. Even after you claimed you believed me, you still haven't introduced me to them," she points out.

My gut dives. All this is true. And it's on me I haven't taken her to my house. I firmly assert, "Once they get to know you, they'll love you. I promise. And you're right. I should have had you meet them a while ago." As I say it, I push the thought to the back of my mind that I need to figure out how to make my family believe in her innocence.

She bites on her lip.

"Dolce—"

"I can't move in there. Not when I'm not welcome," she declares.

"No one said you aren't welcome," I try to assure her, but my chest tightens as I say it. Still, I'm not letting anyone stand in my way of having her. I slide my hands on her cheeks. "Don't you want to go to sleep and wake up next to me every day?"

A hot tear slips down her cheek, rolling over my finger. She says, "Massimo, I can't agree to live with you when your family doesn't even know me."

I clench my jaw, unhappy with her answer. I wish I could deny everything she said about my family, but I can't.

Plus, everything she's saying makes sense. If I brought her home to move in with me, Papà and my brothers would have a fit. They might even kick me out. Still, it doesn't make me back down on my desire to live with her.

"Please don't look at me like that," she chokes out.

I sigh and tug her into my chest, kissing the top of her head. I say the next best thing I can think. "Then let me move in with you."

She freezes.

My heart thumps against my chest cavity, pushing against her. She slowly looks up. "You want to move into my tiny brownstone?"

"It's not that small."

"Compared to your father's mansion, I'm sure it is," she insists.

I chuckle. "Okay, well, it's comparable to my wing."

She arches her eyebrows in disbelief.

I smirk. "Okay, maybe it's about a quarter of the size."

"Exactly!" she replies.

"Well, if I don't care how big your place is, then you shouldn't. Do you want me there or not?" I ask, then hold my breath.

"It's...it's not about if I want you there. Of course I want you there. I always want you with me," she proclaims.

"Good. Then it's settled. I'll move in until you're comfortable with my family, then we'll switch to my place," I firmly assert, but my insides quiver. It's another thing I'm not used to.

She stares at me, swallowing hard.

The notion of ignoring her nervous behavior pops into my mind, but I'm not a coward. "Katiya, what's wrong?"

"I didn't expect... I...are you serious?"

"Of course I am. Why would I ask you to live with me if I wasn't?"

She takes a deep breath then nods. "Okay."

"Okay, what? Okay, you want me to move in with you, or okay, you believe I want to live with you?" I ask.

She cocks an eyebrow, and a tiny smile plays on her lips. "Okay to both."

I grin like an idiot. "Yeah?"

"Yes."

I make a victory fist in the air. Happiness explodes in all my cells. I pick her up and twirl her around.

She laughs, crying out, "Massimo!"

I set her down and kiss her again. "Go to work. I'll see you when your shift is over."

She smiles and pecks me on the lips. "Sounds good."

I pat her ass and watch her walk through the door. When I can't see her blonde hair anymore, I jog down the steps and get in my Ferrari. I rev the engine, turn on some reggae, and pull out. Traffic is heavier than normal for Monday morning, but I weave through it. Horns blare at me, but I don't care. I'm on cloud nine, and nothing is bringing me down, including my family.

My phone rings through the car speaker. Tristano's photo appears. I hit the answer button and chirp, "Bro. What's up?"

"Why do you sound like a giddy schoolgirl?" he taunts.

"Shut up and tell me why you're interrupting my jam session," I order.

He groans. "Let me guess. Bob Marley and your piña colada fantasies are in prime mode."

I chuckle. "And you're calling because...?"

His voice turns serious. "Did you get Papà's message about the meeting this morning?"

My joy deflates a few notches. It's back to all the stresses that I sometimes wish weren't mine. Right now, all I want to do is pack up my shit and get it moved to Katiya's.

It should be a strange feeling. I never thought I'd live anywhere but my papà's, since I have my own wing, and it's the epitome of luxury. But if she's not comfortable, I'm not going to force the issue. I'll make a temporary sacrifice to wake up next to her every day. And everything about it feels right.

If only she were my only responsibility.

The messages from Papà did pique my curiosity, yet I have a feeling it's going to be about something that's a pain in my ass. I haven't seen nor spoken with him since he and Tully lectured us. I grumble, "Yeah, I got it. Any idea what it's about?"

Tristano's voice sounds as irritated as mine. "Not sure. Tully's going to be there."

All happiness disappears. The last conversation with Tully and Papà wasn't fun. I still don't know what Tully will make us do to repay him. And that doesn't sit well with me. It's guaranteed to be something none of us want to do. I snarl, "Tully can fuck himself."

Tristano huffs, "Wishful thinking. How far away are you?"

"Five minutes."

"Okay. Can you keep Papà calm? I'm going to be a few minutes late, and you know how he gets worked up," Tristano states.

I ask, "Where are you?"

"Nowhere interesting. Just keep Papà off my ass, okay?"

It's unlike my brother not to tell me where he is. My suspicion ignites. "What's going on?"

"Nothing is going on," he claims as a woman's blood-curling scream fills the line. Then, "Tristano! Eww! Get this off me! Oh God!"

The voice sounds familiar, but I can't pinpoint it. I question, "Who is that?"

"Shit! I gotta go!" He hangs up, and the line goes dead.

I call him back, but it rings until the voicemail picks up. I hang up and get a text message.

Tristano: *Cover for me.*

Me: *What's going on?*

Tristano: *Nothing. All good. Later.*

Me: *Who was that? Her voice sounds familiar.*

Tristano: *No one you know. See you soon.*

Bullshit.

Why's he lying?

I step on the accelerator and take the curve into the subdivision, speeding down the road until I get to our gate. The guard nods and opens it. I rev the engine past him and park in the garage.

One of our black SUVs enters, pulling up near the door. Dante gets out then reaches in to help Bridget.

I walk over to them. "What are you two doing out?"

"Dropped the kids off. They wanted to try the new breakfast place near their school," Bridget answers.

"Any good?"

Dante shrugs. "I didn't see the big deal. You'd have to eat four plates to equal one. Typical New York hipsters."

"It wasn't that bad," Bridget claims.

"Yeah, it was. I'm going to need to grab some more food to make it until lunch," Dante gripes.

Bridget rolls her eyes, but she's smiling. She kisses his cheek. "You were a good sport."

"That's me," he declares and guides Bridget toward the entrance.

I follow, interjecting, "I'll make a note to never go there. Do you know what Papà called a meeting for?"

Dante halts, kisses Bridget, and says, "Can you excuse us, dolcezza?"

Her eyes dart between us. She nods then smiles. "Sure." She leaves, and we watch her until she disappears.

Dante drills his cold orbs into mine. He crosses his arms over his chest. "Want to tell me what's going on?"

The hairs on my arms rise. My gut says it's about Katiya, and I'm on my last nerve, always having to defend her. Now that she agreed to move in with me, I have to change my family's opinion about her. It all makes me angry. The blood in my veins boils, and I seethe, "Meaning?"

"You're going to play this game with me?" Dante glowers.

I match his stance, crossing my arms. I fume, "I'm not a mind reader, so spit it out, bro."

His nostrils flare, and his intimidating expression irritates me further. I'm not one of his little minions who gets scared or backs down. He may be next in line to rule our empire, but he'll always be my brother first. He glances around us then steps closer. His voice lowers. "Did you think Ettore wouldn't call Papà?"

My gut flips. I wasn't planning on telling Papà and lied to Ettore. Yet I didn't think he'd rat me out within twenty-four hours. I fib, "He didn't give me a chance to tell him."

"Bullshit. You weren't going to tell Papà anything, were you?" Dante accuses.

"Is there a point to this conversation?" I hurl, sick of my brothers interfering in my business.

Dante's scowl grows. "Massimo, when did you stop using your brain?"

"Shut up," I retort.

His face darkens. "This woman you're seeing, she's making you do things you normally wouldn't."

I scoff. "Her name is Katiya. She doesn't make me do anything. And your assumptions about her are just that— false notions."

"She's working for the Abruzzos! You took her to our family jeweler!" he snarls.

I groan and scrub my face. "When are you going to stop stating untruths? She's not an Abruzzo."

"She lives in the same complex Gianni and you snuck into so you could rescue Cara!"

"There are eight buildings in that complex. She's not even near the one where Uberto held Cara hostage. It's a coincidence," I insist, pushing the nagging feeling away. When we pulled up to the building to rescue Cara, I felt sick. But I had it out with Katiya, and I believe her. She even showed me her lease. It's through a slum lord with no ties to the Abruzzos. I did a full background check on him and had my guy follow him for a month. He's not even Italian.

"Jesus! Stop using your dick instead of your brain!" Dante barks.

"Fuck off," I hurl at him, turn, and walk down the hall.

Dante follows, grabs my arm, and tugs.

I spin, warning, "Don't touch me!"

"Why did you take her to Ettore?"

"Papà didn't tell you?"

"No. So what's he going to say?"

Everything feels out of control around my family these days. This conversation only makes it worse. To take back some control and piss Dante off further, I shake out of his grasp, fuming, "I guess you'll find out soon enough." I open the door to the wing of the house Papà's office is in and make my way to it.

Dante follows, cautioning, "You're close to making irrevocable mistakes."

I spin, jabbing him in the chest. "Are you threatening me?"

His eyes turn to slits. "This family runs on trust."

My pulse beats hard in my neck. "So now you don't trust me?"

"Give me a reason I should go into Papà's office and back you up," he asserts.

I step closer and match his leer. In a low voice, I reply, "I shouldn't have to give you a reason, brother."

"This girl—"

"Is innocent. What they did to her—"

"What did they do, Massimo? You always allude to it but never fill us in."

My chest tightens. I want to tell him, but it's not my story to tell. It's personal and private between Katiya and me.

"Just give me something," Dante says in a softer voice. "Please."

I glance over my shoulder then lock eyes with him again. "All I'll say is if you put what Bridget went through and Katiya next to each other, I'm unsure what would be worse."

Dante's dark orbs widen. He stays quiet, and tension fills the air.

I sniff hard, trying to push down the emotions in my chest, hating that I haven't located Ludis yet so I can end his and Leo's life.

"Massimo! Dante! Get in here," Papà's sharp voice booms.

I take a deep breath, turn, and ignore his shocked expression. When I step through the door, Tully and Gianni are there with Boris Ivanov.

"Where's your brother?" Papà barks.

"He's right behind us. There was a small issue at the docks he's handling on the phone," I casually lie, avoiding Dante, and willing Tristano to get his ass home.

"Boris, didn't know you were in town," Dante adds.

Boris glances between Tully and Papà then replies in his Russian accent, "Certain information is better to discuss in person."

Alarm bells go off in my head. Boris turns to me. "If you wanted Petrov information, you should have come to my family."

My gut twists. I stay quiet, feeling all the eyes in the room on me.

"Sorry I'm late," Tristano interjects, stepping into the room.

"Did you take care of that dock issue?" I ask.

He nods. "It's sorted."

"What?" Papà questions.

"Nothing major or anything you need to worry about, Papà. What did I miss?"

Papà's glare turns to me. "Why are you looking for Ludis Petrov? And how did you get his ring?"

The room turns silent. I debate how to answer and finally decide to admit the truth. "I was going to torture and kill him."

"For what reason?" Papà demands.

I stay quiet.

Dante surprises me and comes to my rescue, saying, "Because he's a pig who belongs in the same hell as Bridget's rapists."

My insides quiver like they always do whenever I think about what Katiya went through. I stare at the ceiling, breathing through my anger.

"You can call off the search. Ludis is dead," Boris informs us.

I snap my head toward him. "He is?"

"Yes."

"How do you know?"

Boris grinds his molars then sniffs hard. "That's my family's business. But I assure you, he's dead."

A mixture of emotions passes through me. On the one hand, I'm glad he's dead. On the other, I regret I'm not the one who watched him take his last breath.

"How did you get his ring?" Papà repeats.

I match his stare but stay quiet.

"Massimo!" he shouts.

I run my hand through my hair. "Katiya had it. It needs to get offloaded. I'm not telling you anymore except that she's innocent."

Red rage fills Papà's cheeks. He points at me. "You took that Abruzzo woman to our family jeweler. Do you know what you've done?"

"She's not an Abruzzo," I insist.

"You don't know that!"

"Being raped and held hostage by an Abruzzo doesn't make you one of them! If that were the case, Bridget would be a Bailey and Rossi," I blurt out, tired of this constant battle.

"Watch your mouth," Dante sneers.

"God, you're all hypocrites. And why are you here, Tully?" I hurl.

"Do not disrespect Tully!" Papà barks.

Tully holds his hand in the air. "I'm here to help you."

"Help me?" I say in disbelief. Tully would help my father out instantly, but if my brothers and I are involved, there's always a price to pay.

"Yeah. Get you out of your mess before the Petrovs get wind of what you're up to," he claims.

I shake my head. "No, thanks. Ettore can help me."

"Ah, but how long will it take?"

I pause, study Tully, and my suspicion grows. "Why are you even interested in this?"

His charming grin grows. The green in his eyes glows brighter. "I have my reasons. I'll buy it off Ettore today, but not for what he wants."

I scoff. "And there it is, my brothers. The real Tully is shining through." I step closer. "No. You can't have it."

Papà interjects, "It's yours. I'll tell Ettore to take the full commission out of whatever you give him."

"No. That money is Katiya's. No one is cheating her."

Papà slams his hand on the desk. "Goddammit, Massimo! Do you know the risk you've put this family in by taking her to Ettore's?"

"She isn't an Abruzzo," I maintain for the hundredth time.

"The ring goes to Tully. End of story. And all of you better listen closely," he says, motioning around the room. "No one, *and I mean no one*, is to take any woman or man around our contacts without my approval. Is that clear?"

"Fine. Are we done?" I fume.

Papà shakes his head. "No. There's one more thing."

"What?"

"You're suspended."

The blood drains from my face. "Excuse me?"

"You heard me—no pay for a month."

"You can't be serious," I state in shock.

He glances at Tully. "My sons seem to think they're immune to the law of this family."

"I'm not someone you hired off the street," I seethe.

Papà steps closer and lowers his voice. "Let me make this clear, Massimo. If you continue to put this family in jeopardy with your bad decisions, you'll no longer have us to lean on."

More shock pummels through me. The silent tension in the air grows thicker.

"Out! Everyone out but Tully," Papà orders.

I leave the room, still stunned, not understanding how this is all happening.

Why won't my family trust me about Katiya?

The door to Papà's office shuts, and Tristano asks, "Bro, you okay?"

I say nothing and make my way up the stairs.

"Massimo," Gianni calls after me.

I don't stop. I go to my suite, pack several suitcases of clothes and personal items, then order one of our workers to haul them to my car.

"What's going on?" Gianni asks when the last bag is gone and I'm shutting the door to my wing.

"I'm doing what I should have done a long time ago," I claim, still pissed.

"What's that?" he asks.

"Moving out."

He opens his mouth, but I cut him off.

"Save it." I stalk past him and don't stop until I'm outside of the gates. Only then do I pull over, slam my hand on the steering wheel, and take a minute to digest everything.

For the first time in my life, I don't know if I still want to be a Marino.

8

MC

Katiya

"HERE'S THE NEXT BATCH," MY SUPERVISOR ALICIA ANNOUNCES, wheeling a cart overflowing with books next to the current one I'm emptying.

Ask her.

Not yet.

Massimo is going to get upset if I don't at least ask.

She turns to walk away, and I call out, "Alicia."

She spins, raising her eyebrows. "Yes?"

I put the book on the shelf then rise. My gut twists. "Ummm..." I swallow the lump in my throat then clear it. "I was wondering if I get any vacation time."

Her smile fades. "Didn't HR review the employee benefits package with you after they offered you the job?"

My chest tightens as I panic.

HR? I don't know anything about HR.

My father raised me not to lie, but everything he taught me seems to no longer exist. Not only did I become a thief when I stole Ludis's ring, but it's become second nature to fib. I stick my chin out, answering, "Yes. They did, but I forgot what they told me. I was excited about getting hired. There-there was a lot of information."

Her grin reappears. She tucks a rogue brown strand of hair behind her ear. "Ah. Understandable. Do you still have your booklet?"

The air in my lungs turns stale. I shake my head. "No. I lost it."

"Let me call Cynthia in HR and get a new one for you. I imagine you have a few weeks a year of vacation, plus your sick days," she states.

"A few weeks?" I blurt out, surprised.

Amusement fills her expression. "Sure. It's pretty standard. Do you want to take a week off?"

My gut dives. I square my shoulders, attempting not to look as anxious as I feel right now. I reply, "Yes. If I can?"

She pushes her neon-green glasses up the bridge of her nose then answers, "With proper notice, it shouldn't be a problem. Do you know the dates you're looking to take off?"

I shrug. "Soon, but I don't know the exact days yet."

"Okay. I'll get you the request form. When you have an idea of the timeframe you want off, fill it out and give it to me. I'll approve it on my end if no one else has requested those days, then I'll send it to HR. Should I leave it on your desk?" she questions.

"That would be perfect. Thank you."

"No problem." She turns and leaves.

I should feel excited I have vacation days and about the possibility of a vacation with Massimo, but it's only making me more apprehensive. If I attempt to leave town, Leo will have a fit. His thugs warned me too many times to stay put.

I've never wanted to speak with him before, nor have I had the desire to seek him out. In order to go anywhere, I have to get his permission. Otherwise, he'll hunt me down.

How do I even find him?

Why have I never asked how to contact the Abruzzos should I need something?

Ugh.

The dread in my gut expands. I've gotten to know how Massimo works. If he wants something, he'll do everything in his power to make it happen. I'm only going to be able to hold him off for so long. Unless Leo approves of me going, I can't leave the city.

For the next two hours, I restock the shelves, trying to concentrate on my job and push the lingering worries out of my head.

It's impossible.

By the time my shift is over, I still don't have any answers about how I can get Leo's permission to leave. I put the last book on the shelf, wheel the empty cart to the return desk, and go to my cubicle to get my purse.

I freeze when I look down. As promised, Alicia left me a copy of the employee handbook. I pick it up and flip to the vacation day section. And just like she assumed, it states I get two weeks of vacation and five sick days.

I wish I could feel happy about finding this out, but I know nothing in this pamphlet applies to me. Leo rules my entire life.

I glance over my cubicle and through the glass, catching the back of Massimo's head. His dark, thick hair and broad shoulders are hard to miss. He's speaking with Alicia, and more angst builds within me. I slide the handbook in my desk drawer, hoping to gain more time until I can figure out how to speak with Leo or one of his thugs.

I grab my purse, trot over to Massimo, and put my hand on his back. "Hey. You didn't have to come inside."

He spins, sliding his arm around my waist. "I needed to stretch my legs. Ready?"

"Yes. See you tomorrow, Alicia," I say.

"Have a good night," she replies.

Massimo nods and steers me outside of the library. The moment the doors shut, he tugs me into him, sliding his hands on my cheeks. He studies me for a moment. My butterflies spread their wings. I'm about to ask him what's wrong when he presses his mouth against mine. His tongue parts my lips and urgently teases mine until my knees buckle and he's supporting all my weight against his body. He retreats from the kiss, murmuring, "I've been wanting to do that all day."

My anxiety disappears. Right now, it's just Massimo and me. The world could burn around us, and I wouldn't notice. His steel-blue eyes mesmerize me. The warmth of his hard flesh penetrates against my skin. A different cologne than what he normally wears flares in my nostrils. Hints of amber and cedarwood taunt my senses. Any good feeling I've ever experienced is in this moment. The heat in my cheeks grows hotter, and I ask, "Was it worth the wait?"

Amusement fills his orbs. He leans into my ear. His breath tickles my skin, and I shudder as he asserts, "Definitely. I'll let you know if the other things I've been waiting to do to you are worth it, later tonight." He pulls back and locks his gaze on mine.

Tingles rush down my spine. I reach for his cheek, asking, "What would that be?"

"Tsk, tsk, tsk. Are you looking to get punished by asking for details?" he challenges.

I smirk, keeping my voice low. "Will it involve restraints?"

His face turns stern. "I think it's time for you to learn about self-restraint."

"What does that mean?"

Dark arrogance expands on his face. He declares, "You'll find out tonight." He pecks me on the lips, spins, then leads me through the building. The sun peeks through the clouds, and I tilt my face toward it.

"Spring will be here soon. Did you find out about vacation time?" he asks, snapping me back to reality.

The nerves in my chest reactivate, squeezing my heart. Once again, I lie, "Alicia said she'll find out from HR."

He pins me with his eyes, opening the car door. "She doesn't know what you're eligible for?"

I shrug, tearing my orbs off his, and slide into the car. "She has a lot to manage."

I pull the visor down, pretending to fluff my hair.

He shuts the door and races around the car. He gets in and turns. "So you'll know tomorrow?"

I keep my focus on my hair. "I assume so. Is there anything you feel like eating for dinner? I can make something."

He turns on the engine and revs it. Pulling into traffic, he replies, "I'm taking you out tonight."

I close the visor and turn toward him. "Oh? Where are we going?"

"It's a surprise. Your dress is in the backseat."

Excitement flares through my bones. I shouldn't allow myself to keep feeling these emotions where Massimo is concerned, but I don't know how to stop them. I glance behind me. A deep-purple silk dress hangs next to the window. A see-through bag with *Gucci* written in gold protects the garment. I gape at him. "You bought me a dress?"

"Yep."

"It's beautiful. Thank you."

He reaches for my hand and kisses the back of it. "It'll be beautiful once you're wearing it."

My heart soars. Once upon a time, I could only dream of meeting a man like Massimo. He treats me like a rare gem. And it's not just the gifts he bestows on me. Every aspect of our relationship—sexual, emotional, mental—is more than I could ever have imagined. I never knew real chemistry existed before him. If I didn't have Leo's orders hanging over my head, I'd believe he'd protect me until the end of time. Yet I know our ending will never be what I wish.

Guilt creates emotions I don't want to feel right now. I blink hard, but a tear escapes. I curse myself and try to swipe it away before Massimo sees it, but I'm too slow.

He pulls into a fire lane. I laugh through my tears, choking out, "Do you ever park in actual spaces?"

He removes his sunglasses and turns my chin so I can't move. "Dolce, what's wrong?"

"Nothing. You're very generous," I offer.

"It's just a dress." He caresses my cheeks with his thumbs.

I close my eyes, wishing that everything could be different. It's like having Prince Charming at your fingertips and the insight it's not going to last.

It's the cruelest torture.

His lips brush mine as he says, "Katiya."

I open my eyes. "You're too good to me."

He slowly shakes his head, repeating, "This is just a dress. Your real gift comes tonight."

"Real gift?" I ask, confused.

He chuckles, pecks my lips, then releases me. He puts his hands on the wheel and peels out into traffic. Horns blare all around us, but it doesn't faze him. He weaves in and out of the vehicles and states, "Get used to me spoiling you. I plan to give you everything in life you deserve."

Shame fills me. It mixes with the growing love I have for him. I don't deserve one ounce of his affection based on what I'm trying to trick him into giving me.

"How long will it take you to get ready?" he asks, pulling me out of my pity party.

Based on the gorgeous dress, I don't want to only freshen up my makeup and hair. I want to put in more effort and look as good as possible for him. I reply, "Is an hour too long?"

"Not at all. Our reservation is whenever we show up," he nonchalantly declares.

I stifle a smile. It's typical of Massimo. Everywhere he takes me, the staff rolls out the red carpet and treats him like a king. I lean my head against the headrest and roll my face toward him. I rest my hand on his thigh, asking, "Did you have a good day?"

Darkness passes over his expression. It flickers then fades. He smiles, but it almost looks forced. "Nothing exciting."

"No?" I question, wondering if it's the truth.

"Yep." He accelerates, zooming past other vehicles and cutting a semi off. More horns blare, but he once again seems unfazed. He turns on my street and pulls up to the brownstone, jumping out, then opening the back door to pick up the dress. He rushes around to my door and opens it, reaching for me.

I take his hand and let him help me out of the car. I ask, "What's the occasion?"

"Do I need one to take you out?" he questions, sweeping me across the sidewalk and up the steps.

"I'm sure that dress costs more than my weekly wage."

"Wait until you see the shoes." He wiggles his eyebrows, grinning, then motions for me to go through the door.

I step inside the corridor. "The shoes?"

"Yep. I got them earlier. They're in your bedroom." He freezes then tugs me into him. His eyes twinkle. "Sorry. I should say *our* bedroom."

Zings ping-pong in my stomach. "So you're still serious about moving in?"

His face falls. "Of course I am. I already brought my stuff over."

Surprised, I blurt out, "You did?"

"Enough that I don't need to return to my father's for a while." He studies me, clenching his jaw.

"What?" I nervously ask.

"Did you change your mind?"

I shake my head. "No! Not at all. I guess I assumed it would take a while to move your stuff in."

"I'm a simple guy, dolce."

I laugh. "Sure, you are, Mr. Ferrari, with the Gucci dress."

"Wait until you see the shoes," he repeats, his face turning mischievous.

"Well, don't keep me in suspense," I tease, but I can't deny my excitement. I love shoes.

He leads me up the stairs and slides the key into my front door. Instead of opening it, he spins into me. "Hey."

"What?"

He holds my face, and the vulnerable expression that makes my insides turn to jelly appears. "I love you." He kisses me, and the love he has for me becomes a sheath, consuming the inner depths of my soul.

It's all too much right now—his sacrifice of moving out of his mansion so he can be with me, the way he endlessly spoils me, and his protective manner that I want to pretend will never end but know it's impossible to keep.

I breathlessly pull away, forcing a smile. "I love you, too. I better get ready."

I push past him and go to the bedroom then freeze.

He chuckles. "I thought you'd be surprised."

A pair of Jimmy Choo gold stilettos are sitting on my bed. Massimo caught me staring at them through a window one day when we waited for the coffee shop to open. He tried to drag me into the store to try them on, but I pulled him away, not wanting him to spend any more money on me.

"This is too much," I cry out, picking them up. The smooth leather feels like butter. A four-inch gold heel has a sharp appearance. I wonder if I could poke Leo's eye out if given the opportunity. I almost laugh at the thought but catch myself when Massimo circles his arm around my body, holding out a La Perla shopping bag.

"Don't think I forgot about later tonight," he warns.

I stick my hand in the bag and pull out a delicate purple-and-black lace bra and thong. I run my finger over the soft material. "Wow."

"Don't move," Massimo orders.

I stay still, missing the heat from his body, and wait.

A few moments pass, and he returns with a tumbler of scotch. He takes a seat in the armchair. A smug expression lights up his face. He takes a mouthful of his drink, sits back, and commands, "Strip, dolce. I've been waiting all day to see that little number on you."

I don't take my eyes off his, slowly removing my clothes, loving every minute of how he stares at me. When I'm naked, I state, "Sorry, sexy. I'm showering first."

He curls a finger at me.

I strut over to him, standing between his legs. "What can I do for you, sir?"

His lips twitch. He grabs my hips, leans forward, then deeply inhales. Blowing the air on my pussy, he meets my gaze. "You don't smell dirty to me."

"Oh, but I am," I insist.

"If you're going to shower, I won't get my appetizer before we go out."

I pretend to pout, running my hand through his hair. "Aw, poor baby. You'll be so hungry."

He takes his scotch, swirls a finger in it, then glides it over my clit. "Oops. I guess I need to lick that off."

My pulse races. I try to contain my smile, teasing, "You don't want me to just wash it off?"

His tongue flicks against me, and my knees wobble. I grasp his hair tighter.

In one move, he slides his ass on the floor, tugs my knees on the seat, and holds my body tight to his face.

I reach for the back of the chair, gripping it as he shows me no mercy.

Heat courses through my blood, causing hot pellets of sweat to break out on my skin. I try not to move, begging him to let me grind against him.

"No," he warns, his lips against my pussy. Then he flicks his tongue faster.

"Please, sir! Oh God! Please!" I cry out.

His tongue, lips, and fingers manipulate me until tears drip down my cheeks and I'm hoarse from pleading.

He slaps my ass and commands, "Ride my face and come, dolce!"

The moment I shimmy my hips is sweet bliss. A freight train of adrenaline explodes in my body, creating a wave of endorphins that make me dizzy.

"Massimo!" I scream.

He slaps my ass, over and over, while I continue trembling, riding the O train, not able to comprehend anything but the euphoric state annihilating me.

When my high finally ends, he slides my knees to both sides of his hips, fisting my hair.

My breathing is ragged, cheeks hot, and the smell of my arousal swirls around us. His wicked grin melts my heart further, and he mumbles, "Now you need a shower." He presses his lips to mine in an all-consuming kiss.

I match his affection, realizing the only time I feel whole is with him. It chokes me up, but I kiss him harder through it then mutter, "Want to shower with me?"

He holds my face in front of his. "No, dolce. I'm going to taste and smell you all night on me now."

9

Massimo

M<small>Y DRIVER PULLS OUT INTO TRAFFIC, AND</small> I <small>HIT THE BUTTON</small> to roll up the divider glass. I murmur in Katiya's ear, "You smell like sex and flowers."

She softly laughs. "I showered."

"Doesn't matter. I can smell you. It's going to drive me crazy all night."

She bats her eyelashes, smirking. "Sorry."

I slide my arm around her shoulders and chuckle. "No, you aren't."

Amusement fills her eyes, and the blues twinkle, reminding me of the ocean on a sunny day. All I have to do is look at her when she's happy, and my insides light up. She asks, "Are you going to tell me where we're going for dinner?"

Pride fills me. I answer, "My new club."

"*Your* club?"

"Yep."

She gapes at me.

I chuckle some more.

She turns into me further. "You've never said anything about this. When did it open?"

"Tonight."

"Tonight!" she shrieks.

"Yes. It's the grand opening."

"Wow. Massimo! That's a huge accomplishment. Congratulations!" She gives me a celebratory kiss on the lips.

I return it then shrug, but it *is* a big deal. I've invested in restaurants before with my brothers, but this club is my pet project. It's the only business venture I've done without anyone else sticking their nose into it. I hesitate then ask, "Want me to tell you a secret?"

"Of course!" she chirps.

"I'm normally more of a silent investor, but this club is different. The entire concept was mine. I have to admit, I loved every minute of watching it come together," I confess as my stomach flutters with nerves. I don't doubt it'll be a huge hit in New York, but tonight, all the critics will be at the opening. It's make-it or break-it time, and nothing is in my control at this point.

She runs her hand through my hair, helping to soothe my nerves. She beams at me as she says, "I can't wait to see it."

I kiss the top of her head and take a deep breath, wondering how she's going to react to my next statement. I cautiously add, "I wouldn't want anyone else next to me. Plus, everyone will be here tonight."

My pulse pounds hard between my ears, drowning out the traffic outside the SUV. She locks eyes with me and swallows hard. "Everyone, as in your family?"

I nod. "Yes."

Anxiety takes over her features. She scrunches her face and tilts her head. "Do you...do you think it's a good idea for me to meet them tonight?"

I tug her onto my lap and drag the back of my knuckles over her cheek. "I should have introduced you to my family after we started seeing each other. That's my fault and on me. So, yes, tonight is as good as any other one."

Silence fills the air. Her apprehension doesn't dissolve.

I push my chest out, overpowering the doubt in my mind, and firmly state, "Trust me, dolce. My family will love you."

If only they knew the real Katiya instead of the image they have in their heads.

If they aren't nice and welcoming to her, I'll kill them.

Maybe this is a bad idea.

Too late.

Change the subject.

I ask, "If you could go anywhere in the world, where would you go?"

She tilts her head. "To live?"

"I meant for vacation, but is there somewhere else you want to live besides New York?" I inquire, surprised anyone would want to leave the city I grew up in and love so much.

A tiny smile plays on her lips. She answers, "Yes. I would move, but it would be the same place I would go for vacation, I guess. Not that I take vacations."

Curiosity hits me. "Really?"

"Yes."

"Okay, where would you live and vacation—although vacationing where you live is kind of lame," I tease.

She pushes my shoulder and pretends to pout. "Hey! I'm not telling you now!"

"Aww, come on," I urge, then peck her on the lips.

She hesitates then replies, "St. Pete, Florida."

Surprise fills me at her answer. I've traveled all over Europe, to some parts of Central and South America, and most Caribbean islands. While St. Pete is a great place, it's not a place I would have expected her to pick. I question, "Why there?"

The light in her eyes sparks again, burning brighter as she speaks. "When I was a little girl, my neighbor who babysat me went there on vacation. She had brochures on her hotel and the beach. For months before she went, she'd read them to me and showed me all the photos. When she returned from her trip, she claimed the sand was as white as the pictures and gave me a huge starfish. Something about her stories of the little shops and restaurants sounded idyllic to me."

"So you've never been there?" I ask.

Katiya shakes her head. "No. But did you also know they hold the record for the most consecutive days of sunshine?"

"No, I didn't," I admit.

"768 days!" she exclaims.

"Wow!" I tug her closer to me and grin. "Okay, it's settled, then."

"What?"

"We'll go to St. Pete on our trip," I declare.

Her eyes widen. A flash of panic flies across her expression, but it disappears so quickly, I think I might have imagined it. A smile replaces the fleeing anxiety, and she breathes, "Really? You'd take me there?"

I slide my thumb over her stained lips. "Yeah, dolce. If that's where you want to go, then that's where we'll go."

She blinks hard, and her eyes glisten.

The vehicle pulls up to the club. My stomach flips. I wish I could erase all the nerves over this opening. I'm not used to feeling anything but confidence. I muster all I have, give her a chaste kiss, then proclaim, "If you haven't figured it out by now, whatever you want in life, I'll make it happen."

More emotions overpower her face, and she strokes my cheek. In a low voice, she states, "I don't deserve you."

I huff. "Nonsense. Don't say that ever again."

She takes a deep breath.

I glance out the window at the red carpet, photographers, and press. "Are you ready to fight this chaos?"

She turns her head and mutters, "Wow."

"Crazy, huh?"

She locks eyes with me. "This is insane."

"Don't be nervous. Just stay by me, dolce," I instruct.

"Oh, you don't have to worry about that," she replies.

I kiss her hand. "Good. Let's get past all this madness," I state, then knock on the window.

The driver opens the door. I get out, reach for Katiya, and pull her out of the SUV. When she's steady on her feet, I kiss her quickly then spin into the crowd, proud she's on my arm.

It's another new feeling for me. I've dated models, actresses, and rich heiresses. It's not the first red carpet I've walked. The women were good eye candy, but there wasn't much more to them to keep my interest.

Everything with Katiya is different. When I'm with her, it's as if we're two puzzle pieces that are the perfect fit. She's gorgeous but also intelligent with a bit of naivety. Her semi-cold exterior she often shows the world does something to me. Even with her innocence, she still holds her own with confidence.

And I won't deny that our fifteen-year age difference is a turn-on for me. I've worked hard to keep in shape as I've aged, but her energy makes me feel young again. Plus, she's got a body that would compete with any cover model.

I tug her closer to me and murmur in her ear, "Just keep your chin up and a smile on your face."

She obeys, glancing at me, and I steal another kiss. The purple, strappy minidress I bought her fits like a glove. All I can think about is what I want to do to her while she wears nothing but the gold stilettos and lingerie she has on underneath.

Lights flash all around us. Several reporters call out my name. At the end of the red carpet, I answer some questions, introduce Katiya, and spell her full name for the press. By the time we step inside, I'm ready to be past the media.

"You did good, dolce," I praise. Once my eyes adjust to the darker atmosphere, I lead her past security and into the main area of the club. Soft lights glow on the walls. Ten bars, all made from different colored metals and crystals, already have lines formed. Four floors of VIP suites overlook the main one. The large dance floor is empty, but there won't be any space on it later tonight. Guests occupy different sitting areas, both public and more discreet ones. A band plays indie music but only for the next hour. Then New York's two hottest DJs, Cray Cray and Lipster, will take over.

"The press was nerve-racking," Katiya confesses.

I grin. "You made it look easy."

"I did?"

I brush her lips, saying, "One hundred percent." I kiss her then look up. I catch a glimpse of Tristano's head on the fourth floor. My stomach does a little nosedive.

It's now or never.

My family better give her a chance.

I steer Katiya through the mob of people, nodding and saying thanks to those offering congratulations. We get in the elevator and go to the fourth floor. I quickly whisk her to the suite I reserved for my family.

My brothers, Killian, and Papà stand in a huddle near the private bar, talking. Bridget, Cara, and Arianna sit on couches. Another dark-haired woman is seated with her back to me.

I decide to take the friendlier path to start, leading my dolce to the women. I motion for Katiya to sit on the couch, and I slide between her and Arianna, facing the other woman. Then I realize it's Dante's assistant, Pina.

At one point or another, my brothers and I have all tried to steal her. She's the most efficient assistant any of us have ever had. She runs circles around everyone and always figures out a way to make things happen. But no amount of money or added benefits can sway her to leave Dante. She's loyal to only him.

When I invited her to the opening, I thought she'd be excited. She normally is when we extend invitations to these types of events. One time, she even commented it was perks of her job. Yet, she wouldn't commit to attend and said she'd come if she wasn't busy.

I pin my gaze on her, taunting, "Pina. It's nice of you to grace us with your presence. I'm glad your schedule wasn't full."

She smirks. "My plans changed at the last minute."

"So my event was the second choice tonight?" I ask.

She shrugs. "Sorry."

"Ouch," I tease, pretending to stab myself in the heart.

She rolls her eyes. "Let's not be dramatic now."

"Oh, you know my brother," Arianna interjects, then throws her arms around me. "This place is amazing, Massimo!"

"You saw it a few weeks ago when you flew in to plan tonight. You did an awesome job, by the way," I add, proud of the event-planning business my sister has created. She grew a clientele in both New York and Chicago in little time.

She beams. "Thanks."

I tug Katiya closer to me. "Ladies, meet Katiya." I point to each woman. "This is my sister Arianna, Dante's soon-to-be wife Bridget, Gianni's wife Cara, and Dante's assistant Pina. She secretly wants to work for me and not him." I wink at Pina.

She rises and hugs Katiya. Arianna does the same, but Bridget and Cara only extend their hands, which pisses me off.

What did I expect? For it to be easy?

We sit back in our seats, and the server brings a tray of champagne and one scotch. I hand Katiya a flute, and I pick up the scotch, clinking her glass then taking a large mouthful.

Arianna asks, "Katiya, do you work?"

"Yes. At the library," she replies.

"Oh. That must be—" Arianna stiffens next to me. "Which one?"

My stomach falls.

Time to get this over with once and for all.

I keep my arm around Katiya and lock eyes with Arianna, admitting, "The one you don't like to visit anymore."

My sister's color drains from her cheeks. Her eyes dart between Katiya and me. She puts her hand on her very pregnant stomach and stares at the table.

I put my drink down, grab Arianna's hand, and lower my voice. "She's innocent."

My sister blinks hard and releases my hand. "Excuse me. I need to use the ladies' room."

"I'll go with you," Cara announces, shooting daggers at me, then stepping next to Arianna. I almost say something but bite my tongue. Cara is Gianni's wife, so until he changes his mind about Katiya, I'm unsure what good it'll do to even attempt to sway Cara. I decide I'll talk with my sister later in private, just as Cara leads Arianna away.

The entire atmosphere changes. Tension fills the air. My chest tightens further. I glance at Katiya. Her typical cold exterior is in full force. She sits straight up and pushes her chin out, keeping her line of vision between Bridget and Pina.

I rise and pull Katiya with me. "Let me show you around."

She doesn't argue, and I steer her in the opposite direction of my brothers and Papà. When we get far enough away, I apologize. "I'm sorry about that. I'll talk with Arianna and assure her you aren't to blame for her kidnapping."

Katiya furrows her eyebrows. "It was a bad idea to bring me here. I'm going to go home so you can enjoy your night with your family."

"What? No! You'll do no such thing. I'm sorry for what just happened. I promise you I'll change their minds about you," I vow.

She reaches for my cheeks. "Massimo, they're never going to accept me. You need to be realistic."

"They will," I adamantly reiterate then step closer. "They have to. I'm in love with you. I choose you. So they're going to have to find a way to stop assuming you're part of the Abruzzos."

She squeezes her eyes shut.

"Hey. Everything is okay," I lie, not willing to let her leave.

She opens her eyes, and a tear falls. She swipes at it, but another one replaces it.

"Dolce, don't let them get to you," I assert.

"I'm sorry. I-I just...can you show me where the ladies' room is?" she asks.

I deeply exhale. "Sure." I grab my scotch as I pass the table and steer Katiya to the women's room. Once she's inside, I step against the wall and take a drink.

"What's she doing here?" Gianni seethes.

I fill my mouth with more liquid, swallow, and cringe from the burn. I spin on my brother. "This is my club. I own it. If you can't be respectful toward the woman I love, then get out."

Gianni's eyes nearly pop out of his head. He steps closer. "You're choosing an Abruzzo over me?"

"She's not an Abruzzo," I insist for the millionth time.

He shakes his head. "Wake up, little brother. Your woman is an Abruzzo. And that makes your entire relationship a setup."

Rage rushes through my blood. "A setup? You're one to talk."

"What does that mean?"

"You want to make false accusations about my relationship, but all you are is a hypocrite," I declare.

"About what?"

"You wouldn't be married to Cara if you hadn't tricked her then paid millions for her, would you?" I spout.

"Shut up," Gianni sneers.

I finish my drink. "No. Exactly how many millions did it take to buy your wife? One? Five? Ten? And what does that make her?"

"Are we really having this conversation right now?" he asks.

I sniff hard, wishing I had more scotch in my glass. All the thoughts I've had about the things Gianni did to marry Cara come out with no filter. "It's so easy to judge others when you bought your wife. If you hadn't, she wouldn't be here right now. How big was the transfer out of your bank account? Does she even know you own her?"

Gianni points in my face. "You better watch your mouth."

"Me? I—"

"I already know. It was ten million," Cara interjects, her voice shaking.

The hairs on my arms rise. I glance over his shoulder to see a devastated-looking Cara. I immediately want to crawl into a hole but stand taller. In normal circumstances, I'd never say the things I just said. And Cara's been a part of our family for as long as I can remember. I've never had any issues with her. But I'm still angry Gianni chooses to judge me and bash my woman without even knowing her. To piss him off further, I scoff, "Ten? You didn't tell her, did you?"

Gianni scowls at me for another moment then turns.

"Tell me what?" Cara asks.

Gianni grinds his molars, taking his time to answer.

Cara waits, tapping her foot. A red flush deepens on her cheeks. She fumes, "We've never discussed this. Am I wrong? Did you pay more for me than what I went for on the stage?"

More guilt eats at me for hurting Cara. Yet I'm enjoying every minute of watching Gianni be in the hot seat.

He glares harder, steps forward, then puts his arm around her. He states, "Let's go talk in private."

"Just tell me whatever it is you conveniently forgot. And don't you dare lie to me," she warns.

His voice turns firmer. He asserts, "Let's go talk."

"So you've lied to me?" she accuses.

He reaches for her face, and she steps back.

"Don't you dare touch me!"

"Tesoro—"

"No! Don't you even try to sugarcoat this," she cries out, pushing his chest.

Tense silence fills the air. Neither one takes their eyes off the other. Gianni finally restates, "We need to speak privately." He steps forward, slides his arm around her waist, and steers her down the hall.

Shit! I reprimand myself. *Why did I do that?*

I didn't know she was standing there.

It wasn't my secret to tell.

Now I've hurt her.

"Massimo. Is everything okay?" Katiya asks, placing her hand on my bicep and pulling me out of my thoughts.

I spin and force a smile. "I'm not in the mood for this event. Let's get out of here."

10

Katiya

"WHAT? NO! YOU CAN'T LEAVE. IT'S *YOUR* CLUB!" I CRY OUT.

"Who cares. I sure as hell don't anymore," he states, then circles his arm around my waist. Before I can respond, he guides me down the hall.

As soon as we turn the corner, an older man steps in front of us. Deep wrinkles cover his face. He has the same dark hair and features as Massimo and his brothers. His cold eyes pin Massimo's. In an authoritative voice, he states, "This is impressive, son."

Massimo's body stiffens. He grips my waist tighter. "Thank you. This is Katiya. Katiya, meet my papà, Angelo Marino."

The hairs on my neck rise. I try to smile, but I'm so nervous, I can barely curve my lips. Everything about Angelo Marino exudes intelligence and intimidation. He's either the guy you want on your side or the one you should stay far away from. I manage to get out, "It's nice to meet you, Mr. Marino."

Tension fills the air so thick, I want to run and hide. He keeps his gaze on me, studying me until I'm sure he hates me. But then he surprises me. He leans in and kisses my cheek. "Katiya. I've heard a lot about you."

His cautious tone isn't overly friendly, but I'll take whatever I can get. Part of fulfilling my promise to Leo requires me to get close to the family.

I can't do it. Massimo deserves better.

I have to. There's no way out.

"Hopefully all good," I attempt to joke, but it falls flat. There's no secret he doesn't trust me and believes I'm working for the Abruzzos.

I kind of am.

No, Leo is forcing me.

It still makes his assumptions about me correct.

In a dry tone, Angelo states, "Yes. It seems you have my son wrapped around your finger."

"Papà," Massimo groans.

Angelo locks eyes with him. "Do you want to deny your feelings for this woman?"

"Of course not," Massimo states.

"Well then..." Angelo shrugs then finishes the last bit of alcohol in his tumbler.

"Katiya and I were just leaving," Massimo adds.

Surprise fills Angelo's face. "Oh? Why would you leave your own party? Is something wrong?" he challenges, addressing me.

"I'm the one deciding to leave, not Katiya," Massimo clarifies.

Angelo puts his arm around my shoulder, forcing me to step away from the protection of Massimo's grasp. Angelo sweeps me forward, asserting, "Come, Katiya. Meet the rest of the family. After all, if you're in Massimo's life, you should know who you're dealing with, don't you think?"

My stomach spins, and my skin crawls. Everything about his statement feels like a threat. I don't answer, unsure if he's actually looking for a response. Either way, what would I even say?

"Papà!" Massimo reprimands, staying close on my heels.

Angelo ignores him and leads me to the corner. He motions to each man, introducing them. "This is my son-in-law Killian. And these are my sons Dante and Tristano." He glances around the room. "Where did Gianni run off to?"

"He's with Cara," Massimo states.

"Lass, nice to meet you. What's your name?" Killian questions, leaning down to kiss my cheek.

My insides suddenly feel like a roller coaster. They dive again. Massimo's brothers scowl as I reply, "My name is Katiya."

"She's the librarian," Dante interjects.

My roller coaster drops again.

Killian's smile falls. His eyes grow wider. The green glows hotter, and he pins them on Massimo. "Tell me she's not *that* librarian."

Massimo protectively tugs me into his body. In a firm voice, he insists, "She isn't responsible for what happened to Arianna."

Red burns Killian's cheeks. He looks at me and accuses, "You gave Donato access to that room where he held my wife hostage, didn't you?"

My throat turns dry. I swallow, and it feels like it's cracking. "I-I—"

"Had no idea what he was going to do. And she wasn't working the night he kidnapped our sister," Massimo defends.

Killian's scowl doesn't fade. He shakes his head at Massimo, steps back, then says, "If you'll excuse me, I'm going to make sure my wife is okay."

"Killian," Massimo says, reaching for his shoulder.

"Don't," Killian warns, shaking him off.

All three Marinos glare at me. The air in my lungs turns stale. I blurt out, "I swear I didn't know what Donato would do! And Massimo is right. I wasn't there that night! It was after hours when he took her inside."

"How do you know?" Dante asks, crossing his arms across his chest.

"Massimo told me what happened. I didn't even know about her abduction until he informed me," I admit.

Tristano steps closer. "I believe you."

"You do?" I blurt out.

He nods. "Sure. If Massimo says you're trustworthy, then I believe him. It's nice to finally meet you." He leans down and kisses my cheek.

"Good man," Massimo says, patting Tristano's back.

"Thank you," I manage to get out, overwhelmed with the Marino men and the stress of this evening. We've barely been here an hour, and I'm borderline ready to sweat. If I'm going to gain their trust, I need to at least get them not to scowl at me.

I adamantly repeat, "I swear I didn't know what Donato was planning, nor was I there."

"But say you had," Dante suggests.

"Enough! You're trying to crucify Katiya for something she didn't do, and now you're just pulling at straws," Massimo barks.

Angelo surprises me, stating, "Agreed."

Shocked, I turn toward him. "You believe me?"

"Tristano has a good point. If you convinced my son you're innocent, then who are we to say otherwise?" He smiles, but it doesn't feel super friendly. Still, it's better than nothing.

Dante sniffs hard. "Fine. Nice meeting you." He spins and walks away.

"Asshole," Massimo states under his breath.

Tristano grabs a flute of champagne and hands it to me. "Here. Have a drink." He takes one and knocks it back then pats Massimo's bicep. "Great job, bro. We miss you at the house."

"It's not even been a full day." Massimo chuckles.

"Tristano has another good point. Now that we're all on the same page regarding our misunderstanding, why don't you and Katiya move into your wing? You don't belong in Queens," Angelo remarks, pinpointing his laser stare on Massimo.

Goose bumps break out on my skin. Massimo must feel it because he runs his thumb over them then states, "Katiya and I will discuss it."

Relief hits me. Living with the Marinos could make it easier to find out their contacts. Yet, the calm replacing my nerves can't be ignored.

"What's there to discuss?" Tristano asks.

"Stay out of it," Massimo orders.

"Think about it. Tully's here. I'll speak with you later. Great job, Massimo. You did an excellent job on this project," Angelo compliments. He nods, pats me on the shoulder, and leaves.

Pina steps next to Tristano. "Tristano. How've you been?"

A scowl flickers on his face, but it disappears quickly. He sniffs hard. "I'm great. Best I've been in a long time."

"Is that so?"

"Sure is," he insists, grabs another flute, and hands one to Pina.

She takes it and is about to drink when he stops her.

He demands, "First, we toast."

"To what?" she asks, an annoyed expression on her face.

Arrogance fills Tristano's orbs. He proclaims, "To old dogs who love new tricks but still want to hang on to the past, even though they don't realize that gnawing on the bone eventually destroys it."

"Bro, what the hell does that mean?" Massimo asks.

Pina huffs. "I think what your little brother meant to say is that when a dog's in the doghouse, there's always a reason."

I'm still confused about how this conversation took a turn to this point.

Massimo shakes his head and puts his hand on the small of my back. "Have fun with your dog lingo. Katiya and I will see you later." Before I can say anything, he whisks me through the club. He stops in front of the elevator.

"Where are we going?" I ask.

"It's a secret," he replies.

The doors open, and we step inside. Massimo halts others from getting in the elevator with us. He presses the P and enters a code.

"Secret hideaway?" I question.

He spins, backing me up until I'm against the wall. His lips press against mine, and his tongue urgently slides into my mouth.

When the doors open, I'm breathless.

He retreats, walking backward and pulling me with him. When the doors shut behind me, Massimo spins.

I sharply inhale. It's a clear night. All of New York City is twinkling in front of us. Tiny-looking vehicles whiz by on the bridge. Buildings sparkle with different colored lights.

Massimo slides his arms around my waist. "It wasn't supposed to be finished until next week. They surprised me today when they called to say they completed the remodel."

"This is..." I glance in both directions, amazed at the view. Dark-blue walls, warm-amber lights, and soft music create a sexy atmosphere. I breathe, "This is incredible."

"I'm glad you like it. This is where we should live," Massimo says.

My heart races, and I gape at him. "What?"

I thought I would live at my papà's forever, but honestly, I don't want my family in our business. I meant for this to be a place for me to crash when I'm partying in the city. But when the foreman called today, it seemed like a sign.

Shocked, I glance around the huge space. "You want to move in here?"

"Yes. Tell me you love it and you'll move in," Massimo orders.

I softly laugh. "Of course I love it. I've never seen anything so stunning."

He grins and steps so close, our bodies touch. "So you'll move in with me? Here?"

"Of course I will!" I declare, tearing up. A sharp pain shoots through my chest. This moment is everything a girl could ever dream of experiencing. Never in my wildest dreams did I believe someone like Massimo would love and care for me. All I want is him. This apartment is an added bonus.

"Good. The movers will bring your things tomorrow. In the meantime, I have a gift for you," he states.

"A gift? Massimo, you've already given me enough tonight," I assure him.

"Oh, dolce. That wasn't your gift," he boasts, leading me down the hall. He opens a door and motions for me to go inside.

There's no light on in the room. I carefully take a few steps, and he steps behind me. A light slowly turns on, but like the ones in the main room, it's a warm amber that doesn't overpower anything.

It's as if I'm watching a scene unfold. An oversized bed with dark silk bedding is in the center of the room. Pewter chains with cuffs dangle from the ceiling. Different types of furniture, a luxurious glass shower, and a wall with floggers and paddles all compete for my attention. I ask, "What's in the drawers?"

Massimo kisses the back of my hand and guides me to it. He opens one drawer at a time, displaying all sorts of different toys. Some of them look vanilla. Others make a tiny bit of fear-filled excitement fly through me. He pins his steel-blue eyes on me. "See anything you like?"

I bite my lip as my butterflies spread their wings. I run my fingers over several vibrators and then point to the wall. A thick black leather strap with gold pointed studs hangs next to the floggers. Each end of the leather boasts padded buckles. The middle of the strap is also padded. "What is that?"

Massimo's lips twitch. "It's a thigh sling."

I walk over to it and run my palm over the smooth leather inside. Then I rub the sharp metal studs. I cock my head, asking, "What's it for?"

"It's so you don't have to hold your knees in the air. Allows me to get inside you deeper," he states, wiggling his eyebrows. He traces a D-ring. "I can use these to attach other things to you—or you to them." Blue flames sear into mine.

"Like what?" I ask, unsure why I'm so mesmerized by the leather strap.

He points to the ceiling over the bed. "Those restraints. Or this." He picks up a mouth ring gag. "Of course, I could always attach you to that." He glances at a steel-colored object. It looks like a tool my father would have had in his garage. Yet, there's a pale-pink vibrator in the shape of a cock on it.

"I don't know what that is," I admit, feeling very naive. Gags and restraints were Ludis and Leo's thing. I've never been exposed to toys or most of the things in this room.

"It's a fucking machine," he casually declares.

I furrow my eyebrows, blurting out, "Why would I want to use that when I'm with you?"

Massimo steps behind me, holding me tight to his frame. His hot breath hits my neck, sending tingles racing down my spine. I shudder as he warns, "It's a punishment, dolce. And since you're so interested in it, the next time you disobey me, I'm going to put you in the thigh strap and restrain your hands above your head."

I take a deep breath, imagining my body naked, restrained, spread wide open for Massimo to do what he pleases. My pulse creeps up. I lean my head against his back, inhale his woodsy cologne, and ask, "Then what?"

His hand slides down the front of my body. He bunches the hem of my dress until his palm cups my pussy. His tongue hits the back of my ear, and I shudder. He states, "I'm going to have that machine fuck you for hours, my little dolce. I'm going to record you begging me, crying to let you come. Every time I allow it, which won't be too often, I'm going to watch those blue eyes roll. Then I'm going to slow you down until you're dying to come back up."

His index finger slips under my panties, gliding into my body. I arch my ass into him, taking as much of his digit as possible while moaning.

He drags his other hand over my neck, fisting my hair, then tugging my head back until his face is hovering over mine. Blood heats in my veins. My cheeks flush, and my breath hitches. He mutters, "While the machine is working you over, I'm going to taste your pussy. It's going to make everything more intense. Tears will fall down your sexy cheeks. Your body will be mine to control and manipulate how I see fit. Do you understand?" He curls his finger in my pussy.

"Yes, sir," I whisper, wondering what I can do so he'll punish me sooner rather than later. I've never had a punishment from Massimo I wouldn't want to repeat.

"Ah, but you like your punishments, don't you?" he asks, as if he can read my thoughts.

"Yes. You know I do," I admit.

He yanks his hand out of my panties and spins me into him.

I gasp, my breath shaking and butterflies going crazy.

He grasps my jaw, tracing my cheekbone with the same finger that was inside me. The scent of my arousal permeates around us. A woman's soothing voice sings a long note, making me forget about anything but Massimo and this room.

He studies me. It seems like hours, but I don't flinch, keeping my eyes locked on him. He finally remarks, "I made this room for you—for us. Only us."

My heart soars, and more surprise hits me. "You did?"

"Yes."

"It's beautiful," I say and mean it. Every foreign object represents a new adventure for Massimo and me. It's intimate and naughty yet still classy. "I love it."

His eyes morph into blue crystals. Satisfaction fills his expression. He holds the back of my head and leans closer, lowering his voice so I can barely hear him. "You've been bad again, dolce."

Delicious zings ping around my body. I fall into my role, questioning, "How, sir? What did I do?"

"I told you to find out your vacation time. You didn't do it," he asserts.

Guilt crashes through me, and reality hits. The vision of the employee handbook makes me cringe inside.

This relationship isn't real. He's a means to the end.

I cringe at the thought then think, *the end of what?*

The end of my life.

"What do you have to say for yourself?" Massimo demands.

I push the guilt away then claim, "I tried. Really, I did. I should have the information soon, sir."

He tugs my hair again, this time, a bit stronger. My insides clench. A whimper escapes my lips as he challenges, "Are you expecting me to look the other way, Katiya?"

"Well, I...umm..."

His gaze locks on mine. "Do you think you deserve to get a free pass?"

"No, sir," I reply.

An inferno of blue heat drills into me. He pins his eyebrows together and claims, "You must pay for your sins, my dolce." He leads me to a bench. "Take your dress off. Then bend over this so I can restrain you. Disobedient girls need to learn their lessons."

11

M C

Katiya

THE COOL SILK FALLS TO MY ANKLES. I STEP OUT OF THE purple puddle, leaving my Jimmy Choos on my feet. I widen my eyes, asking Massimo, "Should I take my stilettos off?"

"No, but take your bra off."

I smirk, unable to stop it, happy he wants me to leave the shoes on. Something about it feels naughtier. I reach behind me, unhooking my bra, then let it drift to the floor.

He sniffs hard, his eyes darting over my body, pausing on my breasts, the curve of my waist, and my thighs. He drags his gaze up my body, locking it to mine. He points to the wall. "Before you assume your position, go pick a paddle."

My belly ignites in flutters. Whenever Massimo turns dominant, commanding me to submit, everything lights up in my body. Tingles erupt on my ass cheek, as if it somehow knows what's to come. I bite on my smile and strut over to the wall, answering, "Yes, sir." I pause and assess all the different paddles, unsure of the difference besides the colors and sizes.

He follows me, stepping behind me and circling his arm around my waist. His breath tickles my neck. I squirm into him, and he drops his hand to my pussy. I sharply inhale, glancing up at him. His lips curl into a smug expression. He asserts, "Which ones grab your attention, dolce?"

I tear my gaze off his blues and study the options. Then I motion to several, admitting, "The blood-red leather one, and that black one with three different sizes."

He nods in approval. "We're on the same page."

"Yeah?" I ask, the tingles on my ass intensifying.

Arrogance explodes further on him. He orders, "Go get them."

I take a deep breath and step forward, choosing the red one first. It's intricately made, and I trace my fingers over the raised leather.

Massimo kisses the curve of my neck, putting his finger next to mine. "This has steel in it. You need to trust me if I'm going to use it on you."

The anticipation of what it would feel and sound like, cracking against my skin, intensifies. I blurt out, "I trust you."

He takes it out of my hand. "Good. Pick up the other one."

I reach for the black one, running my fingers over the silver stud decorations.

"It's a three-layer slapper, for three times the discipline," he murmurs in my ear. "Which one do you want?"

I grasp his thigh, rest my head on his chest, and turn my head. He arches his eyebrows, and my pulse beats hard in my neck. I confess, "I've been bad, Massimo. I think I need extra discipline tonight." It's not a lie. I'm a horrible person, plotting against him. Yet, even now, I'm selfish. Every cell in my body wants him to use both these paddles on me.

"So you want the black one," he asks.

I shake my head hard. "No. I-I want both."

Waves of darker blue swirl in his eyes. His body stiffens against mine. He challenges, "Both?"

Adrenaline spins in me, making me slightly dizzy. I'll never understand why I have the needs I do, but if he doesn't do what I want him to, I'll never get rid of the urge exploding inside me. I squeeze his quad, begging, "Please. I need both. Teach me a lesson."

He studies me for a moment. I think he might say no, but then he grabs both paddles and steps back. He points to the bench, ordering, "Face down, hands on the front legs."

The flutters in my stomach go crazy. I lean over the bench, sliding my hands down the legs, grasping the bottom. The leather padding is cool on my bare breasts and stomach. My thighs hug the sides.

Massimo crouches in front of me. He moves my hair to one shoulder then tucks it behind my ear. "What are the rules, dolce?"

"No coming until you permit me. No moving or grinding unless you allow it," I recite.

Satisfaction fills his expression. "Good girl." He pecks me on the lips then clasps the metal restraints around my wrists. "Since you've continued to disobey me, I think your punishment needs to reinforce who's in charge. You need a reminder, don't you?"

Anticipation becomes a hurricane, spinning in all my cells. I breathe, "Yes. Please, sir. Remind me, so I don't forget again."

He sniffs hard, stroking my cheek while taking bated breaths. Every second that passes adds energy to the storm I can't stop growing inside me. It's like Massimo knows the urge I have for him to dominate me. When he gives me commands, I light up in ways I never thought were possible. And the pain he gives me somehow makes the pleasure more intense. He asserts, "There are hundreds of people below us. Are you sure you wouldn't rather be partying with them?"

I don't need to contemplate his question. "No. I want my punishment, sir."

His lips twitch then he rises and walks to the wall. He turns a dial and returns to me. His hot breath hits my ear as he murmurs, "Every sound that comes out of your mouth will get broadcast in the club. It'll mix with the music. They'll all hear you but will wonder how it got in the song. The men will turn hard, but they won't know why it's happening."

"How do you know?" I whisper, excited at the prospect of others hearing us.

Massimo moves his face in front of mine, replying, "There was a study I read years ago. It had women and men on a microphone while they had sex in a club. No one could see them going at it, but everyone heard it in the music. It's why I added this feature to this room. But know this, dolce. Should the DJ take even a few second break between songs, your cries are going to rebound throughout the building. Anyone you speak to after is going to wonder why your voice sounds so familiar."

More adrenaline pools in my cells. Determined to get started, I confess, "I lied."

Massimo freezes then arches his eyebrows. "About what?"

I dig myself deeper into the hole, but I don't want Massimo to hold back tonight. I fib, "I didn't ask Alicia about vacation time."

Tense silence fills the air. His eyes turn to slits, and hurt fills his expression. He holds my chin and seethes, "Why not?"

"She was busy most of the day. Time went quickly and then you were there to pick me up."

"Why did you lie?"

"I didn't want to upset you."

He grinds his molars, and the nervous flutters in my stomach expand. He rises, goes to the drawer, and takes something out of it. He returns and crouches in front of me again, demanding, "Tell me the rules bad girls must obey, dolce."

"No coming until you permit me. No moving or grinding unless you allow it," I repeat.

He scowls. "Should you ever lie to me?"

"No, sir."

"Then why did you?"

"I told you, I didn't want you to be angry."

He scoffs. "So you lie?"

There are so many levels of guilt I experience daily, and right now, it's all crashing around me. Still, I egg Massimo on further. "I lied, and I need you to punish me hard enough I won't do it again."

He studies me then states, "I'm not happy about this."

My remorse grows. I genuinely say, "I'm sorry, Massimo."

His lips twitch. "I don't think you are. And that's why we're going to have to add some things to your punishment." He opens his palm, and a smooth, black oval is in his hand.

"What it is?"

"It's a panty vibrator. I would remove your thong since you have a harder time not squirming when you wear them. But now, it's clear to me I've been too nice in the past," he calmly asserts.

I stay quiet, dying for the first slap on my ass. When he finally rises and steps behind me, I take a deep breath.

His hand slides under my panties, and he positions the vibrator on my clit. A clicking noise hits my ear, and the vibrator turns on. It's slow and torturous. The desire to come quickly floods me, but I know it's just the beginning of the buildup.

"Turn your head to the right," he instructs.

I obey, and there's a noise above me. In a few seconds, a floor-length mirror drops from the ceiling. My almost-bare, exposed skin gleams in the glass.

Massimo returns to the drawers then pulls something else out. He cages his body over my back then places a soft material over my eyes. He murmurs, "Just enough to keep you curious."

My heart pounds harder. He secures it, and the outline of my body and his slowly appears in the mirror. I'm guessing the blindfold is some sort of gauze. And I don't know how he always knows what to do, but the blurry vision I now have only adds to my anticipation.

"You will only call me sir tonight. You are not permitted to say my name unless I change my mind. Understand?" he orders.

"Yes, sir," I answer.

The outline of a paddle in his hand makes me tingle. He gives me no warning, and the leather from one of the paddles slaps my ass cheek.

"Oh!" I cry out, squeezing the legs of the bench to steady myself.

He begins a rotation of slapping me with the different paddles then rubbing his hand over the sting. The vibrations on my clit taunt me. He keeps it at the same speed. All I want to do is grind against it. Every time the paddle connects with my ass, it's a quick pulse of bliss.

"Please, sir!" I cry out, then wonder if the people downstairs really can hear me.

"Please, sir, what?" he provokes, increasing the speed of the vibrator and smacking my ass.

"Oh God!" I moan. Heat burns in my blood. A sheen of sweat covers my skin. The thong I'm wearing sticks to me, and all I want to do is peel it off.

"Answer me," he barks.

"Please, sir! Let me come," I beg.

"Do you think naughty girls who lie to me should get rewarded?" he questions, dragging his fingers over my spine.

Zings bounce in all my cells. I shudder. My breath hitches and comes out sporadically. The desire to shimmy my hips over the bench gets harder to resist. I plead, "Please! Let me move!"

He leans over me until his lips hit my ears. "Do you remember I told you earlier tonight you were going to learn self-restraint?"

"Yes," I whisper, trying to find some moisture in my mouth, but it's dry.

"This is it, dolce. I could have bound your ankles to the bench, but I didn't. I could use the strap under the bench to secure you so tight you can't grind anything. But what would that teach you? Huh?" he goads.

I stare at the fuzzy image of his hard flesh over my much smaller body. Everything about being helpless under him makes me feel like I'm in heaven. I reply in a desperate tone, "Please let me come. Just once."

"Sorry. What did you say?" he asks, moving the remote in front of my face and clicking it.

The sensations begin pulsing on my clit in a new pattern. It speeds up to a point I almost orgasm. Before I do, it changes speed to an excruciatingly slow pulse. I shriek, "Please, sir! I-I-I can't take it anymore."

He slaps my ass with a paddle. I think from the way it continues to ricochet on my skin that it's the three-layered slapper. Each moment of impact drives my body harder against the toy.

"Sir! I'm begging you," I implore as tears blur my vision.

"If you move those ankles an inch, I'll deny you all night," Massimo warns.

The amount of adrenaline sitting in my cells, ready to explode, is past the point of uncomfortable. I don't want to come.

I need a release like oxygen in my lungs.

These are the moments with Massimo where he breaks me. It's as if I can feel my body shattering into pieces, no longer able to stay in one piece, yet not completely destroyed. I cry out, "Sir, please! I-I can't do this anymore."

He tosses the paddles on the floor and jumps in front of my face. He removes the blindfold, grabs my tear-stained chin, and adamantly states, "You can do whatever you choose. Now, what else are you lying to me about?"

My vision is too blurred from my tears. In a moment of delirium, I admit, "I lied. I have the handbook."

Silence fills the room. A chill passes over me, and Massimo turns the vibrator off. He pins his steely blues on me, fuming, "What did you just say?"

Dread fills me. I curse myself for not controlling my mouth. But there's no way to backtrack. All I can do is fess up. I sniffle then repeat, "I have the handbook. Alicia dropped it off on my desk."

"And how much time do you get?"

"Two weeks."

He licks his lips, assessing me, then asks, "Why did you lie?"

Everything in the room shifts. It's no longer a game we're playing. The hurt radiating off Massimo permeates into me. I answer, "I don't know."

"Yes, you do."

"No. I don't," I insist.

"You're going to continue lying to me?" he accuses.

"No. I-I–"

"Are still lying," he interjects.

Thick silence develops between us. My tears continue to fall, and everything I hate about what I have to do to him attacks me.

He enunciates his words, as if he's afraid he'll lose control. "You lied because you don't want to go on vacation with me."

"No! That's not it," I protest.

"Then what is it, Katiya? Hmm?" he spouts.

A few minutes pass, but I don't speak.

He shakes his head, rises, and declares, "Fine. Don't answer me. When you're ready to tell the truth, I'll return. But know this, Katiya." He points to a tiny green light near the corner of the ceiling. "If you move, I'll see it. If you come, I'll know. Any further disobedience, and I'll end all of this between us."

Fear fills me. I cry out, "Massimo! No! Don't break up with me. Please!"

His dangerous, hate-filled eyes rest on mine. It makes me wonder if he no longer loves me, creating more panic. I try to reach for him, but I can't move my hand. He catches the movement and crouches in front of me, swiping at my tears. "Last warning, dolce. You decided to lie to me. Not once but multiple times. If you want my forgiveness and trust again, you're going to have to earn it."

"How?" I barely choke out.

Dark shadows dance on his sharp features. He traces the outline of my sweat-coated hair. "Follow the rules, Katiya. If you want me ever again, show me you know how to follow the rules."

He rises and disappears out of my vision.

"Massimo?" I fret.

"You don't have permission to use my name," he reminds me.

I swallow hard. "Sorry...sir. Please don't leave me."

The tone in his voice makes goose bumps pop out on my skin. "It's too late for that. You need to think about what you've done."

"Please! I-I don't want to be alone. Can't you stay? I promise I'll do everything you want," I vow.

He kisses the side of my forehead then puts his lips on my ear. He murmurs, "Show me you'll do everything I want no matter where I am." He kisses the spot behind my ear then rises.

"Sir!"

His palm makes contact with my ass, and I yelp. He spanks me four more times then rubs his hand in a circle over the sting.

I whimper through it all, confused again about how the pain can heighten my pleasure so much. But I still beg, "Please don't leave."

"You've been naughtier than ever before, dolce. This is nonnegotiable." He uncuffs my wrists and orders, "Go lie on the bed, backside on the mattress. And take your panties off."

I slowly rise off the bench and then stand before him, tilting my head up. "I really am sorry," I state, wishing I had never blurted out the truth and reprimanding myself for creating a new issue I'll have to lie further to cover up.

"It's too late for sorries. Now, are you ready for your punishment, or are we done here?" he challenges.

I'm always ready for Massimo's punishments, but everything in his expression tells me I'm about to experience something totally different.

And I'm unsure if I'm going to like it or how I'll ever get through it.

Massimo

RAGE FESTERS IN MY VEINS, CAUSING ME NOT TO THINK straight. A full-blown state of crazy erupts in my mind. If I don't remove myself from this room, I don't trust what I'll say.

She lied to me.

More than once.

Does she not want to go on vacation? Am I good enough for her day-to-day life but not for extracurriculars?

Katiya's long blonde hair fans across the pillow. She lies naked, her blue eyes full of anxiety, waiting for me to decide her fate.

A million different options fly through my mind. I have an overwhelming urge to crawl on top of her and make her prove to me how much she loves me with her body.

She needs a real punishment.

I can't condone her lying. I don't care how little the white lie is.

I need to step up my game. She's too eager for my punishments.

She doesn't want me to leave. This is how I make my point.

I lower the restraints over the bed, cuffing her wrist and removing the slack. I stop when her fingers are as close to the corners of the mattress as possible. I leave a few feet of slack in the chain.

"Sir," she whispers.

I clench my jaw, resisting the urge to sweep my arms under her. Meeting her gaze, I arch my eyebrows in question.

"I'm sorry. Please don't leave the room," she begs.

My heart wants only to please her. Yet the voice inside my head stops me.

She lied to me.

Liars need to be taught lessons, or they'll do it again.

I don't respond, grab her hips, and tug her body toward the end of the bed. I stop when her ass is on the edge of the mattress then adjust the tension so she can't move her arms. Then I reach for the ankle restraints. I sniff hard then command, "Legs in the air, spread toward the walls."

She inhales a deep breath, furrowing her eyebrows, but the spark of excitement that always lights up her eyes ignites. She obeys, bringing her heels to the bottom of the mattress and then slowly widening her legs. The leg closest to mine moves straight into the air, and I restrain it, pulling the chain taut. I do the same to the other and step back.

She's a work of art. Her legs are spread perfectly in a V, displaying her pink, freshly waxed pussy. It glistens from her arousal, taunting me further. She's like an angel restrained, innocent looking yet tainted by the devil.

That devil is me.

I'm going to stain her with my body before the night is over. But for now, she needs to remember how much she wants me. She needs to beg for what only I can and will give her. And she needs the fear of me not being here when I do it.

Mustering all the control I have, I sit on the edge of the bed and stroke her flushed cheek.

Her bottom lip trembles, and she whispers, "Please stay. I-I don't want to be alone."

I lean over her, kissing her. It's meant to be chaste, but our tongues collide desperately, deepening the kiss until we're both out of breath. My erection strains against my zipper, and I almost lose the willpower to leave.

She needs to learn her lesson.

I caress the side of her head and, in a low voice, state, "I can't let this go. While I'm gone, I'll be watching you. Do you still want me?"

She blinks hard. A tear drips down her cheek, making my heart squeeze tight. She chokes out, "All I want is you. I swear!"

I kiss her tear and then peck her on the lips, not allowing her to put her tongue in my mouth. I keep my face a few inches from hers, calmly directing, "Then show me that I have your full submission."

"You do," she insists.

"Then there's nothing to worry about." I rise, go over to the fucking machine, and roll it toward the bed. I avoid her, going directly to the drawers and opening the fourth one. My eyes dart across the row of penis-shaped silicone. I assess each one, debating what she can handle. I finally choose the second to largest one then coat it in lube.

"Massimo," she says hesitantly.

I return to her, stare at her anxious expression but don't flinch. I secure the dildo on the machine, asking, "What?"

Tears overflow from her blues. She sobs, "Are you going to hurt me?"

My heart sinks. I sit on the mattress and slide my arms under her, stroking her hair. "Have I ever hurt you before?"

She shakes her head. "No."

"That's right. The pain I give you is something you crave, isn't it?" I question. We've never talked about what we do in the bedroom. I've always fallen into my role and she into hers. From the time I met her, I knew she needed to submit to me. Even in the library, I could feel her obedience through her cold exterior. Once we had the opportunity to be together, neither of us had to talk about it. Everything felt natural.

"Yes. I-I need it," she admits.

"Good girl," I praise, kissing her forehead, then pinning my gaze back on hers. "Now listen to me closely. I'm going to be in the room next to this one. Every move you make, I'll be watching. Each cry, I'll hear. But there won't be any pain this time."

Panic explodes on her face. "Wh-wh-wh—"

"Don't forget the rules, Katiya. I want to know if you want to be mine," I warn.

"I do!" she exclaims.

"Then show me." I go to the end of the bed and instruct, "Take a deep breath."

She slowly inhales.

I push the machine forward so the dildo slides in her. Then I go back to the drawer and take out three black silicone clamps. I've never used clamps on her before, and these are a starter pair, so my guess is she's only going to feel them a little.

I connect the chains, leaving one long piece off the third clamp. I put one on each nipple then one on her clit. Her breath hitches. I ask, "Do they hurt?"

"No."

I tug on them.

She whimpers.

"Pain?" I ask.

"No. It...ummm..." Her face flushes redder.

"Tell me," I demand.

"I like how it feels," she states.

My lips curl up. My gut was correct. I kiss her thigh then attach the chain to the D ring on the machine. It's on top, near the base of the dildo. I slide the machine a few inches away from her then turn the knob, grabbing the remote.

"Oh!" she moans as the dildo slides in and out of her pussy, gently pulling the chain. Every time the machine removes the toy, it tugs her nipples and clit.

I flip the switch on the wall, and a mirror comes down from the ceiling. It's bigger than her frame and hangs over her body. I rub her thigh and remind her, "Remember the rules, Katiya. If you break them, I'll come back in here and take you home to your apartment. It's your choice. Me, or no me." I turn the power up a notch.

"You don't need to—oh God!" she shrieks.

"Does it hurt?" I ask again.

"No. It...oh...oh please...don't... Massimo!" she cries out.

Arrogance washes over me. "Good girls get to have me before the night is over. Naughty girls go home. Decide what you want, dolce." I spin and leave before she can respond, shutting the door and locking it from the outside.

The room next to it has a monitoring system. TVs line the entire wall. They're already on, and every angle of her body is on display.

I increase the volume that will mix with the music in the club and make sure the video is recording. Then I pour myself a scotch, taking a large mouthful. It burns down my throat to my stomach, leaving a trail of fire behind. But it barely fazes me. My blood is already hot. I stare at my dolce, spread out and watching herself in the mirror. Her whimpers get louder, and I push the remote so the machine thrusts faster.

"Oh God!" she cries out.

My cock stands so erect it hurts. I unzip my pants and palm my shaft, holding myself back from releasing.

I'm coming in her tonight.

Only if she holds up her end of the bargain.

Come on, dolce. Show me what I mean to you.

I take another mouthful of liquor, my ego soaring every time the clamps tug her body parts and she refrains from moving. Each plea she screams is like a gift from God. Time seems to freeze. It goes on and on until she's sobbing so hard for me to permit her to come or let her move that I can't take it anymore.

She surpassed all my expectations. It's incredible how much restraint she has to control her own body. I leave the monitoring room and unlock the door to the playroom.

"Please! I'll do anything! Please let me come!" she chokes, her voice hoarse.

I go to the top of the bed, kneel, then ask in her ear, "Who do you belong to?" I slow down the machine's thrusts.

"You!" she cries, fresh tears falling down her cheek. "Please...oh God! Don't stop it. Oh God!"

"Shhh," I coo, tucking her sweat-filled locks behind her ear. I kiss her forehead, then nose, then mouth. "Do you want the machine or me?"

"You! Please! Yes, that's what I need," she blurts out.

I caress her cheek. "This mouth of yours keeps getting you in trouble."

"I'm... I'm sorry. Please," she begs.

"Pick, Katiya. My cock or a gag."

She doesn't hesitate. "Your cock."

"You want my dick in your mouth?" I ask, wanting to hear her say it again.

"Please. And put your body on me. Please," she pleads.

I drop my pants. A loud clang fills the air from my belt buckle hitting the floor. I take my shirt off then kneel over her body. "Don't forget the rules," I remind her then guide my cock into her mouth.

She gags then opens the back of her throat, taking all of me. Her tongue and lips create chaos in my veins. I lean on my forearms, positioning them next to her hips. Inhaling deeply, I wait for the dildo to slide out. It tugs at the chain, and I slide my mouth over her clit, flicking my tongue.

"Mmmm," she whimpers, her mouth full of my body. I continue working her clit until she's trembling under me, and I'm worried about coming in her mouth.

I slap the bottom of her ass and order, "Come," repositioning my lips over the clamp and removing it.

I shift my hips, and my cock falls out of her mouth. She weeps, "Sir! Yes! Oh God! Sir!"

I don't let up on her clit. I hit the knob on the machine and turn it off, pushing it farther away. I refocus on eating her out and don't stop until I can't resist being inside her anymore.

In a quick move, I turn on her. I cage my body over hers and slide inside her. I tug at the other clamps then release them, pinching her nipples.

"Masimo!" she cries out then lifts her head, sticking her tongue in my mouth.

I slide my arms under her, not caring how long I last, thrusting faster than I normally do when I first enter her.

She arches her back and grinds her hips in rhythm. I fist her hair, holding her head in front of mine, demanding, "Don't ever lie to me again, dolce."

A mix of emotions floods her face. More tears fall. "I'm-I'm sorry!"

"Shh," I order, returning my lips to hers. I reach for the wrist restraints and release one then the other.

Her arms circle my shoulders. Her nails dig into my back, and her body tenses under mine, spasming so hard, I can't hold back anymore.

I pump into her harder than normal until it seems like her body is draining every last drop of my orgasm it has. When it's over, I bury my face in the curve of her neck.

She continues to quiver in my arms. I release her, unlatch her ankle restraints, then lie on my back. I tug her into me, kissing the top of her head.

Minutes pass in silence, except for our ragged breaths. I finally tilt her chin so she can't avoid me. In a firm voice, I reiterate, "I mean it, Katiya. I won't put up with you lying to me, no matter how white it is."

Her face crumbles with guilt. She tears up again. "I'm sorry."

"Why did you lie to me? Do you not want to go on vacation?" I ask, afraid of the answer but refusing to be a coward.

She squeezes her eyes shut.

I sit up and tug her onto my lap. "Katiya, whatever it is, tell me."

My patience gets tested. She stays quiet, but I don't speak, unwilling to let her off the hook. She finally answers, "I've never taken time off work."

I cautiously reply, "Yes. You said that before."

"I don't know how any of it works. I-I-I just wanted to read everything and know how it works before I spoke to you. I didn't want to sound stupid," she admits, and more tears fall.

I sigh then wipe her face dry. "Dolce, you aren't stupid."

She sniffles. "I'm uneducated."

"That doesn't make you any less bright," I insist.

She turns, straddling me. She holds my cheeks and asserts, "Massimo, I don't want to lie to you."

"Then don't do it again," I order.

She presses her lips to mine, and within seconds, the fire lights back up inside me.

I murmur, "Let me turn the recording off."

She freezes, her eyes wide. She bites her lip.

"What?" I ask.

Her cheeks flush. She asks, "Do you think we could watch it?"

I can't stop my grin. I kiss her then state, "Let me turn everything off. We'll watch it in our new bedroom."

I go to move her off me, but she stops me. "Wait."

I arch my eyebrows.

She leans forward, softly smiles, and declares, "I really do love you."

"I love you, dolce. More than anyone on Earth," I reply.

Her smile grows, but something about it appears sad. She reiterates through glistening eyes, "No. I want you to understand that I really love you, no matter what. My entire heart and soul belong to you. No matter what happens, please don't ever forget it."

Alarms ring in my ears. I swipe my thumbs under her blues. "What are you worried is going to happen?"

She opens her mouth then closes it, jerking her head away.

"Hey," I say.

She slowly refocuses on me. "Nothing. You make me happy, Massimo. I don't want it to change."

I kiss her and tug her into my arms. "Nothing is happening to us, dolce. You're stuck with me for life, and nothing could ever change how I feel about you."

"Promise me," she chokes into my neck.

I tighten my arms around her. "I promise you. Nothing on Earth could ever change how I feel about you. And I'll die before I let anything happen to you. You're my girl."

She clutches me, snuggling further into me.

I rise and pick her up. "Let's get out of here. It's time I showed you our bedroom." I turn off the recording and microphone, carry her out of the playroom, and take her directly to our bed.

Our bed.

She's mine now and always will be.

When I set her on the mattress, my only thought is that I finally have the woman of my dreams. Life is only going to get better from here.

MC

Katiya

MASSIMO'S WARM BODY IS WRAPPED AROUND MINE. IT'S LIKE being swaddled in a cocoon, and I don't ever want to come out.

I told him I lied about the employee handbook.

Why did I admit that?

Ugh.

His lips brush my forehead, and I force myself to wake up. I blink several times to adjust to the morning light, taking in the beautiful, luxurious bedroom.

Panic crashes through me.

Leo didn't permit me to move out of the brownstone.

How am I going to get out of this?

I don't want to get out of it. I want to live with Massimo.

If Leo finds out I've moved out or I'm going on a trip, he might kill me on the spot.

"Morning, dolce," he murmurs.

I need to figure this mess out.

I tilt my head up. "Morning. What time is it?"

"Seven."

I sit up in bed. "I have to get ready for work. I don't have clothes here."

Massimo chuckles. "Yes, you do."

"I do?" I ask, glancing around the room.

Amusement fills his expression. He rises then holds out his hand. "Come on."

I take it, and he helps me on my feet. I question, "Where are we going?"

He leads me to a door and opens it, motioning with his hand. "Ladies first."

I step into an enormous walk-in closet, separated into his and hers areas. Massimo's clothes hang in one section. Women's designer clothes hang in another. I gape for several moments.

This is really happening. How am I getting out of this so Leo doesn't come after me?

I spin into Massimo. "When did you get all these clothes?"

"Yesterday."

175

"Yesterday!" I shriek. "This is a full wardrobe!"

Arrogance grows on him. "Yep."

"You're crazy," I blurt out, still in shock at all the items he selected.

"Wouldn't be the first time someone called me that," he replies.

I run my hand over a row of dresses. Each item feels soft and of high quality. I mutter, "This is insane."

Massimo stands behind me, circling his arm around my waist, questioning, "Why is it insane?"

I arch my eyebrows. "Is that a serious question?"

His lips twitch. "Yep."

I spin into him. "This had to have cost a fortune."

He shrugs. "Not really."

I scoff, reaching for a red Dolce & Gabbana blouse. The tag is still on it. I turn it and declare, "Three hundred dollars! For a blouse!"

"It'll look sexy as hell on you. You know I love you in red," he claims.

"That's a ton of money for a shirt!" I express.

"That's a relative statement," he asserts.

"How?"

He shrugs. "What makes something expensive?"

"Three hundred dollars for a blouse makes it expensive," I reply.

He grunts. "No. Expensive is determined by how much money you have. So, three hundred dollars for a blouse—and one I'm going to imagine removing it whenever you wear it —isn't anything I'll even notice missing in my account."

"Must be nice," I mumble, trying to imagine what it would be like to not notice a three-hundred-dollar dent in my bank account.

"Do you like the clothes?" Massimo asks.

"Yes! I'm sorry. I don't mean to sound ungrateful. I'm just trying to process all this. They're beautiful."

"Good. I'd hate to think my fashion sense is off," he teases.

"Don't worry, Mr. Marino. You have great taste," I assure him. I reach around his shoulders and lace my fingers behind his neck. "Thank you for being so generous to me."

"You don't have to thank me."

"Yes, I do," I insist, then kiss him.

He retreats, and the vulnerable expression I love stares back at me. "I want to make you happy, Katiya."

My heart swells. "You do make me happy. In all ways."

He studies me for a moment then pecks me on the lips and steps back. "You better get ready for work. Want some eggs for breakfast? We didn't eat last night."

I suddenly realize I'm starving. "Sure. That would be great."

"Cappuccino or latte?" he asks.

"Are you going to the coffee shop?"

He grins. "Nope. I had them install a machine in the kitchen."

"Really?"

"Sure did. So, do you want a cappuccino or latte?" he repeats.

"Wow! I guess I'll take a latte, please."

"On it! Towels are in the bathroom on the heaters." He pats my ass and steps out of the closet.

I stare at the clothes in awe again. Then I follow in his footsteps and call out, "Hey, Massimo."

He turns in the doorway. "What's wrong, dolce?"

I throw my arms around him and respond, "Nothing's wrong. Thank you again."

Flecks of blue glimmer in his orbs. He softly smiles, replying, "I'm glad you like it. Now, go shower so you aren't late. You need to stay on your boss's good side so she can approve your vacation week."

My reality hits me again. I blurt out, "I need to read the handbook first."

Massimo's face drops. "Katiya, you can read it tonight. Put in your request for a week."

My stomach flips. All these things are moving way too fast. I can't figure out how to get in front of Leo, and I shouldn't do any of this without his approval.

Massimo sniffs hard. His body stiffens. His voice is firm, but I can hear the hurt in it when he asks, "Do you not want to go?"

I reach for his cheek. "Of course I do. Please don't think it's about me not wanting to go."

"Then what exactly is it about?" he questions, harsher than his normal tone.

"I-I told you last night. I want to know what I should have paid attention to when I got hired. When I ask for time off, it's best if I know what my actual benefits are," I claim, but it sounds weak.

"Last night, you told me you get two weeks. Was that a lie?" he challenges.

"No."

He crosses his arms over his chest. "Okay then. What else is there to know?"

I rack my brain to figure out how to answer his question and buy more time. No solution appears though.

"I'm waiting for an answer."

I blurt out, "I don't know what else there is to know because I haven't read the handbook. What if something is in it I should be aware of?"

"Katiya, nothing will be in the manual regarding your vacation days that should stop you from requesting time off."

I bite my lip, trying to calm my racing pulse. If I request days off, I'm fairly certain my boss will approve it. Leo will have a fit if I leave town without his permission. But Massimo is so adamant, I don't know how to maneuver around this issue. I finally cave so we can end this conversation. "Okay. I'll put a request in."

Satisfaction fills Massimo's expression. He nods. "Good girl. Scrambled, fried, or poached eggs?"

My appetite fades. "Whatever you're having."

He kisses the top of my head. "You better get ready."

I don't argue and go into the bathroom, turning on the shower. The water heats quickly, and I step in, closing my eyes and letting the water drench my body. My mind races with too many fears. Everything leads back to the cold truth.

I'm going to betray Massimo.

It's going to break his heart.

And mine.

Tears well in my eyes. They drip down my cheeks, mixing with the water. The hatred I have for myself seems to be more potent than normal.

I spend more time in the shower than I usually would. When I get out, I use the high-end hair products and makeup. I'm shocked again at Massimo's seemingly endless generosity, no matter what he claims it does or doesn't do to his bank account.

After I style my hair, I go into the closet. The rows of clothes overwhelm me. It takes me a while to put an outfit together. I get dressed and go out to the kitchen. The aroma of coffee, eggs, and bacon fills the air. My stomach growls loudly.

Massimo chuckles. "Just in time. Sit down, dolce." He pulls a chair out.

I sit, and he kisses the top of my head. "You look gorgeous."

"Thanks. It really was very kind of you to fill a closet for me."

"Anything for you. You're my girl," he says. Pride lights up his face.

My butterflies go crazy. I love it when he calls me his girl. I love being it, too.

I won't be forever, flies into my head, making my heart hurt.

He sets plates of food and two lattes on the table then takes the seat next to mine. His hand rests on my thigh. He leans closer and deeply inhales.

"What are you doing?" I ask.

"Smelling you."

I smirk. "Good thing for your nose that I just showered." I take a sip of the latte. "Mmm. Perfect."

He beams. "I'm glad I had them add the machine at the last minute." He shovels a forkful of eggs into his mouth.

I pick up a piece of bacon and take a bite. We chew in silence for several minutes until his phone buzzes.

He glances at the screen and groans.

"What's wrong?" I ask.

"Nothing. Just work crap I need to take care of today." He clenches his jaw.

"Anything exciting?" I question.

"Normal stuff."

"What does normal stuff mean?" I press.

He puts his fork down and wipes his mouth with the napkin. He turns in the chair, studying me.

I nervously mutter, "What?"

He takes a deep, calculated breath. "Katiya, what do you know about my family?"

I lock eyes with him, don't hesitate, and answer honestly. "I know you're a well-known crime family. That's about it. You've always shied away from telling me what you do all day."

His face stays neutral. He declares, "It's for your protection."

I shift in my seat. "I'm a big girl. And I know how to keep secrets."

His stare-down continues until his phone vibrates again. He glances at it, types something, then tosses his phone on the table.

I've been good about not prying until he trusts me. Now that we're living together, I assume we have it. My heart thumps harder against my chest cavity, and I take a risk, asking, "Will you tell me what you do? Like, what's your job for the family? All you've ever told me is you're a businessman."

Minutes pass. The pounding of my pulse between my ears grows louder. His scrutinizing gaze doesn't falter.

I pick up my latte and take a sip, casually adding, "It's okay. You don't have to tell me."

He sighs then picks up my hand, caressing his thumb over mine. Another silent moment passes, and then he states, "I'm going to tell you some basics. Whatever we discuss is between us."

My chest tightens. I nod, cringing inside since anything he tells me might go back to Leo. I lie, "You have my word. Nothing you tell me will ever leave this room."

He tucks a lock of my hair behind my ear, confessing, "I've never told any woman anything about my business."

My guilt eats deeper into me, creating a hole in my stomach.

He takes a mouthful of his latte then taps his fingers on the mug. "So, I am a businessman. I own different businesses."

"Such as?"

He taps the mug faster. "The club, obviously, but some restaurants, too. I also own gyms, construction firms, gas stations, rental properties, and shipping vessels, to name a few."

I gape at him. I only knew what Leo told me, which was that Massimo was involved in jewelry. I clear my throat then compliment, "That's amazing! What business is your favorite?"

His eyes gleam. He replies, "None of the above."

Confused, I look at him in question.

He chuckles and holds a piece of bacon next to my mouth. "Eat."

I accept the meat, chew it, then wash it down with more of my latte.

He adds, "To answer your question, my favorite business is my jewelry one."

The hairs on the back of my neck rise. I freeze, willing the anxiety in my chest to disappear. I debate what to say next and finally decide on, "Is that how you know Ettore? Do you own his business?"

Darkness passes over Massimo's face. "No. He owns his business, but he's very loyal to our family. He and my papà met as children and are good friends."

I play with my eggs, moving them around on my plate. "So, if you don't own his business, how are you involved in jewelry?"

"I guess you could say I'm more involved in gems," he declares.

My insides quiver. I fight the urge to stop this conversation before I learn anything else. Still, the fear of what Leo will do to me overpowers my good intentions. I tilt my head, acting like I know nothing, and question, "What does that mean?"

He answers, "I buy gems directly from the miners."

"Wow! What country do you buy from? Or do you get them here in the United States? Sorry, I don't know anything about where gems come from," I admit.

Amusement replaces the darkness in his expression. He drags his knuckles down my arm. "It's okay. I don't expect you to know anything about it. Some of my gems come from the US, but most are from Africa, Russia, and South America."

My awe is real. I tease, "I'm going to have to call you Mr. International!"

His face falls. He sternly lectures, "Katiya, we don't ever discuss any of this outside of these walls."

"Sorry. I was just kidding!"

He sighs. "Okay. Is that enough for today, or do you have more questions?"

I pause, disappointed I didn't get further but happy he told me something. I shake my head, smiling. "No. But can I reserve the right to interrogate you later?"

"Sure, dolce." He rises, picks up our plates, and announces, "We better leave so you aren't late for work."

"Okay. But you don't have to take me. I can get there on my own," I state.

"No. I'll drop you off. I need to go down to the docks."

"The docks?"

He glances at his phone, replying, "Everything we import comes to us via the docks."

I continue to push for information. "So you have a shipment coming today?"

"No. I have a mess to sort out."

"Oh?"

"Nothing you need to worry about." He rinses the plates and loads them into the dishwasher. "Now, I will need some help at some point."

My stomach flips, wondering what he wants me to do for his business. "Sure. I can do whatever you need."

He cringes, stating, "I'm embarrassed to admit this."

"What?"

"I don't know how to run this dishwasher. When it's full, can you teach me how to turn it on?"

I put my hand over my mouth, unable to stop my laugh.

"Ouch!" he says, holding his heart.

"Sorry. But why don't you know how to run a dishwasher?" I ask.

He shrugs. "I grew up in a household with housekeepers and chefs. There wasn't a need to know."

I reach for his face and pat it. "Okay, sexy. I'll teach you how to use the dishwasher."

"You're making fun of me," he mumbles.

"No," I claim, biting my smile.

"Yes, you are."

"Sorry." I wince, unable to hide my amusement.

He leans down, pecks me on the lips, then pats my ass. "Time to get moving."

We take the elevator to the ground level. It opens into a parking garage. Massimo's Ferrari is parked in the first space, next to the exit. He opens my door, and I slide inside.

Massimo gets into the driver's seat, revs the engine, and backs out of the space.

We get on the main road, and the sun hits the window. I put on my sunglasses, adding, "Spring is finally here."

Massimo steps on the accelerator, weaving through traffic. "Looks like it. Time for our vacation. Ask for the first available week."

The dread I can't shake reappears. In an attempt to buy some more time, I put my hand on his thigh. "Hey."

He glances at me. "What's up, dolce?"

"Can I please read the handbook tonight? I'll put in a request with Alicia tomorrow, I promise."

"Do we have to go through this again?" he seethes.

"Massimo—"

"There's no reason to stall. Look at the table of contents, flip to the page about your vacation time, and read it. I bet it'll take you less than a minute," he claims.

I remove my hand from his thigh and stare out the window.

"Katiya, what is this all about? If you don't want to go—"

"I do want to go. I just don't want to look dumb!"

"You won't look dumb," he asserts.

The city buildings become a blur from Massimo's fast driving. I breathe through my apprehension, wondering how I'm ever going to find Leo so I can get his blessing on all these changes.

"Dolce, I promise you won't appear stupid," Massimo quietly states when he pulls up to the library.

I turn my head toward him, confessing my truth. "Sometimes, I feel super ignorant."

He furrows his eyebrows. "How so?"

I shrug but admit, "You're very worldly. You know how everything in society works. Heck, I assume you've traveled to every continent. All I do is go to work and come home."

He circles his arm around my shoulder then tilts his head. "Ignorance doesn't mean you're stupid. It means you haven't experienced something. There's no shame in how you've lived your life. But all that's going to change, now that you're my girl. I'm going to show you the world, and this ignorance you feel will disappear. You'll see."

My heart soars and dives at the same time.

I want the life he wants to give me.

But it will never be.

Massimo

"SPIT IT OUT, TULLY," I SEETHE, TIRED OF HIS CHARADES. MY brothers and his sons look as equally annoyed as I am. For the last ten minutes, he's been the typical Tully, playing games and wasting our time.

Plus, I swear someone was following me on the way to the docks. I lost them on the expressway, but it's nagging me. When I got to Tully's warehouse, I told my brothers. They wanted to know who it was, but I didn't have any idea. The black SUV looked like one any of the families in New York would have, including ours. And the driver stayed far enough back that I couldn't get a good look at him.

The doorbell buzzes. Aidan glances out the peephole and opens the door.

Papà walks in with Luca in tow. He steps next to Tully and asks, "All set?"

Tully nods, lights up his cigar, takes a few puffs, then exhales. "I was about to tell our boys what they're going to be spending the day doing."

"I thought we were supposed to meet on Thursday night," Tristano points out.

Tully blows a ring of smoke in the air. "Plans change."

"Mind telling us what you're referring to? I don't have all day," Dante seethes.

"Cancel your plans. None of you are doing anything else today," Papà orders.

Aidan groans. "Dad, what's so important you're going to make all of us reschedule our day?"

Papà motions to Luca. "Tell them what you've been working on."

Luca opens a yellow envelope. He removes a stack of photographs and pins each one to the bulletin board. When he finishes, six men I've never seen stare back at us from the photos.

"Who are they?" Gianni demands.

"Your assignments," Tully replies.

Tristano mutters, "And we're back to guessing games."

"He must think we're mind readers," I add.

"Watch your mouths," Papà warns.

Luca taps each photo. "Agent Hopkins, Agent Michael, Agent Dominico, Agent Porter, Agent Rassmussen, and my personal favorite prick, Agent Baskin."

Brody crosses his arms over his chest. He locks eyes with Luca. "Do you have them in custody?"

"No. That's what all of you are doing today," Tully answers.

Dante looks at Papà. "And why are we kidnapping six federal agents?"

"All will be revealed in due time," Tully answers.

"Enough of the cryptic shit, Tully! I'm not kidnapping a federal agent without knowing why," I claim.

Papà points to me. "You'll do what we say. We run the families, not you."

I grind my molars, pissed off about the constant reminder that I'm never going to be the one in charge. It's why I didn't let anyone in my family invest in my new club. I wanted something they didn't have any control over.

Aidan asserts, "I have a new shipment coming in today. I need to be there."

"It's at four," Tully states.

"Right. So you already know I can't miss it."

"Which is why you'll have to have Danny do it," Tully replies.

"He's going to need my help," Aidan claims.

Tully shakes his head. "He can get Jamie to help him."

"Jamie hasn't reviewed shipments before," Aidan points out.

"Time for him to learn. End of topic. You need to concentrate on the task at hand. I want your man picked up in the next two hours," Tully demands, as if kidnapping a federal agent is as easy as taking a walk in the park.

"Why would you have us do this in daylight?" I ask.

"There shouldn't be any issues picking them up," Luca interjects.

"How come?" I question, worried this is the wrong move. Daylight presents issues we normally try to avoid.

Luca lights up a joint and takes a drag. The marijuana mixes with the thick tobacco smoke, suffocating my lungs. I fight the urge to flee Tully's warehouse. Luca slowly exhales and adds, "They're all undercover. Right now, they've infiltrated the Abruzzos and O'Learys. Gianni's guy found out."

Tully sarcastically says, "Way to keep your mouth shut. Now you've taken all the fun out of this."

Gianni scowls at Tully, questioning, "My guy?"

Luca nods. "Your prison friend has turned out to be rather informative."

"Who's that?" Tristano asks.

Gianni's eyes turn to slits. "Garrett Steelworth? How did he find this out?"

"Seems your cell mate has been around the block a few times," Papà adds, but the disapproval in his voice is clear. He's still pissed Gianni got arrested for punching a security guard at Cara's Fashion Week event.

Tully sets his cigar in the ashtray. He pulls an envelope out of his pocket and states, "We're in a prime position to learn everything those agents know about the Abruzzo and O'Leary operations. We take all six of them today." He walks over and holds out the envelope.

"What is this?" I question, taking it from him.

"Open it."

I obey, pulling out a wad of hundred-dollar bills. I lock eyes with Tully. "Why are you giving me this?"

"I already paid Ettore. That's part of your cut," he answers.

My gut spins, my chest tightens, and my fist curls at my side. I snarl, "That ring is worth way more than what's in here."

His lips curl. "You get the rest when you fulfill your assignment today."

Rage fills my bones. I fume, "That's Katiya's money. How much did you pay for it?"

"Anything that woman gets is a bonus. She would have gotten killed had anyone found out she had it. And it's time you told us how she got it," Tully asserts.

"That's none of your business," I hurl through gritted teeth.

His cocky expression makes his next statement worse. "Well, I suppose secrets between a man and his woman can still be a good thing in today's age. But is she willing to keep yours?"

I step forward so I'm inches from his face. "What the fuck does that mean, Tully?"

He puts his hands in the air. "Calm down."

"Don't you dare talk about my woman, make accusations, and tell me to calm down," I bark.

"I didn't accuse her of anything."

"Bullshit," I bellow.

"Enough," Papà orders. "Time is ticking."

"I don't care. You owe Katiya more money," I insist.

Tully's lips twitch. "You'll get the other envelope."

"Other? As in one? No! You'll pay what is fair," I warn.

"It is fair," he proclaims.

I seethe, "Not even close."

Tully maintains his position. "The piece couldn't be offloaded in the usual fashion. I did you a favor buying it so quickly. And, son, the going rate is what someone is willing to pay for it."

"I'm not your son," I fume.

"Massimo, this topic is over. You and Tristano, go pick up Agent Dominico. It shouldn't be hard," Papà claims.

"Why is that?" Tristano questions.

Papà's eyes turn darker, matching his tone. He pins them on me, stating, "For the past two nights, all the agents have been on a drinking spree with the two families. My guess is they'll be trying to catch up on sleep. They have housing in the Abruzzos buildings close to where your girlfriend lives."

The hairs on my arms rise. Oxygen turns stale in my lungs. I grind my molars then reiterate, "Katiya has nothing to do with this."

Eleven pairs of eyes stare at me. Every one of them is full of doubt.

It pisses me off further. I growl, "You weren't being genuine last night, were you?"

Papà waves off my accusation. "Stop being sensitive. Now, all of you get out of here. I want them picked up quickly and brought to our house." He hands me a key and motions toward the door. "Go."

My brothers and I exchange another annoyed glance, then I motion for Tristano to follow me. We step outside, and there's a row of worn-out, older, windowless vans. I open one of the doors and toss a white hazmat suit to him.

He groans and unzips it. "These things are so hot."

I step into mine. "Still don't understand why we can't do this at night."

"Tully just wants us to sweat our balls off," he grumbles.

I zip the plastic around me and pull the hood up. I slide on the mask and my sunglasses. When we get there, I'll put on the dark plastic shield. In the meantime, the mask and sunglasses will keep me incognito.

Tristano follows my lead and becomes unrecognizable. I jump into the passenger side, and he gets into the driver's seat. He turns on the engine and pulls out ahead of the others then asks, "Tully and Papà seem to get crazier, don't you think?"

I grunt. "That's the understatement of the year. I never thought Papà would agree with us kidnapping federal agents in broad daylight."

Tristano turns on his blinker and veers left. Metal clinks in the back, and I shift in my seat, glancing behind me through the small open space. Several restraints slide along a metal rod. I mutter, "Guess Tully got the vans and not Papà."

"Why do you say that?"

I sit back in my seat. "The handcuffs aren't secured. Those agents will slam into the walls. By the time we get them home, they'll have bruises all over them."

Tristano guns the accelerator, and the van's engine skips.

"Easy. This isn't your Lamborghini. We don't need the transmission blowing out," I reprimand.

"Leave it to Tully to give us unreliable vehicles," Tristano states.

I add, "I think he wants something to happen so we have to figure it out. It's like he needs some extra entertainment."

"He needs to get a hobby," Tristano mumbles.

"Yep," I agree. My phone vibrates, and I glance at the message.

Arianna: *I want to talk to you before we leave. When are you coming home?*

I sigh, my stomach pitching. The one person I owed a heads-up to that I was bringing Katiya to the club opening was my sister. I didn't think straight and shouldn't have put her or Katiya in that position.

Tristano weaves around a semi, and the van shakes. He asks, "What's wrong?"

I shift in my seat. "I should have discussed Katiya with Arianna before last night."

Tristano whistles. "Gotta give it to you, brother. No one can accuse you of not having any balls."

"How was Arianna when you got home last night?"

"I didn't go home."

"No? Where were you?" I question.

"Out."

"All night?"

He arches an eyebrow. "Is that a crime?"

I chuckle. "No. I didn't know you were seeing anyone. Who is she?"

He clenches his jaw, refocusing on the traffic. "Just a woman."

"Which woman?" I press again.

"None of your business. So you're sure about Katiya?" he asks, switching the subject.

I don't hesitate. "Yes. Of course I am. And, hey, thanks for being nice to her last night."

He keeps his eyes on the road, gripping the wheel tighter. "Yeah, no problem."

I hesitate then ask what's not been sitting right since the conversation last night. "Do you know why Papà changed his tune about Katiya?"

Tristano shrugs. "Who knows. It's not the first time Papà's flipped the switch about his opinion on someone."

I scratch my chin, pointing out, "But it doesn't happen often."

"Yeah, and when it does, we never understand it," Tristano claims, but I can't argue.

He pulls up to the brownstone where Agent Dominico is then turns off the ignition. We remove our glasses, put on our shields, then get out of the vehicle, walking to the back. One of the other vans passes us and parks a block away.

Tristano opens the back door. There is a large white bin on wheels inside. A small black case is inside the bin.

I reach for the case, remove a syringe, and add the solution. It's a drug Papà had our chemist create. It makes kidnapping easier, and the victim is able to wake up when we force him to by putting another solution over his airway, or after twelve hours on his own. When the syringe is full, I stick it in my pocket and nod to my brother.

He pushes a button, and a ramp lowers to the ground. I grab the corner of the bin and move it to the ground. Tristano drags the handcuffs to the end of the rod so they're out of sight. I place orange cones and a hazard sign around the van.

We make our way into the building. I use the key Papà gave me, opening the front entrance. When we get inside, Tristano locks the door.

I creep up the staircase and slowly turn the knob. I glance at my brother, but his face is covered as much as mine. He points for me to go in, and I cautiously open the door.

Everything seems clear. I nod for him to follow, slip through the main room, and follow the sound of loud snores. I peek into the bedroom and happily find that Papà assumed correctly. Spread out over the mattress is Agent Dominico's large body. He must have been so drunk, he didn't even get under the covers or take his clothes off.

I swiftly cross the room, stab the needle in his arm, and his eyes fly open. He tries to reach for me, but Tristano pins his arms above his head.

Agent Dominico's limbs flail in the air, but not for long. The drug works quickly, and he soon turns limp.

"That's a good fat fucker," Tristano taunts, but in a quiet voice.

"Let's go," I order, not wanting to stick around. Who knows if anyone else is coming to visit. I glance at the desk with papers, a computer, and camera on it. Then I stare at another camera that's sitting on a tripod near the window. The hairs on my arms rise and I walk over to it. I shove my fingers through the blind slats, hit the "on" button, then swallow hard when Katiya's unit appears.

"What are you doing?" Tristano asks.

"Seeing what he was up to," I declare as thoughts race through my head. My gut dives further, and my mouth turns dry. *Was he watching her?*

"Time to go. Clean up isn't our job. I'm sure Papà will send in the cleanup crew," my brother claims.

I grab the camera off the tripod and pull the memory card out.

"What are you doing?" Tristano asks.

I sniff hard, spin, and reply, "I want to see what he knows. Time to go." I point to Dominico. "Should we flip?"

"All you. I got last time," Tristano scoffs, then walks toward the door.

I groan. My brother always seems to get the easy way out. The guy he had to carry was the size of a peanut. Agent Dominico has at least fifty pounds of excess fat on his stomach alone.

But there's no time to argue. I unzip my suit and shove the tiny card in my pocket. I refasten my suit, heave Dominico over my shoulder, then carry him out of the room. I'm about to make my way down the stairs when a photo grabs my attention.

It's my beautiful dolce, gagged and restrained. The slats of the blinds are only partially open, but it's her. And in the corner of the photo is me.

My heart races faster. I try not to breathe in the stale stench of the room. There's no doubt our intel was correct; he's been partying for several days.

I release Dominico, and a loud thud echoes in the room from his body hitting the floor. I tab through the other photos, pulling out a dozen more of Katiya. Some I'm in, some I'm not. Each one I find makes my pulse beat so hard, I wonder if my veins are going to explode.

I grab the photos then shove them in the back of his pants so the pictures aren't visible. I meet Tristano at the bottom of the stairs. I toss Dominico into the bin. Tristano puts a sheet over him, and we wheel him out. When we get to the street, whoever drove the identical van several houses away is also putting their bin back inside.

I ignore them. We get ours in the back and then I jump in and shut the doors. As soon as I sit on the bench, I remove the photos.

Tristano slides into the driver's side, starts the van, and pulls away from the curb. I handcuff Dominico to the rod and sit on the other side of the van, studying all the photos.

Why does he have so many of Katiya?

I'm in several, but I'm not the main focus in any. It's very clear that she's the one who caught his interest.

It doesn't take long before Dominico's body slams against the wall of the van, just like we predicted. In some ways, I have to give Tully credit. He always knows how to add extra injuries to victims.

I remove my face shield and mask. Then I regret it when Dominico's stale alcohol and sweat stench flares in my nostrils. I close my eyes, put my head against the metal, and try to relax during the drive to Papà's.

Yet I can't. Rage stews in my veins, growing hotter each second. There's only one question I need him to answer.

Why was he surveilling her?

When the van's engine finally turns off, I get out, breathing in fresh oxygen. Tristano jumps in and holds a solution-soaked handkerchief over Dominico's mouth and nose.

He opens his eyes, coughing, and then barks, "What the fuck?" He yanks on the rod, but the handcuffs stop him from going anywhere. He attempts to kick us, but Tristano and I both cross our arms and watch him.

Two vans pull up beside ours in the garage. I pull my gun out and hold it to Dominico's head. His eyes widen, and he warns, "I'm a federal agent. If you kill me, it'll come back to haunt you."

The devil in me fills my soul. He's so potent, I can feel the shift. My lips twitch, and I lean closer. "Do you think your threats scare me?"

He clenches his jaw.

I sniff him and then cock my Glock, pressing it harder into his skull. Then I state, "You fucking stink. When did you shower last?"

He remains quiet, but his body shakes.

"When I speak to you, the best thing to do is answer," I assert.

"You don't know what you're doing," he snarls, but he has no leg to stand on. He's my captive, and nothing will change his fate.

I grab his handcuffs and tug him toward the back of the van, ordering, "Look around. Do you see anyone here who's going to help you?"

He lifts his chin, but there's no hiding the fear in his eyes.

Something about his helplessness fuels everything evil within me. I shove the gun in his mouth, and piss drips down his legs. I lean into his ear, lying, "You've got two options. Die now, or try to save your life. What's it going to be?"

His muffled protests fill the air. Everything about it humors me. I glance at Tristano, who's equally amused, based on the gleam in his eye.

The screeching of the fourth van pulling into the garage hits my ears. I remove the gun, step back, and punch Dominico in the side of the head. Blood flies everywhere. I scream, "When I ask a question, I want answers."

His head flops to the side. Tristano steps up, tugs me back, and states, "Easy. We should get him in the dungeon before you start this."

I breathe through my anger. But there's also a nagging fear inside me. I can't shake it.

Why was he watching her?

Katiya

"ALL DONE. SHOULD I HELP CARRIE?" I ASK ALICIA.

She tears her eyes off her paperwork and nudges her multi-colored glasses up on her nose. "That was fast."

I shrug. "Whoever added the books to the cart alphabetized them. It made it easy."

"Horatio needs to take a lunch. Why don't you relieve him?" she replies.

"Okay." I take a step then freeze.

Ask her.

I need to talk to Leo first.

Massimo will kill me if I don't request time off.

Alicia clears her throat. "Katiya? Is there something else?"

I open my mouth then shut it. My chest tightens. I shake my head and force a smile. "Nope. All good. I'll go tell Horatio to go to lunch."

"Tell him not to return late this time," she warns.

"Will do." I stroll to the checkout counter and wait until Horatio finishes checking out a younger woman. When she leaves, I state, "Alicia said you can take your lunch break, but to be sure you stick to the thirty minutes."

He scoffs, waving his hand and leaning closer to me. "Why's she so uptight lately?"

I refrain from rolling my eyes. Everything about Horatio pushes my buttons. He's lazy, constantly late, and sometimes disrespectful to Alicia. I arch my eyebrows and in a cool voice, answer, "She's not uptight. Go to lunch."

He dramatically gasps. "What's up your ass today?"

"Excuse me?"

"Sticking up for the boss? Tell me, what's she done for you?"

My annoyance grows. I step behind the counter and place the pile of books on the cart. He should have done it, but it's not a surprise he didn't. I honestly wonder how he even keeps his job.

Horatio glances toward Alicia's office then smirks, "You must not have noticed her conversation with your boy toy yesterday."

Heat floods my cheeks. "Do *not* call Massimo my boy toy."

"What's wrong with that? I wouldn't mind a little time in playland with him," he claims.

My stomach flips at the thought. Massimo is mine, and no one else's to fantasize about, even if they have zero chance of turning their wishes into reality.

He's only yours for now.

I need to find a way to keep him.

Impossible.

I snap, "Shut up, Horatio. Go to lunch."

His eyes widen. "Oh, sorry. Did I hit a nerve? Well, maybe I shouldn't tell you this, then."

My pulse pounds between my ears. I lock eyes with Horatio, knowing I shouldn't take the bait but unable to stop myself. I seethe, "Spit it out."

Satisfaction appears on his face. His grin widens, making my stomach flip faster. His eyes dart around us, then he steps closer, lowering his voice. "I'm pretty sure something is going on between Massimo and Alicia."

Bile climbs up my throat. It feels like a hand is clawing at my gut. I snarl, "Stop spreading false information."

"Tsk, tsk, tsk," he taunts. "Have you missed all the clues?"

I grip the edge of the desk, holding myself back from slapping Horatio. Unable to stop myself, I continue to engage when I should do nothing of the sort. I question, "What would those be?"

The gleam in Horatio's eyes sparkles brighter. His lips twitch as he states, "The flirting. The touching. The hushed voices."

"We're in a library," I point out, trying to keep my cool. My rationale says Horatio's only trying to start trouble, but his comment is like a seed. He's planted it, and now I need to figure out how to not give it any water so it dies.

Plus, the notion of Massimo and Alicia together is insane. She's slightly older than him, married, and has three kids. I suppose once upon a time she was attractive, but she is five foot nothing and probably weighs close to three hundred pounds. Her gray roots need to be touched up, and she could do with a fashion consult. Her clothes always seem to not fit her body correctly. She's the typical definition of a woman who's let herself go.

I'm not naive enough not to know affairs happen, yet Massimo and Alicia are oil and water. There's no way Massimo would ever be interested in her, but Horatio's comment still bothers me. I hate that it does, but the thought of anyone else with Massimo makes me feel ill.

Horatio grunts. "Go ahead and stay in the dark, then."

"Go to lunch," I repeat, stepping into his space in front of the computer, relieved when a mother and her two children appear. I smile and ignore Horatio, chirping, "Checking out?"

"Yes, please," she replies, stacking a dozen books on the desk.

I focus on her, scanning the barcodes. Horatio steps away, and relief fills me. For the next few hours, there's a steady line of readers. The few moments I have alone, I push thoughts of Massimo and Alicia out of my head.

Horatio is lying.

He's a trouble-stirring jerk.

Massimo wouldn't do that to me.

How do I know? After all, I'm working for Leo, trying to find out Massimo's contacts so Leo can take him and his family down.

Ugh. I hate my life.

"Did you take your lunch yet?" Alicia asks, pulling me out of my thoughts.

I tear my gaze off the computer screen and assess her.

No. There's no way she's his type.

What if something is going on though?

What am I saying?

Goddamn you, Horatio.

Alicia tilts her head, peering at me. "Katiya? Is something wrong?"

A few moments of silence pass as too many crazy thoughts buzz through my mind.

"Katiya?" she asks, putting her hand on my forearm.

I yank it back. "Everything is fine. I'll go now." I beeline to the front door, not even considering eating the lunch Massimo had the club chef package for me.

The moment I step outside, a gust of air blows, slapping my face. It's neither warm nor cold, reminding me that spring is just around the corner. The thought of sunshine and salty ocean water pops into my head.

Maybe he can take Alicia.

What the heck am I saying?

Why am I letting Horatio's stupid comments bother me?

For my half hour, I stroll through the city. I'd normally study the mannequins in the boutique windows or sit on a bench and people-watch. Nothing catches my attention today. I reprimand myself over and over again for letting Horatio get to me.

By the time my break is over, I've regained my sense of peace. There's no way anything is going on between Massimo and Alicia. I'm determined not to think about it anymore and ignore Horatio the rest of the day.

Feeling more confident, I raise my chin and return to work, bypassing Horatio without giving him any attention. I go to my cubicle, pull the employee handbook out of my desk drawer, and find the section on vacation days.

Just as Massimo stated, it's not very long. Based on the time I've worked at the library, I should get two weeks of paid vacation.

I read the section several times then open my handbag. I take out my phone and pull up a photo of Massimo. The flutters I always get when I look at him expand in my belly. Guilt swirls throughout me, and I ask myself for the millionth time how I can ever betray him.

"Katiya, there are three carts in the history section. Alicia wanted me to ask you to shelve them," Carrie states.

I glance up and nod. "Okay." She leaves, and I shove the employee handbook back in my drawer. I leave my office, climb the stairs, and find the overflowing carts. Unlike the last batch I put away, these aren't in any order. Some of the books aren't even history, and I groan. There's no doubt Horatio loaded these carts. He's the only one I work with who wouldn't be bothered to follow protocol.

Deciding it's better to reorganize instead of running each book one at a time to the appropriate place, I toss all the books on the floor and then reorganize them on the cart. I have one half filled when a large hand is placed over my mouth. Heavy musk flares in my nostrils. Heat from his body penetrates my back. Panic paralyzes me, and I freeze.

He asserts, "You've made some wrong moves, little girl."

I close my eyes, recognizing the voice and scent. Leo's head thug, Tommy, shifts closer. He moves his nose above my ear and inhales.

I shudder, reprimanding myself for showing him he intimidates me. He doesn't miss it and grunts in satisfaction.

"What do you want?" I choke out in a whisper, trying to find my voice and further pissed I sound so weak.

He drags his index finger down the side of my throat. I cringe as he threatens, "Cunts like you who disobey receive consequences."

My insides quiver harder. I ball my hands into fists and find my voice, sounding stronger than I am. "I've done no such thing. But since you're here, I want to talk to Leo."

He spins me and slams my back into the shelf.

I yelp, wincing from the pain.

He covers my mouth again, fixing his dark eyes on mine. His tobacco-laced breath makes me feel queasy. I fight the bile trying to rise into my throat while he scolds, "You don't get to make demands."

I attempt to stand straighter, but I can't. He has me pinned. Still, I reiterate, "I need to see Leo."

His scowl intensifies. "Are you deaf?"

"I can't do my job if I don't see Leo," I claim.

His eyes turn to slits. "You don't have room to make stipulations. If you have an issue, you tell me."

Something tells me not to trust him with anything. I need to speak with Leo face-to-face and make sure he approves what I need to do. Who knows how Tommy will spin my words. I don't budge, firmly repeating, "I want to see Leo."

He ignores my insistence, asking, "You think you can move out of the brownstone and make decisions without Leo's permission?"

My pulse races. It doesn't surprise me Leo knows. I should have somehow stopped Massimo from moving my things before I spoke with Leo. I swallow the lump in my throat and answer, "I can't get the information Leo wants without getting closer to Massimo."

He scoffs. "You're fucking him. We all know that. No one thought twice about you spreading your legs."

Scorching heat burns my cheeks.

Amusement fills Tommy's expression, making my embarrassment grow. I fight the tears forming in my eyes, trying to find the cold exterior I normally display.

Tommy continues, "You live in the brownstone. Nowhere else. Understand?"

I shake my head. "No. If you want me to do my job, then you have to let me do it."

His eyes dart down my body. When they meet mine again, his expression sends a cold shiver down my spine. In a hushed tone, he warns, "The thing about whores is, you're all replaceable."

My voice shakes as I blurt out, "I'm not. I can assure you, I'm close to giving Leo what he wants."

"Whores also lie," he adds.

"I'm not lying," I insist.

He arches his eyebrows. "No? Then what have you discovered?"

"I-I met the family. All of them," I inform.

He takes a lock of my hair and wraps it around his finger until it feels like he's going to pull it out.

"Ouch!" I whine.

"You have nothing!"

"I-I do!"

"Yeah? What?" he challenges.

My knees tremble. Tommy presses closer, and the shelf digs into my back, causing more pain. I cry out, "You're hurting me."

"Do you think I care? I want information. Now!" he fumes.

I stay silent, wondering how I'm getting out of this situation alive.

He threatens, "Either give me information, or I'm taking you to Jacopo."

My lungs close up. I'm unable to take any more oxygen in them. Leo's brother is ten times worse than him. I've witnessed how he punishes women. At times, I've had night-mares from the visuals I can't escape. "N-no! Don't take me to him."

"Why shouldn't I? You're wasting everyone's time," Tommy glowers.

There's no time to think. There's only the fear spiraling all around me in a hurricane. I divulge, "He introduced me to his jeweler."

Tense silence fills the air. My skin crawls, and remorse for betraying Massimo immediately assaults me.

Tommy's ice-cold glare studies me. He demands, "Who is it?"

I pause, tearing my eyes off his.

He grasps my neck and forces my head up. Pain shoots through my skull. "Stop stalling."

"His name is Ettore," I state, hating myself further but desperate for him to release me.

More moments of excruciating silence ensue. Tommy finally inquires, "What else have you found out?"

My anxiety grows deeper, squeezing my heart until sharp pains are coursing through it. A tear drops down my cheek. I admit, "That's it."

Tommy purses his lips in disapproval.

I quickly add, "But he trusts me now. I-I'm close to finding everything out. Even his papà likes me now."

Tommy assesses me again then releases me, stepping back. He points in my face. "When I return, you better have more information."

"I need to talk to Leo," I restate.

"You go through me for Leo."

In an attempt to protect myself, I cross my arms over my chest. As firm as I can, I insist, "No. I need to speak to Leo."

"Are you—"

"Katiya, is everything okay?" Alicia asks, her eyes darting between Tommy and me.

Tommy slowly turns his head toward her. He declares, "This isn't your business."

"You're pushing the boundaries," she claims without hesitation.

"Oh? Should we discuss boundaries?" Tommy questions, but it's a threat.

"Alicia, I'm fine," I state, trying to diffuse the situation.

Tommy steps in front of her.

She stays planted, which surprises me. Tommy's a big guy. One look, and it's clear he's dangerous.

He lowers his voice, asserting, "Doing your job requires minding your own business."

She fires back, "Not when you're about to call attention to yourself. What good is that going to do?"

"You think you're so smart, don't you?" Tommy rants.

Arrogance floods Alicia's face. She scoffs. "I guess that's why I'm in my role, and you're in yours."

Goose bumps pop out on my limbs. I open my mouth to warn her she can't talk to him like that then freeze. Everything hits me and becomes clear.

They aren't strangers. She's not butting into this conversation to help me out. She's involved with the Abruzzos, too.

A wave of dizziness crashes into me. I grab the shelf so I don't fall.

This entire time, she's been watching me.

Why did I never assume she was involved with them?

"I liked it better when you took care of yourself," Tommy states, dragging his eyes over her body and pausing on her protruding stomach.

She points to the stairs. "Out. Now. Or I'll call him myself."

Tommy shakes his head, muttering, "I don't understand why he keeps you."

"I can say the same for you. Now, out," she repeats.

He assesses her one more time then nods toward me. "She gets the info, or I'm taking her to Jacopo."

Alicia squares her shoulders and pulls out her phone. "Then let the girl do her job. Now, go, or I'm calling Leo and telling him how you're about to ruin his operation."

My heart pounds so hard against my chest cavity, I think it might burst through it. The silent minutes that pass by only make it worse.

Tommy turns toward me. "You better have more to give me the next time I'm here." He steps toward Alicia and leans into her ear, adding, "You should consider stomach surgery. You've really let yourself go since we were together."

More shivers roll down my body. *She used to be with Tommy?*

She pins her eyes on him, and it's the first time I've ever seen hatred in them. In a disgusted tone, she replies, "I also used to have horrible taste in men."

He snorts then shakes his head. He looks back at me and warns, "Don't underestimate me, Katiya." He moves toward the stairs, and I watch him until he disappears.

Alicia glances over the railing, I assume watching him until he's gone. She turns to me and points to the cart. "Make sure you put those back correctly." She steps toward the stairs.

I gape at her then rush over and grab the back of her arm. "Alicia!"

She spins. "Do your job, Katiya. Every aspect of it."

"You-you work for them?" I cry out.

"Forget about this conversation. Just get him what he wants," she orders.

"I-I'm trying," I claim.

Her eyes turn to slits. "Try harder."

I stare at her, trying to process this entire situation.

She moves down the stairs, and I snap out of it, following her.

On the landing, I reach for her again. "Alicia!"

"What?" she snarls. "Do you have any issues doing your job, Katiya? Do I need to replace you? Because it's not just your ass on the line. Got it?"

A storm of emotions rages through me. I demand, "Please call him. I need to speak with him."

She shakes her head. "No. He doesn't answer to you. If you need to get a message to him, then tell Tommy or me. One of us will make sure he gets it."

Blood bashes against my brain. I contemplate my options, unsure if I can trust her.

"Tommy or me," she repeats.

I decide to hedge my bets with her instead of him. I choke out, "Massimo moved me in with him. I couldn't get out of it. And he wants to take a vacation. He's relentless about it, and if I don't go, I'm not going to continue to earn his trust."

She clenches her jaw.

"Alicia—"

"I will relay the message."

"I need Leo's permission," I state.

She nods. "Yes. You do. I will get it for you."

"You will?" I question, unable to fully put all my faith in her.

She tilts her head then reaches for my face. She tucks a lock of my hair behind my ear and calmly declares, "From now on, if you need something, you come to me. Understand?"

I don't answer.

"Do you understand me?" she repeats.

I nod, unable to find words. So many questions swirl in my mind.

How does Alicia have access to Leo?

What kind of power does she hold in the Abruzzo family?

In an eerie voice, she murmurs, "I expect an answer."

I do the only thing I can. I whisper, "Yes. I understand."

"Good. Now, get back to work." She steps down the remaining stairs, and I watch her waddle away.

I'm unsure if I should be happy she has access to Leo or not. My gut says that Tommy may be physically stronger, but I should be more frightened of the power Alicia holds.

Once again, the fact I have zero control over anything in my life blinks loud and clear. Only now, I know I'm being watched all day long by Alicia. Something about that sends new fear through me.

16

Massimo

THE PIT IN MY STOMACH GROWS, CREATING ANGER SO POTENT inside me, I don't just *want* to kill Agent Dominico.

I *need* to kill him.

It's only been fifteen minutes since I told my brothers I'd meet them in the dungeon, but the fast-forward button gave me all the information I needed. The entire five-hours' worth of footage focuses on my dolce in her brownstone. The only time the camera moves is to zoom in on her or move to the other rooms in her place.

Since the slats of her blinds are usually only halfway closed, there's plenty Dominico captured—including the other day when I had her gagged and tied up.

I curse myself for being so stupid. I'm not naive. I should have flown her miles away and taken her to a private sex club. Others could have watched, but it would have been void of possible local threats. I could have had control over who saw and who didn't, or even just told her others were watching but left the viewing room empty.

What was I thinking?

I let my dick get in the way of her safety.

But why is Dominico watching her?

Papà will get his other footage.

A new panic seeps through my bones. I shut my laptop screen, pace my office, and try to figure out how to intercept the other videos before Papà watches them.

I need to know what's on those memory cards.

How am I going to get them from Papà?

My phone buzzes. I glance at the screen.

Tristano: *Where are you? Papà and Tully are getting antsy to start.*

Me: *On my way.*

I take the card out of the reader and lock it in my safe. I leave my office and go straight to the dungeon. When I get to the bottom of the stairs, the moans and cries of the agents fill my ears.

The desire to slice through Dominico is so strong, I have to pause outside the cell door. I need to find out why he's watching Katiya, so I can't kill him right away. This is going to take every ounce of discipline I have.

What if he reveals something I don't want Papà or anyone else to know?

For the first time in my life, I'm unsure if I want to know the truth.

Katiya is a good girl. There's an explanation for all of this, I try to convince myself. Yet the nagging dread I can't shake only grows.

The door flies open. A cloud of cigar smoke seeps out of the room. Tully arches his eyebrows. "Coming in?"

I shove past him, still pissed he had us kidnap federal agents in broad daylight and about all of his antics. I don't have time on a normal day for the constant guessing games Tully plays, much less today. Now that my girl's involved, I have zero patience. I'm two steps from ripping his head off.

The crowded cell instantly feels suffocating. It's the biggest one we have, but the Marinos and O'Connors, along with the six naked, restrained agents, fill the space. Tully's cigar smoke, the residual smell of death, and stale alcohol mix with the rancid odor of sweat and urine.

Tristano gives me a funny look, but it quickly disappears. He tosses me a pair of black rubber gloves. Then he dips a pizza cutter in acid and holds it out to me. "Thought we'd try something new today."

I slide my hands into the gloves, curl my fingers around the wooden handle, then watch the liquid drip off the steel blade. There's no room to be careless in the dungeon, especially with our chemicals. The acid Tristano picked will burn through your skin right to the bone in seconds upon contact. It's perfect for a slow, torturous death. Not too much blood with maximum amounts of pain. And any infection will set in long after I'm ready for them to take their last breath.

Tristano steps in front of Dominico, holding a metal tongue depressor dipped in acid. He taps it on Dominico's leg, and the skin disappears, displaying a part of his kneecap.

Dominico screams.

Tristano shakes his head at me, declaring, "Amateurs." Then he steps closer to Dominico, asking, "You've been to the doctor, right? I assume you know what this is really for?"

Dominico's eyes grow wider. The other agents' shallow breaths fill the room. Every scent seems to intensify.

Tristano leans into his ear, stating loud enough for everyone to hear, "Let me refresh your memory. It's meant for your tongue. So you have two options. The first is to open wide. The second is to answer our questions without any hesitation. Which one will it be?"

Dominico's nostrils flare as he tries to control his breathing. His eyes dart from Tristano's face to the depressor.

The debate in my head about how to get him to answer questions about Katiya without the others finding out ends. There is no way out of this, and I have to know before he dies.

I step next to Tristano and hold the pizza cutter in front of his face. "My brother is too nice. I won't let him use that tool on your tongue. I'll slice it off with this." I roll the blade from his shoulder to right above his belly button, and his cries fill the air. His skin melts like plastic on a bonfire. One of his ribs pokes out of his body, and for extra pain, I roll the pizza cutter over it.

He screams louder while the sound and smell of piss from another agent swirls around us.

I order, "Tell me why you were monitoring Katiya."

The eyes of both families turn on me, and I try to ignore them as best as possible, keeping my focus on Dominico. I expect him to cave, but, to my surprise, he keeps his mouth shut.

Luca dips his gloved finger in the acid bucket then steps next to the agent next to Dominico. He holds it in front of him. "Your turn, Baskin. Want to answer the question?"

Baskin spits, hitting Luca below his eye.

A sinister smile grows on Luca's lips. He leaves the spit on his cheek and steps closer. "After all our history, I was hoping you'd say that." He drags his finger down Baskin's arm then circles his elbow.

Baskin's screams are more muffled than Dominico's. He never takes his eyes off Luca. I don't know about their history, but I get the impression there's no love lost between the two.

The skin around Baskin's arm fades away until it's only his raw elbow. Luca presses his finger on the bone, and Baskin's cries get louder as it begins to disintegrate. He holds out his hand toward me. "Give me your tool."

I hand him the pizza cutter.

In a swift move, Luca rolls it over the remaining bone, and Baskin's entire body convulses. His shriek is so loud, I wonder if the staff above can hear. Luca demands, "Why was Katiya being monitored?"

Tears fall down Baskin's cheeks, dripping on the dirt floor. He blurts out, "Leo ordered it."

The hairs on my arms rise.

"Leo? Why would Leo Abruzzo want you to watch Katiya?" I ask.

He grinds his molars, and I lose all my patience. I grab the pizza cutter from Luca and jump to the first agent. I slice his waist then keep moving down the line until every agent has skin dissolving just under their belly button.

The shrill sound of pain fills the cell. I go back across the line, this time, above the same spot. The wails get louder. Acid burns one of the men's intestines. He sobs like a baby and goes into shock.

"Tell me," I roar in Dominico's face.

"He never said," Dominico replies.

"Liar!" I scream, slicing his quad muscle.

"It's true," he yells.

"Bullshit!" I bark, slashing his other leg then stepping in front of Baskin, commanding, "Tell me the truth!"

"I don't know! But he visits her," Baskin states.

I freeze. A cold shiver rolls down my spine. My mouth turns dry. I hold the pizza cutter in front of his face, fighting my rage. With as much control as I can muster, I claim, "You're lying."

"I'm not! I swear!" he asserts.

"Liar!" I move my hand toward his cheek, but Luca grips my arm.

"Wait!"

Breathing hard, I glance at Luca.

He arches his eyebrows and firmly repeats, "Wait."

I take a few deep breaths and lower my hand.

Luca tugs Baskin's hair so he faces the ceiling. Luca leans over him. "Why would he visit her?"

"I don't know."

"Don't lie to me, Bruce."

"Luca, I swear," he grits out.

I lose all control, push Luca out of the way, and slash the pizza cutter over Baskin so many times, Tristano and Dante pull me back.

"Chill out," Dante orders.

But it's too late. The front of Baskin's body has barely any skin left. Some of the acid eats his organs. His cries become faint, and he either passed out or is dead. His head hangs toward the ground. If he is still alive, it won't be for long. Too much damage occurred.

"Jesus Christ, Massimo," Luca mutters.

I avoid his pissed glare and turn to Dominico. My insides tremble, and I enunciate my words, repeating, "Why did Leo visit her?"

More tears drip down his cheeks. He chokes out, "I don't know. Leo never said. But Tommy also visits from time to time. It's-it's all on my surveillance. If-if you let me go, I can show you."

His words only incite more rage within me. As far as I'm concerned, these men are worthless. They were Leo's pawns and had no hesitation monitoring Katiya. I sniff hard, no longer able to smell the stench around me. I stare at him and in a calm voice ask, "Tristano, do you know the difference between a local cop and a federal agent?"

He steps next to me. "No, bro. Tell me."

"A local cop is a baby pig. They run around the pen, learning how to fatten up. A federal agent, well, they're a full-blown hog. They think they have all the power, but they have none at the end of the day. Do you know who has the real control?"

Tristano presses the tongue depressor on Dominico's jaw. The skin melts until bone is visible.

He shrieks and begs, "Please, stop!"

"Who has the power?" Tristano asks.

I take my fingers, shove them past Dominico's lips, and force his mouth open. "The farmer. Right when they're the fattest, he slaughters them." I meet eyes with my brother.

A spark flashes in Tristano's eyes. He shoves the depressor on Dominico's tongue, and the acid destroys it.

I hand my pizza cutter to Tristano. "Have at it." I turn to Papà, ignoring all the others' stares. "Where's the footage?"

He pins his dark orbs on me. "In my office."

I don't ask permission. I tear off the gloves, tossing them on the floor, then bypass the others. I slam the cell door, thud up the stairs, and go directly to Papà's office.

A box sits on his desk. I grab it, take it to my suite, then fast-forward through the first memory card.

Some of the Abruzzo thugs appear on it but no Katiya. I pop the next card in, but it's the same. I get through a dozen videos before she appears.

My skin crawls as I watch it. Leo and several of his goons are in her place. Since I can't hear the conversation, it only makes me antsier. At first, Katiya wears her cold exterior. As the visit progresses, it appears as if they're threatening her. At one point, Leo grabs her neck. The fear in her eyes makes my gut somersault. I squeeze my hand into fists, trying to figure out what they converse about and why they're in her place.

Why didn't she tell me?

I can protect her from them.

What if Papà is right? What if she is an Abruzzo?

Sweat pops out on my skin. I watch the storm of men leave her place, and Katiya sinks to the floor. Within seconds, she's sobbing.

My heart twists so tight, I struggle to breathe. I rewind the video, watching it several times. I slowly review the rest of the footage, but nothing else catches my interest. I toss all of the cards in the box and then put the one with Katiya and the Abruzzos in my safe.

I should give it to Papà, but I can't. I grab my Glock, lock the safe, and race down the stairs.

I open the door to the garage, and Papà's voice cuts through the air. "Massimo."

I freeze, my heart thumping hard, and close my eyes for a brief moment. I force myself to spin, sniffing hard, pinning my gaze on my father's cold eyes. I blurt out, "Don't start. I'll get to the bottom of this."

Instead of being angry, Papà's expression and voice soften. "It happens to the best of us."

"What?"

A minute of tense silence passes. He steps closer, admitting, "We fall for an enemy."

"She's not an enemy."

"You don't know that."

"Neither do you," I point out.

He sighs. "Massimo, I speak from experience. I know how easy it is to believe what you want instead of the truth."

"Yeah? How's that?" I hurl.

He grinds his molars a moment then squares his shoulders. "Before I met your mamma, there was another woman. Let's just say that I learned a very hard lesson."

I cross my arms, hating how I can feel my heart pounding against my bicep. Even though I don't know what the situation is, I maintain the same position. "Katiya isn't one of them. You'll see." As soon as I say it, my heart twists.

"Massimo, don't be a fool," Papà warns.

"You're wrong," I state again, then spin and open the door, stepping into the garage.

"Massimo!" Papà calls out.

I ignore him, grab the keys for my Land Rover, and rev the engine. I peel out and honk before I get to the gate so the guard opens it sooner. It's barely open as I surge through it, an inch away from avoiding the metal bars scraping my doors.

It takes me half the time it normally does to get to the library. I pull into the fire lane and take a few breaths. If I'm going to find out the truth, I have to play my cards right.

I get out of the SUV, race up the steps, then enter the library. Instead of looking for Katiya, I glance around to find Alicia. I spot her in the childrens' section and approach her. "Hey, Alicia."

She spins and glances at her watch. "Massimo. You're here a bit early. Katiya has two hours left in her shift, and we've been busy all day."

"I can wait. I actually came to speak with you," I confess.

Surprise fills her expression. "Oh?"

My chest tightens, and my pulse pounds hard against my neck. "Did Katiya ask to take a vacation week?"

Alicia sets a paperback on the shelf then shakes her head. "No, but I haven't chatted with her today. As I said, we've been busy."

I put on my most charming smile, saying a prayer Alicia helps me. "Understandable. Since I have your ear, can I take a few more minutes of your time?"

"Sure. What's going on?" Her forehead wrinkles, and she shifts on her feet.

"I wanted to take Katiya on vacation. She's never really gone anywhere. Any chance you could do without her the next week? I'd like to surprise her," I state.

"Oh. That's...well..." Alicia puts her hand on her hip.

I interject, "I know there's no notice, but if there's any chance, I'd appreciate your help. And I promise to bring you back a really nice thank-you present." I flash her another smile.

She curls her fingers. "Follow me."

I obey, and we go into her office.

She picks up her calendar and studies it for a moment. Time seems to stand still. If I'm going to find out the truth from Katiya, I need to get out of New York. The farther we are from my family and the Abruzzos, the better.

Alicia smiles, pinning her brown eyes on me. "Go ahead and surprise her."

Relief consumes me. "Really?"

"Yep. Don't forget my awesome gift though," she teases and winks.

I chuckle. "I won't. Thank you."

"When are you leaving?" she questions.

"Tonight," I claim, hoping it's not too late to get a flight plan together. The laws have gotten stricter, and even private jets have had some issues.

"Where are you going?" Alicia asks.

I gaze behind my shoulder then turn back to her, lowering my voice. "Can you keep a secret?"

She pretends to zip her lips.

"I'm debating, but Bora Bora or Fiji," I reveal.

She gapes, blinks a few times, then says, "Wow. That's far and pretty amazing, I imagine. Why there?"

"No reason, really. I've never been there and think Katiya will like it."

"I bet!"

"Tell you what," I say, stepping closer. "When's your next vacation?"

She shrugs. "No idea."

"Well, once you know your dates, let me know. Since you're being so flexible and helping me, your next trip is on me—anywhere in the world, only five stars, including the private jet."

Her mouth drops.

I chuckle again and hold out my hand. "Deal?"

She takes it and shakes it hard. "Deal."

I wink, feeling happy, even though I shouldn't right now. "Thanks again. Let's keep this between us, okay? I want to surprise her."

She nods. "Of course."

I thank her again then leave, getting back into the Land Rover. Over the next two hours, I secure the jet, book a bungalow over the water in Bora Bora, and order a slew of clothes for Katiya and me. I instruct the personal shopper I work with to deliver them to the jet before we leave.

By the time Katiya's shift is over, everything is in motion. I debate about all the ways I can get her to admit the truth to me. The only definite is I'm not leaving Bora Bora without it.

Katiya

ALL DAY I'VE BEEN RATTLED. MY BRAIN'S SPINNING A thousand miles a minute.

How could I have missed that Alicia was an Abruzzo?

Is she though? Or is she forced to do their work like I am?

She and Tommy have a history.

Ugh! I need answers.

Since our discussion, Alicia has kept me busy restocking shelves. Every time I look up, there's another unorganized cart next to me. A few times, I caught myself placing the books in the wrong area and had to start all over. I reprimanded myself after each incident, yet my concentration didn't seem to improve. Now I'm second-guessing all the work I did today.

I sigh, finish emptying the last cart, and go to the main area. Massimo is sitting on a tabletop with his arms crossed. The moment our eyes lock, he grins. "Ready?"

"Is it five already?"

He glances at his watch. "Five-fifteen."

I wince. "Sorry. I didn't mean to make you wait."

He shrugs then hands me my purse. "No problem."

Surprised, I ask, "You went to my cubicle?"

"Guilty," he admits and rises, tugging me into him.

I inhale his woodsy scent, wanting to melt into him and never escape.

If only that were my reality.

He kisses the top of my head, murmuring, "Let's get out of here."

I let him guide me out of the library. He opens the door to a Land Rover. I ask, "New car?"

"Nope. It's a year old." He motions for me to get in.

I obey, inquiring, "How many vehicles do you own?"

"Five," he states, shuts the door, and rushes around the car. As soon as he's inside, he turns on the engine and pulls out. He asks, "How was your day?"

"Fine," I lie, forcing myself to smile. "How was yours?"

"Oh, you know—same shit, different day." He slides his hand onto my thigh. "I'm glad to see you though."

My heart swells, and the guilt spins in my stomach. There are too many competing emotions, and I have an urge to cry. Somehow, I avoid it. I reply, "I'm glad to see you, too."

He squeezes my thigh, removes his hand, and places it on the steering wheel. We ride in silence as he zips through traffic. My thoughts continue to race, and I don't realize he's not taking us home until I read the Teterboro Airport sign.

The hairs on my arms rise. I question, "Why are we here?"

He speeds up then parks the Land Rover in front of a humungous jet and black SUV. A man gets out of the passenger side and waits.

Nerves continue to expand in my belly. I put my hand on his arm. "Massimo?"

He grins. "I spoke with Alicia. She cleared you to take the week off. We're leaving for vacation."

I gape at him. My insides quiver, and Leo's face pops into my mind. I blurt out, "I-I can't go!"

His eyes darken. "Why not?"

Anxiety plagues me. I answer, "Work."

"I just told you Alicia said you can have the week off. I took care of everything, so stop worrying." He gets out of the vehicle and comes around to my side.

What if Leo doesn't approve?

Alicia will get him to.

I don't know that.

The man on the runway gets in. "Ma'am," he says as Massimo opens my door.

"Ummm...hi," I reply, then refocus on Massimo.

He chuckles. "You should see your face right now. Come on. We have a flight plan to adhere to." He takes my hand and helps me out of my seat.

Massimo guides me to the stairs. Not knowing what else to do, I climb them with him in tow. At the top of the steps is a red-haired woman. She wears it pinned in a neat French twist. Her lipstick matches her hair and nails. Her pressed navy-blue uniform is flawless. She chirps in an accent I can't determine, "Welcome aboard, Ms. Nikitin and Mr. Marino. I'm Chanel."

Overwhelmed and still freaking out, I nod and let Massimo guide me to the middle of the plane. I barely take in the luxurious tan leather seats before Chanel holds a glass of champagne in front of me.

I take it, and Massimo accepts one for himself. He holds up his flute. "Cheers."

"Cheers," I say, clinking the glass and then taking a sip. I stare at the bubbles, telling myself to calm down.

"Can I get either of you anything else?" Chanel chirps.

"I'm okay. Katiya?" Massimo questions.

I shake my head. "No, thank you."

"Very well," she replies and leaves.

Massimo slides his arm around my back and leans into me. "Stop worrying."

I blurt out, "We don't have clothes."

Arrogance crosses his face. "Of course we do."

"But I—"

"Have a suitcase full of resort wear," he boasts.

I stare at him, trying to process it all. I finally ask, "So we're going to St. Pete?"

He shakes his head. "No."

Confused, I ask, "But I thought you said that's where we'd go."

"We can go to Florida anytime. Let's have a real vacation. One we won't forget," he declares.

My stomach flips. I take another sip of champagne, but it does nothing to calm my nerves. I question, "So where are we going?"

He wiggles his eyebrows. "Bora Bora."

My gut drops further. Bora Bora is on the other side of the world. If Leo doesn't approve, he'll kill me.

Massimo leans closer and tugs me into him. "Why do you look like I just gave you a death sentence? I thought you'd be excited."

I turn to him. "I-I am. Excited... Sorry. I ummm..."

"What is it?"

"Just blown away by all this," I say, which isn't a lie.

He kisses my forehead. "Don't let it overwhelm you. Everything is taken care of, and there's no reason to worry."

I stay silent, still freaking out.

He moves my chin so I can't avoid him. "Katiya, do you trust me?"

The air turns stale in my lungs. My emotions get the best of me, and a tear drops down my face. I swipe at it. "Sorry. Yes. Of course I do." It's not a lie. He's the only person on Earth I trust. The entire situation hurts worse every day, and I don't know how to stop it.

He pulls me onto his lap. "Hey, dolce. Are you okay?"

I sniffle. "Yes. Sorry. I'm just..." I take a deep breath and place my hands over his cheeks. "You're too generous. Thank you."

He studies me, and another worry flares in my belly.

I nervously ask, "What is it?"

He shakes his head and smiles. "Nothing. I'm glad we can finally go away."

I nod and kiss him. It leads to a deeper kiss, and his hand slides under my shirt. His warm palm caresses my spine. I move my body so I'm straddling him.

He retreats and fists my hair so my face is inches from his.

"What's wrong?" I question, my anxiety reigniting.

His face stays neutral, but the blue in his eyes swirls like a twister gaining speed. He doesn't answer me.

"Massimo?"

He deeply inhales then pecks me on the lips. In a cautious voice, he suggests, "Maybe we should never come back to New York."

I stare at him, surprised he would ever leave the city. Massimo thrives in New York. Anywhere we go, he makes heads turn. Being around him, especially on his arm, is like an injection of energy. I blurt out, "You love New York. It's your home."

"What if you were my home?"

I hold my breath, blinking hard again, attempting to harden my expression so I don't lose it. I reply, "What do you mean?"

Several moments pass. My heart feels like it's going to explode out of my chest. Massimo keeps his cool expression on his face, responding, "I don't know. We're happy together, aren't we?"

"Yes. Of course."

"Okay. So we could go anywhere. Escape all this chaos."

My stomach flips. "What chaos? Did something happen with your family?"

An expression I'm unsure about crosses his face. He sniffs hard then smiles. He traces my lips with his thumb. "Nothing happened. Just thinking out loud."

I tilt my head. "Are you sure everything is okay?"

He nods. "Yep. I guess I'm in la-la land. You can't be on vacation forever, right?"

A mix of relief and sadness fills me. I'd run away with Massimo in a heartbeat if I could have a guarantee Leo wouldn't hunt me down. But I know that's not possible. If Massimo told Alicia we were leaving, then Leo definitely will know. Yet a new thought appears. *Maybe it is possible to disappear.* I question, "Does Alicia know where we're going?"

"Yeah. I told her. Stop worrying about work," he orders.

All my hope dissolves. I look away and blink as hard as possible to stop the disappointment from flowing down my cheeks.

I'm never escaping Leo.

Massimo and I will never be able to be together.

I'll have to betray him.

"Katiya, what's going on?" Massimo asks, moving my chin toward him.

I breathe through my emotions and shake my head, fibbing, "Nothing is wrong. Thank you for talking with Alicia. This is going to be an amazing adventure. I love you." As I say the words, I cringe inside. My heart belongs to Massimo. But what kind of cruel person hurts the person they love?

He pecks me on the lips. "I love you, too, dolce."

There's a ding, and the pilot says over the loudspeaker, "Please buckle up. We're ready to start our journey."

I give Massimo another kiss and slide off his lap. We fasten our belts, and the jet moves forward.

Different nerves expand in my gut. I put my hand over my belly.

Massimo leans into my ear. "Are you a nervous flyer?"

"I've never flown before," I admit, then bite my lip.

He arches his eyebrows. "Never?"

Heat creeps into my cheeks. "No."

"Wow."

"How many times have you flown?" I question.

He shrugs. "Too many to count. I lost track when I was a child."

The jet rolls faster down the runway, lifts into the air, and my stomach lurches.

Massimo chuckles, tightening his arm around my shoulders. "Breathe, dolce." He mimics deep breaths.

I follow his lead, wishing the aircraft would level off. My entire body feels pressed against the back of the seat. I couldn't get up if I tried. Something about it freaks me out.

"Five, four, three, two, one," Massimo counts, and the plane changes its angle.

Gravity resumes to normal. I sigh in relief, but then my ear canal fills with pressure. I put my hands over them, cringing.

"Yawn," Massimo orders then does it himself.

I force myself to yawn, and my ears pop. "Oh, wow!"

He squeezes my thigh. "Good now?"

"Yes. Thank you! How long is our flight?"

"Close to twelve and a half hours."

I gape at him.

His lips twitch. "Something wrong?"

"That's half a day!"

"Yep. We'll sleep through most of it," he claims.

I press the button, and my seat moves back. "Okay. I guess it's good these chairs are so comfy."

He grunts. "We aren't sleeping in these chairs."

"No?"

He rolls his head so his cheek is against the seat. "There's a bedroom in the back of the jet."

"Is it hard to sleep during a flight?"

"Not at all. Plus, I don't plan on you having any energy to stay awake," he adds.

Flutters overpower all the nerves I had. A new flush replaces the embarrassment I felt earlier. I lick my lips, try to contain my excitement, then ask, "Why? What are you going to do to me?"

His eyes dart down my body then back to my face. "Let's eat dinner first. You're going to need the extra calories."

Zings race through my cells. I bite on my smile. I can't get enough of Massimo, no matter how many times I'm with him.

He leans closer. "Do you know what's different about this aircraft?"

The anticipation builds, and I swallow hard. "No. Tell me."

He purses his lips, assessing me as my cheeks grow hotter. The look in his eyes is one I crave. It's like a wild animal trying to determine when it's the right time to pounce on its prey. Every part of being on the receiving end of his punishments sets my soul on fire. He drags his knuckles down my cheek, creating a blaze of fire underneath, while stating, "There are few planes in New York designed for punishments. This is one of them."

My butterflies spread their wings, fluttering like they're trying to escape an enemy.

He points at the ceiling, adding, "Look around, dolce. What do you see?"

I glance up, and tingles race down my spine. Discreet, round metal pieces, perfect for attaching handcuffs or other restraints, are positioned around the plane. If you don't know what they are, they look decorative.

He continues, "See the speakers?"

"Yes," I breathe.

"See that button?" he motions toward a red one on the wall.

"What is it for?" I ask.

"It's for my discretion."

"Your discretion?" I question.

He glides his hand up my inner thigh and cups my pussy. His thumb pushes against my pants, adding pressure to my clit.

I gasp, rolling my hips into his hand.

Arrogance washes across his face. It becomes the catalyst for a round of fireworks exploding in my cells. Everything resides in that look. It exudes confidence that he knows exactly what to do to me. It showcases that his desire to dominate me is as potent as mine is to participate. And then there's the danger in his appearance that'll never escape him. It's ingrained in him so deeply, it's not able to be hidden.

His expression fuels me. It reiterates the faith I have in him. He's able to give me all the things I never knew I needed before he showed up in my life. There's no denying I don't just love what it represents. It fuels me, breathing life into the parts of my soul I wish I could stay in forever. When I'm not with him, I'm just existing. There's no other way to describe it. Every touch, every command, every moment he holds my fate in his hands is pure utopia. But it's not only for me. It's his nirvana as well. And it's no secret between us.

The longer he stares at me, the more impatient I become to experience his punishment and know what his discretion means.

His lips curve, turning cockier. He finally answers, "It's my discretion to make the pilots and flight attendant listen to you beg me for hours. It's my choice to let them hear the desperation in your voice. It's my option to never let you come."

My heart races faster.

He continues, "I'll create tension so extreme in this jet that they'll excuse themselves to the bathroom and take care of their own needs. And at that point in time, your voice will have turned hoarse. Your agonizing pleas will torture them. They'll all wonder how I can continue to torment you. They'll silently wish I would give it to you."

"Yes," I whisper, closing my eyes, wanting Massimo to take me to that place.

His hot breath hits my ear. "But I won't, dolce. I won't until I'm positive I've broken you. When you get off this plane, you won't be able to look at any of them without your cheeks burning. But if you had to do it all over again, you'd say yes and let me. Because you crave what I give you. Every dirty word. Every filthy touch. Every indecent act you need. I see it, dolce. I know the wildness that resides in you. I feel it. You're a bird trying to escape the cage, aren't you?"

I open my eyes and stare at him. His blue eyes turn to ice. My pulse increases. Fear he knows about Leo and what I'm supposed to do to him fills me.

His hand slides up my shirt and under my bra. Two fingers roll my nipple. My breath hitches, and he lowers his voice, demanding, "I expect answers."

"Yes," I reply breathlessly.

"Yes, who?"

"Yes, sir."

"Yes, sir, you're what?" he challenges, his eyes turning colder as he lifts his brows in question.

I square my shoulders and stick out my chin. Nothing has ever seemed truer. Maybe he knows, maybe he doesn't, but his analogy isn't false. "Yes, sir. I'm desperate for you. I-I want to escape the cage."

Satisfaction morphs into his expression. He picks up my hand, kisses the back of it, then presses the call button.

Chanel appears, beaming. "What can I get for you?"

"Dinner," Massimo states. "And don't leave anything out. My dolce needs her energy."

Chanel nods. "Right away, sir." She turns to leave, but I don't miss the faint flush in her cheeks, as if she knows what is about to happen.

Massimo rises and reaches for my hand.

I take it and he pulls me onto my feet. He points to the back of the plane. "Go into the bedroom. Put on the outfit that's on the bed."

"What is it?" I ask, a new thrill racing through my blood.

He undresses me with his eyes then locks them with mine, replying, "Something that's going to make Chanel jealous on too many levels."

"Why is that?"

His lips curve into a confident grin. He answers, "Because no one is as sexy as you, my dolce. And there's no way anyone can look at you in the outfit I chose, without their panties turning wet."

I bite on my smile once again and step past Massimo. The thought of sitting in lingerie while Chanel serves us should make me uncomfortable. It does the exact opposite.

Now, everything about it only makes dinner seem like a torturous event.

A delicious, explicit, sordid affair.

Nothing could make me not want to partake.

18

Massimo

"Eat the last bite so we can begin," I order, holding the forkful of tiramisu to Katiya's lips.

She doesn't argue. The light in her blue eyes grows, and her chest rises and falls faster. Every second of this dinner has been full of sexual tension. I intentionally made it last longer than it should have, forbidding Chanel to bring the next course until everything was off our plates. Every new course that arrived, I conversed with Chanel. I included Katiya in every discussion so that the women couldn't avoid each other.

From time to time, I'd slip my hand between my dolce's thighs when she was speaking to Chanel. We didn't get through the appetizer before she was wet and the smell of her arousal swirled among the aroma of the food.

Mid-course, I was so hard from watching Katiya try to maintain her composure, I almost broke. A few times, she squirmed against my hand. It was subtle but didn't get past me. I made a mental note to punish her for it. And now, as the last bite of the rich dessert goes into her mouth, I'm ready to deliver it.

I let her chew then swallow. She dabs her lips with the cloth napkin and takes a sip of water. I watch her, studying her every move, questioning how all this could be an act. If she is working for the Abruzzos, she's the best actress in the world.

I push the button that turns the speakers on. I turn the dial to maximum volume so even whispers can be heard by the crew. Something about knowing everyone can hear my dolce, but the only one who can have her is me, turns me on more than I've ever experienced. Not taking my gaze off Katiya, I relay, "Chanel, we're ready for dinner to end."

Katiya takes a deep breath. Her expression lights up, and it's as if she's intentionally torturing my dick. My erection grows harder, and the tension in my pants turns into sheer suffering.

Patience. Don't blow your wad before the fun begins.

The indecent part of me that needs to dominate and control the woman I'm with won before I got on this plane. I should be spending every second finding out why the Abruzzos were in Katiya's place, but I convinced myself I'd figure everything out in Bora Bora. For now, I'm going to pretend nothing has changed—that I didn't see with my own eyes Leo grabbing my dolce's throat, or her arguing with them, or her falling to the floor and sobbing after they left.

Right now, I'm going to do what gets me off in a safe environment. The guilt that's eaten me all day over those federal pigs catching our activities on camera makes my head spin. No staff member will ever discuss or see what we do in this plane. Every employee Papà hires signs a confidentiality agreement. And no one would dare cross my papà's orders. They receive higher pay than they would get if they flew for someone else, but with that comes stipulations.

Everything and anything goes on this plane. Nothing is off-limits.

Not one word ever gets uttered outside of it.

The penalty for breaking my family's trust is more than someone losing their job. And everyone in Papà's employment knows the consequences.

Papà and each of my brothers have their own jet, just like me. It was our present on our twenty-first birthdays. Sometimes we use the other's plane, but each of us decided how to decorate and accessorize the one we were gifted. We also hand-picked our staff. Papà insisted he approve our human capital selections at the start. My staff has never broken their contracts or given me any reason to replace them. They've been with me for almost two decades.

My pilots are in their fifties. Chanel is younger than me; she was only sixteen when she arrived in the United States. Her father was a highly trained spy for Giuseppe Berlusconi, the head of the Italian Mafia in Italy. Papà is still loyal to Giuseppe, even though my brothers and I don't understand why. However, he sent Chanel's father to New York to assist Papà in some matters.

The day they arrived, Chanel and her father stood in Papà's office. She had already graduated from our high school equivalent and wanted a job. Papà suggested she become my flight attendant, and I've never regretted it. All sorts of lewd activities have gone on inside this jet. There's been blood-shed, ridiculous amounts of sex, and important business meetings requiring the utmost confidentiality. Not once have I worried about my staff. And everything about that means this is the safest setting for me to dive into my kinks with Katiya.

Chanel appears with her friendly smile plastered on her lips like usual. She turns to Katiya and pauses, staring at her, then stating, "By the way, you're really beautiful." My dolce's cheeks burn brighter, and I make a mental note to give Chanel a bonus.

From the hundreds of flights I've taken on this plane, I've often gotten the impression Chanel enjoys my antics as much as the women who accompany me. There's never been a discussion, but the knowing spark in her eyes gives it away. Her perfectly timed comment is almost as if she's playing a strategic game. Then again, it's my job to know everything about my employees. And I'm too aware that Chanel is into voyeurism. She's a frequent guest at the sex club the crime families all attend, often watching instead of participating.

Of course, it wouldn't be the first time I gave her a bonus with a note stating that her efforts with my female guests didn't go unnoticed. So I'm pretty sure she caught on to what I approve of, and anything that makes my woman slightly uncomfortable and flushed deserves acknowledgment.

"Thank you," Katiya says.

Chanel freezes, locking eyes with Katiya. I wait, enjoying how my dolce shifts in her seat.

Chanel turns her attention on me. "Is there anything else I can get for you, Mr. Marino?"

"Not at the moment, but I'd like your feedback," I respond.

"Oh?" She tilts her head, arching her eyebrows.

I decide to do something I haven't before and order, "Katiya, stand up."

Her eyes widen. She opens her mouth then shuts it.

I give her a challenging stare but not for long. She submits like the good girl she is and rises.

"Turn," I demand.

Katiya squares her shoulders, standing straighter. Her hand slightly shakes, and I hold in a groan. It's her tell that she's trying not to squirm. I know because she admitted it once.

I drag my finger down her almost-naked spine, and she shudders. When I reach the blue thong, I trace its top then the tiny string between her crack, stating, "Katiya's disobeyed me. I need to punish her. Should I mark her right or left cheek?"

Chanel doesn't hesitate. "Right."

"Why?" I ask.

"You're right-handed."

"So?"

Chanel's green orbs sparkle. "Your thumbprint will be near her panties."

A drop of juice rolls down Katiya's thigh and catches my eye. I drag my finger over it and place my hand on her hip. "Katiya, turn your head but not your body."

She obeys, her blue eyes burning brighter, her cheeks so red, she could mesmerize people for weeks with her beauty. And while some women may think my perverted self is going over the line, the fact my dolce gets off on this as much as I do makes me push the boundaries harder.

I lock my gaze with hers, ordering, "Look at Chanel."

She obeys, taking short breaths.

I rub my palm on her ass, asking, "Chanel, can you imagine my handprint on my dolce's perfect ass?"

"Yes."

"And?" I press.

Chanel doesn't miss a beat. She states, "It'll be a work of art."

Katiya licks her lips, her hand shaking harder.

"How should Katiya address me?" I ask.

"Daddy."

Surprised, I arch my eyebrows at Chanel, asking, "Why daddy and not sir?"

Neither woman tears their gaze off the other. Chanel replies, "I guessed from the age difference, but that's what she wants."

"Oh? How do you know?" I question.

"By the tiny gasp she tried to hide. She's as excited as you are," Chanel says.

Katiya bites her lip.

"You really are beautiful," Chanel tells her.

Satisfied with this little pre-game show, I offer, "That's all for now, Chanel."

"Thank you, sir," she replies, then takes the dessert tray away.

When she pulls the curtain and disappears behind it, I rise and guide Katiya to the couch. I stand behind her, my arm circled around her waist and body flush to hers. Leaning down to her ear, I murmur, "You loved every minute of that, didn't you?"

"Yes," she whispers, slightly trembling against me. She grasps my thighs and closes her eyes.

"Whispering isn't going to hide anything. The microphones all around us may be tiny and hidden, but they pick up everything," I admit.

She opens her eyes and pins them on mine. The same look she gave me before I restrained her in front of the window and put on the ball and gag fills her face.

"It's time for your punishment. Daddy isn't going to be easy on you," I warn, adding, "But you don't want me to be, do you?"

"No, Daddy. Please. Don't go easy on me," she breathes.

I almost ask her if she knows what she did to be punished but decide against it. Microphones can't be on when I make her admit she's hiding something with the Abruzzos from me. Instead, I push it as far to the back of my mind as possible and question, "You agree you've been naughty?"

"Yes."

"Yes, who?"

"Yes, Daddy."

"I'm only smacking the right cheek. It's going to sting more than normal. Is that what you want me to do?" I taunt, not doubting she wants it.

Her voice cracks as she replies, "Please, Daddy."

Satisfaction sears through me. It's like a flower blooming, taking in all the sunshine. I release her, sit, and pat my legs. "Assume your position."

She bites her smile then crawls over my lap so her ass is in the air. She turns her head, bats her eyes, and asks, "Is this okay, Daddy?"

"It's a start," I declare, open the drawer next to me, and pull out a pair of handcuffs. "Fingers laced together."

Katiya obeys, and I close the cuffs around her wrists.

I demand, "Stretch your arms as far as possible."

She pushes them out in front of her on the seat. I push a button, and a chain drops from the ceiling. I attach it to the O-ring then hit another button. It moves the restraint farther away until there's no slack.

"Face to the left," I order. There's a mirror on that wall, and I don't know if Katiya likes to watch others, but she gets off seeing herself. Plus, I need to see her eyes to know when to stop.

She turns her head, and her growing excitement is reflected in the mirror.

"Daddy's going to make you watch. Bad girls need punishments, and you'll watch every part," I order.

She locks eyes with me in the mirror and swallows hard.

I study my dolce, wearing only the dainty lace bra and thong. Her creamy skin is beautiful, and her arousal flares in my nostrils. I take several breaths, calming my insides, finding the control I need to do this without truly hurting her.

It's a delicate balance between pain and pleasure, and I'm fully aware this requires discipline. I caress her ass with my left palm. I run my right hand up her spine, and a tiny whimper flies out of her mouth.

I raise my hand in the air then bring it down on her right cheek.

"Oh!" she blurts out, jerking her hands. The sound of the chain scraping the leather seat hit my ears.

"You'll address me as Daddy," I remind her, then smack her again.

"Oh, Daddy!" she cries out, louder than before.

I rub her cheek then smack her five times, ordering, "No more hiding things from me, Katiya."

Guilt flushes all over her face. My stomach lurches. I didn't plan on bringing it up right now. However, her facial expression confirms what I already know. I remind myself now isn't the time and slide my left hand over her pussy, positioning my index finger over her clit. Circling it at a slow speed, I glide my thumb inside her.

"Daddy," she moans.

I work her pussy then take my right hand and smack the same cheek but slightly harder.

"Daddy!" she calls out, her body trembling.

"Have you learned your lesson?" I taunt, knowing we're only getting started.

"No," she says, shaking her head as much as possible against the seat.

"No? No, who?" I ask, then smack her again, continuing to manipulate her sex. "Maybe I need to stop."

"No, Daddy! No, I haven't learned my lesson," she asserts, pushing her bottom against my hand.

"Stop moving, Katiya," I bark.

Her body turns limp. Her breath comes out ragged, and I meet her eyes again.

"Please," she whines.

I push my thumb in and out of her faster and change the motion of my finger on her clit. Instead of circling it, I rub it side to side.

"Oh God! Daddy, please!" she begs, her skin glistening in the reflection of the mirror.

I smack her again then rub the red mark, but my handprint will be there for a while. No amount of rubbing is going to erase it. I've marked her, and everything about that drives me to keep going.

"Please, what?" I taunt.

"Let me come, Daddy. Please!" she pleads.

I lean down, scrape my teeth over the red mark on her ass, and intensify playing with her pussy. She moans, and her body trembles.

I pull my hand away from her cunt and smack her, roaring, "You naughty little girl. You think you can hide things from me?"

The previous guilt mixes with lust, creating an expression on her so powerful, my cock pulses. It makes me angry, worried, and so damn ready to be inside her, I cave.

I slide out from under her and rise.

"Daddy? Please! Don't stop. I-I've been so bad. I-I need you to punish me," she declares.

I drop my pants and fist my cock, rubbing the pre-cum on my thumb that was inside her. Then I cage my body over hers and slide my thumb in her mouth.

She moans, sucking it hard.

I position the tip of my cock at her entrance then lean into her ear. I murmur, "I know you've lied to me, Katiya."

Her eyes widen with worry, and I keep my thumb in her mouth, not wanting to hear her deny it. Her floral scent wafts in the air, mixing with the smell of sex, making me borderline dizzy.

I slide my thumb out of her mouth and grasp her chin. "Admit to me you've not been honest."

Tears well in her eyes. She blinks hard, but they fall. She chokes out, "Massimo..."

"Admit it," I order again, suddenly needing her to confess so she can't deny it later when I bring it up. I thrust my cock an inch into her.

"Oh," she moans, then moves her hips back to take more of me in, but I stop her.

"I want the truth, dolce, or I stop," I threaten and pull out of her.

"Massimo," she cries out again.

"Tell me, and I'll give you what you want," I demand.

She stares at me. More tears fall.

I soften my voice, kiss below her ear, and state, "Whatever it is, we'll figure it out. I need you to admit this one thing. If you love me, you'll confess," I add.

She sniffles several times.

I freeze over her. "Okay, we're done."

"No! I-I'm sorry. I've lied to you," she divulges.

Relief fills me. It makes zero sense, but something about her admission gives me hope. Maybe it's false, but it makes me feel like whatever is going on, she'll tell me, and I'll fix it.

"Good girl," I praise and slide into her. "Tell me what you want Daddy to do."

"Harder, Daddy," she cries out.

I obey. "What else?" I ask, grabbing her knee and pushing it toward the back of the seat, then thrusting deeper in her.

"Yes," she whimpers.

"What else?" I demand again. "What else do you want from your daddy?"

"Don't stop, Daddy. I-I need you not to stop," she begs.

I push her leg up more and thrust faster.

"Oh God!" she screams, her body trembling under me.

I grunt in her ear, "No matter what, I'll take care of whatever is going on, dolce. No one, and I mean no one, will fuck with you or me. Understand?"

She gets more emotional but moves her hips faster, meeting my thrusts eagerly.

"Answer me," I order.

"Yes, Daddy. I understand," she relays, with tears falling at record speed. Her fingers grasp the chain tighter, and her entire body convulses.

"Look at me," I growl.

Her glistening eyes meet mine in the mirror.

"Whatever it is, I'll fix it," I promise, and it's a vow I mean to keep.

MC

Katiya

ADRENALINE SURGES THROUGH MY BODY, CREATING A HIGH SO powerful, I can't stop shaking. It mixes with the emotions I no longer have any control over, and I wonder if I've become delirious.

How does he know I'm lying to him?

Did he find out what Leo wants me to do?

Oh God. Maybe he'll kill me, and this is his last hurrah with me.

In a swift move, Massimo flips me onto my back. His warm frame is a perfect contrast against the cool leather. He slides his hand up my arm, wrapping it around my fingers that still grip the chain.

"Relax, dolce," he instructs.

I release my grasp on the chain, but I'm still shaking.

He drags his knuckles over my cheek, pinning his blues on mine. He praises, "Good girl."

All the guilt I constantly have spirals faster. I take a few shaky breaths.

He flips his hand and swipes at my tears. In a firm voice, he declares, "We aren't talking about this now. We'll discuss everything in Bora Bora. Understand?"

Too many questions plague me. More tears fall, and I hate myself for being so weak. Plus, I don't understand why he's being kind to me when he knows I've lied to him. I rack my mind some more, trying to figure out if there's anything else I've lied to him about, but everything has to do with Leo.

"I need you to tell me you understand," he says.

I nod. My cheeks grow wetter, and I choke out, "Okay."

He inhales deeply, not removing his authoritative gaze from me. My heart beats against his chest and his against mine. I wonder how two people can fit together so perfectly when one is supposed to betray the other. And then it hits me that this will be the last time we're together. Whatever he knows, he isn't going to sweep it under the rug. Maybe we aren't even going to Bora Bora. Perhaps this flight is only to get me far away so he can kill me and then dispose of my body.

It's better than dying at Leo's hand. At least if Massimo kills me, it's because I deserve it.

The entire notion that this is it and my seconds on Earth are limited creates a new panic in me. I lift my head, getting an inch from his lips, and admit, "No matter what, I love you. I've never loved anyone before, but I do love you. Please believe me." His face turns blurry from the fresh emotions that besiege me.

He tightens his fist around my hands, caresses my cheek, and leans closer until his lips press into mine. I desperately slide my tongue into his mouth, wanting all of him and needing to show him that I'm not lying about how I feel about him. I wrap my legs around his thighs, lift my hips, and attempt to have him slide back inside me, but he freezes.

His eyes harden, returning to the dominant expression he wears whenever we do anything sexual. Even with all my worries and sorrows, the butterflies in my gut go crazy. He questions, "Do you think your punishment is over?"

"I-I..." I blow out an emotion-filled breath of air.

"You want Daddy's cock?" he asks.

"Yes. Please, Daddy," I whisper, falling right back into my role. New endorphins ignite in my cells. Calling him Daddy turns me on, adding to my confusion. This entire plane ride has been full of surprises. I should have felt humiliated when Chanel studied me, or when she told me I was beautiful, or when she instructed Massimo to use his right hand when he slapped my ass. Instead of feeling shame, it added to my anticipation, lighting me up to the point my nerves were buzzing.

Massimo adds fuel to my perversion when he says, "Everyone on this plane knows you're a filthy, naughty girl. And you still want more?"

"Yes," I answer without hesitation.

"You came without my permission. I should tie you up in the bedroom and leave you there for the rest of the flight," he threatens.

"No! Please, Daddy," I beg.

Moments pass in a haze of sexual tension. I hold my breath as he studies me until I can't take it anymore.

"Please. I won't come again until you permit me," I promise.

He remains silent. Every second feels like torture. More arrogance floods his sharp features. He finally questions, "Why should I believe you? You don't handle punishments with my cock as well as others."

It's true. I have the hardest time not coming when he's inside me, but I'm desperate for him to set my body on fire while ordering me not to fall over the cliff. And I know he's the most dominant when he punishes me like this. I beg, "Please. I promise you. I'll wait until you tell me to come."

He sniffs hard then grabs a fistful of my hair and tugs my head until it's as far back as possible.

I gasp, push my hips closer to him, and whisper, "Please, Daddy. Punish me."

He murmurs in my ear, "If you come before I permit you, I will tie you up in the bedroom and leave you there. There won't be any second chances, Katiya. Do you understand?"

"Yes," I agree.

"Last chance. Are you sure you want my cock for your punishment?"

"Yes! Please!"

"Then ask appropriately," he orders.

My pulse increases, and tingles roll down my spine. I implore, "Please, Daddy. Punish me until I can't take anymore."

"Ah, but that's where tonight is different, dolce," he says, then steals a quick kiss, teasing me and leaving me wanting more.

I don't understand. I ask, "How is it different?"

He palms my head and leans over my face, declaring, "I'm pushing you past that point. And if you disobey me, you'll be naked, chained, and on your own in the bedroom for the next ten hours." He kisses me then pauses. "On second thought, I'll chain you out here and only release you when we land. The entire staff will see you at my mercy."

I bite my lip, my flutters kick into overdrive, and my pussy pulses.

Why am I tempted to make him follow through on that threat?

I reprimand myself for even contemplating it, but it's too late.

It's like he can see right into my innermost thoughts. His lips twitch. "Fuck, you're naughty. You'd like that."

My short breaths only serve to increase the endorphins spinning through my body. I open my mouth, shut it, then push my hips closer to him.

The plane vibrates, creating a loud rattling noise. Massimo slides his other hand up my arm, pinning me beneath him, and thrusts into me.

It's sweet agony mixed with different sensations from the vibrations.

A ding breaks into the air, and the pilot announces, "Looks like we've got some turbulence. Please secure your seat belts."

Massimo's expression challenges me. He buries his head into the curve of my neck and nibbles on it while slowly thrusting.

"Oh God!" I cry out as the sound of the plane fighting the turbulence gets more intense.

"Who loves you?" he mumbles in my ear.

"You do, Daddy," I answer.

"And what does my cock love?"

"My pussy," I respond.

"How do I love it? Tell me how I love it," he orders.

"Wet. Pulsing. Oh...oh..."

"Don't you dare come, dolce!" he barks.

I close my eyes and do everything in my power to stop the onslaught of adrenaline from taking over.

"Look at me," he demands.

I obey, and he pins his cold, controlling gaze on me. The shaking stops, but only for a moment. It resumes but is rougher than before, adding more vibration and making it harder for me not to release.

He asks, "What else do I love about your pussy?"

"I'm tight," I breathe, then moan as new sensations from his shaft tease my walls.

He groans, clenches his jaw, then speeds up his thrusts.

"Massimo," I cry out.

"Who?" he snaps.

"Daddy! Oh God, Daddy!" I scream over the loud aircraft.

"You know what daddies do?" he barks.

"Make me feel good," I respond, gripping the chain and pulling, but there's no slack.

He grabs the back of my thighs and pushes them, sandwiching them between my chest and his. He scoops his arms under me, holding me tight. His erection sinks deeper into me, filling me like never before.

"Daddy," I gasp.

He circles a palm around my neck and squeezes. I can still breathe, but it adds an element of danger, heightening all my sensations. His blues assess me, then he bites my collarbone.

The sounds that fly out of my mouth are incoherent. It's a whirlwind of pleasure tainted with sharp pain from his teeth. My pussy clutches his shaft, and sweat breaks on the surface of my skin.

He sucks and bites me in a rotation. His fingers squeeze and release the pressure on my windpipe, taking me to the edge of dizziness. He thrusts inside my body like he owns it and knows it better than I do.

Maybe he does. How can someone create so much euphoria for another without that knowledge?

Every skilled touch is torture. He continues tormenting me, reminding me at times he didn't permit me to come yet. Several times, he backs down, giving me a slight break before escalating his intensity.

I become a pleading, desperate woman. The longer he makes me wait, the louder I beg. When the tears fall down my cheeks, instead of permitting me to release like he normally does, he roars, "Do not come, dolce!"

"Daddy! Please!" I wail, needing the high so much, I think I'm on the edge of dying.

"No. Your punishment needs to fit the crime. You lied to me," he barks, the anger and hurt in his eyes bursting into blue flames.

All my guilt comes racing back. I sob, "I'm sorry. I really am."

He squeezes my neck harder. The turmoil in his expression grows more potent. He asserts, "You don't lie to me. Never. You should know this, dolce."

I panic. Is this my last moment? Will he tighten his grip just a little bit more and cut off my air supply?

He releases his grasp and kneels next to my hips, keeping my legs pushed to my chest. He moves his forearms across the back of my thighs, thrusts a few times, then smacks my ass.

"Daddy!" I choke out as the sting travels right to the inner core of my pussy, mixing with the sweet sensations of his shaft. I yank on the chain, but my arms still can't move out of the rigid position.

"What does your daddy do for you?" he snarls, his eyes lit with a crazed expression. He continues thrusting but slows it way down.

"Oh," I moan, trying to stop my eyes from rolling.

"Tell me," he demands.

"Everything," I reply.

"What does that mean?" he pushes.

I don't know how to answer him. My mind is stuffed with too many thoughts, while my body is aching for the release only he can give me.

"Answer me!"

"I-I-I...oh God! P-please... I...oh...oh..."

"Do not come," he growls.

"Please, Daddy!" I scream, my body quivering and walls spasming.

He stops moving and palms my cheeks, locking his gaze on mine. "I take care of you, dolce. If you have a problem, you come to me. No matter who it's with, I'm the one to whom you disclose the truth."

The longer we stay in silence, eyes pinned on the other, the more the sensations fade away. A wave of emotion over-powers me, and this time, it's not from sexual acts.

He knows about Leo. There's no doubt.

But what does he know?

"Do you understand what I'm saying?" he questions.

I blurt out in a sob, "You can't save me."

His eyes turn to slits. In a firm voice, he replies, "I will. No matter what's going on, I promise you that I will."

I shake my head, wanting to believe he can but knowing the extent of the Abruzzo wrath. Their power is unlike any I've ever seen, including the Petrovs', which I would have thought was impossible when I was under Ludis's roof.

The turbulence dies down, and everything turns calm, except for the tension between us.

More determination fills his expression. He claims, "I will kill anyone who threatens or harms you."

I blurt out, "But you haven't." As soon as the words leave my mouth, I regret them.

He freezes, and the color drains from his face.

"Massimo, I didn't mean—"

He lurches over me, unlocks the handcuffs, and jumps off the couch. Before I can move, he picks me up and reaches for the microphone button, turning it off.

I wrap my arms around his shoulders, embracing him tightly and saying, "I didn't mean it. Forget I said it, please."

He says nothing, takes me into the bedroom, and puts me under the covers. He leaves the light off, slides in next to me, and then tugs me into his arms.

Blood pounds between my ears, matching the hard thumping of my heart. I place my hand on his chest and find his heart beating as fast as mine. For several moments, I take deep breaths, reprimanding myself for saying that to him and wondering where it even came from.

Not once did I ever think it was Massimo's responsibility, nor did I believe he was even capable of killing Leo. There are too many men surrounding him, watching and protecting him against all enemies. Massimo is capable of murder, but getting to Leo is another story. Anyone who tries ends up dead. The last thing I want is Massimo to be Leo's next victim.

In a calm, low voice, Massimo states, "I will kill Leo. It's only a matter of time. And Ludis is already dead."

Goose bumps flood my skin. I shiver and blurt out, "What do you mean?"

Massimo kisses the top of my head. "Ludis was killed a few years ago. I didn't know. I was searching for him but just recently got confirmation of his death. I wanted to kill him and Leo together."

"I-I don't understand," I admit, wondering how that could even be possible. I try to process that Ludis can no longer get to me. Then the realization hits me that I've been living in fear not only of Leo but also of Ludis someday trying to get me back. I swipe at the new tears that escape my eyes.

Massimo sniffs hard, confessing, "You can never repeat this."

I nod. "Okay."

He flips on a wall switch. I blink several times to adjust my eyes to the soft light. He holds my chin so I can't avoid him and questions, "Can I trust you, dolce?"

"Yes."

"But you've been hiding things from me."

I bite my lip, trying to stop the tears, but it's pointless.

He adds, "Things about the Abruzzos."

My gut flips. Hearing him admit he knows I'm hiding things makes me ill. I sniffle, confessing, "I'm sorry. I don't want to. I-I don't want to hurt you or do any of it."

His eyes darken. He grinds his molars. So much anger appears on his face, it scares me. But it also makes me think that I deserve whatever he's going to do to me. His nostrils flare a few times, and he states, "Tell you what. Why don't you tell me everything? No lies. Just whatever Leo is threatening you about, you tell me."

My insides quiver hard. Paralysis takes over, and I don't even breathe.

"Katiya, if you don't tell me, I'll find out on my own. You have a choice to make. Choose me. Choose us. We'll figure out how to deal with whatever is going on. If you don't tell me, then you're on your own. And when I do find out the truth, I won't show mercy to anyone when I deliver the consequences. That includes you. I won't be able to protect you from the Abruzzos or my family. Do you understand?"

Everything crashes down around me. I sob into his arms, so far into the secret life I never wanted that I don't know what to do. I want to tell him everything, but I still have a deep fear about Leo killing me. I'd rather receive the wrath of Massimo or his family than any Abruzzo. The Marinos may be as dangerous, but at least I would be paying for my sins.

"Katiya, choose me," he orders, but I hear the fear in his voice, too. It's the only time I've ever heard it. New pain shoots through my heart. I hate how he thinks I'm even contemplating not choosing him.

I roll into him more, tilting my head and stating, "You think I'm not choosing you if I don't tell you, but did you ever consider it's the exact opposite?"

"What do you mean?"

I shake my head, so tired of the deceit and position Leo's put me in. The exhaustion from it all overwhelms me. Even if I told Massimo everything and there was no threat to him, I wonder how I could ever admit it. Once I do, he'll never love me again. I'm a monster. No one, not even a dangerous man like Massimo, could ever continue giving his heart to a woman willing to betray him. It doesn't matter if I was under Leo's orders and fearful for my life. I didn't have the courage to try and kill Leo myself or let him end my life. I took the easy way out.

Massimo pushes. "Katiya, what did you mean by not telling me you're choosing me?"

"He'll kill you. If I tell you everything, you'll go after him. It'll be a suicide mission. You'll end up dead, and he'll string your head in his courtyard for the vultures to eat," I declare. My stomach pitches thinking of all the decapitated, bloody heads Leo put on display, sending a message to everyone in his house that he's the boss.

Anger flares on Massimo's cheeks. It's the opposite of what I expected, and now I'm reprimanding myself for once again being naive. Why did I assume he would be thankful I'm trying to look out for him?

His anger turns into disappointment, and in a deadly voice, he proclaims, "I've been wrong about you."

My chest tightens. I stay quiet as my heart continues to break into millions of pieces. This is it. There will be no more us after this conversation.

"You don't know the first thing about me, do you?"

Confused, I question, "What do you mean?"

"If you knew me, you'd know that I'm not scared of Leo Abruzzo. The only one who will have access to anyone's head is me. When I get done with him, his body will be in *my* possession. It'll be mutilated beyond recognition and tossed to the dogs. When the bones are the only thing left, those will disappear into thin air. And you know what else?"

The hairs on my neck rise. I slowly shake my head.

Massimo's eyes darken. "I'll enjoy every minute of torturing him."

20

Massimo

THERE'S SO MUCH ANGER FLARING THROUGH MY BONES, IT'S hard to maintain my composure. I promised myself I wouldn't talk to Katiya about this until we got to Bora Bora. If I got her far away from New York and Leo, I assumed she'd open up and tell me what's going on.

My plan to distract both of us until we're in the sunshine failed. I couldn't keep my mind off it. The need to make it clear to her I knew she was hiding things from me only grew more intense.

I reprimand myself for screwing all this up.

Her hesitation to divulge the truth and assumption I can't handle Leo isn't doing much to help me keep my cool. I'm giving her every benefit of the doubt, but Papà's nagging voice is growing louder in my head.

It happens to the best of us.

We fall for an enemy.

My gut twists. I'm running out of time. My family and the O'Connors know the Feds were watching Katiya. They are aware Leo was visiting her. I need an explanation and fast. Not only to prove my family wrong but to protect my dolce from whatever is going on. And if I don't get to the bottom of this, I don't trust my family to not take matters into their own hands.

I should have killed that bastard months ago.

The more time passes and she doesn't speak, the more agitated I get. I seethe, "You think I'm weaker than that thug?"

"No! I never said that," she claims.

"But you choose not to trust me enough to protect you from whatever this is," I accuse.

She closes her eyes, whispering, "Massimo—"

"Don't sugarcoat it, Katiya. One thing I'm not is stupid," I interject.

She stares at me. Anguish is all over her expression. She turns away, and a tear drips down her cheek.

It cuts me to the core. I always assumed I was immune to others affecting me in this way, but it's clear I'm not. I clench my jaw, take several controlled breaths, and reach for her chin. I force her to look at me and ask, "Are you working for the Abruzzos? And don't you dare lie to me."

Her bottom lip trembles. She scrunches her face, and her tears become a solid stream.

275

My heart drops. I don't need her to answer. I can't deny it anymore. Everything about the truth makes me naive, and what I just told her I wasn't—stupid.

Rage builds inside me, boiling my blood. Part of me wishes I didn't know this information. The other part curses myself for being such a fool. I snarl, "What do you do for them?"

Her entire body trembles. She chokes out, "Massimo. I-I-I didn't want any part of it. I swear I didn't. I-I love you."

I grind my molars. For the first time ever, I question if she does. If she's working for the Abruzzos, she's one of them.

How can an Abruzzo love a Marino when they hate us as much as we hate them?

Does this new information change everything I feel toward her?

I wish it didn't hurt, but it does. If only I didn't love her or imagine us married, spending our lives together.

Why did I let myself fall so hard?

I hurl, "You didn't want any part of what?"

"What Leo wants me to do."

"What's that?"

She puts her shaking hands over her face.

"Stop stalling!" I order as another thought pops into my mind. I swallow my pride, ignore the pain in my heart, and ask, "Did you lie to me about what Ludis and Leo did to you?"

Shame fills her face. She wipes it, but it's pointless. "I didn't lie about that."

"No? How do I know you didn't tell me that just to fool me?" I angrily reply.

She lifts her chin. "You think I'd lie about that? You think I have it in me to make up the gruesome things they did to me?"

Guilt eats me. The sick feeling I always get when I think about what she told me spins in my gut. When I got her to open up, the detailed account of their sordid actions made me nauseous.

I sigh, softening my voice, and admitting what I shouldn't. "Make me believe you, Katiya. More than anything, I want to trust you and believe what you tell me. But you can't continue this lie anymore. The Feds have you on tape. They recorded your meetings with Leo."

"What?" she asks, the color draining from her cheeks. "I-I don't understand. Why would they be watching me? I've not done anything illegal."

I glance at the ceiling, working through my frustration about all of this. Then I refocus on her, stating, "You're meeting with Abruzzos. That's enough for them to be interested in you."

"I didn't want to," she claims again.

Tense silence fills the air. My insides quiver, mimicking her body. "Time's up. I need to know everything. Now."

Emotions plague her expression. She reaches for my face and firmly repeats, "I didn't want any part of this. I love you. I need you to believe me."

I remove her hands and reply, "Keep the love talk to yourself. Spill it."

She swipes at her cheeks and sniffles. Her voice cracks as she says, "I don't know where to start."

"Pick a place," I demand.

She closes her eyes, takes a few breaths, then pins her glistening blues on me. "I lied about how I escaped Leo."

"Go on. I'm listening," I tell her, crossing my arms over my chest, trying to stop the anger from burning through my lungs.

She hugs her knees then divulges, "I got too old for him. He...he brought a new girl to the house. Then he moved me into the brownstone and told me I needed to work at the library. I was responsible for my living expenses except for housing."

My chest tightens. "And what were you supposed to do at the library? Were you there to make sure my sister was held captive?"

"No! I swear! A long time passed where I only went to work. I convinced myself Leo had forgotten about me. One day, Donato showed up at the library. I-I didn't even know who he was, and I swear I had nothing to do with Arianna's kidnapping! I never lied about that!" she claims.

I breathe through more anger. I kick myself for not taking Donato out when I could have. He should never have gotten to my sister.

"You have to believe me!"

I'm not willing to acknowledge whether I do or don't. Until I know everything, I'm unsure what to think. I reply, "So he put you in the library so Donato would get access?"

She shakes her head. "No. I don't think so. I mean, maybe it was part of it, but I'm unsure. It...it..." She bites her lip and scrunches her face.

"It what?" I seethe, wanting answers and fast.

She swallows hard. "You wouldn't stop coming in."

My stomach pitches. "What are you talking about?"

"You kept coming into the library. Leo...he...he always has people watching me. I never know who. Even Alicia surprised me. I had no idea."

The hairs on my neck rise. "Alicia? What does she have to do with this?"

Katiya releases a long breath. "She's one of them. I found out the other day. The Abruzzos are always watching me. No matter what, I can't escape, and they'll always know what I'm doing."

The pit in my stomach grows. I blurt out, "I told Alicia where we're going."

Katiya nods. "I know. I'm hoping she tells Leo and he doesn't disprove, or he'll have my head when I return. It's why I didn't ask for time off. I didn't have his permission. I already got in trouble for moving in with you."

"Trouble? How?"

"Do you know Tommy Abruzzo? He's his head guy," she relays.

I grunt. "Yeah, I know the douchebag."

She nods. "Well, he came into the library. It's how I found out Alicia is an Abruzzo. They even used to date or something."

I rise and pace the small space, tugging on my hair.

"Massimo?" Katiya asks.

"I'll be back in a minute. Don't leave this room," I command.

"What's wrong?" she frets.

I turn in the doorway. "Leo knows where we're going. We can't go there."

More anxiety floods her features. "But he'll be even more pissed if he sends his guys to follow me and I'm not there."

I bark, "Jesus, Katiya. When are you going to understand I will protect you from him? Do you honestly think I'm allowing you anywhere near him when we get back?"

She rises on her knees. "He'll kill me."

"I will protect you," I insist.

"You-you can't! You don't know what he's capable of doing. I-I've seen it. I've experienced it," she shrieks.

I open and close my fists at my sides. She could be telling the truth or lying, but my gut says she wouldn't be so terrified if she weren't being honest. I can only imagine what Leo exposed her to that she hasn't discussed with me. Yet, I still need her to understand I'm capable of way more than Leo Abruzzo. I reiterate, "I need you to believe in me. If Leo attempts to come after you, he'll have to get through me first. And that's not happening."

The fear doesn't leave her face.

I sigh, take two steps back to the bed, and kiss her on the head. I wish I could turn off my affection for her, but it's impossible. I state, "I'll be back in a few moments."

She reaches up and grasps my bicep. "Massimo."

I freeze.

She opens her mouth then hesitates.

"What is it, dolce?"

Her face crumples. She chokes out, "I do love you. More than anything."

Pain shoots through my heart. I want to stay and fix this. It's what I do—solve problems. But I don't even know what I'm solving, nor can I afford to have Leo's guys showing up in Bora Bora. I reply, "We'll talk more when I return." I leave the bedroom and shut the door. I go straight to the cockpit and open the door.

"Massimo. Something wrong?" Sy, the co-pilot, asks.

"We can't go to Bora Bora," I blurt out.

Sy, and my other pilot, Josh, exchange a worried look. Both of them are former Air Force fighter pilots. They've experienced war and secret missions.

Josh questions, "Anything we need to be aware of?"

"I just learned we may be followed to Bora Bora. I'm not looking for company," I state.

Josh nods. "Got it. Anywhere you want us to divert to? We'll need to change the flight plan and have it approved."

MAGGIE COLE

There are so many things racing through my mind, I can't even think of anywhere besides Bora Bora. I answer, "I'm open to suggestions. Somewhere far from New York and preferably with sunshine."

"Hmm. It's still pretty chilly in Europe this time of year," Sy states.

Josh suggests, "The Maldives should be nice. You been there?"

"No, can't say I have. It's nice?" I ask.

"Yeah. They have some higher-end luxury resorts. I'm sure Chanel can book something before we land," he answers.

"Done. Let me know if there are any issues with the change in the flight plan," I order, then shut the door. I spin.

Chanel smirks, "On it, boss."

"Thanks. I want the most private suite you can find."

"Consider it done," she chirps, pulling out her laptop.

I return to the bedroom and find Katiya sitting on the edge of the mattress. I shut the door and take a seat next to her.

"Where are we going?" she asks.

"The Maldives."

More worry appears on her.

I tug her onto my lap. "Listen to me, Katiya. In order for me to protect you, I need to know everything. Even if you think it puts you or me in more danger, I have to know everything. Why was Leo visiting you, and what did you mean when you said I wouldn't stop coming in?"

She takes a few shaky breaths then answers, "To the library. You kept coming to visit me and asking me out. Someone—maybe it was Alicia—told Leo. I'm unsure how many people Leo has watching me. But someone told him you were interested."

It feels like a claw is scraping my gut. "So he wanted you to spy on me?"

She nods.

The claw scrapes faster. I push, "And find out what?"

She bites on her lip. It's trembling again, as are her hands. I tighten my arms around her. She lifts her chin higher, admitting, "He wants to know who all your jewelry suppliers are and how to contact them."

Bile rises in my throat. My family has been in the gem business for years. No other crime family has been able to successfully tap into the market as we have. I swallow hard and try to stay calm, demanding, "And?"

She furrows her eyebrows. "What do you mean?"

As calm as I'm trying to stay, I fail. I belt out, "So you were going to try to find out and give him what he wanted?"

"I didn't want to."

"But you were?"

Her cheeks turn maroon, making her blues appear brighter. My cock twitches, and I hate myself for it. Even when she's telling me she'd betray me, I find her more beautiful than anyone I've ever met. She closes her eyes and says, "I didn't want to. I..." She licks her lips and swallows hard. Her eyes open. She squares her shoulders, asserting in her cold demeanor, "It doesn't matter, does it? Now that you know the truth, there's only one ending to this, isn't there?"

My pulse pounds between my ears. I ask, "Meaning what?"

Her chest rises and falls faster. She tries to maintain her cool exterior, but her voice cracks, and tears fill her eyes. She declares, "There's no more us."

My heart shatters into millions of pieces. The air in my lungs turns stale, like it's trying to suffocate me. The thought of her and I not existing as an us almost kills me. I shouldn't feel this way. Common sense tells me to turn her in to my family and let them deal with her, since there's no way I can. Maybe it means I'm weak, but I couldn't hurt her if my life depended on it.

Her next words don't give me any comfort. "It doesn't matter if I really do love you, does it?"

I continue to stay silent, fighting the emotions expanding in my chest.

Is it possible she does love me and just didn't know how to get out of Leo's grasp?

She was going to betray me.

She had no choice.

She could have told me at any time. I would have protected her.

Ludis and Leo abused her in some of the worst ways. She's petrified of them.

It doesn't excuse her willingness to betray me.

Or does it?

Is it possible we can get past this now that I know the truth?

My silence only makes things worse.

She straightens her back, sitting as tall as possible. With the cold voice she normally reserves for others, she asks, "Can I make a request?"

"What's that?" I question.

She looks at the floor, quietly asking, "After you kill me, can you sprinkle my ashes over my father's grave? It's an unmarked city plot since I had no money to buy a headstone when he died. But I can write down how to find it."

Everything I thought I knew about myself, I now question. I assumed if anyone ever conspired to betray me, I'd take them out without a second thought. I'm unsure if I'm more upset because she doesn't understand how deep my love for her goes and is presuming I'll kill her, or if I'm more pissed I don't even know if I have the guts to turn her over to my family so they can do it for me.

The only thing I'm sure of is that the thought of her dead and sprinkled over her father's city burial plot makes me want to die alongside her.

I officially have the biggest problem I've ever faced.

21

Katiya

"WHO SAID I'LL KILL YOU?" MASSIMO ASKS.

I glance at him. "I just told you everything."

He clenches his jaw, assessing me. I force myself not to squirm under his leer. In a flat voice, he states, "Maybe I'll keep you locked up in a room. Make you suffer longer for your sins."

I tear my eyes off him, focusing on the floor and twisting my fingers in my lap. The last thing I wanted was to be in this position. He's hurt by my admission. It's written all over his face, and I've always known this day was coming. Fighting more tears, I mumble, "Eventually, I'll die. Could you at least give me my final wish?"

I've only been to my father's burial plot a few times. It's hard for me to go. Everything that's happened to me since he died brings me shame. As soon as one situation ends, another one seems to pop up. I'm not living the life my father intended for me to experience. If he were still alive, it'd kill him. And I hate how I can't afford a proper tombstone for him. At least if I'm sprinkled on top of the dirt, he won't be alone.

Massimo replies, "Who says I'll cremate you?"

I squeeze my eyes shut. It was stupid of me to make this request. Did I really think the man who holds my fate in his hands would show any mercy upon me? I mutter, "Forget I said anything."

Tense silence fills the small room. The whir of the engines, Massimo's deep breathing, and the pounding of my heart are the only sounds. I can't take the stress between us anymore. I rise.

He reaches for my arm. "Where do you think you're going?"

My lips and hands tremble harder. I spin, responding, "I'm tired."

He lifts the covers and tugs me on the bed in a quick move. I gasp, and he slides next to me and spoons me. "Then it's time to sleep."

The warmth of his body is like a torture device. I sink into it, fitting next to him like a puzzle piece. It feels safe and full of love, but there's no hiding the reality of our situation. It chokes me up further. The more I try to hide my emotions inside, the worse the quivering in my belly gets.

He tightens his hold on me, cocooning me against his hard flesh. He sighs then quietly says, "Nothing is happening tonight. Close your eyes and sleep."

Nothing I do allows me to stop shaking. I've never felt so out of control of my emotions. Even when Ludis and Leo would have their way with me, I held a lot inside. Now, it's like I escaped Pandora's box. Every ounce of strength I have is gone. The guilt and shame over my life since my father died thickens. My lungs seem unable to take in any more air. I break down, sobbing.

Massimo sighs, kisses my head, then presses his lips to my ear. "How would you have done it?"

I freeze.

"Tell me your plan," he demands.

Blood pulses in my veins. I sniffle then admit, "I don't know."

He softens his voice, "Please don't lie to me. Not now."

I turn to him. "I swear. I don't know. Leo kept threatening to kill me since I wasn't giving him any information."

Massimo adds, "But he didn't."

"Not yet. He would have," I insist.

We hit more turbulence. The jet shakes harder and louder than before. Everything rattles around us, and I wince from the sound.

He slides his hands over my ears, pinning his blues on me until the noise subsides.

After everything I told him, the way he continues to try and protect me only hurts my heart more. I blurt out, "I'm sorry. I love you. I swear I do."

He clenches his jaw. His chest rises and falls faster as he studies me, inches from my mouth.

I slide my hands on the sides of his head and beg, "Please. Tell me you believe me. Even if you still kill me. Just tell me you know I love you."

He sniffs hard, saying nothing, then glances at my lips.

My instincts take over. I lean closer and kiss him, parting his lips with my tongue and putting everything I feel into it.

He doesn't return my affection.

I scoot closer, restating, "I love you." I slip my tongue back into his mouth.

He resists for a moment, then he palms my ass, tugging me as close to him as possible. He finally reciprocates, sliding his tongue against mine and matching my urgency.

In a few minutes, we're naked. He cages his body over mine, supporting himself on his elbows, holding my face while he continues kissing me.

My legs wrap around his hips. I lift them up, pushing myself toward him. He thrusts inside me until I'm filled with his cock. As his erection pushes against my walls, I gasp, holding my arms around his shoulders and digging my nails into his back.

"You betrayed me," he mutters through a kiss, thrusting slowly.

"I'm sorry. I didn't want to," I reply, tears falling from my eyes. I tighten my limbs around him, as if it'll somehow solve our issues and keep us together.

"How could you?" he mumbles, dragging his teeth down my neck.

I whimper, saying nothing.

"Answer me," he orders, biting the curve of my neck.

I blurt out, "I'd rather have you kill me than him." A flood of tears bursts through the damn.

He lifts his head out of my neck and positions it over my face, freezing mid-thrust. "You think I'm not capable of what Leo is?"

"No. I know you are. But I'd rather die by your hand than his," I reiterate.

"Why?"

"Because I'd deserve your wrath. I-I don't want him to get any other part of me," I declare, sobbing harder.

The coldness in his eyes fades. He resumes his slow thrusts, firmly stating, "I could have protected you. If you only trusted me."

"I do trust you," I claim.

"You didn't think I could handle Leo," he adds, returning to the spot on my neck he bit and sucking.

"Oh God!" I cry out. A sharp pain mixes with a shot of endorphins. My pussy clenches his shaft.

"We're so good together," he mumbles.

"Yes," I agree, then moan as he increases the friction on my walls.

"Your lack of faith destroys us," he proclaims.

"No! I-I...oh... Massimo!" I shudder as a wave of heat courses through me.

"Don't you dare come," he barks.

Sweet sensations ripple through all my cells. "I...oh...oh..."

"If you trust me, show me. Fully submit," he orders, sliding a hand between us and manipulating my clit.

"Massimo! Oh God!" I shriek.

He slows his thrusts, matching the rotation of his fingers. "You love me, you say? Then show me," he demands.

"Please," I beg, ready to fall over the edge, putting everything I have into not releasing.

He sucks on my breast, and my body arches into his. He does it to the other and drags his teeth on the edges of my nipples.

"Mass—"

"Who am I?" he growls.

"Daddy! Oh God! Please," I plead. More adrenaline rushes into my cells, but I refrain from letting it overpower me.

"What does your daddy do for you?" he barks.

"H-he...oh..."

"Answer me!" he commands, increasing the speed of his hand and thrusts.

"Makes me feel...oh...so...good," I barely get out.

"What else," he snarls.

"Come," I whisper in a hoarse voice.

He moves his lips an inch from mine. In an angry voice, he insists, "I protect you."

I nod, breath hitched, trying to keep my eyes open.

"From everyone," he says, his chest pushing into mine harder with each inhale he takes.

I lean up to kiss him, but he retreats.

He creates more tension in my body and demands, "Do you understand how this works between us?"

Bright light hits my eyes. I fight my orgasm, unable to answer.

"I'm the one you trust," he declares, thrusting faster. "I'm the one who protects you. There won't be any more lies between us going forward."

All I can reply is, "I love you." Sweat pops out on my skin. A wave of heat rushes to my cheeks, making me dizzy.

"Tell me you agree, Katiya," he orders.

"I... I... I agree...oh God! Please let me come. I...can't...oh..."

"Don't you come," he barks again.

"Massimo," I cry out, fresh tears falling as my body clutches his shaft. "Please!"

"You're not coming, dolce. You'll take more of me," he states.

"Please," I beg again. I'm at the point I love the most. Everything is overwhelming. The sensations shooting through every atom of my being are ones I crave when we're not together. All I smell and feel is him. It's as if he's a part of me. Everything about giving him my full submission and letting him take over control of my body is pure heaven. I dig my nails deeper into his flexing shoulder muscles as he pounds into me harder.

He reaches toward the headboard, and the sound of metal hits my ears. "Hands up," he demands.

I obey, and he cuffs my wrists. The light in his eyes changes to the crazed, dominant man I'm obsessed with, but everything about it appears darker than normal. A morsel of fear pops in me, turning into tingles racing down my spine.

A whirring sound fills the room. Massimo rises on his knees and reaches above us.

I glance up, and my butterflies dance. Two more cuffs, one on each side of us, lower to the bed. He quickly snaps them around my ankles and orders, "Legs in the air, spread out."

I lift my limbs, and he hits a button on the headboard. The chains move up until pulled taut. I think I'm in position, but he pushes my legs closer to the headboard so my ass is in the air. The chain continues to get shorter until I can't move an inch.

The whirring stops. Massimo moves his face in front of me, dipping his fingers inside my wet heat and circling his thumb on my clit.

I whimper, wondering how much more I can take. I whisper, "Please."

His lips curl. "Please, what?"

"Please, Daddy. Make me come," I beg, swallowing hard.

"You want what I give you?" he asks, arching his eyebrows.

"You. All of you. I-I need you. Please forgive me," I blurt out, wanting him to tell me the impossible.

"Why should I believe you?" he questions.

I catch my breath, finding more control within me not to come, and reply, "Deep down. You know I love you."

"Prove it," he says again. Then, "Give me your full submission."

"You...oh God...oh...y-you have it," I choke out, then incoherent sounds fly out of my mouth.

"Then tell me you deserve a new punishment," he orders.

"P-punish me," I agree, willing to do anything to regain his trust and love.

As soon as the words are out of my mouth, his hand slaps my already-sensitive ass. The fingers of his other stay inside me. He scissors his fingers while rubbing my clit faster.

"Yes! Punish me," I whisper, closing my eyes and yanking on the cuffs, but they don't move. A tremor rolls through my bones.

"Look at me," he growls.

I pin my blues on his. Every emotion swirls in his dark orbs, making him appear wild and out of control. It's as if he's more dangerous than ever.

All it does is intensify my sensations. I should be petrified, but all I want is whatever punishment he'll give me.

"If you come, we're through. There will be no second chance unless you earn it," he states.

"I won't," I say, determined to be his once again.

"You'll thank me each time," he demands.

"Yes, Daddy."

His lips twitch. Concentration deepens on his face. He slides a hand over my sweaty thigh and pulls it back, slapping my ass cheek.

"Th-thank you, Daddy," I say, then moan as he teases my G-spot, fighting the O-train from annihilating me.

He leans down, rubs the sting, and suctions his lips to my clit.

"Oh...my...oh!" I cry out.

He flicks his tongue and smacks me again.

"Thank y-you, D-Daddy," I manage to get out.

"Louder," he orders, reaches for the wall, and turns a dial. He repositions his mouth on my pussy and resumes my punishment.

Sweat coats the sheets underneath me, sticking the fabric to my skin. Tears roll down my face, and my voice turns raspy. Every smack he gives me, I thank him. Each flick of his tongue on my clit or finger inside me pushes me past any previous limit. I muster all my self-control, somehow refraining from losing all inhibitions. My body buzzes from the swirling mix of pain and pleasure.

"Please. I-I can't do this anymore," I finally beg, feeling like I'm bathing in a mess of my bodily fluids and the smell of my arousal.

He slides onto his knees, moves flush against my ass, and pushes his cock inside me.

"Daddy!" I cry out.

He grasps my hands, pinning them and his forearms to the headboard. A salty bead of his sweat drips off his chin, hitting my lips. He takes several ragged breaths, not tearing his gaze off mine, then begins to thrust hard and fast.

"Please," I scream. "I... I...oh..."

"Thank me," he demands.

"Th-thank you, Daddy," I whisper, blinking hard to try and keep him in focus, but my body begins to betray me.

"What else?" he demands. Tingles erupt on my ass cheek from his warm pelvis every time he thrusts.

"I love you. I'm-I'm sorry, Daddy!" I blurt out. Then beg, "Please, I-I can't—"

"Come," he shouts.

Adrenaline surges through my exhausted body. Endorphins attack me like a machine gun firing at its enemy. His cock pumps hard, expanding my walls until I think he'll tear through them.

He groans, thrusting faster. I spasm around him, and a stream of my juice erupts from me, drenching us.

His orgasm seems to go on forever, continuing to keep me high. When he finally releases everything into me, he effortlessly unlocks the cuffs and cages his body over mine.

Our breaths merge, our chests heaving against the other. He reaches for the wall and turns off the microphone. Then he stares at me, still catching his breath.

"I'm sorry. Please forgive me," I beg again.

He rolls onto his back, tugs me into his arms, and wraps his legs around my body. His voice turns calm. All the anger disappears. He commands, "Tell me how it'll be going forward, Katiya."

Hope ignites that a miracle might occur for the first time in my life. I sniffle, answering, "I trust you and don't lie to you. You protect me."

He wipes the tears off my cheek then pecks me on the lips. "That's right. But do you believe it?"

"Yes," I answer, still fearful Leo will harm him or me but wanting Massimo's claim to be the truth.

"Are you sure? I can't have you wavering on this, dolce."

I swallow my emotions, nodding. "Yes. I'm sure."

His eyes darken. "Then from here on out, I'm making the decisions. And you won't fight me on them."

"Okay," I agree, sliding my palm on his cheek.

He gives me another chaste kiss then asserts, "We need to clean up. Let's get in the shower."

"So...umm...you still want me?" I ask, new tears forming.

He tucks a sweaty lock of my hair behind my ear. "Don't ask me questions you already know the answers to."

Relief rushes through my cells. I kiss him. "I really am sorry I didn't tell you."

His face hardens as he pauses to study me. New fear ignites that he's changed his mind. "I'm in love with you, dolce. If you make a fool out of me again, you might as well cut my heart out. But there won't be another chance."

"I won't need to ask for one," I promise. "Please, believe me."

He assesses me some more. Then shock fills me as he states, "When we land, we're getting married. And you aren't taking your birth control pills anymore."

22

MC

Massimo

MY DOLCE'S GLISTENING EYES WIDEN. I DEBATE WHETHER SHE'S in shock or isn't interested in marrying me and having my babies. I give her a moment, hating the doubt I have in my mind and pissed off that I'm unprepared to ask her the right way. But everything about today makes our reality glare in my face.

Katiya finally speaks, "I don't understand."

"You don't want to marry me?" I blurt out.

She climbs onto my lap, straddling me, claiming, "No. That's not it."

"You don't want my babies?"

Her chest rises and falls faster. An expression I'm unsure about floods her. She bobs her head side to side, answering, "Kids? I don't know what kind of mother I'd make."

The anxiety in my chest lessens. I stroke the side of her head and insist, "You'd make a wonderful mother to our children."

"I would?"

"Yes."

"How can you be so sure?" She licks her lips and scrunches her face.

I cover her heart. "Because of this."

She closes her eyes then mumbles, "I don't know how to take care of a baby."

"You'll learn. Plus, we'll have help." I move my hand and cup her cheek. In a firm tone, I declare, "If you're my wife, you'll have my babies. And I'm not getting any younger, so it's now or never. Plus, you're a perfect age to start popping them out."

Pink creeps up her neck. She replies, "I just told you what kind of person I am. Now you want to marry me and have babies?"

It's not abnormal for me to make decisions with my gut, even when others wouldn't. When this happens, rationale doesn't align with my choices. In some ways, it's what makes men fearful of me. It's also always paid off for me. I take bets others won't, and it's helped me get ahead in many ways. So while this might be considered crazy, I'm trusting my instincts, which haven't failed me in the past.

Maybe I should be running from Katiya. If any of my brothers' women were plotting to betray them, they'd get as far away from them as possible. Yet it's only made me more determined to fully make her mine. While it's true I'll experience great satisfaction when Leo finds out she's no longer going to do his dirty work, it isn't only that. She'll be untouchable under the umbrella of my family's protection. He'll know I've won, and he's lost.

Then I'm going to show him my real wrath.

Still, she stares at me with those big blue eyes, full of so many doubts and questions. I assert, "I thought you said you loved me."

"I do!" she insists.

"Then what's the real problem?" I inquire, my anxiety growing. The longer she doesn't change her perplexed expression, the tighter my chest gets. I add, "If you love me, you'll marry me—willingly."

She gasps slightly. "Willingly? You would force me?"

My heart races faster. Everything about Gianni and Cara's wedding was unkosher. They had a long history of being on and off. Cara hated Gianni when they got hitched. While they didn't share all the details of their unethical nuptials, it's not a secret he forced her down the aisle.

However, it's a question I don't think I should answer. If Katiya didn't want to marry me, I'd have a harder time protecting her. The best way to ensure that is for her to become my wife. And I don't want to be like my brother, but there's no way I'm not marrying her. If she said no, I'd find some way to lure her down the aisle just like Gianni did with Cara.

As much as I despise Katiya's admission that she was working for Leo to betray me, I can't let her go. Learning about it only intensified my urge to keep her as mine forever. I'm not blind to what she could have done, but she didn't follow through with it.

Plus, I'm a man who tries to put myself in others' positions. It's not for empathy. It's usually to get in their minds and see how I can take advantage of them. It's a skill I worked hard at developing. I saw early on how you can manipulate someone if you know their situation. So as unhappy as I am about Katiya's betrayal, I understand why she thought she had no other choice.

Leo plays mind games to scare others into doing what he wants. Katiya would have witnessed many of his fear tactics. On top of that, he spent years brutalizing her. A man in my position, one who understands violence, torture, and threats, knows Leo inside and out. I'm too aware of how those past events won't fade easily. They'll never fully disappear from Katiya's mind. I'd do anything to change that reality, but some things you can't alter.

So the truth drives me to make sure I keep her so close, she'll never have another opportunity to waiver again.

She'll never again be at Leo's mercy.

There won't be any opportunity for her to get caught in any other thug's trap again.

"Massimo? You would force me?" she repeats, horror growing in her expression.

I wouldn't force her, but I would manipulate things until I convinced her to say yes. Still, I tell a half lie. "No. I wouldn't force you. Now, tell me you want to marry me."

More silence fills the room. She bites on her lip and pulls on her fingers. The thumping of my pulse between my ears grows louder. She tilts her head then asks, "How would that work?"

"You say I do. I say I do. We work extra hard to put my baby in your belly," I tease, wiggling my eyebrows.

A tiny laugh escapes her lips, then her smile falls. Lines form on her forehead as she pins her brows together. More confusion plagues her expression. She replies, "How does it work with Leo?"

Anger ignites in my belly. Leo's on borrowed time right now. I thought I made it clear, yet she still doesn't trust I'll handle him. I snap, "You still don't believe me when I say I'll protect you, do you?"

She opens her mouth then shuts it.

"Say whatever it is you're thinking," I demand, irritated over her lack of belief in me.

She scoots closer and places her hands on the sides of my head. She confesses, "This is all new to me, Massimo. I've lived in fear of Leo for so long, I..." She turns away and blows out a big breath of air.

Her statement tugs at my heartstrings. That monster put her through so much that I can't even fathom how she survived. I soften my voice, turn her chin toward me, and demand, "Finish your sentence. I want to know what you're thinking."

She squeezes her eyes shut then pins them on me, tugging on my heart strings further. She frets, "I don't know how to do all this."

"Do what exactly?"

She slowly shrugs, confessing, "Be Mrs. Massimo Marino. Have babies. Become part of your family when they already hate me. Once they find out what I was going to do to you..." She takes a deep breath then continues, "They'll never accept me."

I tighten my arms around her. "Do you trust me?"

"Yes. You're the only person in the world I trust."

"Is that true?" I question.

"Yes."

"Okay. Then stop worrying. You marry me, become my wife, and all the baby stuff we'll figure out like every other couple. You leave my family to me. They will accept you. In fact, I promise you, they'll eventually love you as much as I do," I vow, determined to fulfill my statement.

"Love me? How?"

"Leave it to me, dolce."

The anxiety doesn't leave her face. A few moments pass, and she yawns. I realize I'm tired, too, and notice the red in her eyes. I slide down the bed and tug her with me. She rests her head on my chest, palming my heart, then asks in a tiny voice, "Are you serious about marrying me?"

I tilt her chin so I can look in her eyes. "I've never been so sure about anything in my life."

She blinks hard. "Really?"

I peck her on the lips. "Yes. Now, tell me you'll marry me and have my babies."

She softly laughs. A spark lights in her exhausted orbs. She smiles then nods. "Okay. I'll marry you."

Happiness shoots through every atom of my being. I tighten my arm around her and slowly kiss her, deepening it for several moments until my erection returns. I hold in my groan and retreat, asserting, "Good girl. Now try to sleep. We still have a long flight ahead of us."

Silence fills the cabin, but she breaks it. "Massimo?"

"Yeah, dolce."

She clears her throat. "Are you sure your family will learn to accept me?"

I refrain from sighing and muster all the conviction I have. "Yes. Once they know you're not a threat and get to know you, they'll shower you with affection. You'll see."

She takes a shaky breath then curls into me further. She yawns again.

I kiss her head, ordering, "Go to sleep. When you wake up, we'll be in the Maldives."

"I don't even know where that's located. See how naive your future wife is," she admits, but there's also excitement in her voice, which only makes me happier.

"It's an island country in the Indian Ocean. It's part of South Asia," I inform.

"Wow!" she sleepily exclaims.

I chuckle. "What's wow about it?"

She pins her tired gaze on mine. "I never thought I'd go to Asia."

I smile and press my lips to hers, murmuring, "I plan on taking you all over the world. Create a list when we get home. I'll make sure we go anywhere you want."

Her eyes widen. "Seriously?"

"Yeah, dolce. Now, go to sleep," I repeat.

It doesn't take long before she's asleep. The sound of her breathing pattern relaxes me, and I fall asleep until the loudspeaker dings several times. I barely hear the pilot announce, "Please put on your belts to prepare for landing. We'll be on the ground in the next twenty minutes."

I blink a few times, taking in the small space and realizing I'm on the plane. The events of the day spin in my head.

She was going to betray me.

She agreed to marry me.

I'm going to kill Leo.

"Mm," Katiya whimpers, curling into me further.

I glance down. She looks peaceful, still sleeping, with her long blonde locks slightly tousled.

I lean into her ear. "Dolce, wake up."

"Mm," she replies again, but a smile forms on her lips.

Unable to resist, I press mine to hers. She kisses me back yet doesn't open her eyes.

I chuckle, stroking her hair, stating, "We're going to land soon. Time to open those pretty eyes."

She blinks a few times until her vision focuses on me. Her smile grows. She whispers, "Hey."

More happiness fills me. If I get to wake up next to her every day until my last breath, I'll die a lucky man. Everything about her makes her my dream girl.

She was going to betray me.

It's Leo's fault.

I need to kill him. The sooner, the better.

I push the thoughts out of my head. While the threats loom in New York, they aren't in the Maldives. No one knows we're here, nor will they find us. For the next week, I'm doing nothing but appreciate the view of my dolce in a string bikini with the water glistening around her. I'll rub suntan lotion on every inch of her body and make her beg me every day for hours.

I peck her on the lips and sit up, taking her with me. "We should go out to the main cabin and put our belts on."

She arches her eyebrows in amusement, biting her bottom lip.

"What's so funny?" I ask.

"I didn't picture you as Mr. Safety," she teases.

"Ha ha. You'll thank me when we have a rough landing one of these days. Come on, let's go," I order, rising and opening the closet. I hand her a set of clothes and put fresh ones on myself while she dresses. Then I hold out my hand.

She takes it, and I pull her up, then lead her to our seats. We buckle our belts, and Chanel appears.

"Ah. I was coming to wake you, but I see you're up and ready for landing," she chirps.

I slide my arm around Katiya. "Did you secure a good resort?"

"The best," she boasts.

"Great. Did you book for yourselves as well?" I inquire. Wherever I go, my jet stays on the ground until I'm ready to fly. If anything pops up, my staff is never far and can get me back in the air.

Chanel smiles bigger. "Everything is booked for the pilots and me. Do you need anything before we land?"

"No. We're all set. I hope you brought your bathing suit," I answer.

She beams, "You know me. I've always got one stashed in my bag."

"That's good," I respond.

Chanel nods and leaves.

When she's no longer visible, I lean into Katiya's ear. "Who's more upset? You or Chanel?"

Katiya turns to me. "Upset? What do you mean?"

My cock turns hard, thinking about the beginning of our journey. I answer, "I didn't let her check out your bare ass again."

My dolce's cheeks flame red. She bites hard on her lip, and her chest rises and falls faster. To my surprise, she blurts out, "Why am I into it?"

"Others watching you?"

She nods. "Yes. I-I'm not into women, but..." She blows out a nervous breath. Her eyes dart to the floor.

I force her to look at me then wait several moments until she squirms in her seat. I claim, "But the thought of Chanel, or anyone, male or female, listening and watching you makes that tight pussy of yours clench."

She inhales deeply, admitting, "Yes."

I tuck a lock of her hair behind her ear, put my lips on her lobe, then murmur, "There's nothing wrong with what you like. Hell, I love it. The thought of others seeing and hearing you when I know they can't have you is hot as fuck, little dolce. And you shouldn't feel any shame in it."

"No?" she whispers.

I retreat then command, "Look at me."

She turns, locking eyes with me.

I declare, "Let others look. Let them listen. But there's one rule you can never break."

"What rule is that?" she asks.

I fist her hair, tug her head back, then position my face over hers. She gasps and reaches for my thigh, digging her nails into it. My erection strains against my zipper. Everything about her turns me on. Right now is no exception. I assert, "There will be no touching. Are we clear?"

"I don't want anyone else to touch me," she proclaims.

Satisfaction rages through me. "Good. If anyone does, I'll kill them—especially once you're my wife."

Her lips twitch, and my heart soars higher. "So I didn't dream you asked me to marry you?"

My mouth curls into an unstoppable grin. I declare, "No, dolce. Nor did you imagine everything about the babies. And I'm going to spend all week trying to knock you up."

A mix of anxiety and excitement fills her expression.

Arrogance grows inside me. I state, "Your panties are turning wet again, aren't they?"

The flames on her cheeks turn maroon. She admits quietly, "Yes."

I grunt. "Take them off."

"What?"

"You heard me." I unclasp her belt.

She slithers out of the thong.

I grab it, sniff deeply, then bunch it in my fist. I order, "Buckle up."

She obeys just as the jet begins to descend to the ground.

Within minutes we're on the tarmac, and the seat-belt sign turns off. I hit the speaker, saying, "Chanel, can you come here?"

"Sure," she replies, and within seconds, she appears next to my seat. "What can I do for you, Mr. Marino?"

"I have a job for you."

"Oh?" Chanel asks.

I dangle the delicate thong in front of her and order, "Hold on to these until our return trip."

Her eyes light up. She glances at Katiya, and my dolce's lips slightly tremble. Chanel replies, "No problem, Mr. Marino. Will you need them washed?"

"Do you want to wash them?" I ask.

Katiya loudly inhales, holding her breath.

Chanel glances at her and then pins her gaze on mine. "No, sir."

"Why not?"

Chanel smirks. "I'd rather look at them all week and think about what you're doing to her."

"Because you're attracted to women?" I ask, which is a question I've always wondered.

She shakes her head. "No, sir. I only like men."

I'm half surprised, half not. I inquire, "But you like to watch women?"

Confidence floods her face. She raises her chin, answering, "I like to watch sex. Women and men are both beautiful. Any more questions?"

I hold in my chuckle. "No, Chanel. You've been very helpful. Thank you."

"In that case, have a great week in the Maldives," she replies, winks at Katiya, and disappears with the slightly damp panties.

Katiya

MASSIMO GUIDES ME TO THE DOOR OF THE PLANE, AND I GASP. Clear turquoise water sparkles only a few feet from the runway. A fluffy cloud moves across the sky, and the sun shines even brighter. The warm air feels too good to be true after the cold New York winter that's slowly ending.

I've never seen anything so majestic. It's beyond breathtaking, and I continue gaping, at the top of the stairs.

Massimo chuckles, boasting, "Pretty amazing, huh?"

I tear my eyes off the landscape, turning toward him. "This is incredible. Pinch me so I know it's real!"

"It's real, dolce." He pinches my ass.

I jump, screeching.

He laughs again and states, "I guarantee you it's more fun if we're off the jet."

"Oh! Sorry!" I reply, flustered. I make my way down the staircase, and he follows.

Massimo leads me to a black sedan. The driver opens the door. We get inside, and Massimo says, "Get comfy. It's about an hour to our destination."

There's so much to take in during the trip, I barely take my eyes off the window. White sand beaches, palm trees, and greenery are everywhere. By the time we get to the resort, I can barely contain my excitement.

Then we pull up to where we're staying. A dozen secluded bungalows perch over the water. Each one is about half a mile away from the other. They have private pools, hot tubs, and lounging areas. You can be under the shade or get full sun. I get out of the car and utter, "Holy crap!"

Massimo follows, glancing around. "Not bad for a change in plans. I imagine it feels the same as Bora Bora."

"It's amazing! Who needs Bora Bora when you have the Maldives!" I exclaim, reach up, pull his face toward me, and kiss him.

He grins and squeezes my ass. "I think it's time for you to get that bikini on."

"Don't have to tell me twice!"

"Mr. Marino. Ms. Nikitin. It's nice to have you here. I'm your butler, Dekel. Can I offer you a drink?" a dark-haired man, with an Indian accent, holding a tray of champagne, asks.

Massimo takes two and hands one to me. "Nice to meet you. I assume that's ours?" He points to the bungalow in front of us.

Dekel nods. "It is. Do you want me to show you the main building, or would you prefer to see your bungalow?"

Massimo glances at me in question.

Excitement expands all around me. I clasp my hands together, as if I'm praying, and assert, "Bungalow, please."

Massimo's grin widens. He kisses my hand then says to Dekel, "You heard the woman. Bungalow it is."

I clap then take Massimo's arm. Dekel leads us down a wooden dock. The water's so clear, I can see different brightly colored fish swimming around us. Pockets of soft corals, forming a boulder-type appearance, have a palette of different pastels. Fiery reds and oranges dance among lavender, pink, yellow, and blue species.

We get to our bungalow, and Dekel takes us to the private deck in the front. A dolphin jumps high in the air, creating a splash in the water only a few feet from us.

"Oh my gosh!" I blurt out, overwhelmed with all the tropical beauty.

"That was awesome," Massimo states as two baby dolphins soar through the air simultaneously.

Dekel laughs. "Looks like you've got a show."

"Are they always here?" I ask.

"Quite a bit. We keep a supply of small fish and squids for the guests to feed them," he answers.

"Oh! I want to feed them!" I exclaim.

"Where's the food?" Massimo asks.

"On land. If you like, I'll have a bucket brought down immediately and refill it with fresh fish each morning," Dekel declares.

"That would be great. Thanks," Massimo replies.

"Yes. Thank you," I echo.

"As you can see, you have a private pool, hot tub, sun area, and outdoor dining space. If you prefer to swim in the salt water, the ladder is to your right. Rafts, snorkeling gear, paddleboards, and kayaks are all available," Dekel informs us.

"Where are they?" Massimo asks.

Dekel opens the door to a small outdoor closet. "You'll find everything in here. If there's anything you don't find satisfactory, let me know, but it's all new as of this morning."

"Perfect," Massimo replies.

Dekel motions toward the open doors, saying, "Please, go inside."

I take a few steps then freeze. The inside is as breathtaking as the outside. A king-size bed is covered in white linens and has purple petals strewn on it. Almost the entire building is windows, displaying a magnificent panoramic view.

"The shades can give you more privacy if you desire. It's harder to see inside during the day, but at night, it's so dark here that any light inside will showcase your entire room unless the windows are covered. Many of our guests have everything covered but the one overlooking the ocean. Would you like me to close them each night?" Dekel inquires.

My flutters take off.

Massimo pins his sultry gaze on me, answering, "No. I don't think that will be necessary. If we change our minds, I'll let you know."

Heat filters into my cheeks. Elation flies through my bones. I squeeze my thighs closer together, taking a deep breath as Massimo's eyes drift over my body.

Dekel doesn't flinch. "Very well. This button is the same as on the wall outside. All you have to do is push it, and I'll appear."

"Like magic," I tease, feeling like the weight of the world has been lifted off me.

Dekel grins. "Yes. Fresh towels and toiletries are in the bathroom. Fresh fruit and chocolate are on that tray," he points to a silver-covered dish, then continues, "I instructed the chef to prepare a tray of fresh tuna, fried yams, Aluvi Boakibaa, and Saagu Bondibai for lunch. Will that be okay, or would you prefer something else?"

Massimo slides his arm around my waist, arching his eyebrows and replying, "Not sure what those last two things are, but I think we're open to anything. Our palates are pretty diverse, right, dolce?"

I nod. "Yes. We'll try it all."

"Great. Would you like me to prepare the sun deck for a day of lounging?" Dekel asks.

"Yes, please," Massimo responds.

A bellhop appears with luggage. Dekel instructs him to unpack our things as a server arrives with a cart full of food.

It doesn't take long before Massimo and I are in bathing suits, sitting at the outdoor table, alone at last. I state, "This place is amazing."

"Glad you like it. Hungry?" he asks.

"Starving, actually," I admit, then pick up a spoonful of the little white starchy spheres. Dekel said it was the Saagu Bondibai and made from the spongy cores of tropical palm stems. It resembles rice pudding. I pop it in my mouth and moan. "Mmm."

"Starting with dessert first?" Massimo teases.

"Try this," I order, then hold a spoonful in front of his lips.

He takes it and groans. "It's good."

We take our time, filling our bellies with the local cuisine. When we finish, Dekel magically appears and removes our dishes. Massimo goes over to the lounger and lies down. Instead of following him, I take a few steps to the water's edge and dive in.

The water's the perfect temperature. It's refreshing but not too warm. I swim as far out under the water as I can, until my lungs need fresh air, before popping above the surface. I lean back, run my hands over my hair, and lick the salty water off my lips.

Massimo pops up next to me. "Didn't know you were a swimmer."

Nostalgia runs through me. I admit, "My father used to take me to the ocean once a year in the summer. It wasn't clear like this—well, you know how the water is at the Jersey shore. But he taught me to swim. He said it was an important skill everyone should have."

Massimo grabs my waist.

I wrap my legs around his hips and ask, "Are you standing?"

"Yep." He pecks me on the lips then states, "Your father was right. Glad to see you aren't afraid to get your hair wet."

I scoff. "Contrary to popular belief, I'm pretty simple."

Massimo shakes his head and pushes my wet locks behind my ear. "There's nothing simple about you, dolce."

Whenever he looks at me like he is right now, the zings I always get return. It's as if he can somehow see right through to my soul. My heart grows so big, it's like it might explode from the love I feel for him.

He wants to marry me.

How is this possible?

He wants me to have his babies.

A mix of fear from the unknown and happiness fills me. My expression must change because he asks, "What's going on in that head of yours?"

I blurt out, "Why are you so good to me? You shouldn't be. After everything I admitted, you should want nothing to do with me."

Darkness weaves through his features. He stares at me for a moment then slowly exhales, replying, "Maybe it's because deep down, I always knew."

My pulse races faster. I gape at him until I can muster, "What do you mean you knew?"

He glances behind him then back at me. Lowering his voice, he confesses, "I knew your ties to Leo and Ludis. The story about how you won your freedom from Leo was far-fetched." He clenches his jaw then swallows.

"You didn't believe me?" I ask, shocked, since he seemed to never doubt me.

He shakes his head. "No, I believed you. None of my brothers or Papà would have ever fallen for it."

Confusion fills me. I question, "Then why did you?"

The vulnerability I see so often on his face appears. He reveals, "I think I wanted to."

"Why?"

He tightens his hold around me. "Have I not made it clear?"

My butterflies spread their wings. I reply, "You love me."

He shakes his head. "No."

"No? You don't?"

"Of course I love you. But I meant I'm crazy about you. Once I met you, I couldn't see straight. I thought about nothing until you agreed to go out with me. The thought of you working for that bastard wasn't something I could believe," he divulges.

"I'm sorry. I'm so—"

He puts his finger over my lips. "Shh. We aren't going to talk about this again. Right now, we're in paradise. Tomorrow, we're getting married."

"Tomorrow?" I gape.

"Yes. Tomorrow. Your dress will be here later this evening. I'm making you mine, and everyone is going to know. The Abruzzos. My family. Everyone. If Leo or any of his thugs try to come near you, they won't live to see the next day," he confidently states.

I stay quiet, trying to process it all. I can imagine how angry Leo will be when he finds out. A part of me is fearful, but the other is happy—so joyful, I don't ever remember feeling this way.

Massimo strokes my cheek. Disappointment fills his expression. "You don't think I can protect you from him?"

"No! That's not it," I assert.

"Then what is it?"

I decide it's best not to admit a tiny part of me is afraid. I know Massimo will kill for me. There's not a bone in my body that doesn't believe he'd jump in front of a firing squad to protect me. But years of threats and too many nightmares I can't escape aren't easy to forget. Still, I reassure him, getting a bit teary, claiming, "I wish my father were still alive. He would have loved you."

Compassion fills Massimo's face. He gives me a chaste kiss then adds, "I wish my mamma were alive. She always wanted more daughters, but after Arianna, she couldn't have any more children. She would have loved you."

"Really?"

He nods. "Yep. She told me once that I'd know when I found the woman that was meant for me. And you know what?"

"What?"

"She was right. I felt the earth shift when I saw you behind the checkout desk. I actually heard her say in my head, 'she's the one.'"

I blink hard. "You did?"

He holds up his fingers. "Scout's honor."

I laugh. "I still can't believe you were a Boy Scout."

"Cub Scout, dolce. I didn't get promoted, remember?" he replies with pride on his face.

I lace my fingers in his hair. "That's right. You shot everyone with wine."

"You better hope our kids aren't anything like my brothers and me. We were always getting into trouble," he admits, wiggling his eyebrows.

A warm, fuzzy feeling grows in my stomach. I lean closer to his face, admitting, "I hope we have a son and that he's just like you. He'll be brave, full of personality, and all the girls will be after him."

Massimo snorts. "You'll hate that—the part about the girls. Trust me. My mamma couldn't stand most of the ones we dated. And Arianna, well, she sure knew how to pick them at times, too."

My happiness dives in my gut and gets replaced with worry. I fret, "Arianna is going to hate me forever, isn't she?"

His smile falls. "She doesn't hate you."

"Yes, she does," I insist.

He shakes his head. "No. She doesn't know you. Once she gets to know you and what you've been through, she'll realize you didn't have anything to do with her abduction."

I bite on my lip, unsure if I believe him. I want his family to like me. Ever since my father died, all I've craved is to have a family again. But I don't see how any of them will ever be on my side. I blurt out, "I don't want you to be at odds with your family over me."

His face hardens. He asserts, "I won't be."

"How do you know?"

"As I said before, leave it to me." He glances past me then says, "Dekel brought fresh drinks. Want to get out for a while?"

"Sure."

We swim to the dock, climb the ladder, and take a coconut with a straw in it from Dekel's tray. I inquire, "What is this?"

"Our special resort beverage. Alcohol is illegal in the Maldives unless you're at a private resort. This is a special blend of red wine and tea, along with some other secret ingredients," he informs us.

I take a sip of the sweet drink. "It's good."

"What do you think, sir?" he asks.

Massimo shrugs. "Honestly, I'm not a fruity-drink guy. By any chance, do you have a beer?" He sets the coconut on the table and sits on the double sunbed mattress. He pats the seat.

Dekel replies, "I'll be right back." He scurries away.

I sit near him then take another sip. "I'll drink yours. This is super-yummy."

He chuckles. "Might want to see how you feel after that one. I have a feeling that coconut's going to hit you hard."

I take another large mouthful and then set it on the table. I roll into Massimo and place my hand on his chest. He palms my ass and tugs me closer. I open my mouth to speak, but his phone rings.

He groans. "I thought I turned it off."

"Who is it?" I ask.

He glances at the screen. "Tristano."

"Aren't you going to answer it?"

"Nope." He hits the red button.

I tilt my head. "Why don't you want to talk to him?"

He slides his hands on my cheeks. "Because I'm here with you in the sunshine. The last thing—"

His phone rings again.

I grab it and hold it out to him. "I think you should get this. It must be important."

Massimo sighs and answers, "Make it fast, Tristano."

I whisper, "Don't be rude."

Annoyance flashes in his eyes, and he sits up, then rises. He walks to the edge of the bungalow and freezes. He barks, "What the fuck are you two doing here?" Red flies into Massimo's cheeks. He scowls at me and then walks down the dock.

I get up and follow him. When I turn the corner, Tristano and Pina are strutting toward us. She has a coconut drink like mine.

We meet in the middle, and Massimo repeats, "I asked you what you're doing here. And why are you with Pina? No offense, Pina," he says, glancing at her.

She waves her hand. "Dante owed me a vacation. Tristano said he needed my assistance. I make things happen."

"What are you here to make happen?" Massimo seethes.

Tristano motions for Massimo to follow him. "Let's talk in private."

Massimo

"SPIT IT OUT, TRISTANO," I ORDER, PERPLEXED ABOUT HOW HE knew where I was and why he and Pina are here.

Tristano crosses his arms. "I want to know what's going on. Why are you and Katiya halfway around the world?"

"One, it's not your business, little brother. Two, you could have called to ask me this. Three..." I glance back at the ladies. Pina is waving her hands around, and Katiya looks as bewildered as I am. I pin my scowl on Tristano, snarling, "How did you know where I was?"

He sniffs hard, assessing me.

"Tristano," I bark.

He leans closer. "Answer my question first."

"I'm on vacation with my fiancée. Now, talk," I demand.

His eyes widen. "Your fiancée?"

"Yeah. And you better not say one disrespectful word about her," I warn.

His dark eyes dart down the dock then back at me. "Are you crazy?"

I grab him by the shirt, but he pushes back, crying out, "Get off me!"

"Do not disrespect her!" I yell.

His nostrils flare. Red fills his cheeks just like when Papà gets upset. He jabs me in the chest and says, "She's working for Leo!"

My hands turn into fists. "Little brother, you're one step from getting punched off this dock," I threaten.

He doesn't back down. "It's true! She's trying to find out all the details about our business contacts!"

I clap slowly. "You haven't told me anything I don't already know."

Horror fills his expression. He takes a moment then demands, "Why are you with her, then? Tell me you haven't turned against us, Massimo."

Rage fills me. I roar, "Turned against you? And done what? Joined the Abruzzos?" I say it sarcastically, but Tristano's expression tells me everything I need to know. I seethe, "You believe I would ever be part of that family?"

Through gritted teeth, he repeats, "Then why are you here with her?"

I shake my head, stopping myself from slapping him. "We're on vacation. Not that it's your concern."

"Have you lost your marbles? She's an Abruzzo," he growls.

I reach back and am about to punch him, but Katiya grabs my arm.

"Sorry! I tried to keep her away!" Pina blurts out.

I freeze then address her. "You're here to trick Katiya?"

"Well...umm..." Pina looks guiltily at both Katiya and me.

"Goddamn it, Pina! You work for Dante! Not Tristano!" I remind her.

She winces.

More disappointment fills me. "Dante knows why you're here?"

"He is my boss," she replies and cringes. "Sorry to be the bearer of bad news, but honestly, Massimo. What the heck are you doing?" She puts her hand on her hip and arches her eyebrows like I'm her child.

"Fuck off, Pina. And mind your own business," I fume.

"Don't talk to her like that," Tristano warns.

"Or what? You're both out of line," I assert.

"You just admitted she's an Abruzzo trying to betray us," Tristano says and glares at Katiya.

I pull my dolce into my side. I'm so pissed, I can't think to reason. I roar, "So what?"

Pina gasps, but I ignore her.

Tristano steps closer, but Katiya interjects.

"I didn't want to!"

He gives her an exasperated look. "Sure, you didn't. And now you're going to fuck with my brother's head some more."

"No! I—"

"Don't waste your breath on him," I instruct, then add, "I'm only going to tell you one time. I know all about it. She didn't betray us and is as much of a victim of Leo as Arianna or Cara were to the Abruzzos."

"How is that?" Tristano sneers.

"None of your business," I claim, unwilling to answer to him and still angry he thinks I would ever go over to the dark side by joining the Abruzzo family.

"I beg to differ," he snaps back.

"Beg all you want. Get the fuck off my dock," I demand, then spin with Katiya.

I take two steps with her, and she tugs on my arm. "Wait."

I stop, barking, "What?"

"We have to sort this out," she insists.

I shake my head, throwing daggers at Tristano and Pina with the glare I send their way. "No. We don't need to sort anything out. I'm done. And tell Dante I'm done with him, too," I say to Tristano.

"Massimo! Don't say that!" Katiya cries out.

"Yeah. If you're through with the family, she can't get what she wants," Pina interjects.

I wag my finger at her. "You're about to go into the water with Tristano."

He lunges forward, shouting, "Don't threaten—"

"Ludis Petrov and Leo Abruzzo both owned and raped me. Leo tossed me out when I got too old for his taste. He put me up in a brownstone, made me work at the library, and for a long time, I didn't know why. I swear to you, I had nothing— and I mean nothing—to do with Arianna's kidnapping except to give Donato the key. I had no idea what he was going to do!" Katiya maintains.

"Sure, you didn't," Tristano replies.

"You're an asshole." I glower at him.

"Takes one to know one," Pina mutters.

"Excuse me?" I say in shock.

She tilts her head. "Really? Every one of you and your brothers are assholes."

"Gee, thanks," Tristano mumbles.

She chirps, "Sorry. Just telling the truth."

"We are not assholes," he proclaims.

"Of course you are," she restates.

"Fine. We're assholes. Whatever. But you sure like our paychecks," I add.

She grins. "I earned every single one of those."

"Didn't claim you didn't," I state.

She smirks then turns toward Katiya. "Can you finish, please?"

"You aren't buying this, are you?" Tristano utters, scrubbing his face in frustration.

Pina ignores him and nods to Katiya. "You were saying?"

My dolce takes a deep breath. "For a long time, I worked in the library, thinking he forgot about me. But Leo's always watching. He has eyes everywhere."

"Don't doubt that," Pina states.

"Right. So, besides Donato, I never had to deal with him. But then...well..." Katiya nervously locks eyes with me.

I interject, "I wouldn't stop going into the library to ask her out. Leo found out, and he wanted Katiya to learn about our jewelry contacts."

"And you were going to do it, weren't you?" Tristano accuses.

I tug Katiya closer to me and say the first lie that comes to my mind. "No. She told me right away. We've been playing Leo the entire time."

Her body stiffens against my frame.

I squeeze her hip. "Isn't that right, dolce?"

She squares her shoulders and lifts her chin. "Yes. Massimo is correct."

Tristano's eyes turn to slits. He studies us briefly then asks, "How exactly were you playing Leo?"

"It involves me killing him, not that it's any of your business. All you need to know is that I knew about her association with the Abruzzos all along. She was helping me. Now drop it."

"Why didn't you tell us?" he asks.

"Because I'm going to kill Leo, and you know how Papà is lately about making moves on high-ranking crime family members. I wasn't going to risk him saying no."

"You could have told us. We could have helped you," Tristano claims.

"And risk Dante going to Papà? No, thanks," I say, coming up with my story as I speak. I change the subject, adding, "But I do want to know how you knew I was here. The only possibility is you followed me," I claim, and my stomach flips.

Tristano's face once again reveals everything.

My gut drops like I'm on a roller coaster. "Are you serious? You followed me?" I glance at Pina, but she's got her poker face on.

No one speaks.

I demand, "You've been following me? And Dante knows about this?" His guilt grows. I hold Katiya tighter so I don't feed him to the next vicious fish that swims by us. I roar, "What the fuck, Tristano?"

"You've been making bad decisions," he claims.

New anger swells through my blood. "You put trackers on me? Do you have my plane bugged, too?"

"Seats five and eight, and the bedroom," Pina admits.

I gape at her. "You little—"

"You heard us in the bedroom?" Katiya frets.

"Nope! There was too much interference, but we did hear some rather interesting things in the main cabin," Pina smirks.

Katiya's cheeks turn red.

I shake my head at Pina, snapping, "Hope you enjoyed the show."

"I actually think Chanel is the most interesting character," she admits.

"What?" I ask in shock.

"Sure. She's into girls...but not. I wonder if she's ever been to the club. I bet she's watched a lot of things," Pina states.

"What club?" Katiya questions.

Pina dramatically opens her mouth then replies, "What? Massimo didn't take you to the club yet? Especially with what you're into?"

"Meaning?" Katiya pushes.

Pina's smirk grows, but it's also laced with disgust. She turns to Tristano. "Ask him. He was there just the other night."

"I told you I had to go for work."

She puts her hand on her hip. In an annoyed voice, she answers, "Sure. I could work on Fifth Avenue at two in the morning, too. Would you like that?"

He groans. "How many times—"

"This is the thing about men in their thirties. You only know how to play," she argues.

He slides his hands in his hair. "Are you kidding me? This is getting old, Pina."

Holy shit.

"Are you two fucking?" I ask incredulously.

They freeze. The color drains from their cheeks.

"You are!" I shout.

My brother sniffs hard.

Pina spins and claims, "I never confirmed that."

"You didn't deny it, either," Katiya mumbles.

"You don't have a place to talk. This is about you two and your issues. Not—" She snaps her mouth shut.

Katiya glares at them. "Not about you two?"

"Kind of hypocritical, don't you think?" I say to Katiya.

She nods. "Totally."

Uncomfortable silence fills the dock. I finally break it by saying, "Dante's going to kill you."

"Shut up," Tristano barks.

I chuckle. "Come on, dolce. We're on vacation. Just ignore them while they sit on their high horses."

She lifts her head higher, and we return to the bungalow. When we get to the end, I've cooled off. This new little revelation of my brother's is too good for me not to find out more. I glance back and ask, "Well? Are you coming for a drink or not?"

Pina shoots Tristano a look of death then marches toward me. He follows while scowling.

"Sit," I order, pointing to the chair.

They take seats, and Katiya and I return to the sunbed. There's a bucket full of beers and two brand-new coconuts with straws. I hand a coconut to each of the women and give a beer to Tristano. I grab a beer for myself and sit next to my dolce. I take a sip then command, "Tomorrow at this time, Katiya will be my wife. You will treat her with respect. You will apologize for your rude behavior. You will not ever again have me followed. Do you understand?"

Tristano stays quiet and scowls.

I pick up my phone. "Should I call Dante right now?"

"No! Please don't!" Pina begs.

"I don't care. Call him," Tristano orders, then takes a mouthful of beer and turns his glare on Pina.

Pina shakes her head. "Massimo. I'm begging you."

"What's it going to be, Tristano?" I threaten.

"Tristano," Pina pleads.

He sighs then pins his eyes on Katiya. "I'm sorry for being rude."

She offers a tiny smile. "It's okay. I promise you, I hate the Abruzzos as much as you do."

He clenches his jaw and stares at me. "Put the phone down."

"Tell me you won't have me followed anymore," I repeat.

"Fine," he agrees.

I drop it on the mattress. "How long were you following me?"

"A few months."

"A few months!" I seethe.

He holds his hands in the air. "Easy."

Abhorrence and embarrassment explode in me. "So the person following me wasn't an Abruzzo? It was our men?"

"Luca, actually," Pina mumbles.

"What? You had Luca on me? Are you kidding me?" I explode. Luca's one of our best men, our cousin, and used for only the most important jobs.

Tristano jumps out of his seat. "You would have done the same thing. You weren't acting rationally."

"Fuck off," I hurl.

The sound of the tide picking up and the waves rolling on the shore fills the tense air.

Katiya questions, "How did you know Leo wanted me to find out info about your contacts?"

Pina scoots her chair closer. "Tristano got it out of one of his men."

"Who?" my dolce asks.

"Tommy," Pina answers.

Katiya gapes. "He told you? No way!"

"He didn't have a choice. Tristano made him," Pina informs us.

It hits me that Tristano's not just fucking Pina. He's telling her about torturing the Abruzzos, and who knows what else. She may work for Dante, but this is past her level of clearance. I accuse, "You shooting your mouth off?"

Tristano hurls, "Shut up."

"I'm not stupid. I know all about the dungeon but not from Tristano," Pina states.

In frustration, I glance at the sky, then ask, "What are you talking about?"

"Oh, please! Don't try to cover it up. Do you know the number of times I had to pick Dante up off the couch over the years? He was always drunk and moaning over Bridget and whatever he was up to that week in the dungeon," she claims.

"Dante? Drunk and talking? No way," I say.

Tristano nods. "Yep. Pina knows more about our family than we do."

"Then why are you telling my brother?" I growl.

She jumps. "It's...it's only Tristano!"

I point at both of them. "You two are idiots."

"I'll remember that next time you want concert tickets, or an impossible reservation, or—"

"Knock it off, Pina! I'm not in the mood. Tristano, you better tell me how you got Tommy to rat out Leo," I demand.

Arrogance expands on his dark features. His lips twitch as he replies, "He went to Katiya's brownstone two nights ago. When she didn't answer, he used a key to get inside."

"And?" I ask.

"I picked him up. It didn't make sense he was there with a key if she's not an Abruzzo."

"Then what?"

The devil appears behind Tristano's eyes. I've seen him in my little brother's orbs since he was six. Tristano licks his lips and relays, "Pizza cutter."

"I personally can't use one anymore," Pina cringes.

"Why?" Katiya asks.

"Well, he likes to—"

"No reason. Forget you heard anything about it," I say, glaring at Pina. The last thing I need is for Katiya to start having nightmares about pizza cutters. It's bad enough she wakes up sweating and crying sometimes.

"Long story short, Tommy sang like a canary and will no longer be of use to anyone," Tristano announces.

Katiya takes a deep, shaky breath. I slide my arm around her. "You okay?"

She nods. "Yes. It's a relief but hard to believe."

"Oh, believe it! He's—" Pina takes her hand and pretends to slice her neck.

My dolce shudders, and I reprimand Pina again. "Knock it off."

Pina rolls her eyes then glances around the bungalow. "Can you have the butler bring my bag? I could at least be getting a tan right now."

"They're in our place," Tristano states.

"Your place? Let's get back to this little issue you two have," I scoff.

Pina rises and drops her T-shirt and shorts, showcasing her lace bra and thong.

"Pina," Tristano growls.

"What? It's no different from a bikini," Pina claims, then grabs Katiya's hand. "Let's go for a swim. Let the brothers talk. Don't forget to give him the box."

"What box?" I ask.

Tristano holds up his finger.

"Three, two, one," Pina says, then pushes Katiya in the water and dives in herself.

"Pina!" I shout, rise, and then step to the edge, but Katiya bursts through the surface laughing.

Tristano stands. He reaches into his pocket then pauses. "Let's go inside a minute."

"Fine." I lead him through the slider wall and cross my arms. Just to piss him off, I react, "You and Pina? Seriously? Isn't she a tad old for you?"

"Shut up, dickhead. She's only a few years older," he declares.

"Dante's going to kill you, no matter your age gap," I repeat, which isn't a lie. But I can't totally blame my brother for going after her. Pina's always been a ten. Age hasn't done anything but make her more attractive.

Tristano snorts. "That's rich when you're what...fifteen years older than Katiya? And I'm not scared of Dante."

I ignore his age remark. I'm fully aware of our age difference, and I don't care what anyone thinks. I advise, "Then tell him."

"I would, but Pina won't let me," he replies.

I offer, "Sucks to be you, then. Now, where's this box."

"Are you sure you want to marry Katiya?" he questions.

"Man, are you trying to disrespect her again?" I boom.

"No. I'm just asking. How do you know she's the one?" he inquires.

I sigh, admitting, "Never been so sure about anything in my life."

He stares at me a moment then pulls out a ring box. "Then you should have this. Ettore gave it to me before I left."

Katiya

The Next Morning

"KNOCK, KNOCK," PINA'S VOICE CALLS OUT.

"Mm," I mutter, turning into Massimo's warm body and burying my face in his chest. After the initial surprise visit and interrogation, we all had a great time until late last night. When we returned to the bungalow, it was after midnight. Massimo kept me up for hours, begging him. By the time we fell asleep, the darkness of the night was fading.

Pina chirps, "Time to get up, sleepyheads."

Massimo tugs me into his body. "Go away. We're on vacation."

"Not today, you aren't. Come on. We've got work to do," she states.

I groan, questioning, "Work?"

"Yep! Besides, it's bad luck for you to see each other before the wedding," she adds.

Wedding!

I'm going to be Mrs. Massimo Marino!

So much joy rushes through me, I can't contain my smile. After everything I've gone through, and even after Massimo learned the full truth, he still wants me to be his. It's a reality I never thought would be possible. I almost ask him to pinch me again.

Massimo orders, "Let us sleep. We don't get married until four."

Tristano chuckles. "It's already after noon."

Massimo and I both sit up. I've not even seen my dress. It arrived last night while we were at dinner, but Massimo and I were too into each other to care. I fret, "What time is it?"

Tristano's lips twitch. "Only ten. But you do need to get up."

I relax, but Massimo doesn't, questioning, "Why is that?"

"Tsk, tsk, tsk," Pina taunts.

"Enough of the dramatics," Massimo reprimands.

She points at me. "You need to come with me."

"Where?" I ask.

"Hair. Nails. Makeup. Massage. We need to go, or we'll miss our appointments," she states.

"Appointments?" I question, still bewildered.

She smirks. "Of course! Thank God I'm here since Massimo didn't think of the important stuff."

"No, I didn't think about that, but it's because she's a natural beauty. She doesn't need all that crap," he replies and squeezes my hip.

"Please. Save it," she demands, then beams at me. "We have a full day of pampering ahead of us, all on Tristano." She pats his shoulder. "Right, babe?"

He drags his eyes down the length of her body.

She pretends to ignore him and shifts on her feet. "Katiya, time is ticking."

I've never been to a spa or had any pampering. I'm still trying to wake up, not to mention process a day at the spa.

Massimo snorts. "You lost a bet, didn't you?"

Tristano disregards his question. "We have stuff to do as well. Let's go."

"Like what?"

"Man stuff."

"Such as...?" Massimo inquires.

"Breakfast. Drinking by the water. Lunch. More drinking by the water." He grins.

"Fun day. I approve," I tease.

Massimo shifts on the bed but keeps me tight to him. "I still vote you let us sleep."

Pina grabs the blankets. "I can pull these off if you want."

"We're naked," I blurt out.

"Aren't you two into that?" She smirks.

"Shut up, Pina," Massimo growls.

She turns to Tristano. "You didn't tell me your brother was such a grouch in the morning."

"Not everyone can be as chipper as me. It's a good thing we're here to make sure they get their shit in order," he replies.

Pina motions to us, claiming, "You two are lucky you have such a devoted wedding party."

"Wedding party?" Massimo questions.

She nods. "Yeah. You can't get married without a best man and maid of honor."

"Says who?" he asks.

She scoffs. "Don't be ridiculous."

"Yeah, and it's not like I'm not your favorite brother," Tristano declares.

"Is that so?" Massimo replies.

"Anyway, time to get up," Pina repeats, tugging on the blankets again.

Massimo and I grip them tighter. He orders, "Get out and let us put our clothes on."

"Come on, Pina. Let's grab one of the mimosas Dekel left on the breakfast tray," Tristano suggests.

I sit up straighter, clutching the sheets to my chest. "Dekel was here? While we were sleeping?"

"Yep. That cat's more like a mouse. He's sneaky and quiet," Tristano claims.

Pina lifts the silver platter in the corner of the room then calls out, "Want me to butter you a piece of toast for the ride over to the spa? Or maybe add some jam?"

"No. I'm okay," I answer.

"Take the cart on the deck and make me a plate. I'm starving," Massimo orders.

She spins and puts her hand on her hip. She bats her eyes and says in a sugary voice, "You didn't say please. And I was asking Katiya. I'm not on the clock. It's Saturday."

Arrogance fills Massimo's face. "Really? Since when aren't you on the clock? Dante know that?"

She rolls her eyes and spins. She steps onto the deck and adds, "You have ten minutes to get ready."

Tristano grabs a piece of toast, bites into it, then drops it on the plate. "Needs butter." He wheels the cart outside and disappears.

Massimo lies back on the pillow.

"What are you doing?" I ask.

He flips me on my back and rolls over me.

My butterflies take off. I hold my breath.

His grin widens. "They can wait."

"I heard that, and no, we can't," Pina sings.

He groans and drops his head on my chest.

I kiss his forehead and laugh. "We should get in the shower."

He sighs then rises, holding out his hand. I take it, and he pulls me up. He studies me a moment then says, "I meant what I said. You're beautiful. Don't let them talk you into anything you don't want."

"I won't," I reply.

He pecks me on the lips. "Good girl. Let's get in the shower." He pats me on the ass.

I go into the bathroom and turn on the shower. When I spin, Massimo is naked and down on one knee. He's holding the most enormous ring I've ever seen. The flawless, sparkling diamond sits high on top of an intricate band. Platinum, yellow gold, and rose-gold metals twist around each other with the same colored gems filling different shapes. I've never seen a piece of jewelry so detailed. I gape at it, unable to close my mouth or stop staring.

Massimo's voice tears my eyes off the stunning piece. He takes my hand and claims, "The moment I saw you, I had to have you. I knew you were the one. It was like my whole life unfolded in front of me. Our first kiss, I thought Thor himself struck me with a lightning bolt. No one, and I mean no one, dolce, ever affected me how you did."

Tears fill my eyes. I blink, and they overflow, dripping down my cheeks.

He continues, "You're everything to me. And I promise you that I'll never lose sight of that if you marry me. I'll protect you, worship you, and love you until I die. If anyone ever tries to hurt you, I'll kill them. Hell, all they have to do is think about harming you, and I'll take them out. The same goes for our babies. And all I ask is the same from you. Have me be your everything now until we die."

"You are my everything," I choke out, putting my shaking hand on his cheek.

"Then marry me. Tell me you'll marry me."

"I thought I already did."

He grins, but it's blurry through my tears. "Say it again."

"Yes, I'll marry you," I affirm.

He slides the ring on my finger. My eyes dart between it and him, and he says in a relieved voice, "Thank God it fits."

I laugh, and he rises. He picks me up and spins me then sets me on my feet and kisses me until I'm breathless and he's hard.

"When did you get this?" I ask, unable to take my eyes off the exquisite details of the ring.

"I met with Ettore and told him what I wanted him to design."

"When?"

That vulnerable expression I love so much pops onto his face. "Shortly after I met you."

More flutters erupt. I whisper, "Really?"

He nods, kissing me again. "I always knew you were the one for me."

I sniffle then open my mouth but shut it.

"What is it?" he asks.

I close the bathroom door then question, "Why did you lie and say you knew what Leo wanted me to do all along?"

He cups the side of my head and strokes his thumb over my cheek. "You're the most important person in my life."

"You're mine," I reply.

"My family used to be number one. Now they're second. And I told you I'd take care of them, and they'd love you. That was the easiest way of doing it. Since I doubt you're going to rat me out, I think our secret is safe," he declares, winking at me.

I put my arms around his shoulders and hug him. "Thank you. I love you so much."

He kisses the top of my head. "I love you, dolce."

"Three minutes," Pina shouts.

Massimo groans, yelling, "You're a pain in my ass, Pina!"

"Unlike you, Tristano doesn't like it when other men—or women—comment on my ass," she calls back.

Heat burns my cheeks, but I laugh, muttering, "We're never living our plane ride down."

"Sorry my brother's boring in bed," Massimo bellows.

"Speak for yourself," Tristano roars.

"Go shove more food in your mouth," Massimo orders, then motions for me to get into the shower.

I shampoo, condition, and wash quickly. When we get out, I crack the door open. I peek through it and call out, "Do I need to dry my hair?"

Pina and Tristano magically appear in the doorway. She answers, "Nope. They'll do it. Ready?"

"I need clothes."

"Thought you didn't like to wear them in front of others," Tristano replies.

"Watch it, little brother," Massimo warns.

I ignore the heat reigniting on my face and step back into the bathroom.

"I'll get you clothes. Disregard everything they say," Massimo states, wraps a towel around his body, and leaves the room.

I comb my hair, and he returns with a sundress, undergarments, and sandals. "Here you go, dolce."

"Thanks." I take the clothes, put them on, then step out of the bathroom. "I guess the next time I'll see you, we'll be ready to say our vows?"

I've never seen him smile so big. Everything about his happiness makes my soul sing. He tugs me into him. "Don't have second thoughts and leave me on the beach next to Tristano."

"I won't. I promise," I vow, then peck him on the lips. "I better go before Pina gets out her whip."

"How did you know I have one?" she states.

Massimo arches his eyebrows at Tristano. "You into that, bro?"

"Shut up," Tristano demands.

"Pina, I can give you some pointers on what kind of floggers to buy if you want," Massimo teases.

"Not necessary. I'm fully capable of choosing." She beams at us.

Tristano turns slightly red, and he groans, scrubbing his hands over his face. "I'll be on the deck."

"No shame in your game, bro," Massimo shouts after him.

"Shut up, dickhead," Tristano orders.

Pina grabs my hand and tugs me toward the deck. "Time to go. We're already late."

"It's island time," Massimo says.

She groans. "Showing up late is not cool." She continues pulling me away from the bungalow.

"You and I would not get along on vacay," Massimo mutters.

"Maybe that's why I never asked you to go on one with me," she chirps, releasing my arm.

"Bye," I shout and follow her down the dock.

At the end is an oversized golf cart and driver. He says, "Good morning, ladies. Ready for the spa?"

"Yes! So ready!" Pina says.

"Sounds fun," I reply, still clueless and a bit overwhelmed about a spa day.

We climb in the second row, and the driver takes off. I ask Pina, "How long has Tristano been your boyfriend?"

"Mmm...not sure if I'd call him my boyfriend."

"Oh? Why?" I inquire, surprised. They were all over each other last night, especially Pina, who straddled him for hours at the club.

She shrugs then points to the water. "Look!"

A pack of baby dolphins plays in the water. The one I assume is the mama jumps high in the air, creating a huge water ripple.

"They're majestic," I utter.

"Yeah," Pina agrees, then grabs my hand. "Damn, girl, Massimo sure did well on this one!"

Pride sweeps through me. "Yes, he did."

"I need to get on some sunglasses!" she exclaims.

"You're wearing them," I point out.

She peers closer, turning my hand to watch the sparkles. "Then I guess I need darker ones. This rock is to die for!"

The golf cart pulls up to the spa. The driver says, "Have a great day."

"Thanks," we say in unison, get out, and go past the man holding the door open for us.

We spend a few minutes getting checked in. Then a staff member shows us to the dressing room. She demonstrates how to secure the lockers and open them then takes us to the private saltwater pool area and two other quiet rooms.

Over the next four hours, I get immersed in spa services. I have a massage, pedicure, and manicure. I review several different makeup styles and choose a natural look, but with a red lipstick close in color to the one I know Massimo loves. After a lot of debate, I decide to wear my hair in beach waves.

My wedding dress gets delivered to a private room in the spa that Pina reserved. When we arrive, I unzip the bag and pull it out.

Everything about it screams that Massimo chose it just for me. It's a form-fitting, sheer white, strapless dress with ruched panels. You can see just the right amount of skin on every part of my body. The bodice shows off the perfect amount of cleavage. One side is cut at the top of my thigh. The other runs down to my ankles.

"Wow! That's...wow!" Pina whistles.

"I love it," I say, running my hand over the delicate fabric.

"Let's get you in it." Pina unzips it and takes it off the hanger. She hands it to me.

I step into it, and she zips me up.

"There's no veil," she states.

I shrug. "I don't want one."

"No?"

I shake my head. "Nope!" I slide into the designer white-and-silver flip-flops and stand in front of the mirror, admiring myself.

Pina slides into a sundress and steps next to me.

I tell her, "You look nice."

Her smile is wide. "You look like the sexiest bride I've ever seen!"

I laugh then take another minute to enjoy the moment.

There's a knock on the door. A woman cracks it open and declares, "It's time to go. Oh, don't you look gorgeous!" She steps in and smiles, scanning me over.

"Thank you," I reply, squaring my shoulders and lifting my chin to deal with the overwhelming nerves growing in my gut. I'm not used to the focus being on me unless I'm with Massimo.

Pina grabs my arm and leads me through the spa. We get into a private car. The driver takes us to a very exclusive beach. There are only five people on it—a DJ, a photographer, the wedding officiant, Tristano, and Massimo.

The moment I step on the sand and his eyes meet mine, I tear up. He looks as handsome as ever, in white linen pants and a matching dress shirt. His dark features appear extra sharp. The vulnerable expression I could get lost in overtakes his features and his dark gaze studies me, igniting an entirely new slew of flutters.

The sun hides behind fluffy clouds, making the light not as harsh. Waves crash against the shore, and birds squeal in the sky. I walk toward Massimo, barely hearing the music, so full of love and happiness, I could burst.

He takes my hand when I reach him then kisses me. I feel every ounce of affection he has for me and return it all. When he drags his lips away from mine, I mumble, "Aren't we supposed to wait?"

He strokes my cheek and smiles. "No. Nothing about us is ordinary. We do what we want, dolce. You and me. For the rest of our lives, we call the shots."

The officiant states, "With that statement, is it okay if we get started?"

Massimo chuckles. "Yeah."

The ceremony doesn't take long, but I prefer it that way. Massimo and I both pledge our lives to each other. When it's over, I've never had so many emotions sweep through me.

I'm Mrs. Massimo Marino.

For the first time in my life, I feel untouchable—that *we* are untouchable. It's as if nothing bad ever happened, and nothing ever will again. I have him, and he has me. We're indestructible.

"You're my wife. There's no going back," Massimo murmurs in my ear when we get into the car to go to the private dinner.

I turn and kiss him, teasing, "You're stuck with me now."

Tristano and Pina get into the car. The driver takes us to a restaurant outside of the resort. We pull up to the valet area, but as he reaches for the door, Tristano shoves the lock down and shouts, "Go! Go now!"

Massimo fumes, "Tristano, what in God's name—"

"Get down!" Tristano shoves Pina's head to her knees, and he reaches for my head, pushing me down. He cries out, "His men are here!"

2 6

M C

Massimo

"Drive faster," I instruct our driver, wishing one of our guys were behind the wheel. I'm pretty sure he's never speeded in his life. He did make a few moves that put the car following us behind several vehicles, including a large semi, but it won't be long until he's on our rear end again.

"Fuck this," Tristano says and leaps over the backseat and into the passenger seat. He grabs the wheel and slides his foot next to the driver's, which is on the accelerator.

"What are you doing?" the driver frets.

"When I say move, you get out of the seat. Take your seat belt off," Tristano orders.

"What! No! I can't—"

"Do it! Or you're going to die," I threaten, pointing my Glock at his head. There's no time to deal with his lack of courage to get out of the driver's seat. Leo's men will be right behind us in a few moments, and they won't hesitate to shoot.

"Don't kill me!" the driver yells.

I roar, "Then get your ass out of that seat!"

"Move!" Tristano yells, pushing his body toward the window.

The vehicle veers sharply to the left, and Tristano tugs on the wheel before oncoming traffic hits us. Our driver tries to get out from under Tristano, but he struggles due to the size of his stomach.

I yank him to the side, and once he's in the passenger seat, command, "Put your seat belt on and get down." I glance at Pina and Katiya, who still have their faces between their knees.

Tristano hits the accelerator and maneuvers through more traffic. I text my flight crew to get the plane ready for immediate takeoff then turn so I can see how close the Abruzzos are, but I don't recognize any of the vehicles.

"Did you lose them?" I ask.

Tristano glances in the rearview mirror. "Shit, they're back within view."

Adrenaline builds in my cells. I spin again and cock my Glock and point it, preparing to shoot the back window out if needed. I admit, "I don't see them!"

"Behind the red truck," Tristano replies.

Horns blare. I look again as the black sedan moves into the other lane. It barely gets in front of the truck, coming close to a head-on crash.

Tristano makes a sharp turn, and the wheels squeal. The driver screams then begins praying. Katiya and Pina slide to the other side of the car since there aren't any seat belts in the back.

Pina's shoulder slams hard against the window. She cries out, "Ouch!"

"You okay?" Tristano questions.

"Yeah," she claims, wincing.

"Dolce? You all right?" I worry.

"Fine," she replies, locking scared eyes with me.

"Keep your head down," I order, pushing their heads back to their knees.

"Shit!" Tristano shouts.

I turn around. The car passes several other vehicles and is only four away from us. I add, "They're getting closer!"

Tristano veers into a narrow alley. He barely misses the car scraping against the brick wall. We get to the end, and he turns right as the black sedan enters the alley.

"They're on us," I warn.

Tristano increases our speed. He weaves his way through several alleys. After the third, I assert, "I don't see them."

The smell of urine fills the car. Tristano mutters, "Fuck. Dude, the women didn't even piss their pants." He cracks his window then shoots down the main road, accelerating to over a hundred miles per hour, then getting on the expressway. After several miles of not seeing them anywhere, I state, "I think you lost them."

The driver continues praying, and the smell of his urine intensifies. Pina looks up and wrinkles her nose. I roll my window down halfway and tell Katiya, "You can look up, dolce."

She slowly sits up. Her expression is full of fear. She questions, "How did they know we're here?"

"I don't know. I'll find out later," I vow.

"Pina, you okay?" Tristano asks.

She puts on a brave face. "Yeah. All good."

Tristano doesn't slow down. He continues speeding past the other cars.

My phone vibrates. I glance at the text:

Chanel: *Ready in ten minutes.*

Me: *On our way.*

I demand, "Tell us where to go to get to the airport."

The driver keeps praying.

Tristano flings the back of his hand on his shoulder. The driver yelps then covers his face with his hands. "Please don't kill me!"

"I'm not! Now tell me where to go!" Tristano barks.

He points to the exit ramp sign stating we're several kilometers away.

Tristano speeds up and maneuvers us off the ramp. There's an airport sign and arrow. He follows it, turning right.

It takes several more minutes to get to the private landing strip. Tristano pulls up to the jet and tells the driver, "As soon as we're on that plane, you drive away. And fast!"

I open the door and help Katiya and Pina out. Tristano follows, and we race up the steps. When I step inside the jet, the driver accelerates the vehicle away from us. I push the staircase away and close the door.

"Leave as soon as you can," Tristano orders the pilots.

"We have ninety seconds," Sy relays.

"Put your seat belts on," I instruct the women, including Chanel, then take the seat next to Katiya. I grab her shaking hand and kiss it. "Everything will be fine," I insist, trying not to jump out of my skin during the longest ninety seconds of my life.

When the wheels begin moving, and we lift off the ground and into the air, relief fills me. I lock eyes with Tristano and ask the question I already partly know the answer to. "How did they find us?"

He shakes his head. Red rage fills his cheeks. He seethes, "I don't know. We have to have a rat in our house."

I grind my molars, exchanging unspoken words with my brother. Whoever it is, they're going to pay. I slide my arm around Katiya and kiss her head. "You sure you're okay? You didn't get hurt?"

"No. I'm fine."

"Shit! You're bruising!" Tristano exclaims, then orders, "Chanel, bring Pina some ice for her shoulder as soon as you can."

"It's fine," Pina claims, but she winces when he touches it.

"No, it's not. Bring some pain meds, too," he adds.

"Got it," Chanel replies.

The jet continues to move higher in the sky. When it finally levels off, the seat belt sign dings.

I remove mine and pick up my cell. I dial Dante.

"Massimo, what the hell are you doing? Pulling a Gianni on us isn't cool," he reprimands.

"We have a traitor," I snarl.

The line turns silent. Dante clears his throat and demands, "What happened?"

"The Abruzzos were here in the Maldives. We're on our way home," I inform him.

He questions, "Anyone hurt?"

I glance at Tristano and answer, "Pina's shoulder got bruised when it slammed against the car door."

"Shit! I'm going to kill Tristano for convincing me to let her go!" he claims.

"Why did you?" I ask, curious how he could let her go and not suspect anything.

"Blame our little brother. He came into the office during my weekly meeting with her. He said he would track you down, and his new assistant just quit. Then he made a stupid bet with me to take her, and I lost. It was a stupid bet on my part I won't fall for again. And all of you need to stop trying to steal her from me. It's getting old. But didn't he tell you?"

Pina's worried eyes meet mine. She mouths, "Don't tell him! Please!" She puts her hands in a prayer pose.

As crazy as it is that she and Tristano are together, I'm not going to be the one to break it to Dante. No one saw this coming, and I still believe Dante will go ape shit. Pina's been his assistant for over twenty years. He values her more than us at times. I quickly wink at Pina and lie, "Yeah, he did, but I didn't believe you'd fall for it. Thought you were smarter."

"Shut up," Dante growls.

Relief fills Pina's expression. She whispers, "Thank you."

"Pretty shitty of you to have me tracked," I hurl at him.

The line turns quiet again.

"Yeah, I know all about it," I point out.

"We'll talk about it when you get back," he asserts.

"Oh, we will. For sure," I proclaim.

He changes the subject. "Which Abruzzos were there?"

"I don't know. I didn't recognize them. Tristano did."

"Let me talk to him and Pina," Dante demands.

I hold the phone out. "Dante wants to speak to both of you."

Nerves fill Pina's expression.

"It's fine," I mumble so Dante can't hear.

She breathes a sigh of relief.

Tristano rises and grabs the phone. "Let's take this in the back."

She gets up and follows him into the bedroom.

I turn to my bride, pissed her life was in danger and our wedding night got ruined. I promise, "I'll make this up to you."

"Massimo, you didn't know. I'm just grateful Tristano saw them," she replies.

I reach for her jaw, stroking my thumb over her cheek. She leans into my palm and closes her eyes. I peck her on the lips and admit, "I promised to protect you."

Her eyelids fly open. "You did protect me."

We should never have assumed they wouldn't find us. Tristano and I should have both had bodyguards with us. I sniff hard, pledging, "I'll do better going forward."

She rises and straddles me. I circle my arms around her, holding her tight, still freaked out by what could have happened. She slides her hands to the sides of my head then states, "There's only so much you can do, Massimo. Leo has eyes everywhere. I know this from experience. I need you to promise me something."

My chest tightens. I peer closer at her. "What's that?"

She hesitates a few seconds then demands, "If they ever recapture me, don't do anything stupid."

"What does that mean?" I bark.

She lifts her chin higher and swallows hard. "I don't want you blaming yourself when the inevitable happens."

Anger digs into my bones. I roar, "The inevitable? You still believe I can't protect you, don't you?"

She moves her head in tiny bobs. "Massimo, I have full faith in you. But Leo...he..." She closes her eyes and sighs then adds, "Has ways of finding people."

"Yeah? Well, so do I. And you're my wife now. I'll be damned if he comes near you. Until I have him in my custody, you're not leaving the house," I declare.

She tilts her head and asserts, "It'll be easy for him to get to us above the club."

"No. I meant my place at Papà's. There's no way he'll have any chance of hurting you there," I contend.

She doesn't speak, biting her lip.

"Don't be nervous. My family will treat you like you've always been ours," I claim.

"How?"

"Do you feel uncomfortable now around Tristano and Pina?" I ask.

"No. Of course not."

"Then stop worrying. I'll take care of everyone. You'll see," I maintain.

"Okay. Umm..." She bites her bottom lip.

I stroke her spine. "What's on your mind, dolce?"

She takes another moment then asks, "Is it true what Pina said?"

"About?"

"You have a dungeon under the house?"

My pulse races faster. The dungeon isn't something anyone should know about or discuss. When Arianna caught me going down to it when she was a teenager, Papà gave me a week of no pay and reiterated to all of us the importance of keeping the dungeon on the down-low. I'm unhappy Dante's drunk ass used to moan to Pina about it.

Still, Katiya is my wife now. All the women in our family know about it and how we deal with our enemies. I confess, "Yes, there is. You can't discuss this with anyone, understand?"

"Of course. Besides, I don't have any friends. You know this," she adds.

Her statement makes me sad. She had her childhood ripped from away her. At twenty-five, she should have a slew of girlfriends and not know anything about the horrors of my world. I tighten my arms around her and claim, "You're young, dolce. Once I kill Leo, these threats will be over. No one will come after you. Every crime family will know you're my wife. Things will be safer for you to start over."

"Start over? What do you mean? I-we're married!" she frets.

"Sorry! I didn't mean us. I just meant that you can figure out what you want from your life outside of being Mrs. Massimo Marino," I relay.

Confusion fills her face. She quietly admits, "I don't understand."

I answer, "Hobbies? A career? Volunteer work? Whatever you want to do. You'll meet people through those things and make friends."

Her face falls. "I guess I won't be working at the library anymore."

"You're upset about that?" I question.

She shrugs. "I've never done anything else. I'm good at my job."

"Yes, you are, but there are many things you'd do well."

She doesn't look convinced.

"Stop worrying, dolce. You don't need to work. If you want to, you can, but it's not necessary. There's plenty of time to figure out what you want. Plus, you're young, and now you have unlimited resources. The world is in the palm of your hand," I proclaim.

"But the library is out," she states.

I nod. "I'm afraid so. But there's something else out there you'll love to do. I promise."

A tiny smile curves her lips. "You seem so sure of everything."

Arrogance fills me. I tease, "Of course I am. That's why you married me."

365

She laughs, and her face lights up.

"That's better. I much prefer you happy than worried. Leave the latter to me," I order.

She gives me a salute then says, "Yes, sir."

"I think you mean Daddy," Chanel voices.

Katiya's cheeks flush, and we glance up to see her smirking.

She wiggles her eyebrows. "Did you two get hitched, or did your plans get interrupted?"

"Oh!" Katiya glances at her dress. "Yes."

"Our dinner got interrupted. I assume there wasn't time to grab a lot of food?" I ask.

Chanel beams. "There's plenty on board for me to whip up. Just don't expect anything fresh."

"Deal." I turn to Katiya. "You hungry?"

"Yeah. Starving, actually."

"I'll bring you some bread and get started on the rest," Chanel states.

"Great. Thanks," I reply.

Wickedness fills Chanel's green eyes. She clears her throat then studies Katiya.

My dolce nervously questions, "What's wrong?"

Chanel shakes her head then pulls out the pair of Katiya's panties I gave her. She holds them in the air, not saying anything as my dolce's cheeks turn fire-engine red. Her breath hitches. She slowly tears her gaze off the thong and pins her blues on mine.

Chanel asks, "Mrs. Marino, would you like these back?"

"Did you wash them?" I inquire.

She dangles them closer to my face. "No."

The slight scent of my dolce's arousal flares in my nostrils. I breathe deeper as Katiya squirms on my lap. I drag my knuckles down her cheek, and she shudders. Testosterone flares in my veins, giving me an instant erection. I pin my stare on Chanel, firmly ordering, "Make extra food. My wife needs her energy. And you can keep the panties for now."

Chanel's lips twitch. She grins at us, her gaze lingering on Katiya. My dolce digs her fingers into my shoulders, lifting her chin. Chanel replies, "Thank you, sir. And can I say you look beautiful, Mrs. Marino."

"Thank you," Katiya replies, her face lighting up again.

Chanel shoots us another naughty grin then disappears.

I move my hand to Katiya's zipper then lean into her ear. "How long do you think they'll be in the bedroom?"

She takes a deep inhale and shifts her wet heat over my cock. "I don't know. Can we make them stay back there?"

I chuckle then peck her on the lips. I move her off me and rise.

"Where are you going?" she asks.

I fist her hair, tug it, and lean over her face. She gasps, and I answer, "To lock them inside so I can play with you, Mrs. Marino."

Massimo

MY DRIVER PULLS THROUGH THE GATES. KATIYA FURROWS HER
brows and bites her lip, glancing in the darkness at Papà's lit-
up mansion.

I squeeze her waist and murmur in her ear, "Don't be
nervous. Everything will be fine. You'll see."

"Papà won't be upset with you. It's Massimo whose head is
on the chopping block," Tristano adds.

I snap, "Shut up."

He snorts. "It's true. How are you going to explain all this?"

Katiya tears her gaze off the house. She frets, "You mean me?"

Tristano shakes his head. "No. I mean the fact Massimo knew
what Leo wanted, didn't tell Papà, and was secretly going to
kill that bastard."

The SUV stops in front of the large staircase. I open the door and order, "Keep your comments to yourself, bro." I reach in for my dolce and help her out. More anxiety builds in her expression. I assure her, "Stop worrying. Everything will be fine." I peck her on the lips and don't wait for the others to get out. I lead her up the steps, and one of Papà's bodyguards opens the foyer entrance.

As we cross the threshold, Papà steps out of his office with Dante and Gianni.

"We'll skip the part where you congratulate us. It's late, and I'm showing my wife to our wing, so save your breath a few more minutes," I state, brushing past them and guiding her up the stairs.

"Massimo," she utters.

I keep moving farther up and reassure, "Everything is fine. I'll show you around tomorrow morning." I get to the top and turn down the hallway into my wing, steering Katiya into the bedroom suite. We step inside, and I shut the door.

She spins into me. "Your papà looked mad."

"He's always upset about something," I claim, which isn't false. Lately, my brothers and I are always upsetting him. "Why don't you take a bath, get in bed, and try to sleep. I'm unsure how long my meeting is going to take."

She doesn't move. The worry in her gaze intensifies.

I slide my hand on her cheek. "Please trust me. Everything is fine."

"I'm sorry I've caused issues between you and your family," she whispers.

I scoff. "You haven't caused anything. This is Leo's fault." I spin her and move her toward the bathroom, stopping in front of the jacuzzi tub. Lit candles create a soft glow. Bubbles and rose petals lie on the surface of the water. The floral scent flares in my nostrils. Soft, romantic music plays on the surround sound.

"Is your bathroom always like this?" she asks.

I grin. "Nope. But if you want it to be, I can make that happen."

She bites on her smile. I unzip the back of her wedding gown and slide the white dress off her. It glides to the floor and pools at her feet. I take a minute to appreciate her curves then admit, "Not the wedding night I imagined. I promise I'll make it up to you."

She circles her arms around my shoulders, lacing her fingers around my neck. "You have nothing to make up to me."

"Oh, I'm going to make this up to you," I reiterate, trying to hide how pissed I am that I have to deal with my family issues tonight. I pick up a claw clip I had my staff member put on the side of the tub and pin her hair so it won't get wet. I push her thong down her legs and order, "Now, get in the tub."

She obeys, sinking into the water until the bubbles cover her chest. She sighs. "This feels so nice. It's not fair I get to sit in this without you."

I lean down and peck her on the lips. "I'll try to be quick, but don't wait up. Make yourself at home. Whatever's in this wing is now yours."

She reaches up and caresses my cheek. "I love you. I'm so lucky to have you."

"I'm the lucky one, dolce." I kiss her again then rise. "Enjoy your bath." I leave and shut the door to the bedroom. For several moments, I stand there and breathe deeply, debating how I want to deal with Papà and my brothers. I go over the story I told Tristano and Pina in my head so I don't get caught. This might be the most important lie I've ever told.

I make my way down the stairs and pass Pina outside Papà's office. She's pacing while tapping her fingers on her thigh. I cautiously ask in a low voice, "What's going on?"

She freezes then exhales. An anxious expression appears on her face. It's new for me. I've never seen Pina not confident. She answers, "Dante wants to talk to Tristano and me."

"About what?"

"He didn't say." She glances at the ceiling and takes several slow breaths.

I pull her to the corner of the hallway, away from Papà's office. "Why don't you just get it over with and tell him?"

"No," she firmly replies.

"Why not? If you and my brother are an item, then just—"

"Who said we're an item?"

I cross my arms. "You slept with Tristano, and it's just fun and games?"

Her face hardens.

"Tell me you aren't that stupid," I add.

"Why don't you ask your brother that."

"Meaning?"

She huffs. "You know Tristano."

"Still not following."

Her anxiety changes to disgust with a hint of sadness. "This is a conversation you should have with your bother, not me. I'm not the one with the issues."

"What issues?"

"End of conversation," she claims and brushes past me.

"Pina!"

She looks over her shoulder, firing darts at me with her eyes, and commands, "Stay out of it, Massimo."

I hold my hands in the air. "Fine. I have enough of my own problems."

"Yeah, you do," she mutters.

For two minutes, I regroup, doing the same thing I did before walking down the stairs. Then I ignore Pina and enter my father's office.

Papà stops mid-sentence. His scowl deepens. He seethes, "Nice of you to join us."

I go into defensive mode. "If you don't mind, my bride is alone in my bed. Let's move this conversation along."

Papà jabs me in the chest, roaring, "You don't decide to take a head member of a family out without my approval. How many times do I need to tell all of you this?" He glares between my brothers and me.

Stick with the story. Katiya's future relationship with my family hangs on this conversation.

I sniff hard, crossing my arms. "Maybe if you weren't so closed-minded, we could tell you our plans."

"But you didn't tell us, either, did you?" Dante accuses.

Anger builds in my veins. I hurl, "Let's not pretend all of us don't have our secrets."

"Like what?" Papà demands.

The room turns silent. My brothers and I don't move. Each of us tries not to appear guilty.

"What else are all of you hiding from me?" Papà interrogates.

"I'm not hiding anything," Dante asserts. He goes over to the bar and pours himself a scotch. He takes a large mouthful, swallows, and grimaces. "And I'm with you on this, Papà. None of you can continue to make these decisions without approval. It's irresponsible."

I sneer. "Now you side with Papà? It was fine when you wanted us to blow up the sex club when Papà instructed us not to."

Dante's face hardens. "Shut up, Massimo."

"Why? Because you're next in line? It's okay for you to go against Papà's orders, but we can't make our own decisions?" I hurl.

Papà slams his hand on the desk. "None of you—and I mean none..." he pauses, locks eyes on Dante, then continues, "...are to touch any crime family head unless I approve it. From this point forward, if I catch any of you going against me, that's it. You're out!"

"Out?" Gianni questions.

It only angers Papà more. He shouts, "Yes! Out! All privileges revoked. No more taking part in any family business. And you'll move out of this house. Does that clarify?"

"You can't do that," Tristano mutters.

Papà's dark eyes gleam black. He grits his teeth and threatens, "Watch me."

The tension in the room grows. The more time that passes, the redder Papà's cheeks turn. He never flinches, assessing each of my brothers and me.

I decide I need to move this conversation on. I sniff hard and state, "Leo needs to die. He'll come after Katiya."

Papà turns back toward me, seething, "Did you ever stop to think? If you came to me, we could have solved this together."

My chest tightens. I didn't expect this response from Papà, just another lecture on not taking out the head of crime families.

Gianni comes to my defense. "Maybe if you weren't constantly saying no to everything, we'd bring things to you."

"It's my job to say yes or no," Papà asserts.

"You don't trust us," Gianni points out.

Papà sarcastically laughs. "Trust you? Sometimes I wonder if the four of you are trying to test me. You have more power than I did at your age, yet it seems to only result in your arrogance. You all think you know better than me."

"Leo needs to die," I reiterate, not into the lecture.

Papà spins to me and jabs my chest. "Now that you've done what you have, there's no other choice, is there?"

"No, there isn't," I agree, happy he's cornered, then add, "But why are you so pissed about it?"

"There are ramifications when you take someone out," Papà declares.

"Not this again," Tristano mutters.

"You! Out!" Papà roars, pointing at him, then continues, "All of you except Massimo. Get out!"

My brothers give me a sympathetic glance and go to leave. When Tristano opens the door, Tully steps inside.

As soon as I see him, I demand, "Where's Katiya's money?"

The smile I hate so much appears on his lips. In his equally annoying voice, he replies, "Is that any way to welcome me to your house?"

"Cut the shit, Tully."

"Do not disrespect him," Papà barks.

I refrain from saying anything. Papà's idea of who should have respect and who shouldn't is different from my and my brother's opinion.

"Pretty sure you want the information I have," Tully gloats, focusing on me.

I tighten my arms to my chest, trying not to react. Everything about Tully gets on my last nerve lately. I respond, "Such as?"

He lights up his cigar, puffing a few times, creating a cloud of thick smoke around us.

I step a few feet back and wave the smoke out of my face. A lot of guys I know love cigars. To me, it's always felt like it was smothering my lungs. Plus, I prefer to stay in shape. Not being able to breathe while working out doesn't sound appealing to me.

He takes a few more drags then slowly releases more toxic air. He states, "Leo's ordered a raid on your club."

The hairs on my neck rise. "What are you talking about?"

Papà hands Tully a tumbler of whiskey.

Tully takes a mouthful, swallows, then calmly answers, "Our contact inside just relayed the message. Leo's men planted drugs in it. The FBI is raiding it in ten minutes."

"You're lying," I accuse, but my gut says this isn't one of Tully's games. He spoke without dragging it out like he usually does.

Papà's color drains from his cheeks, but it's quickly replaced with rage. He snarls, "Leo set us up with the FBI?"

It's a crime family rule no one breaks. We deal with our problems between families. Unless they're on your payroll, getting law enforcement agents involved is a huge sin. It opens all the families up to legal issues. Plus, the stronger we all are, whether we're on the same side or not, the harder it is for the police to hurt any of us.

"He did."

I tug on my hair and mutter, "Jesus. Ten minutes..." I focus on Tully. "What are they planting?"

"Heroin."

"Fuck!" I yell. Then I point out, "And you knew but did nothing?"

Tully takes another puff of his cigar, like we're playing a game of cards or something.

It irritates me but also gives me a sense of relief. I freeze, realizing he's back to playing games. He'll only do it if he's in control of something.

Now I'm going to owe him again.

Shit.

Better than having the FBI on my back, I suppose.

"Tully?" Papà demands.

After another mouthful of whiskey, Tully responds, "My guys went in and removed the drugs."

Yep. I'm going to owe him big-time.

"When?" Papà questions.

Tully finishes his drink. "Twenty minutes ago."

"They got everything?" I ask.

"All of it. But now my inside guy's compromised," Tully announces.

My gut dives. I'm going to owe Tully double. This isn't some little favor. It takes years to penetrate your guy into another crime family.

"You're sure they got it all?" Papà asks.

Tully nods. "Every last packet."

Papà pats him on the back then takes his glass. He refills it then hands it to him. "Thanks. We owe you. I'll call the attorney to meet Massimo over there."

Tully's lips twitch. "What are friends for if you can't intercept an Abruzzo. Right, Massimo?" He smirks at me, making it loud and clear that I owe him.

There's no point in stretching this out. I demand, "What do you want?"

He shrugs. "Not sure yet. But I'll let you know." He winks at me.

I refrain from groaning. I open and close my fists at my side then reply, "Fine. Now, where's Katiya's money?"

A few moments pass. Tully gives me his arrogant grin, and more tension mounts.

"Tully—"

"Calm down," he reprimands, reaching behind his coat and pulling a thick yellow envelope out of his back pocket. He hands it to me.

I open it up. It's all one hundred bills but still less than what Katiya should have gotten. I blurt out, "You seem to have forgotten the majority of it."

Tully sticks his chest out. "Nah. I think the favor you owe me, along with what you think is missing, is more than fair...considering I lost an undercover man to save your ass tonight."

"This is Katiya's money, not mine," I seethe.

"Well, since you're married now, it's both yours, right?" Papà interjects, arching his eyebrows in a challenge.

"Married? Did I miss my invite?" Tully questions.

"No. My sons seem to think our family traditions don't apply to them," Papà answers, and I can't help but hear the hurt in his voice. Gianni and Cara's nuptials without my father present didn't go over so well. I guess mine are no different.

"What a shame. I love a good Marino wedding," Tully replies.

My blood boils, but there's nothing I can do. I owe Tully, and there's no way I'm getting more money from the ring.

"What did your bride expect to get for the ring?" Tully questions.

I shift on my feet, not answering him. Katiya and I never discussed figures.

Tully's face lights up. "Ah. She has no idea what it was worth, does she?"

I stay silent, not wanting to give him the satisfaction of being correct but unable to deny it. I only lie when it's necessary, and this isn't. Plus, I imagine what Tully didn't pay for the ring doesn't cover the cost of him replacing his man.

Tully chuckles. "Give your bride the money. She'll be more than happy to have that cash."

"We done here?" I ask Papà, tired of this entire scenario.

He assesses me then responds, "For now. We'll talk more later."

"Looking forward to it," I mutter, then swallow my pride and tell Tully, "Thank you for taking care of the situation."

He nods, and I leave.

My phone rings. I pick it up, ignoring the heated conversation between Tristano, Pina, and Dante, going straight to our suite. I answer, knowing what's coming, "Jenifer. Everything okay?"

"The FBI is here. They have a search warrant," she frets.

"Let them do their jobs. I'll be there in a few moments."

Before I open the bedroom door, I stand against the wall and close my eyes, trying to get a handle on everything that's happened. No matter how much I attempt to calm my quivering insides, the rage only grows.

Leo's gone too far. He was a dead man before he tried to set me up with the FBI. Now, there's a silver lining in his actions.

There's no way Papà or my brothers would ever attempt to stand in my way. As soon as I deal with the Feds and return from the club, I'm insisting Papà put all of our resources on taking him down. Leo's about to learn what happens when you fuck with a Marino.

28

Katiya

WHEN THE CLOCK HITS TEN IN THE MORNING, I OPEN Massimo's bedroom door. I don't know where he is, but I've been up for the last few hours. I must have fallen asleep as soon as I got out of the jacuzzi and my head hit the pillow.

My stomach somersaults as I step into the hallway. I attempt to retrace my steps from last night, but I'm unsure if I'm going in the right direction. Not that I have any clue where I should go at this moment; the house is huge. I'm aware his family probably still doesn't think too highly of me, and I don't know where Massimo could be hiding.

Why hasn't he come back to the room?

Did he speak with his family, and they changed his mind about me?

Is he intentionally staying away?

The pit in my stomach grows with every step I take. Plus, the long corridor doesn't help. Its gold-and-maroon walls should feel warm, but everything about it screams money, serving as a reminder that this isn't my house.

Perhaps our nuptials were too good to be true?

No. Massimo is committed to me. He wouldn't have married me if he weren't.

His family wasn't there to change his mind.

He's a stronger man than one who listens to others.

I turn the corner, and the staircase comes into view. A touch of relief erupts, even though I still don't know where I'm going. I make my way down it and step off the landing, continuing past an office and several sitting rooms. I get to another corner and run smack into Angelo.

"Oh my gosh! I'm so sorry!" I blurt out. I step back and almost slip.

He swiftly circles his arm around my waist. "Whoa," he says, then pins his dark, brooding eyes on mine.

My pulse skyrockets. I breathe a few times, trying to figure out what to say.

"You have to be careful on the marble. It's wet and slippery when that sign is out," he states, pointing behind me.

I glance several feet behind me at the glaringly yellow sign, feeling stupid I didn't see it. "I'm sorry. I—"

"Missed it. Yes. It's easy to do," Angelo claims, the corners of his eyes crinkling softly.

I nod, adding, "Well, thank you for not letting me fall."

He releases his arm from me and claims, "Marinos don't let other Marinos fall."

Silence fills the air. I rack my brain about how I should respond, but I can't seem to form any coherent sentence. All I see is Angelo's intimidating stare assessing me. I'm undecided if he's angry or okay with our marriage.

He breaks the tension, declaring, "I'm sorry I missed the ceremony."

"You are?" I blurt out, then reprimand myself for questioning him.

His lips twitch. "Of course. I prefer to welcome my new daughters-in-law into the family before they say their vows."

More anxiety floods my chest. I reply, "I'm sorry. It just…it just happened."

His eyes turn warmer. I can see resemblances he shares with all his sons and even Arianna. It calms me a bit. He asserts, "Yes. Well, I know my son. When he gets something in his head, there's no stopping him. He does it on his timeline."

I smile, still not trusting my words to be the right ones.

Angelo surprises me again, reaching around me and giving me a fatherly hug. Something about it pulls at my emotions. I blink hard to stop the tears from falling.

I return the hug as he states, "Welcome to the family. Once you get to know everyone, I'm sure you'll fit right in."

Hope swirls with doubt. I want to be part of the Marinos. Besides Massimo, I don't know them well. Yet, I would love to feel like I'm part of their family. Family is something I've craved since my father passed.

Angelo kisses me on the cheek, pulls back, and asks, "Have you had any breakfast?"

I shake my head. "No, but umm...do you know where Massimo is? I don't think he came back to the room last night. His side of the bed was perfectly made."

Angelo's face darkens. The energy around him turns serious. He answers, "He had some business to take care of at the club. I'm expecting him shortly."

Panic fills me. "He's okay?"

Angelo puts his arm around my shoulder. "Yes. He's perfectly safe. Now, let me show you to the dining room. The ladies were still there when I left. They were discussing some final details for Bridget and Dante's wedding."

"Oh. I wouldn't want to interrupt," I claim.

"Nonsense," Angelo replies, then stops outside a doorway. The women's voices fill the air, and he motions for me to go inside. "I have some work to take care of, but help yourself to anything. If you don't see something on the table, the chef can make it for you."

I hesitate.

He orders, "Don't be shy. Go eat."

"Okay. Thank you," I say, then step into the room.

Cara says, "When do you want—" She catches me out of the corner of her eye then turns her head.

Bridget and Arianna spin in their seats.

My heart pounds so hard, I think it's going to burst. I don't move, wishing I'd stayed up in Massimo's room.

"Katiya. Did you sleep well?" Bridget asks.

I nod, unable to speak. Arianna's glare looks meaner than Massimo's. I can't tear my eyes off them as I try to stop my quivering insides.

"I'll take that as a no. Come sit," Bridget says, then rises and pulls out the chair next to her.

I force my feet to move, obeying her orders. When I'm safely in the chair, my stomach growls.

Cara lifts a few silver platters, asking, "Eggs? Bacon? Waffles? The chef can make you an omelet if you want."

"Coffee?" Arianna pours a mug and slides it toward me, still glaring.

I swallow the lump in my throat, managing to get out, "Thanks."

She crosses her arms and sits back in the chair. She tilts her head and asserts, "You should eat while it's still hot."

My stomach growls again, but I'm cautious, suddenly wondering if Arianna poisoned anything. I tell myself it's ridiculous, but now I can't get the thought out of my head.

"Yeah, have some food," Bridget gently adds, picking up my plate and dumping a spoonful of scrambled eggs on it. She adds strawberries and toast then sets it in front of me.

I clear my throat. "Thanks." Silence fills the air. The women are staring at me, waiting for me to eat. Poison becomes harder to get out of my mind.

"Go on. Eat," Cara demands.

This is silly. She didn't poison it.

I don't know that.

I pick up my fork then pause.

As if she can read my mind, Arianna smirks. "Don't worry, I didn't poison it. I didn't know you were coming down here to prepare."

"Arianna!" Bridget reprimands.

"What? Don't stick up for her and act like she's an innocent bystander in everything. I could have been raped or killed!"

"I didn't know why Donato wanted access to that room," I declare.

"That's convenient for you." Arianna huffs.

"It's true!"

"Sure, it is." She scowls.

I scoot my chair out and rise. "Sorry I interrupted your breakfast."

Bridget grabs my forearms. "Katiya, wait! Don't go!"

I lock eyes with her.

She nods to the seat and softens her voice. "Sit down."

"Sorry, I'm not very hungry anymore."

Massimo's voice rings through the air, scolding, "Arianna, you have it wrong. All of you have it wrong."

I spin, relieved he's okay and happy to see him, even if this is super uncomfortable. But my relief is short-lived.

The lines around his eyes and forehead look deeper than usual. His eyes are bloodshot, and it's clear he didn't sleep at all. He steps next to me, puts his hand on my lower back, and leans down to kiss my head. He locks eyes with me and questions, "Did you sleep okay?"

I respond, "Yes. Is everything okay? Your father said something happened with the club?"

He grinds his molars for a moment. "Things are taken care of for the time being. I'll fill you in later."

His answer doesn't relieve all my anxiety, but I'm glad things are okay for now.

He turns to Arianna. "We need to talk."

"Yeah, we do. Don't we?" she claims.

Massimo squeezes my waist. "I'll be back soon. Have some breakfast. You need to eat." He walks over to Arianna and holds out his hand.

She refuses to take it, grasps the table's edge, and pries her very pregnant self out of her seat. After giving Massimo another look of death, she leaves the room with him in tow.

More tense silence builds. I blurt out, "I'm telling the truth! I didn't have anything to do with her kidnapping except for showing Donato how to access the room. And that was weeks prior to when he abducted her!"

Bridget and Cara exchange a look I'm unsure how to interpret. I say, "Fine. Don't believe me." I turn to leave, and Cara grabs my arm.

She demands, "Sit down, Katiya."

"Why should I? Neither of you believes me. Or maybe you don't want to," I hypothesize. And I wish I wasn't disappointed, but I am. I shouldn't have thought things could be fine between the Marinos and me. Perhaps they'll always think the worst of me.

"I believe you," Bridget offers.

Surprised, I glance at her. "You do?"

"Yes."

"Why? No one else does."

"Not true. I do, too," Cara claims.

I jerk my head toward her. "But you don't act like it."

"What did I do?" She arches her eyebrows.

I take a few deep breaths, trying to vocalize it, but I can't.

Bridget pats the chair. "Katiya, you're part of the family now. Massimo will straighten Arianna out. Everything will be fine between you both. You'll see. Now sit down and eat."

My stomach growls again, and Cara snorts. She taps my fork on the plate. "Eat."

I cave, sit down, and take a sip of hot coffee. The acidic drink hits my tongue, and I wince.

"You didn't tell us what you wanted in it," Cara states, her lips twitching.

"Oh." I reach for the creamer boat and sugar jar. It's too far.

Bridget pushes it toward me.

I fix my coffee how I like it then take a sip.

"Good now?" Cara asks.

"Yes. Thank you."

Bridget orders again, "Eat."

I take a bite. Cara and Bridget watch me, but once I take the first mouthful, I no longer care. I shovel the food in as fast as I can, trying to fill the emptiness in my gut. Then I take a break from the food, washing it down with more coffee.

Humor fills Bridget's expression. "When did you eat last?"

I shrug. "On the plane. Not sure what time."

"Well, you're just in time to discuss the bachelorette party," Cara chirps.

I furrow my eyebrows. "Bachelorette party?"

"Yep. Bridget and Dante are getting married in a month."

"Oh! Right. Sorry. My mind is all over the place," I admit, then turn to Bridget. "Congratulations."

She beams. "Thank you. I hear congrats are in order for you, too, Mrs. Massimo Marino."

My heart swells with pride. The few times I've been called Mrs. Massimo Marino, it's done the same. I don't know if I'll ever get used to it or stop feeling so happy about the title.

"Yes! Congratulations. I heard your wedding was a bit like mine," Cara states.

"Oh? How?" I ask.

She scoffs. "Oh, you know. Last minute. Private. Unannounced, shall we say?"

"You didn't have a big wedding?" I question, surprised. Everything I've heard about Dante and Bridget's upcoming wedding makes me believe there are hundreds of guests invited.

"Nope. Don't think Angelo will ever forgive Gianni or Massimo," she admits.

"How did—"

"Ladies, have you seen my wife?" a familiar voice says, and I turn.

Killian's smile falls. He tears his eyes off me and addresses Bridget. "Where's Arianna?"

"Talking to Massimo. You should go speak with them. Things aren't what you think," she replies.

He drills his green orbs into mine. "Is that right?"

"Yes, it is," I assert, trying to ignore my quivering insides.

"Katiya's your sister-in-law now, so you might want to offer her your congrats," Cara chirps.

He gapes then shuts his mouth. He licks his lips then questions, "You married Massimo?"

I lift my chin and sit straighter in my chair. "Yes."

"When?"

"Yesterday. At least, I think it was yesterday. The time change has me confused about what day it is," I confess.

"Where was this?"

"The Maldives."

"Tristano and Pina were there," Cara adds.

Killian scrunches his forehead. "Why were they there?"

"Oh, you know. Family business." Bridget bats her eyes.

"Such as..."

Cara shrugs. "You'd know more than us, wouldn't you?"

Killian shifts on his feet. "How would I know?"

"I think your dick gives you leverage in this family, doesn't it?" Cara quips.

Killian gives her an exasperated look then states, "I'm not answering that. Where's my wife?"

"Who knows where they went. Want some toast? I'll put some extra butter on it while Arianna isn't here," Bridget offers, waving a piece in the air.

Killian glances behind his shoulder then steps forward. He lowers his voice, "When did they leave?"

"A few minutes ago," Cara says.

He gazes behind him again then tells Bridget, "Go on, then. These pregnancy hormones have Arianna on a bigger health kick than normal. If she tosses my butter one more time, I swear I'm going to lock her in a room until the baby comes."

"Wow. You must really love butter," I mutter.

He locks eyes with me again. I think he's going to reprimand me about Arianna, but he claims, "It's not just butter. It's Irish butter."

"What's the difference?" I ignorantly question.

Killian scrunches his face. He shakes his head at me then instructs Bridget, "Please tell our new sister-in-law what kind of sin she just committed."

Bridget tries to hide her amusement. With a straight face and serious tone, she states, "There's nothing better than Irish butter."

I glance at Cara, who's biting her smile. I answer, "Good to know."

Killian grabs the piece of toast from Bridget and shoves it in his mouth, quickly chewing it until it's gone.

Cara hands him a glass of water, and he downs that, too.

"Okay. Off to find my wife." He spins and freezes.

"I saw that," Arianna claims.

"It was dry," Killian lies.

"Sure, it was." She huffs then leaves the room.

He follows, and Massimo comes over and sits next to me. He slides his arm around my shoulders, tugging me into him and pressing his lips to my forehead. "You okay?"

"Yeah."

He studies me for a moment then pecks me on the lips. "Don't worry about Arianna. Everything will be fine. She just needs to process everything."

I stay silent, unsure she'll ever like or trust me.

"Don't worry, dolce." He points to the table. "Someone hand me a plate. I'm starving."

29

MC

Massimo

One Week Later

"Leo's in the back of Fat Tony's Pizzeria for the next few hours," Luca relays, stubbing out his joint in the ashtray and releasing a big cloud of smoke.

The hairs on my neck rise. "Fat Tony's? Tell me I heard that wrong."

"That motherfucker," Tristano mutters.

"You did not hear it wrong." Luca scowls, taking his Glock out of his pants and checking the chamber.

"When did Fat Tony turn?" Tristano asks.

"We had our suspicions about a month ago," Papà informs us.

My stomach dives. Fat Tony is Tristano's and my guy. We recruited him, trained him, and convinced the family to allow us to do so. I seethe, "And you didn't bother to tell us?"

Papà calmly sits at his desk. He takes a mouthful of sambuca then rises. He pours another tumbler and stands at the window, gazing at the night sky.

Tristano angrily shakes his head at me then questions, "Papà, what's your reasoning for hiding this from us?"

Another moment passes. He finally turns and declares, "I'm the head of this family. I watch everyone. All our men. All the time. It's my job."

"But you should have informed us," I insist.

Papà grunts, finishes his drink, then sets the glass down on his desk. He crosses his arms over his chest, replying, "*You* should know your men. If you were watching them, you would know. I kept waiting for you to come to me with this information, but you never did."

I sniff hard, shifting on my feet. He's right. I hate that he is, but it is Tristano's and my responsibility to watch our men and know what they're doing.

"So what was it, Papà? A test? You should have disclosed your suspicion. That's unfair," Tristano states.

Papà's eyes turn to dark slits. He steps in front of Tristano and jabs him in the chest. "Unfair? Don't you dare talk to me about disclosure! Or did you already fully inform your brother of your personal affairs?"

Tristano's eyes widen, and his cheeks turn red. His face hardens, and he stays quiet.

Papà puts his hand on Tristano's cheek. "You need to grow up. Real men don't hide things from their family—especially a woman."

Anytime I try to approach the subject of Pina with Tristano, he clams up. I even asked him what happened with Dante the night we got back from the Maldives, but he refused to tell me. All he said was, "Keep Pina's and my business to yourself and tell Katiya to do the same. Dante isn't to know anything until Pina is ready to tell him."

Since it isn't my business, and I have enough of my own problems, I did what he asked. And while I agree with Papà that he needs to come clean to Dante, I'm not in their shoes. From what I could tell in the Maldives, Pina's the one stopping Tristano from telling Dante, but I don't know her reasons for keeping it a secret.

Still, I feel bad for my brother. I'm pretty sure Dante isn't going to be okay with their relationship. I know what it's like not to have our family on board with your decisions. Plus, I'm unhappy with Luca. I wonder if there will ever be a point where he chooses our confidence over Papà's. So I break the tension, interjecting, "Let's have this conversation another time. We've got a limited window of time to take Leo out."

Papà and Tristano glare at each other another minute, then Papà steps back. "Leo's already on his way here."

"What are you talking about?" I inquire.

"I sent Dante and Gianni to take care of it. They left an hour ago with their crew."

My pulse shoots toward the ceiling. I fume, "Leo is mine. I've made it clear from the start."

"Your brother's team will handle picking him up," Papà asserts.

I step closer, barking, "He raped my wife."

Papà lowers his voice and says, "Which is why I didn't send you."

"That makes zero sense," I claim.

Papà's lips curve into a sinister smile. "Doesn't it?"

My chest tightens as the air in my lungs turns stale. I shake my head, insisting, "No, it doesn't."

Papà's phone rings. He glances at it then looks at Luca. "Why don't you explain it. This is Giuseppe. I need to speak with him in private."

"So he can promise more things that'll never happen," Tristano mutters.

"Do not disrespect Giuseppe!" Papà roars.

"Let's go," Luca states, pointing toward the door.

My brother and I leave as Papà answers the phone in Italian. As soon as his office door shuts, I spin to Luca. "Are you ever going to have our backs?"

Luca clenches his jaw, giving me a peeved expression. He finally answers, "Do you really think it's wise for me to ignore Angelo's orders? Or did you forget he runs this family?"

"You could have said something," Tristano claims.

Luca stands taller. "No, I couldn't have. So stop blaming me. Take this out with your papà. He's the boss. I'm not. It's pretty clear, so get with the program."

I take a few calculated breaths, trying to calm down. Everything Luca is saying is correct, yet I hate how he kept this from Tristano and me. Fat Tony was one of our first recruits. He's been with our family for years.

"Are you over your pissy fit so I can tell you why your papà didn't send you?"

"Fine. Tell us," Tristano orders.

Luca points between us. "You two would have shot the place up, including Fat Tony and Leo."

"Give us some credit," Tristano claims.

Leo scoffs then focuses on me, arching his eyebrows.

I glance at Tristano, stay quiet, and clench my jaw tight. I can't deny that it could have happened.

Luca continues, "I thought you wanted to make Leo pay for his sins."

"Of course I do," I state.

Luca's phone buzzes. He glances at it then orders, "Go tell your bride you'll be a while. They're five minutes away."

I gaze behind my shoulder to make sure no one else is around then demand, "No one touches Leo. He's mine. Understood?"

"I get Fat Tony," Tristano claims.

Luca motions toward the staircase. "Then go warn your bride she might not see you tonight."

The buzz in my veins grows. It always happens before I'm about to go into the dungeon. By the time I get to the library in my wing, I'm antsy.

Katiya's reading a book. She looks up and smiles. "Hey! Is it time to get ready for dinner?"

I sit on the couch and tug her onto my lap.

She smiles and cups my cheek, tracing my jawbone with her thumb. She tilts her head, asking, "Why do you look serious but happy?"

I decide it's better not to lie. "Leo's here."

"What? Where?" she frets, looking around.

I tighten my arms around her. "Not up here. In the dungeon."

She inhales sharply then freezes. Her hand shakes against my cheek.

I cover it with my palm and state, "He's going to pay for what he did to you. Tonight."

Her eyes well with tears.

I swipe at one that falls. "Dolce—"

"Let me do it," she chokes out.

It's my turn to freeze.

"I-I could do it," she claims, but it sounds like she's trying to convince herself.

"No."

"But—"

"No. I won't have you involved in this."

She bites her lip, and the tears freely fall. "I-I thought so many times about killing him. I imagined how I would do it."

Her confession doesn't surprise me. I acknowledge, "I know. But you aren't doing this. You'll never get it out of your mind if you do."

She sniffles and turns her head.

I move it back so she's facing me. "Let me do this for you, dolce."

She stays quiet.

"Trust me to inflict and extend his pain," I demand.

She finally nods, blinking hard.

I hug her then rise, setting her on her feet. She glances up, and I say, "Come on."

"Where are we going?"

"I'm taking you to Bridget. You hang out with her tonight, okay?"

"I'm okay on my own," Katiya claims.

"No. I might be all night. Spend time with Bridget and the others until bedtime. It'll be easier for you," I insist.

She takes a deep breath then agrees. "Okay."

I kiss her on the lips. "Good girl. Daddy will give you a reward when I get back." I wink.

A soft, emotion-filled laugh escapes her lips.

"Come on," I repeat then walk her to Dante's wing.

Bridget's in the combined office-sitting room he had remodeled for her. I knock, and she looks up from the desk, smiling. Her face falls, and she asks, "What's wrong?"

"Dante and Gianni picked up Leo. I'm going to be busy for a while. Can Katiya hang here?" I say.

She rises. "Of course! Fiona and I were going to have dinner and watch a movie later tonight. She was going to ask you and Cara to join us anyway."

I spin Katiya into me. "Don't wait up for me. Okay?"

She nods and kisses me. "Be careful."

"You don't have anything to worry about, dolce. It's the dungeon," I assure her.

She still looks anxious.

"Tell her, Bridget," I demand.

"It's true." She takes Katiya's hand. "Let's go find the others."

"Thanks," I say, then leave the room, going straight to the dungeon.

When I get to the bottom of the steps, Luca's waiting outside the cell.

"Why aren't you inside?" I question, glancing in to confirm Leo and Fat Tony are there.

"What's your tool of choice tonight?" he asks.

I stare past him at Leo. His naked limbs stretch as far as possible, his toes barely touching the ground. His arms are shaking, probably a mix of the fear he's trying to hide and his body reacting to the restrained position. I curl my hands into fists at my side, admitting to Luca, "I haven't decided."

Luca's lips curl. "Great. I have a present for you."

"What is it?"

He answers, "A slow, painful death. Cabinet B. Shelf five."

I arch my eyebrows, but his arrogant smile only grows. "Guess it's cabinet B, shelf five." I pat him on the back and go directly to the area we keep our tools.

When I open the cabinet, I can't help but look back at Luca and grin. He wasn't exaggerating about slow and painful. I pull out a five-gallon bucket of deck stain, open it, then grab a set of paintbrushes. Most are smaller, more like what an artist would use. They're appropriate for painting on canvas, not ones you'd use on a deck. There's only one bigger one. I carry everything over to where my brothers are and set it down.

"We're making pizza tonight," Tristano states, glaring at Fat Tony and Leo. It's a crapshoot who in my family hates traitors more. Tristano is no exception.

I glance at the table full of different kitchen utensils. I pat Tristano on the back. "Pace yourself, brother."

Papà and Luca step into the cell. Papà goes to the small bar and pours six shots of sambuca. He hands one to each of us and holds his glass high in the air, toasting, "To the fall of the Abruzzo empire!"

"Saluti!" my brothers and I chime in then toss the alcohol down our throats.

The heat burns from my throat to my gut. I pick up a brush, and Luca passes me a mask. I put it on then dip it in the deck stain. I step in front of Leo, and all the rage I've felt since learning what he did to my dolce burns hotter than the alcohol.

He swallows hard, clenching his jaw, but his legs are now shaking as badly as his arms. I drag the stain over his top lip so he'll have no choice but to inhale the deadly fumes all night. He winces and coughs, his face turning red. I grab his hair, yank his head back, and he spits at me.

I duck the wad of saliva and slap him. "You motherfucker. You can't even spit correctly."

He tries again, but it's weak since he's still trying to find fresh air. I dodge another wet ball of phlegm and tug his head to the point if I go any farther, I'll break his neck.

"Easy. We wouldn't want this to end too soon," Dante cautions.

I make a mental note to stay in control so I don't make a mistake I regret. I hold my hand behind me and order, "Give me the bigger brush."

Someone hands me the one-inch wide one soaked in the harsh chemicals. I lean over Leo, trailing the brush down his bare chest and torso until I reach his pelvis. He tries to spit again, but it's a sad gag. I murmur, "When you raped and threatened to kill my wife, you chose your fate." I barely touch his flaccid cock with the bristles.

"Don't!" he chokes out.

Even though I'm wearing the mask, I need to get some fresh air from the fumes. The combination of my adrenaline and the stain is making me slightly dizzy. Yet, I'm unable to step back. I snort then stab his lower region with the brush. He winces, which only makes me giddy. I coat his lower abdomen, cock, and balls with several layers of stain.

His face contorts, and his lower body squirms. When his lower extremities are a redwood color, I step back, needing the distance for a moment from the harsh scent. I stand next to where the others are watching. It's a tiny area that's well ventilated for these situations. Cool air blows above me, and another vent is suctioning out the fumes.

Tristano steps next to me. He crosses his arms and scowls at Fat Tony, stating, "I'm still debating what to do with this fat fuck. I'm leaning toward the pizza cutter."

I grunt, pull my mask down, and tilt my head toward the ceiling where the fresh air is coming out. Then I hand Tristano a brush and reiterate, "We can use it later."

He studies Fat Tony further but finally takes the brush and puts his mask on.

I replace mine, dip my small brush in more stain, then move back in front of Leo. I ask, "Did you know your skin is your body's largest organ? Whatever you put on it gets absorbed. Right now, your kidneys and liver are trying to fight the toxins." I take the brush, grab his hair, and yank his head back.

Leo tries to fight, but his body only flails against the restraints. The sound of liquid dripping on the concrete floor hits my ears, and I glance over at Fat Tony. Piss pools at his feet.

Tristano slaps him hard, shouting, "Fat slob. You can't even keep control of your own body."

"Please. You have it wrong," Fat Tony claims.

"Oh yeah? How's that?" Tristano asks.

He roars, "I'm not an Abruzzo."

Leo's face scrunches tighter. He chokes out, "Motherfucker."

"So you haven't been spending time at the Abruzzo whore-house?" Tristano seethes. If there's one thing Marinos can't stand, it's how crime families like the Abruzzos force women to work in their whorehouses.

Fat Tony's eyes widen. He shakes his head. "No!"

Luca steps forward and plays a video on his phone. "So that's not you?"

Fat Tony's stomach rolls begin to shake. The color in his face drains as he watches the video.

"For every lie you tell, I'm extending your life by five minutes," Tristano warns.

Luca demands, "Now, I want to know—"

"Shut your mouth," Leo threatens.

I laugh. "Or what? You'll hurt him? Kill him? Have you not realized you no longer have any power?"

He tries to spit at me again, but it only dribbles down his cheek.

"Piece of shit," I mutter, then slide the smaller brush up his nostril.

He gags, and I step away before his puke hits me.

Gianni claps loudly. "Now we're getting somewhere."

"Give me the cheese grater," I order.

Dante hands it to me. The flat stainless steel is smooth on one side. The back has sharp, raised metal.

I release Leo's head, take the grater, and press the rough side under his shoulder. In a swift move, I slide it over his nipple, slicing bits off.

His scream sounds like an animal in pain. It echoes in the small cell, mixing with his whimpers.

Fat Tony's sweat runs down his body, and he cries out, "I swear I'm not an Abruzzo."

Tristano shakes his head. "So, what? You just take advantage of the women they enslave?"

"Because who would choose to fuck him? Look at the slob," Gianni states, then steps up and gets into a boxer stand. He pummels Fat Tony's stomach a dozen times like a punching bag. His stomach jiggles like jelly as he cries, begging Gianni to stop.

When he does, bruises begin forming on Fat Tony's stomach. Purple and red color the skin, and his stomach swells even more.

I refocus on Leo, sweeping the grater between his legs so it destroys his balls. New screams fill the air. Luca hands me the larger paintbrush, dipped in fresh stain. I hold it in front of Leo's nostrils, waiting for his sobs to lessen.

"Not such a scary motherfucker anymore, are you?" Luca taunts.

Leo's bloodshot eyes won't stop watering. I assume it's a mix of tears and toxic fumes. He sobs, "Please. Just get it over with."

New rage surfaces within me. I bark, "Is that what my wife begged you?"

He doesn't answer. His breath continues coming out in ragged bursts, and his head hangs toward the floor.

"Hold his head up," I order.

Luca yanks it back, and I land a right hook on his face as hard as possible.

Blood spurts everywhere. The cracking sound of his nose fills the small space. It moves to the side of his face, under his right eye. There's so much swelling, I can barely recognize him.

"Nice hook, bro," Dante praises.

I bark, "Admit that you threatened my wife to work for you, even though she didn't want any part of your twisted game."

His eyes swell so much, they're almost shut. He mumbles, "She's a whore."

I slam my left fist, and his nose moves to the left side of his face.

"Massimo, take a breather," Papà orders.

I glance at him in question.

He holds a shot glass in the air, giving me the look. He uses it when he's afraid we'll kill someone too soon before getting information out of them. He reiterates, "Come. It's my turn."

I reluctantly step away, down the sambuca, and spend the next few hours letting Papà and my brothers interrogate Leo and Fat Tony about the Abruzzo operations. From time to time, I step in and escalate the punishments.

Most of the information comes from Fat Tony, who sings like a canary more and more every time Leo weakly orders him not to speak.

We learn about the Abruzzo's plans to infiltrate our gem business, more men who are traitors, and several more FBI raids scheduled for our other businesses in the city. When it's clear there's only a window of time left before Leo takes his last breath, Papà motions for me to resume my activities.

I coat his entire body in stain then order the others, "Step back."

They obey, and I pick up the flamethrower, move several feet away, and blast the fire at Leo.

His body erupts in flames. The smell of stain fumes and burnt flesh turns so thick, we all leave the room and shut the door.

I rip off my mask and watch him burn through the fireproof glass. Fat Tony gags from the smoke until his body hangs lifeless. When nothing but Leo's bones are left, I go to the bathroom to shower and clean up.

It takes about an hour until my insides calm. It's only then I climb up the stairs to the main level of the house.

It's dark. I glance at the hallway clock. It's five-thirty in the morning. I continue to my wing, and when I open the bedroom door, my dolce is there, pacing.

"Hey," I say, rushing over to her.

Anxiety fills her expression. She throws her arms around me and asks, "Is...is he dead?"

I tighten my arms around her and reply, "Yeah. And I made him pay."

30

MC

Katiya

Two Weeks Later

"Dolce, do you have a few spare hours for me?" Massimo asks, popping his head into the bathroom. He's wearing a grin that brings instant joy to me.

Ever since Leo's death, I've slept better than ever.

I finish my last curl and set my iron down, unable to hide my smirk. "That would assume I had a job or something on my schedule."

Massimo steps behind me and slides his hands down my arms. I tilt my head back. He gives me a peck on the lips. His eyes twinkle as he states, "I'm good if you want to be barefoot and pregnant for the next decade."

"Next decade!" I shriek.

He chuckles. "Yep. We could have a little team of Marinos."

Laughing, I shake my head and spin into him. Since the night before we got married, a day hasn't passed where Massimo hasn't talked about knocking me up. The idea of kids is growing on me now that the threat of Leo coming after me is over. For the first time since my father was alive, I feel safe and loved. It's allowing me to think about a future, which I used to avoid. I lock my fingers through Massimo's thick head of hair, asking, "So what's going on?"

Arrogance fills his expression. "It's a surprise."

My flutters explode. Massimo's always taken good care of me, but he has a new surprise for me daily. I claim, "You're spoiling me."

He declares, "I think you're going to really like what I have in store for you."

"Because I didn't like the other amazing things you've done for me?" I tease.

"This is different."

"How?"

"You'll see."

My butterflies spread their wings. Heat flies to my cheeks as I question, "Is it more of what you did to me last night?"

He cocks his eyebrows. "Which part? The part where I restrained you to the balcony in the dark so the guards could hear you beg me? Or the part where I turned on the lights in our room and fucked you against the glass?"

The burn on my face intensifies. I meekly reply, "Either?"

He chuckles and squeezes my ass. "It's not that type of surprise, dolce. But I'll make sure I take care of your needs later."

I get on my tippy-toes and kiss him, then chirp, "Deal."

"When can you leave?" he inquires.

"Hmm." I pretend to look at a watch even though my wrist is bare. "Since I have absolutely nothing planned for today, I'd say anytime you're ready."

"I kind of like you at my beck and call," he adds.

I smack his shoulder, laughing.

"It's warm outside. I don't think you need a jacket or anything," he states.

"Awesome!" I exclaim, happy the sunshine is returning to New York.

"Let's go," he instructs, takes my hand, and leads me through the suite, then the wing, and down the staircase. We step outside into the warm spring air. His black SUV and driver are waiting. We slide inside and take off.

"Are you going to tell me where we're going now?" I ask.

He shakes his head. Amusement fills his blues. He answers, "Nope."

I pretend to pout. "Aww. Please?"

He leans his head next to mine. "Say that again."

"Pleeeeeease," I reply with a smile.

He picks up my hand and kisses it. "Sorry. I can't tell you."

"Really?" I question.

"Yep." His phone rings, and he groans. "I have to take this."

"It's okay," I assure him.

He answers in Italian and has a fairly long conversation. I spend the time glancing out the window, admiring the spring colors that are finally starting to pop. He hangs up and says, "Sorry."

I shrug. "No worries. How far are we?"

He points to the exit marker on the side of the road. "This is us."

The SUV veers off the ramp. We drive several more blocks before pulling into Green-Wood Cemetery. It's the place where the elite of New York gets buried.

Confused, I question, "Are we going to a funeral?"

Massimo's face turns neutral. "No."

"Then why are we here?"

He answers, "My mamma's burial plot is here. My papà will also get buried here. Actually, all the Marinos have plots."

"Oh."

The driver turns down several roads then stops. Massimo gets out of the SUV and reaches in for me. I grab his hand, and he helps me out.

We walk across the green grass until we get to a large mausoleum shaped like an angel hugging a heart. It has several Marino names on it, including Nicoletta Marino.

"Do you come here often?" I ask Massimo, feeling guilty I haven't been to my father's grave in a while. The sting of his early death also hits me, but I try to shove it down.

"Not a lot," Massimo admits, then adds, "But I wanted to show you something else."

"What?"

He moves me several feet to another plot. The dirt looks fresh, as if it was recently added. I look at him in question. He tugs me closer to him and informs me, "Your father got moved here this morning."

A chill runs through my veins. I gape at Massimo, unable to speak. My vision turns blurry from my tears.

He continues, "I'm having your mother's casket transferred from Russia to here as well."

My mouth falls wider.

He adds, "I didn't order tombstones yet. I wanted you to pick them out."

Too many emotions fill me. I barely remember my mother or leaving Russia. All I ever knew was my father, but I know he fiercely loved my mother. He never dated anyone else to my knowledge. I heard him speaking to his best friend a few times about how much he missed her and hated how her grave was in Russia.

I glance between the dirt and Massimo, too shocked to put words together.

"Say something, dolce," he orders.

I finally choke out, "I-I don't know what to say!"

"Are you happy? Or upset? I can't tell," he confesses.

I toss my arms around him and squeeze him, sobbing, "So happy! I-I don't deserve you!"

He embraces me tightly, muttering, "I'm glad you like it."

When I retreat from him, I look back at the empty dirt.

My father is there.

My mother will be here soon.

How is this possible?

A fresh set of tears fall. "Thank you," I restate.

Massimo kisses the top of my head. "You don't need to thank me."

"Yes! I do!" I insist.

We spend a few more minutes at the graves, then he asks, "Do you want to go pick out the tombstones?"

I nod, choking up again about having my parents buried next to each other.

Massimo leads me to the SUV, and we drive to a nearby building. He guides me inside, and a bald older man greets us.

"Good morning, Mr. Marino. I assume this is your wife you told me about?" He holds out his hand.

Massimo shakes it, answering, "Yes. This is Katiya."

"Mrs. Marino, what a pleasure. I'm Daniel, the monument mason here. I can design and create anything you want. Your husband tells me you're looking for a headstone for your parents?"

"Yes," I reply.

"Great. I take it you've never had to do this before?"

I shake my head. "No, I haven't."

"Okay. So, the trick is to not be intimidated."

A nervous laugh escapes me. "Sounds easy."

He grins. "That's the spirit." His face turns serious. "Let me show you how we categorize things. It'll make the process easier."

"Thank you," I state. Massimo and I follow Daniel into a private room with a large table. Catalogs are spread all over it. He spends the next hour showing us different tombstones. By the time I decide on the oversized butterfly piece that's big enough for both my parents, my head is spinning.

Massimo and I get back in the SUV. Silence fills the vehicle. My thoughts are all over the place, but one thing is certain.

I hit the button for the divider window to go up then straddle Massimo. "Hi."

He tucks a lock of my hair behind my ear. "Hi. You doing okay?"

I circle my arms around his shoulders. "I can't believe you did that for me."

He runs his thumb over my jaw, asserting, "You're my girl."

All the happiness in the world feels like it's inside me right now. Never in a million years could I ever imagine I'd not only be out of the Petrov and Abruzzo grasp but also married to a man like Massimo. I reiterate, "Thank you so much."

He smiles then kisses me like I'm everything to him. And I return every ounce of his affection tenfold, because that's what he is to me—my everything.

I retreat, asking, "What are you doing the rest of the day?"

He shakes his head. "No major plans."

The light inside me grows. I lean into his ear, murmuring, "I think we need to spend the day trying to start our Marino squad."

He beams. "That's the first time you initiated the conversation about kids."

The flutters in my stomach expand. I unzip his pants and free his cock then slide my panties to the side and slide over him.

He groans and fists my hair, tugging my head back. He positions his face over mine and asks, "Is that what you want, Katiya? A houseful of my babies?"

There's no longer any doubt. Whatever I need to do to be a good mom, I'll figure it out. It's impossible not to. I have Massimo at my side.

I circle my hips and admit, "Yeah. I want lots of your babies."

His grin explodes. He grabs my wrists and pins them to the ceiling. "Then let's get started."

EPILOGUE

MC

Massimo

A Few Weeks Later

KATIYA STEPS INTO THE ROOM, AND MY HEART SKIPS SEVERAL beats. The blue silk dress hugs her curves perfectly, ending mid-calf.

My eyes dart between her popping cleavage to the curve of her waist. "Spin," I demand.

Her lips twitch, and she obeys.

God, her ass is perfection.

I step forward, circle my arm around her waist, and tug her into me. She's four inches taller in her new stilettos. The top of her head is eye level with me, and I stare at us in the full-length mirror. I murmur, "You're a goddess."

"You look as hot in a tux as you do naked," she claims.

Arrogance fills me. I assert, "I think you prefer me naked."

She laughs, her cheeks flushing pink. Her grin widens. She turns to me and holds my cheeks, stating, "Pinch me."

I chuckle then pinch her ass.

"Great! This is still my life!" she exclaims, which is something she says several times a week.

I admit, "I hope that the excitement hasn't died off when I'm old and decrepit and you're still young and hot."

Her face turns serious. The hint of her Russian accent I love so much gets thicker. She tilts her head, firmly answering, "Of course it won't. I'm Mrs. Massimo Marino."

My cock turns hard. Every time I hear that, I get a full-blown erection. I tug her as close to me as possible then nibble on her ear, claiming, "We're going to need to find a dark corner."

Her breath hitches. "Maybe not too dark?" She bites on her lip, making my cock pulse against her abdomen.

"Massimo! Time to go," Gianni roars, knocking hard on the door.

I glance at him. "What's the rush? The wedding isn't for a few more hours."

"You know how Papà gets. And Dante's pacing."

"Wedding nerves?" Katiya asks.

"No. Something else," Gianni states.

The hairs on my neck rise. "What is it?"

Gianni glances at Katiya then me. He declares, "Tristano is missing."

"Missing?" I question.

Gianni nods. "Yeah. No one's seen him since last night when he left the rehearsal dinner. He's not answering his phone. Papà pulled me aside and told me to call Pina. I don't know why, but she's not answering, either."

Katiya and I exchange a guilty look.

Gianni notices it and steps inside. He shuts the door. "Massimo, do you know why Papà wanted me to call Pina?"

My gut dives. I don't want to break Tristano's trust, but I also don't want to lie to Gianni. It's been a little over a month since we got back from the Maldives.

"Massimo?" Gianni barks.

Katiya puts her hand on my thigh and squeezes it. "I'm going to go to Bridget's suite now." She tilts her head and kisses me.

"Okay, dolce."

We watch her leave, and Gianni steps closer. "What do you know that you aren't telling me?"

I sigh but don't see any other options. "Pina and Tristano are seeing each other."

The color drains from his cheeks. "What are you talking about?"

"Just what I said. Pina didn't want to tell Dante."

Gianni scowls, shaking his head. "What the fuck?"

"I know."

"Dante cannot find out about this today."

"Fine by me. But why isn't Tristano here?" I question.

Worry fills Gianni's expression. "It's not like him to bail on an important occasion. Something is wrong."

"You don't know that. I'm sure he'll be here shortly," I state, hoping I'm right.

"Gianni! Massimo! Come quick!" Papà's voice blares through the speaker system.

My brother and I exchange a quick look then race through my wing and down the staircase. Papà and Dante stand at the bottom, their faces as white as a ghost.

A horrible feeling skyrockets through my body. I ask, "What's wrong?"

Papà scrunches his face. He holds the table to support himself, informing us, "The police just called. Tristano and Pina..."

Gianni locks eyes with Dante. "Tristano and Pina what?"

Dante's eyes turn darker. "There's been an accident. Tristano's motorcycle...it's...it's destroyed."

My head spins. "They were on it?"

Dante's face says it all. "Tristano's in surgery now. It's..." He takes a deep breath then continues, "He may not make it."

Gianni swallows hard. "What about Pina?"

Dante closes his eyes. "A van sideswiped them. They peeled Pina off the ground and raced away from the scene."

Who was it?" I ask.

Papà sniffs hard. Anger and hatred infiltrate his face. He seethes, "The footage isn't super clear. But there's no doubt. The Abruzzos are involved."

Ready for Tristano and Pina's story?
READ CARNAL - BOOK FOUR OF MAFIA WARS NEW YORK!

One work meeting created an obsession neither of us could shake.

My boss's brother was a friend...until the day he turned his dark-brooding eyes on me.

For years, I studied Tristano at the club.

I'd mimic his commands, dominating the most powerful, dangerous men.

Now, he wants me to submit to him—the opposite role I usually play.

So we make a deal.

But the urges we think we'll overcome, we can't.

When we finally come to terms with our secret, his enemy tries to destroy us.

Then I wake up, not remembering anything.

And the man who claims I'm his makes my skin crawl.

If only I could understand the flashbacks of the dark-haired, chiseled-faced man.

READ CARNAL - BOOK FOUR OF MAFIA WARS NEW YORK!

PINA DE LA CRUZ
CARNAL PROLOGUE

$$\mathcal{MC}$$

Pina De La Cruz

Darkness fades as faint noises grow louder. A chill runs down my spine while sweat breaks the surface of my skin. My heart pounds harder, and the sound of metal slamming together is followed by horns blaring.

A gruff voice heckles, "Stupid motherfuckers. Look at those idiots, Kiko."

Kiko? Who is Kiko?

I blink, and the sunlight blinds me. Hammers pound in my head. I squeeze my eyelids shut, wondering why my mouth is so dry.

Why does my body feel so sore?

A whistle rings in my ears. Another man's voice replies, "That's not getting fixed. Too bad. That Porsche deserves better."

"Good thing I didn't bring my new Vette down to this dump."

Where am I?

I need to wake up!

"Still think you should have gotten red over the blue, boss," Kiko claims.

The other man grunts. "When you pay for it, you can choose it."

"Suit yourself."

I blink again and attempt to sit up, then whimper when pain shoots through my entire body.

"Biagio, she's awake!" Kiko exclaims.

The throbbing agony almost convinces me to stay asleep and not face whatever situation this is, but the voice inside my head tells me not to fall back into the dark abyss. I try harder and keep my eyelids open, letting everything come into focus.

Faded, chipped yellow paint covers the walls. A large window with dusty half-open blinds explains the sunlight. A brown door sits open across from me, and the hallway looks as worn as the room I'm in. Two men study me. One appears a lot older. He's maybe late fifties or early sixties even. The bald spot on his head is shiny, as if he polishes it. Several scars indent his face, and he wears a white tank top. So many tattoos run up his arms and neck, I can't see any skin without ink.

The other man could pass for being in his late thirties. Dark, thick hair fills his head along with a short goatee. He's in better shape than the older man. He has an arm sleeve tattoo and his designer T-shirt hugs his body, displaying his muscles. They're so big and veiny that he has to be on steroids. Unlike Kiko, he doesn't look like a thug. It's clear he's in charge.

Who are these men?

Panic washes over me. A flashback of me at a conference room table, typing, and warm, muscular arms sliding around my shoulders, pops into my mind. The scent of tonka bean, cedarwood, and geranium briefly filters through my nose. However, almost as soon as it appears, it's gone. The present replaces it. I try to sit up again, but the bald man pushes me down.

"Easy," he orders. I assume he's Kiko, based on his voice.

I freeze, unsure if I should try to fight, even though my body feels like I can barely move it.

Biagio lights a cigarette. The sound of his Zippo flicking makes me wince. Smoke seeps into my airway, and I cough. Sharp pain like nothing I've ever felt before erupts in my lungs.

He steps to the opposite side of the bed and reaches for a metal chair. He pulls it closer, turns it backward, and sits. A few moments drag on as he stares at me, never blinking, keeping his intense gaze on mine. Then he leans closer to me. His stale, cigarette breath flares in my nostrils.

"Wh—" I barely make a sound. I try to swallow the raw feeling in my throat, wincing from the pain.

"I've been waiting a long time for you to wake up," he asserts, then moves his hand toward my face.

I flinch, my breath hitches, and more pain assaults my chest. A tiny whimper escapes my lips.

He holds his hands in the air. "Easy. You've got a few broken ribs, a concussion, and extensive bruising."

"What?" I whisper, confused about how my body is so battered. Several beeps come from the machine next to me, and I glance at it.

He cautiously runs his finger across my forehead, tucking a lock of hair behind my ear, causing me to I cringe. He sees it but doesn't move his hand off me. His lips twitch and he slides his palm over my cheek, holding me firmly. "Did you forget who we are?"

My pulse pounds between my ears. *We? What is he talking about?*

My lack of response answers his question. Instead of disappointment flooding his expression, it's as if he expected my reaction, which only adds to the confusion.

My voice cracks as I claim, "I-I-I don't know you."

He nods, insisting, "You do. In time you'll remember."

"Do you know your name?" Kiko interjects.

I tear my gaze off Biagio, turning toward Kiko. The longer I stare at him, the more horrified I get.

What is my name?

Oh God! Why don't I know my name?

"It's okay, baby. The doctor said there's a good chance it will all come back," Biagio declares.

I snap my face toward him and grimace from more stabs of pain. "What will come back?"

"Your memory," he responds.

My heart pounds harder against my ribcage, creating more horrible sensations. "I lost my memory?"

Biagio glances at Kiko and motions with his head for him to leave the room, ordering, "And shut the door."

Kiko obeys, and once the lock clicks in place, more fear pummels me.

Biagio places both palms on my cheeks. "Everything is going to be okay. I promise."

"Wh-who..." I squeeze my eyes shut, needing hydration like never before.

He grabs a glass of water off the table. "Here, baby. Have a sip." He holds it to my lips.

I drink, relishing the moisture in my mouth and throat.

"Better?" he asks, his dark eyes softer than before.

"Yes. Thank you."

He sits the glass down, then picks up my hand. He kisses it, then tilts his head, reassessing me.

"Please say something," I beg, unsure what question I should ask first and feeling too foggy to put my anxiety into words.

He takes a deep inhale, strokes my cheek, then answers, "The doctor said you have amnesia."

"What?" I try to sit up again, but he holds his forearm against my neck so I can't move. It freaks me out, but I'm too hurt to fight.

"Pina, stop moving. You need to not make any quick movements, or you could hurt yourself further," he directs.

Pina. My name is Pina.

Is it?

Oh God!

I freeze, blinking hard, but tears fall. *Why can't I remember anything?*

"Listen, baby. You don't need to worry about anything right now," Biagio declares.

"Why can't I remember anything?" I sob.

"Shhh. It's okay. The doctor said it's probably temporary," he reiterates.

"But I... I don't..." I squeeze my eyes shut and try to stop the emotions overpowering me, but I can't. More pain shoots through my ribs as my chest heaves with scared sorrow.

He firmly holds my face in his hands and orders, "Pina, look at me."

I manage to obey.

He asserts, "Everything will be okay. I'm going to take good care of you, just like I always have."

"But I don't remember you," I cry out, and more tears roll over his fingers.

His eyes stay in control. There's no emotion in them, only confidence. It strikes me as odd, but I can't pinpoint why. He replies, "Yes. And one day, you will. In the meantime, I'm going to take care of you. All you need to know is that you love me, and I love you."

Love? How can I love a man I don't remember?

I shake my head, and more hammers pound into my skull.

He holds my face tighter. "Stop moving."

I obey again, unable to fight.

"Good girl," he praises, but it makes me cringe inside. The machine next to me beeps faster, and he arches his eyebrows. "Your IV is empty. I'll send the nurse in to change the bag."

"What is it?" I ask.

He shrugs. "Hydration. Vitamins. Everything you need to make you well enough for me to move you."

Goose bumps break out on my arms. I don't know where I am right now, but something about leaving this room scares me. "Move me?"

He runs his thumb over my lips. " Yes. You don't think we live in this dump, do you?"

My eyes dart to the paint-chipped wall and dusty blinds. I refocus on him.

"Well?" he asks.

"I-I don't know," I admit.

He smiles. "You'll love my place. It's unlike this one."

"Then why am I here? Why aren't I in a hospital?" I interrogate.

His eyes turn to slits. He purses his lips for a moment, then chuckles. "That's the Pina I know. Always asking smart questions."

His remark sends a bolt of pride through me. I think, *At least I'm not an idiot.*

He adds, "The doctors and nurses are the best in the country. I can assure you that your medical care has been nothing less than superior. I had to bring you here until the risks were over." The machine beeps again, and he reaches for it and then pushes a button. The loud noise stops.

My agitation grows. "What risks? I don't understand."

A dark storm swirls in his orbs. He snarls, "The Marinos."

"Who are the Marinos?" I ask.

"Our enemy," he fumes. He leans down and pecks me on the lips. The hairs on my neck rise. I turn my head and blink hard.

Biagio moves my face toward him again. Arrogance replaces the anger in his expression. He claims, "I'm your fiancé. Soon enough, you'll be all over me again."

My lips quiver. I whisper, "Fiancé?"

He smiles, but nothing about it comforts me. "Yes. We were starting to work with the wedding coordinator to plan our big day."

"We were?" I ask, unable to recall anything about a wedding.

"Yes," he confirms, then releases me and sits back in his chair. "Any more questions before I send the nurse in?"

I take a few breaths, trying to prioritize my thoughts.

"Pina?"

I blurt out, "How did I get hurt?"

His face darkens so much I can see the evil in it. He seethes, "You were on a motorcycle."

I attempt to remember it, but I can't. I ask, "With you?"

His voice oozes with hatred. He responds, "No. With *him*."

"Him?"

He grinds his molars before replying, "Tristano Marino."

Everything stays blank. I ask, "Who is Tristano Marino? And why was I on his bike if I'm with you?"

His nostrils flare into wide triangles. He grabs my hand and traces his thumb over my knuckles, answering, "He attempted to kidnap you. But don't worry, baby. I stopped him."

A burning sensation fills my belly and climbs up my chest. "Why did he want to kidnap me?"

"Because you're mine," Biagio states.

Maybe I should feel good that this decent-enough-looking man is claiming me as his, but I still don't remember anything. So I stay silent, trying to process all of this. I finally ask, "Is he okay?"

"Why do you care?" Biagio barks.

I jump, then wince from the bruises on my back.

"Shit. Sorry," he says in a softer voice, but something tells me he isn't.

I reprimand myself for questioning him when he's my fiancé.

In a controlled tone, Biagio declares, "He's still in the hospital. For now, he's alive. But I guarantee you it won't be for long."

My stomach flips. I can't say why. I don't know this man Tristano who kidnapped me. I shouldn't care about his life after what he did.

Biagio kisses my hand and rises. "I'll send the nurse in to change your IV. As soon as I can bring you home, I will."

Too tired to argue or figure any more of this out, I just reply, "Thank you."

He hesitates, then arches his eyebrows. "Any more questions?"

I start to shake my head, then stop. "Who are you?"

Pride fills his face. He lifts his head and puffs his chest out. Something about his answer sends chills to my bones, but I have no idea why. He states, "I'm Biagio Abruzzo. Son of Jacopo and next in line to rule the family. And you, Pina dela Cruz, will be queen of the Abruzzos."

READ CARNAL - BOOK FOUR OF MAFIA WARS NEW YORK!

READY TO BINGE THE ORIGINAL 10 BOOK MAFIA WARS SERIES? GET TO KNOW THE IVANOVS AND O'MALLEYS!

He's a Ruthless Stranger. One I can't see, only feel, thanks to my friends who make a deal with him on my behalf.

No names. No personal details. No face to etch into my mind.

Just him, me, and an expensive silk tie.

What happens in Vegas is supposed to stay in Vegas.

He warns me he's full of danger.

I never see that side of him. All I experience is his Russian accent, delicious scent, and touch that lights me on fire.

One incredible night turns into two. Then we go our separate ways.

But fate doesn't keep us apart. When I run into my stranger back in Chicago, I know it's him, even if I've never seen his icy blue eyes before.

Our craving is hotter than Vegas. But he never lied.

He's a ruthless man...

"Ruthless Stranger" is the jaw-dropping first installment of the "Mafia Wars" series. It's an interconnecting, stand-alone Dark Mafia Romance, guaranteed to have an HEA.

Ready for Maksim's story? Click here for Ruthless Stranger, book one of the jaw dropping spinoff series, Mafia Wars!

ALL IN BOXSET

Three page-turning, interconnected stand-alone romance novels with HEA's!! Get ready to fall in love with the characters. Billionaires. Professional athletes. New York City. Twist, turns, and danger lurking everywhere. The only option for these couples is to go ALL IN...with a little help from their friends. EXTRA STEAM INCLUDED!

Grab it now! READ FREE IN KINDLE UNLIMITED!

CAN I ASK YOU A HUGE FAVOR?

Would you be willing to leave me a review?

I would be forever grateful as one positive review on Amazon is like buying the book a hundred times! Reader support is the lifeblood for Indie authors and provides us the feedback we need to give readers what they want in future stories!

Your positive review means the world to me! So thank you from the bottom of my heart!

CLICK TO REVIEW

MORE BY MAGGIE COLE

Mafia Wars New York - A Dark Mafia Series (Series Six)

Toxic (Dante's Story) - Book One

Immoral (Gianni's Story) - Book Two

Crazed (Massimo's Story) - Book Three

Carnal (Tristano's Story) - Book Four

Mafia Wars - A Dark Mafia Series (Series Five)

Ruthless Stranger (Maksim's Story) - Book One

Broken Fighter (Boris's Story) - Book Two

Cruel Enforcer (Sergey's Story) - Book Three

Vicious Protector (Adrian's Story) - Book Four

Savage Tracker (Obrecht's Story) - Book Five

Unchosen Ruler (Liam's Story) - Book Six

Perfect Sinner (Nolan's Story) - Book Seven

Brutal Defender (Killian's Story) - Book Eight

Deviant Hacker (Declan's Story) - Book Nine

Relentless Hunter (Finn's Story) - Book Ten

Behind Closed Doors (Series Four - Former Military Now International Rescue Alpha Studs)

Depths of Destruction - Book One

Marks of Rebellion - Book Two

Haze of Obedience - Book Three

Cavern of Silence - Book Four

Stains of Desire - Book Five

Risks of Temptation - Book Six

Together We Stand Series (Series Three - Family Saga)

Kiss of Redemption- Book One

Sins of Justice - Book Two

Acts of Manipulation - Book Three

Web of Betrayal - Book Four

Masks of Devotion - Book Five

Roots of Vengeance - Book Six

It's Complicated Series (Series Two - Chicago Billionaires)

Crossing the Line - Book One

Don't Forget Me - Book Two

Committed to You - Book Three

More Than Paper - Book Four

Sins of the Father - Book Five

Wrapped In Perfection - Book Six

All In Series (Series One - New York Billionaires)

The Rule - Book One

The Secret - Book Two

The Crime - Book Three

The Lie - Book Four

The Trap - Book Five

The Gamble - Book Six

STAND ALONE NOVELLA

JUDGE ME NOT - A Billionaire Single Mom Christmas Novella

ABOUT THE AUTHOR

Amazon Bestselling Author

Maggie Cole is committed to bringing her readers alphalicious book boyfriends. She's been called the "literary master of steamy romance." Her books are full of raw emotion, suspense, and will always keep you wanting more. She is a masterful storyteller of contemporary romance and loves writing about broken people who rise above the ashes.

She lives in Florida near the Gulf of Mexico with her husband, son, and dog. She loves sunshine, wine, and hanging out with friends.

Her current series were written in the order below:

- All In (Stand alones with entwined characters)
- It's Complicated (Stand alones with entwined characters)
- Together We Stand (Brooks Family Saga - read in order)
- Behind Closed Doors (Read in order)
- Mafia Wars (Coming April 1st 2021)

Maggie Cole's Newsletter
Sign up here!

Hang Out with Maggie in Her Reader Group
Maggie Cole's Romance Addicts

Follow for Giveaways
Facebook Maggie Cole

Instagram
@maggiecoleauthor

Tik Tok
https://www.tiktok.com/@authormaggiecole?

Complete Works on Amazon
Follow Maggie's Amazon Author Page

Book Trailers
Follow Maggie on YouTube

Are you a Blogger and want to join my ARC team?
Signup now!

Feedback or suggestions?

Email: authormaggiecole@gmail.com

twitter.com/MaggieColeAuth
instagram.com/maggiecoleauthor
bookbub.com/profile/maggie-cole
amazon.com/Maggie-Cole/e/B07Z2CB4HG

Made in United States
Orlando, FL
30 June 2024

48462851R00275